Trials of Friendship

Trials of Friendship

Hazel Hucker

St. Martin's Press New York

A THOMAS DUNNE BOOK.
An imprint of St. Martin's Press.

Library of Congress Cataloging-in-Publication Data

Hucker, Hazel.
Trials of friendship / Hazel Hucker.
p. cm.
"A Thomas Dunne book."
ISBN 0-312-17051-3
I. Title.
PR6058.U27T75 1997
823'.914—dc21 97-25071
CIP

First published in Great Britain by Judy Piatkus (Publishers) Ltd

First U.S. Edition: January 1998

10 9 8 7 6 5 4 3 2 1

For Cynthia, Jackie, Kathy, Susan and Veronica.

Chapter 1

When Polly Ferrison realised that she had fallen out of love with her husband Neville she was shocked: monogamously inclined, she had expected to love to the grave. But there was nothing she could do to recover the lost emotion; it eluded her totally. She tried not to let the change affect her life; there were the girls to be considered, appearances to be kept up. At first she felt lost and bewildered, as if she had suffered a bereavement. And she felt sorry for Neville; after all, he was bereaved too.

Her friends must never know, Polly reflected, as she sat in her little garden on a warm day in late April, especially not her university friends, particularly on her mind this morning, who had viewed their hard beginnings. There must be none of those comforting confidences that never remain confidential. She was determined, at this strange juncture of her life, and with their twentieth wedding anniversary approaching, to preserve the rosy image she had taken care to paint over the years of a marriage settled, content, inviolable. She had little else.

There was unexpected comfort in the thought that their relationship had never been a demonstrative one; in this, at least, Neville had been austere. So, no obvious closeness, no surreptitious yet visible squeezing of hands, no fleeting exchanges of glances, lack of which might draw attention to the change. She remembered how once in their early days together she had taken his arm on leaving the cinema, hugging it, giving a little skip, leaning against him. He had disengaged himself. 'Must you bounce like a spaniel?' he had reproached her. 'Do have some dignity.' Hurt, Polly had straightened her back and cultivated decorum.

It had not proved easy. The spaniel simile was an apt one: Polly had the silky reddish hair, the large eyes, the trusting nature and all the exuberance of the species. But she struggled to please Neville because she was giddy with amazement and delight that he chose to allocate her any part of his precious time. He was of a quite different breed from the men in her year at the London School of Economics. She was doing her finals, but he had come from Oxford with a first in Politics, Philosophy and Economics to study for his doctorate, his thesis something to do with the economics of transport management. 'Profoundly boring,' he had told her with a rueful smile, 'but politics and philosophy do appear a touch esoteric in the basic world of the job market, and a job, I'm instructed, one must eventually have. Personally I'd rather have immersed my mind in developments in modern philosophic thought, but where Uncle holds the purse strings, Uncle dictates.'

As well as being both clever and scholarly, Neville had startling good looks. When she first met him in her friend Vanessa's company in the college pub, The Three Tuns, Polly had wanted to stare endlessly, for she had never before seen any male, never imagined one, so perfect. But she had not dared to stare, for it seemed rude, childish, pathetic even. Besides, in Vanessa's eyes as they flickered from one to another of the group of friends sitting there, Candida, Mary, Jane and herself, she had read not only a desire for their admiration of her new acquisition, but a challenge that erected invisible boundaries around him. Yet in surreptitious glances Polly had taken him in: the lean, solid shape of his head, the thick fair hair, the sexual promise implicit in the heavy-lidded eyes, and the long languorous elegance of him as he leaned against the bar in clothes of a different cut from the student crowd milling behind him. He was a star in a firmament of grubby jeans and jumpers, and she yearned and yearned.

It was not only his looks that she found so terrifyingly attractive, but his conversation also. He spoke of the theatre, of recent startling productions which he and Vanessa had seen but the others had not, moved on to modern literature and experimental writing which he could describe and expound upon equally with admiration, scorn or laughter. She heard of structuralists and Leavisites and formalists; she became dizzy with excitement and new conceptions. Polly had always found herself weak-kneed before intelligence and Neville was the most knowledgeable and articulate man to whom she had ever had access. Her lecturers and professors were not accessible, they were God-like creatures who appeared on the platform of a lecture theatre, dispensed theories and learning and removed themselves to another world, where she never had the nerve to pursue them. She longed to sit, literally and metaphorically, at Neville's feet, though later she could hardly remember the discussions, only the glory of them. But it was enough. This was why she had gone to university.

In the warm spring air Polly sighed as she arranged the shabby rectangular iron table before her. She had brought out paper, pencils, address book, cookery books, a thermos of coffee and a freebie tiger's head mug from the local garage, ready to work on her plans. Two decades ago. It was yesterday and it was forever. Soon they would meet again, the friends who had been there that evening, joining together with their husbands and partners and children for their annual Sunday lunch party, keeping the relationship running on its course, though the subscribing members of it had changed and led very different lives. Sentimentality and tradition held them together, she supposed. Would the friendship hold if anything real were to try it – rivalry, say, or infidelity? Impossible to imagine. Polly returned to her cookery books.

This year it was her turn to give the lunch party and she dreaded it. They were five, Candida, Vanessa, Mary, Jane and herself, but if all their men and children turned up, and it was likely they would, the total could be seventeen. Seventeen in her house, in her garden? It could be done, but at a cost of crowding and discomfort that made her shudder with embarrassment. She would have to borrow extra tables and chairs. And plates and glasses. And cutlery. In the early years Polly had found the idea of these reunions delightful, now she groaned at such sentimentality and cursed the work involved. Besides, while by no means a competitive woman, she detested the thought that her friends might pity her puny efforts on their behalf. Last year Candida's housekeeper had produced exquisitely dressed salmon with a wide choice of original salads. The puddings had been melt-in-the-mouth confections, the cheeses ripe to perfection. The cutlery had been heavy silver, the glasses had glinted in the sunshine on the long terrace. There had been champagne and Pimms. Polly poured herself coffee and stared furiously at the tiger on her mug; the tiger stared back, expressionless. Her budget would barely rise to supermarket Australian wines. Somehow she must save on the housekeeping; she was the poorest of them all.

She scanned a cookery book for ideas. Her approach to entertaining resembled a climber's to his mountain. Pre-planning was essential to avoid pitfalls, chasms and precipices. She used charts, lists, manuals, determined to succeed in her lone assault on this dangerous territory. As a busy teacher in a comprehensive school she had to think ahead. The new term started on Monday. Plans must be made now. Lists turned amorphous clouds of worry into mastery and order; Polly, her life full of worry, found comfort in her lists.

'I'm off!' a voice called from the house.

Polly turned. Neville was standing in the French windows, dressed in a polo-shirt and sailing trousers, one hand raised in farewell. As he turned his head sunglasses flashed.

'Pleasant sailing!' she proffered to the dark lenses.

'Thank you. Remember, no dinner for me this evening. We'll have something on the boat or in a pub, it'll give us longer out.'

'Fine.'

'In fact, if the wind changes, we may stay out all weekend. Simpler if you expect me when you see me.'

As he turned to go out through the house, so Rose emerged, pushing him to one side. Rose was their eldest daughter, tall, slender and lovely, a redhead with the quick temper said to accompany the hair, and a sharp tongue.

She assessed Neville at a glance and remarked: 'Off to have fun without Ma again, Pa?'

'I've plenty to do here,' Polly said hastily.

'Of course,' Rose said. 'As usual you work while Pa plays.'

Neville sighed. 'Am I to give up my sailing because your mother isn't the sort to relish the wind in her hair? Offend my friends by refusing their kind invitations? Invitations, incidentally, that I can't return because of the costs of bringing up my children.'

'Mother pays most of those costs,' Rose said scornfully. 'I've seen her write the cheques from her own bank account. You don't suffer much. Whatever Papa wants, Papa gets.' She switched her attention to his dark glasses. 'Ray-Bans, I see. More flashing of the wallet? I suppose you hope they'll give you an air of idle wealth. Or is it anonymity you seek?'

Ignoring Rose, he swung on his heel and left.

'You shouldn't be so rude,' Polly told her tiredly. She flicked in a desultory way at the pages of the cookery book.

'Why not?' Rose asked. 'He's so selfish. That's rude if you like. Why doesn't he take you sailing with him? Wouldn't you like to go?'

'I wouldn't mind,' Polly admitted. 'But it's Geoffrey Brookes' boat and Joanna detests the water. So it's always a boys' day out. It would be selfish of me to insist he stay at home.'

'Or so he tells you!' Rose observed shrewdly. She sat down opposite her mother, picked up a lavishly illustrated book called *Delicious Desserts* and began to leaf her way through it. 'You should break out, Ma. Pay him back in his own coin. Go to parties without him, get sloshed and stay away all Sunday. Have fun!'

'No one invites me to parties,' Polly said, 'not on my own.'

'You don't give out the right signals, emit the right messages.'

'No?'

'No. You're a worthy woman.' Rose slapped the book shut and leaned towards her, laughing. 'But you could still break out.'

'How, for heaven's sakes?'

'Ah,' Rose pounced. 'You'd like to then, wouldn't you? There are pent-up desires in you, Ma, buried somewhere. Unseen depths. I think you should take a lover.'

'Rose!' Sometimes she went too far. But telling her so made her worse; one had to take her lightly, joke back and laugh. 'School-teachers can't take lovers – think of the scandal! And why should I want to, anyway? Neville and I are fine.'

'He may be, but you're not. You're withering fast into nothing.'

'Oh, thank you!'

'Don't interrupt, Ma. I don't mean that nastily. Sorrowfully, rather. My friends used to say how pretty you were and what fun. They couldn't say that now.'

'I'm growing older,' Polly pointed out, and flinched at the thought of the fading and fretful forties.

'You could still be pretty if you tried. But the problem isn't just in your looks, it's inside you. The bounce and the zest for life I remember have gone. You're disappearing into some private place where no one can touch you.'

'Nonsense.'

'No, truth. I think you're depressed. Which isn't surprising seeing how hard you work and how little fun you have. You've a long way to go before you're old – but waste no more time, buy yourself sexy clothes, send out the signals and rejoice in nefarious fun!'

'You're talking tosh. Quiet now, and let me get on with my work.'

'What work? What are you doing?'

'Planning a lunch party for my friends.'

'What? The old girls you went to uni with? You're not still doing that!'

'Won't you want to keep up with your friends when you leave Cambridge?'

Rose was reading English at Girton and planning to go into publishing. Rose shone as the single success in Polly's life.

''Course!' she said. 'But not in your solemn way. We'll have an evening out, go to see the latest play – or something lovely and sexy like the Chippendales! Male bodies – whee!'

Polly laughed but shook her head. 'Our family lunches are fixed in amber now. Besides, just think, darling, they're much the cheapest and easiest when you've got children. And – though it may be surprising to you – we're interested in one another's offspring.'

She thought of those offspring: her own two, Rose then Emily, two years younger and working for her A levels; Candida's two lively sons, annoying their father by doing as little work as possible at an expensive prep school; and Mary and George's three, a boy and two girls, placid, pleasant, and, Polly thought, with a passing impulse of malice, dull.

Mary's eldest girl was fifteen, but she would never look as Rose did today, erratic and exotic in a flame-coloured shirt floating over flowery ethnic trousers that ended at a pair of heavy ankle boots. Odd, Polly ruminated, how the young insisted on wearing clothes that had no relationship one with another. Was it a form of disguise or a desire for attention in any guise? Or was it the uniform of the young that the boots implied? Neville had once been unwise enough to enquire, receiving the answer: 'Oh, God, Pa, you're so crass. Don't you understand about fun?' But Neville, Polly remembered, had never interpreted fun in the clothes sense. Even as a student he had insisted upon a classic style. He liked Mary's girls, neat in crisp cottons.

'So what will you give this mob to eat?' Rose wanted to know.

'No idea,' Polly admitted. 'Salads would be easiest, but they're a bore to prepare, and besides, all of us have had them, every time.'

'Something different, then.'

'But what?' Polly moaned. 'Anything exciting is bound to mean exotic ingredients and wines and cream galore, and that demands money and we're broke. And besides . . . oh, hell, hell, hell! I've just remembered, Vanessa has gone vegetarian. She announced it on her Christmas card.' She picked up another illustrated volume and turned its leaves furiously.

'Got it!' Rose exclaimed, making Polly jump. 'Have a curry lunch. Curry's your best dish by far. There you are – problem solved.'

Polly blinked, contemplated and smiled. 'Good idea . . . Yes, I like it, I truly do. Lamb korma, tandoori chicken, aloo gobi . . . side dishes like yogurt and cucumber raïta, channa dahl.' She rolled the words over her tongue, then added: 'Plus a courgette and aubergine curry – Vanessa can eat that – and there you are! Cheap, too. Rose, you're brilliant.'

'I know,' said Rose. 'And I'll go to the pick-your-own place for lots of luscious strawberries for the pudding. Or we could send Pa. He never helps. You should make him. It isn't good for a man to be such an egoist as he is. You deserve better.' She spoke with gruff affection, avoiding Polly's eyes. 'Like I said, you work too hard and worry all the time. You try to treat it as a joke, but I know you've got real money problems. And I'm not surprised, not with Pa's determination always to make a show – hand-made suits, a new car every other year, seats at the opera. No, don't leap to his defence, I'm not interested. I've an essay to write on Sir Philip Sidney's "Apologie for Poetrie" and it'll take me hours to knock it into shape. I came out to tell you not to interrupt me or bother to feed me for the next twenty-four hours – I'll grab bread and cheese when I must. With Emily in London with Granny all weekend that means you needn't cook unless you want to. Okay?' She slouched off into the house without waiting for an answer.

Polly stared unseeingly after her, noting Rose's assumption that Neville would not be back that night, shook her head to clear it, then stood and followed her inside to telephone her friends. Candida must be consulted first about the date for the lunch, Candida had the busiest social life.

'Could I speak to Lady Gough, please?' she requested when the Goughs' housekeeper answered, and was annoyed to hear her voice adopting a slight but distinct drawl. 'It's Mrs Ferrison – Polly Ferrison.'

'Are you the press?' the voice on the other end enquired with suspicion.

'Certainly not,' Polly retorted. 'I'm an old friend.'

'Oh, very well. We have to be careful, you know.'

'Bitch,' Polly muttered to herself. She had met the housekeeper on several occasions, but the woman invariably failed to recognise her or her name. She suspected it was her way of letting Polly know that her elderly little car, her chainstore clothes, her lack of jewellery, were really not quite up to the Gough mark.

'Darling Polly!' came Candida's voice. 'How lovely to hear you. What are you up to?'

'Organising the usual summer lunch-party date,' Polly responded, 'and starting with you because I know you're bound to be off shortly to America or the South of France or Italy, and I have to nab you and pin you down while I can!'

'I'd adore to be pinned down,' Candida replied. 'It'll be such fun to see you all again. When are you thinking of? Hold on while I find my diary.'

Candida gave the impression that the invitation was the very thing she had been waiting for. Just to hear her voice raised Polly's spirits. Candida had the knack of always appearing to be in the best of moods; in their LSE days she had been the insouciant one, the one who accepted an essay savaged by her tutor with a wry joke, who tossed off problems with a shrug. She had said once to Polly: 'Life's a bowl of cherries – you can concentrate on the stones as if they were the pits of the world, or you can spit them out as I spit out Dr Karp and relish the lovely juicy fleshy parts!' And she had flashed her eyes with glee. She had certainly concentrated on the juicy fleshy parts of life, Polly reflected wrily. In those days, when asked what she planned to do after she graduated, she would say with a chuckle: 'I'm going to marry a millionaire!' and no one ever persuaded her to a more sober answer. It was the more surprising then to witness the world's shock and amazement when, at twenty-seven, Candida became the second wife of the renowned industrialist Sir Bernard Gough, chairman of the Gough Group and older than her by eighteen years. Now the insouciance had gone, to be replaced by the poise and dignity her position demanded, but the wry wit and charm were unchanged.

'Diary at the ready.'

They fixed on the second Sunday in June, with an alternative should it prove unsuitable.

'Now listen,' Candida said when those had been duly noted. 'What are you up to today? Have you lots of things booked?'

Polly thought of her empty diary and of Neville sailing across the Solent. 'No,' she said baldly. 'Nothing.'

'Wonderful. Then come and rescue me. Please, dear sweet Polly, come and have lunch with me – Bernard's rushed off to Strasbourg or Bonn or somewhere dreary where wives aren't welcome, and the boys have gone to join their cousins for a few days, and I'm all my own. I ought to do all sorts of worthy administrative things for my charities, but it's much too lovely a day to waste. I intend to relax in the sunshine on the terrace every moment I can and it's occurred to me how good it would be to have you come and relax with me. Please?'

Polly experienced a rare glow of pleasure at being regarded as a desirable companion by someone whose life was so full and fascinating. 'I'd love to,' she said.

'You could stay to dinner. No, wait, better still, stay till tomorrow night. Yes, that's it, stay till then and we'll laze and drink and gossip like we haven't been able to do for years. Could you get away from Neville and the girls?'

Thoughts flashed across Polly's brain in a series of images: Neville shocked and disconcerted at arriving home to find no dinner; Rose, cheerfully rude, refusing his demands that she should run around after his needs; Neville, aggrieved, sulking in a chair over a couple of clumsily made sandwiches. The images were not shocking or disconcerting to Polly, they were of no importance, or now she thought of it, even pleasing.

With a liberating feeling of excitement she responded: 'Yes!' Candida, I can't think of anything I'd relish more. Be with you in an hour.'

Chapter 2

Candida also lived in Hampshire, and only twenty-three miles from Polly, but she lived in another world. Polly's spirits, which had lifted in affectionate response to the invitation, survived packing her battered overnight case (no Louis Vuitton luggage – the housekeeper would raise her snobbish eyebrows), but began to droop as the car climbed the long hill out of Winchester. The engine was not exactly knocking, but it sounded as tired as she was herself and she suspected big bills were looming. Candida's large silver Mercedes was regularly replaced with a new version; there was no hope of a replacement for Polly's banger.

It was against Polly's nature to fret, but fret she must. There was no money for items other than day-to-day essentials, not while Neville considered the expensive amusements that consoled him for the tedium of life as all essential. With a large assurance he told her not to worry. Worrying was a drab activity, he said, it demeaned her. As deputy head of the history department at the Durngate Comprehensive School her salary should rise to a new car to take her there, surely? he added, but left the room when she tried to explain why it wouldn't. He refused to discuss the vulgar details of money. As the engine of her ten-year-old Austin Metro spluttered, Polly changed to bottom gear and winced.

Her life, she felt, was one long climb uphill – but to what? Gone were her ambitions of twenty years ago for the whirl of an exciting career, for the dashing clothes and holidays in farflung places that success would bring her. Ahead stretched year upon year of the same plodding job, the same plodding poverty, and worse, the loss of her children. Their smiles, their softly breathed confidences, their trust in her ability to make everything right for them, had made it all endurable; more, had given her real happiness. Now those children were grown up and all but gone, and it seemed to her sometimes that every stage of their development had been one of severings, of bereavement. The final suckling, the first day at school, the time when their friends became more important than their parents, leaving home time. She thought, You pour out love and anxiety, energy and time. You owe them the utmost that is in you to give, and in the end they owe you nothing. You wave them goodbye and say: 'Keep in touch!' They go to find a brave new world, and you find that a great chunk of your world has disappeared. And gone too was her old hazy vision of developing a new and closer life with Neville as they relaxed in the knowledge of a job well done, and revelled in the afterglow of their achievement. Her lips twisted scornfully as she viewed that past deluded self. 'Closeness' had never been a word in Neville's matrimonial vocabulary.

She changed gear upwards and the car, the hill conquered, purred briskly between the sunlit Hampshire fields. Polly opened her window and the air smelt sweet. She felt as though she were escaping, and suddenly she wished she *could* escape, not just to Candida, but outward and onwards to a different existence.

Her classroom overlooked this distant countryside, and sometimes she would stand by the window and stare out, longing to be on the road, driving away to somewhere, anywhere, that was away from the stuffy classroom with its smell of chalk and books and overwarm adolescent bodies. But she had to have a reason for running; disillusionment with her husband and her life was not enough, she had to be committed to some new purpose. Polly was committed to nothing. Panic hit as she realised the emptiness of her future. She thought: Oh, God, what can I do? Where are my choices? In novels women with empty lives take lovers, like Rose said, relishing the excitement of illicit admiration. But middle-aged and drab as I am? Who'd fancy me? Only some pot-bellied creep, thrown out by his wife. And Polly had forgotten how to flirt, how to give the *come-on* messages that advertise availability.

She had married soon after graduating, by then four and a half months pregnant with Rose and overwhelmed that Neville was actually condescending to marry someone as ordinary as her. For that was how they both saw her: ordinary. She was average in height, with a good figure and a lively face lit up by big eyes and flyaway red hair, but Neville didn't care for red hair, and anyway, she hadn't the looks, she felt, to compare with him. And while she had once been the brightest girl in her school, at university where everyone was perforce of high intelligence, Polly was just, well . . . ordinary. She graduated with an upper second, nothing to Neville's Oxford first, but comforted herself with the thought that out of her friends only Jane, at twenty-four more mature than the rest of them, had done better.

Neville and Polly were married in church, at their mothers' insistence. Neither had a father to produce; Polly's had died ten years before of an early heart attack, Neville's had simply walked out one day and his wife had not bothered to discover his destination – she did not care enough. Neville had suggested that Polly have an abortion, Polly had refused. She was terrified of being left alone to bring up the child, terrified of the disgrace, (which in those days was still considerable), but she couldn't bring herself to have it aborted: she adored Neville and longed to have his child, while the thought of the bloody, messy and unnecessary dispatch of the foetus made her retch with revulsion. The mothers had met together in annoyance and suspicion over tea at The Ritz (the only place Mrs Hart could call to mind) and held a discussion that came to reveal a shared passion. Mrs Ferrison, strikingly good-looking and dashing, was an art college lecturer. Quiet Mrs Hart was a quarter French and a quarter Austrian; being trilingual she earned her living as a freelance translator, working mainly for educational publishers. And it was here that their interests converged, in a life-long fervour for education and the development of the intellect. Each having revealed their disgust at the trap in which the other's progeny had ensnared her own, a conversation abounding with insinuations and bland offensiveness, they settled to speaking with pride of the brilliance of their respective son and daughter (both were only children), and of how extraordinarily early their special qualities had appeared, moving on to the infant in Polly's womb, its certain talents and its future education. Here they were at one: with Neville and Polly as its, or rather, *his*, parents (they were convinced their mutual grandchild would be a boy), he would be sure to be a genius, and in an almost ritualistic way they conspired towards the wedding which would ensure his legitimacy and a childhood watched over by great and cultivated minds. Awash with Earl Grey tea and an odd mixture of decision and sentiment, they decided to eat dinner together, and walked to Brown's Hotel. At midnight they tottered back on to the pavement clutching each other's arms, slightly drunk, sworn friends for life and adamant. Neville had no chance; even the reception venue had been selected.

With the promise of a down payment on a house from his uncle if he did the right thing, the baited trap closed upon Neville. He was out of control of his destiny and drifted out of LSE and into marriage and a job with Hampshire County Council, comforted by Polly with the thought that he could work on his PhD in the evenings, and eventually, when she was able to work and keep them, would return to full-time study and complete his course. Why a job in local government, no one who knew him could fathom. But Neville had found job-hunting impossible: more and more he yearned for the academic life painted in such glowing colours by his mother, but scorned by his uncle for its low financial rewards. 'With your expensive tastes, Neville, that would be a disaster.' No post outside the universities could compensate for the life he had lost, he mourned to his sympathetic mother and Polly – and besides, other offers were not forthcoming. Eventually, calling it a temporary expedient, he accepted the offer Hampshire County Council made to him, saying that working for the Education Committee was at least roughly in his line, that a cathedral city like Winchester was the sort of place one could bear to live in, and moreover, thank God, houses there would be cheaper than in London.

Two years after Rose, Emily arrived. Neville was not particularly interested. That they were bright little girls made their noise and mess and pranks bearable, but the marriage trap had been baited by the prospect of a son. More children could not be afforded, Neville never had his son, and privately Polly doubted he would have been any more enthusiastic a father had a male child arrived. He was already accumulating shelves of books and notes for his projected work on a philosophy for the end of the twentieth century and on the evenings when he was not out with his friends – 'Marriage needn't mean suffocation for late-twentieth-century man, need it, my Polly?' – he shut himself into the spare room which he had appropriated for his study, and lost himself in the contemplation of great minds.

Downstairs in the sitting room Polly marked exercise books (she taught history to nearly three hundred eleven to sixteen year-olds) and prepared lessons. She did not loathe teaching, as one of her colleagues had confided he did, but she did not love it either. When Rose turned five and started school, Polly left Emily with a child-minder neighbour and started school too, having completed a year's post-graduate course at the local teacher training college. 'Nothing,' said Polly, gritting her teeth that first morning as she buttoned Rose's coat, 'nothing fits with school like more school.' She endured the noise, the unsightly buildings, her 'temporary' pre-fabricated classroom which leaked every winter, the chronic lack of money for new desks or new textbooks or paint to cover the graffiti, her boredom in the repetitive nature of her work. The money she earned was desperately needed, and while the amount was ludicrously low beside the salaries her old college friends earned it did pay off several debts and a hefty bank overdraft in her first year. There was now no hope of Neville returning to a post-graduate course; they were both locked into the jobs they had.

The village of Chilbourne was dozing in the April sun. Polly drove past the fourteenth-century church, past the thatched and slated huddle of the cottages in its shadow, and on for a hundred yards up a slight rise to the pretty but long-empty gatehouse guarding the drive of Chilbourne House. Here she turned in; the drive curved round a stand of Spanish chestnuts and suddenly the house was in view. It was a handsome brick building of the 1730s, calm and classical, low and wide. Vanessa had been heard to describe it snobbishly as 'a small stately home'. Usually it gave Polly a frisson of pleasure to see it, but certain memories of Vanessa here last year spoiled that pleasure. She parked her car to one side in the shade of a vast holly tree, to hide its shabbiness. In front of the house was a shiny Jaguar.

As she raised her hand to tug at the jangly old bell by the great doors, the left one opened abruptly and the Goughs' housekeeper appeared, ushering out a large woman with an overbearing air of confidence, who was talking in a strong carrying voice. She stopped when she saw Polly and bent upon her a stare that seemed to penetrate straight through her blouse and skirt to her shabby underclothing and her National Health appendix scar.

'Ah. Mary, isn't it?'

'Polly,' said Polly.

'Mrs Ferrison,' the housekeeper identified her, not to be outdone.

'Of course. Polly. One of Candida's little friends. I'm her mother – but of course you'll remember me. Mrs Jamieson-Druce.'

She was tall, she was stout, her nose was hooked, her bosom was a cantilevered cushion, but from her head to her heels she was chic. Her suit was too immediate even to have reached *Vogue*, the tiny shoes crammed on her plump feet were an extreme version of the shoemaker's art. Polly recalled Candida saying that her mother had ruled her childhood: her father had been useless and soon vanished. Almost from the start Mrs Jamieson-Druce had had to make her way from nothing, and *with* nothing but a small house at the Fulham end of Chelsea and an even smaller income. She had helped the wealthy and famous: 'A helping hand to a friend, my dear, nothing more!' acting as secretary, companion, flower arranger, or whatever: 'On a purely ad hoc basis.' She also had rich lovers: 'A very old friend from childhood days – he stays with me occasionally and takes me to the opera. Isn't that charming?' Presents of beautiful things made her little Chelsea home a treasure house, and if the beautiful things sometimes vanished to be replaced by other treasures, no one would have dreamed of suggesting she was a dealer. She knew everyone and everything that was worth knowing. Candida had once confided that the elegant appearance she and her mother made had been achieved by knowing the managers of the smartest dress agencies, and why didn't Polly buy her clothes similarly? But Polly could not fancy other women's clothes, however briefly worn, however fashionable.

'Goodbye, Candida,' Mrs Jamieson-Druce's voice suddenly boomed. 'I'll see you tomorrow. And, darling, for Heaven's sake, make up your face. No woman past thirty should have a naked face. Enough to put dear Bernard right off.' She surged out to the Jaguar.

The housekeeper tightened her lips and shut the door behind her, then ushered Polly across the wide hall, through the drawing room and out on to the terrace.

'Darling, at last! How lovely.' Candida gave Polly kisses on both cheeks, stepped back to look at her, said: 'Unchanged, as always!' a comment which Polly was unsure how to take, and added to the housekeeper: 'We'll have Pimms out here, please, Ann, and lunch too. The weather's too gorgeous to waste.'

Chatting together, they crossed the terrace to lean on the balustrading. The garden was on a gentle slope that fell away beneath them, layered with brick walls, statues, fountains and spring flowers. Beyond and below these an arrangement of box hedges and small specimen trees made the vista look longer than its reality, while beyond an invisible ha-ha was a borrowed landscape of the soft Hampshire countryside, a double *trompe l'œil* that Polly marvelled at.

'This is tremendous,' she murmured, snuffing the scents on the air and remembering the expensive landscape gardening and interior design courses that Candida's mother had insisted she attend after she left LSE. 'More focussed than finishing school,' she had proclaimed. Once Polly had asked Candida why on earth she had gone to LSE – such an unlikely place for her mother's daughter. Candida had opened her eyes wide: 'But, darling, to annoy Mummy, of course. Besides, I wanted to be in London and LSE was different.' Mummy had informed her friends that the LSE had quite forsaken its old left-wingery and was now THE place where the international community sent its hopeful youngsters: 'Surely that hasn't escaped you?'

Polly supposed that Sir Bernard must appreciate his wife's grasp of City affairs. He certainly should respect her other talents. The gardens at Chilbourne House featured regularly in glossy magazines, as did its interior. Sir Bernard had bought the place soon after he married his first wife. 'Dear God, you should have seen it,' Candida had once remarked to Polly. The interior had had the unconvincing air of a palace, with a lavish use of pretentious gilding and far too much bullion on the curtains, while the planting in the herbaceous borders was padded out with busy lizzies and begonias. Imagine! It caused Candida to blench. However, like Mr Brown, she had seen capabilities. She had altered panel mouldings, suppressed gaudy gilding, and redesigned the gardens. Now Chilbourne House was satisfying as a large but lightly informal country house and much admired by the cognoscenti.

'Ah, now, I mustn't forget,' Candida said, putting the jug of Pimms down after she had filled both glasses. 'It was your birthday recently – many happy returns – and I let it go unmarked. I do apologise.'

'Not at all,' said Polly. 'Forty-one. Hell! Something I'd rather forget.'

'The more reason to cherish you. And I do have something for you. It's upstairs on my bed. Bring your drink.'

The Gough marital bed was a four-poster with a handsome arched cornice and painted fluted posts. In its centre lay something wrapped in tissue paper. Candida tossed it to Polly.

'Try it on,' she commanded. 'I could only guess at your size.'

It was a grey-green silk shirt, the very shade of the very colour that suited Polly best. She put down her glass of Pimms and removed her cotton blouse. The silk slid coolly over her flesh; she fastened buttons and walked to Candida's mahogany dressing-table to study herself in its pretty bevelled oval glass. Perfect.

'Perfect,' she said aloud. 'I love it. The exact colour I'm always looking for but never seem to find.' It was also the extravagance she could never afford. 'You are clever. Thank you.'

Candida studied her and remarked with candour: 'You look positively young still with that Titian hair, but your face needs colour.'

Polly grinned. '*No woman over thirty should have a naked face!*'

'Oh!' A chuckle. 'Mummy. I used to think she was just a brute – now I think she's a hugely shrewd brute. But she watches over me like a broody dragon, you know.'

'Goodness, why?'

'Because her life depends on my impeccable behaviour and Bernard's goodwill. She lives in one of his houses in the village, rent free, cleaner and gardener provided. If anything goes wrong, if I misbehave and we divorce, Mummy loses everything.'

Polly almost blenched as she contemplated the horrific picture of Mrs Jamieson-Druce with her loud voice and imperious ways constantly hovering on her doorstep and for the first time saw flaws in Candida's outwardly alluring life. Was Candida tempted to infidelity? Was Bernard, come to that? She knew he had been unfaithful to his first wife. The words: '. . . enough to put dear Bernard right off!' floated into her head.

As if Candida were reading her thoughts she said: 'We'll decorate our middle-aged faces together. Paint over the cracks. Use my stuff. God knows I've enough of it.'

Polly looked. The dressing-table was covered in expensive pots and bottles and sprays in every conceivable shape and size, more probably than she had owned in all her life, and she could see through a door that there were still more in the marble bathroom.

She sat on a stool beside Candida and drank Pimms and experimented with fascination on her skin, her eyes, her lips, finally spraying herself with an expensive and alluring rosy scent that seemed to complete her transformation into a different person. 'Lovely,' she said, and knew herself to be slightly intoxicated and more attractive than she could remember for years. It *was* possible still to paint over the cracks. Maybe men might still fancy her? She felt elated.

Candida swept up the bottles and jars Polly had used. 'Let's put them in your room,' she said. 'Then you can have fun with them again. You look so pretty when you try.'

They ran back down to the terrace, flinging themselves on to big soft garden chairs, curling their feet up beneath them.

'More Pimms,' said Candida, leaning across to fill Polly's glass.

'Heaven,' she said, sipping and reclining back and admiring the south front of the house. 'How I'd love to live in a handsome place like yours – or no, this would be too big, but somewhere old, somewhere with character and charm.'

Candida's triangular eyebrows lifted. 'I thought you liked your present house? You were thrilled when you moved – when was it? – five years ago?'

'Seven. And these things are comparative. A four-bedroomed house on the edge of an estate is infinitely to be preferred to a cramped three-bedroomed one in its noisy centre, but neither exactly fits my dreams of thatch and roses or Georgian symmetry.'

'No, I suppose not. Yet you've always given the impression of contentment.'

Polly sipped and sighed. 'People who complain all the time are bores.'

'You mean *you* have something to complain of *all* the time? That's not like you. Tell me what's wrong?'

Polly agitated the drink in her glass and watched the fruit swirl while her mind seemed to twist this way and that. In falling out of love with Neville she had had a vision into the depths of reality. Once she had loved him with all the emotion in her nature, and while in the grasp of that emotion she had found it impossible to believe that Neville did not love her. His frequent and vigorous demands for sex, their marriage, their children, all had convinced her. It was a natural illusion in someone of her warm temperament and one so wishful of being convinced. She told herself that though he was undemonstrative, emotion lay buried deep in him, perceptible to her alone. Now she was chilled by his coldness and repelled by demands for sex detached from any affection. But she could not say this to Candida. In her marriage there might be nothing left but the outward show, the visible framework that still stood, but that carefully painted exterior was necessary to her. She could not see herself standing alone, open to all the winds of life; she needed some shelter still, for the girls and for herself. To settle for second-best appalled her, but it was infinitely better than nothing. For what would she be without her marriage? She spoke instead of a different problem.

She said: 'Teaching in a comprehensive school never enthralled me. Now it has lost whatever fascination it once had. But I see no way out of it.'

'Why ever not?'

'No other qualifications but a stale degree. Little chance of retraining at my age.'

'You've done it for what . . . fourteen years? What's suddenly become so bad about it? I've always thought of it as a horror story, that's for certain, but then I'd never have started.'

Polly shrugged her shoulders. Sometimes she felt guilty about her lack of dedication. Teaching, her tutor at the training college had told his students, was not only a profession, it was a vocation informed by dedication. Many students had been uplifted by his words; not Polly. She taught for convenience's sake, and subtly, steadily, over the years had felt punished for that lack of commitment. She had tried, though. She was a conscientious teacher, moderately popular, trusted by the children. Yet the process gave her little pleasure.

'What's so bad? Marking, endless marking. The lack of money for new textbooks or any sort of teaching aid. Coping with the ever-increasing number of unhappy and disturbed children who come from broken homes, without being able to offer them any real help. Implementing the endless changes within the schools that have been inaugurated by the government's National Curriculum or the latest fads in teaching practice. It stuns individual initiative, it stuns enthusiasm.' She thought of certain of her colleagues, particularly her head of department who, with only three years to go to retirement, got by on the minimum of work, whose results were passable through long years of practice, but who despaired of the whole system. She told Candida, ending: 'I teach or act as tutor to nearly three hundred children every year. How can I hope to know each one individually as I should? I can't forget the two sisters I found hiding in the cloakrooms rather than go home to the unemployed stepfather who was sexually abusing them, or the boy we have to watch all the time because he ran amok at his last school and did eight thousand pounds worth of damage. But the quiet average child sinks out of sight. I've no hope of doing the job to the standard it should be done. None of us has. Morale is at rock bottom these days. Yet still I plod on. Oh, I know I should come to it afresh every year, with renewed enthusiasm, but I can't. I love history, but not this factory process.'

Candida sat up, embracing her knees, interested. 'This is a new Polly, a cross Polly. Why have you never said anything of this before? I've recently joined the board of governors of the local prep school, Hamlins, and I've already been roped in to help raise capital for new dormitories and the latest computers for the children. I thought the staff there had problems, but they're nothing in comparison with yours. But there must be some avenue of escape for you. Couldn't you teach economics at a higher level?'

'No. I'm years out of date with the theory. And I think I prefer history – at least it's credible! And I couldn't teach history at a higher level because I haven't a history degree.'

'A pity.' Absently Candida poured the remainder of the Pimms, the last pieces of fruit jostling on the lip of the graceful glass jug to plop out heavily. 'But whatever the problems of change, don't give in. Resignation is appalling, it's wasteful of so much talent, it's . . . it's sickening. Life is intended to be rich and varied and full of colour. So tell me, if someone waved a magic wand, what would be your dream come true? What would you do?'

The housekeeper arrived with a tray and began to lay the table for their lunch. Polly watched her silently.

'Come on, Polly darling, don't be shy, tell.'

Polly suspected she had told enough already, the drink lubricating her tongue, spilling anger and resentment she had never revealed before, but suddenly had felt impelled to tell. Still, why shouldn't she? The housekeeper removed herself and her tray briskly; as her ample backside disappeared into the dim reaches of the house Polly took a deep breath and said simply: 'I'd write. I'd be a novelist.'

Chapter 3

'Would you?' Candida sat up in surprise. 'A novelist? Well! You've always seemed so serenely unambitious in comparison with the rest of us, yet now you come out with something distinctly demanding.'

'I first dreamed of it when I was fourteen. I was a bookworm – only children frequently are – and the books I read led me to create my own fantasies. Then one day I heard a writer talking on the radio about how she put her plots together and built up sub-plots, how she planned her characters' looks and ways. I was entranced. I longed to do that myself. And it's still my ambition.'

'How amazing. What sort of novel would you write?'

'Historical, naturally! My first would be about the start of elementary education for all in the late-nineteenth century and how it changed the lives of the poor, particularly my chief character, a girl whose illiterate father objects to her "being taught to look down on the likes of me".'

'The origins of the empowerment of women! Polly, that sounds terrific. Tell me more.'

'She's bright and ambitious, she struggles to break new ground for women and achieve success in her work – but then a colleague betrays her and she's sacked for marching with the suffragettes . . . I shan't tell you how she fights back because I'll give away all my plot if I do!'

'It would need tremendous research.'

Polly shook her head. 'I've packed folders of notes and references. Remember I've been teaching this sort of stuff for years. But although I've found plenty of novels written on the horrors of child labour in Victorian times to recommend to the children, there's little on schools and education then – except *Jane Eyre*!' She laughed. 'I'd help children to empathise! That's one of the new fads: "Imagine yourself a Board School brat, being taught to know your duty and keep your place".'

Candida leaned forward, her heavy-lidded eyes intent. 'Then if you're so inspired, go for it.'

'How? When? Find me the time in my packed life,' Polly challenged her.

'Simple. Get up at five-thirty.'

'Horrors! That isn't a time, it's a pain in the arse.'

'Nonsense. I ride then and it's wonderful. The world's full of birdsong and fresh clean breezes. You could find time on Saturdays, too. Let the house and garden go hang! Come on, I challenge you, do it!'

'All right, damn you!' Polly said, antagonistic and cross. 'I will. I bloody well will!'

Candida laughed. 'Good,' she said. She leaned across to Polly and hugged her shoulders. 'I know you,' she said. 'You can do it.'

Polly was suddenly excited; the sun and the drink and the conversation had gone to her head so that she saw everything in a dancing golden haze. All through the delicious lunch the housekeeper brought out she was conscious of a sensation she had almost forgotten: happiness. Now she would have an endless source of interest and amusement in her life: she would live with the characters in her manuscript, exploring their lives, creating intrigues and stratagems, loving with them, arguing with them, grieving with them.

Over coffee she turned to contemplate her friend, one hand reposing on the gently rising and falling ribcage, the other flung across her forehead as if in dissatisfaction with some thought. Born in the summer, she was still forty: forty, a notorious year for women's disquiet. Polly had earlier looked at her present life and disliked what she saw. How would Candida assess her own achievements? Financial success and a modicum of fame, that was self-evident, but through a marriage the world concluded was made in greed – hers for money, his for a lithe young body once more in his bed – but which had lasted now for well over a decade, and, so far as she knew, without gossip or innuendo. No career, not like Jane, advancing steadily up the higher ranks of the Civil Service, or Vanessa, a solicitor. Candida worked on interior and garden design commissions from time to time, as well as her charitable works which were largely concerned with children's needs. To Polly she had observed: 'One has to do something, otherwise life would descend to the levels of sex and shopping described in those positively pornographic novels. But Caesar's wife must be above suspicion.'

Did such words indicate that Candida was? It would not be hard for her to find a lover, Polly mused, looking at the long smooth face with its high cheekbones, the odd triangular eyebrows that had a volatile charm all their own, and the lean model's body. She would age elegantly, look lovely for years yet, as those with her bone structure did.

But if she were faithful to the powerful Sir Bernard, then her looks had not had the success that those who built their lives around such assets would desire: one man and he almost sixty. Many would think that a waste. Others found power and wealth strong aphrodisiacs. Polly had no clue as to Candida's thoughts there. (How sexually active were sixty-year-old men, anyway? She had no information on that score either.)

Two sons. She had given Sir Bernard two sons, already developing the big bones and solid flesh of their father. There Candida had been more successful than any of them, (including the first wife, whose contribution had been one weedy daughter). Only Mary beside Candida had a son. Candida was lucky with her boys, Polly thought enviously. How basic the longing for male children was in all countries. Asians sighed over daughters, the Chinese had been known even in recent years to abandon girl babies to die. The Western nations were less extreme, but they too yearned for sons. She thought with annoyance of Neville. Why? The combative strength of the male; the male seed dominating, the female merely a receptacle? The man's biological rôle was brief but exciting, the female's long and demanding; even the most ardent feminist must envy men. In England, all interest is focussed on the eldest son and his family, especially where fortune and an historic house are involved; a younger son is a reserve heir; the family solicitor sighs at the birth of daughters. It's the effect of primogeniture. Power again, the male power that Candida was passing on.

But Candida had had other successes. She was the *châtelaine* of the distinguished Chilbourne House. Moreover she didn't simply exist within its spacious walls, complacent and inert, she contributed constructive thought and the house reflected her taste, her knowledge and charming whims, and when, twice each summer, together with the gardens, it was opened to the public to raise money for her charities, Candida was available to talk, regaling her audiences with personal anecdotes about the problems that beset the owners of large and ancient properties, and with wit and point making them laugh.

Was her own life 'rich and varied and full of colour', or did it only seem so to the outsider? This weekend she had spoken of Polly rescuing her from boredom. A brief blip?

At this point sleep suddenly overcame Polly, a dreamless oblivion under the sun from which she woke with the impression that endless æons of time had passed, and that for once it didn't matter. She stretched like a cat, breathing deeply. She felt refreshed and peaceful.

Candida was talking softly on her cordless telephone. 'Mmm . . . mmm . . . I'm sure you're right. No . . . No . . .! So silly to think otherwise. Isobel, I must go now, I have a friend here for the weekend, a girl friend of many years' standing. 'Bye. Yes . . . Yes, you mustn't worry.

Goodbye.' She put the telephone back on the table, sighed, shrugged, and seeing Polly awake, said in a wry voice: 'Oh, my dear, what does one do, what does one say, when a friend rings up to tell you that some miserable bitch has hinted that her husband is being regularly unfaithful and the poor thing's longing, just longing, for you to reassure her?'

'And is he unfaithful?'

'Oh, God, yes. With anything of the right shape that moves. But she says pathetically, "Surely I'd know if he were having an affair? I'd sense something. But there've never been any signs, Candida, never." I feel so useless making reassuring noises.'

'How do you know about him?' Polly asked, curious.

'He boasted to Bernard years ago about the shooting weekends he goes on. The shooting isn't of the variety his wife imagines. Besides he's tried his charms on all the wives round here. I imagine he's had his successes too – if they're the sort who thrill when he warms his genitals against them at Hunt Balls.'

'Yuk. How does he get away with it?'

'He doesn't have affairs, he has sex. Wherever he can manage it. One night stands or weekends with like-minded friends don't leave tracks.'

'A real four-letter man.'

But Polly spoke without heat; an unknown man married to an unknown friend of Candida's was too remote to rouse her. Without Neville's demands, without thoughts of marking or the myriad repetitive tasks of the house to perform, she could suspend all bothersome preoccupations and relish whatever Candida had in store for her. She had not enjoyed such idleness for years. 'What do we do this afternoon?' she asked.

Candida had a new bay mare to show her, that was the first thing, so they strolled to the stables and the mare was brought out and looked over, not that Polly knew anything of the points to look for in horses, but she made admiring sounds at the glossy animal and tried to say the right things, and the mare nodded her head and nudged her new mistress and Candida told her she was the most gorgeous creature in the whole country. Then they walked to see the old wild garden that had been the scene of Candida's latest project and which was now carpeted with blue and white and pink anemone blanda and wild flings of narcissus, while in the dappled light under the blossoming trees the chequered flowers of the snake's head fritillary were just beginning to bloom. Polly was almost speechless with admiration; she had seen nothing like it in all her life, and said so.

'It's come off well,' Candida conceded. 'The photographers from *House and Garden* came yesterday – all part of keeping the Gough profile high!' After a moment she added that the garden had been one of the many ploys that had kept her busy this last year. Too many ploys, she sometimes thought: her house, her garden, her charitable concerns, in the holidays her sons and their friends, the business entertaining that her life with Sir Bernard inevitably demanded: 'And crashingly boring that is too – Americans and Germans whose wives have knuckleduster diamonds on their fingers and no conversation!' Moving between their Kensington house and here, riding and occasionally hunting. 'It's a good life,' she shrugged, 'but it's splintered. There's no continuity, no whole. *I'm* splintered.'

'You achieve a lot,' Polly said.

'Do I?' she replied. 'Sometimes I wonder what it's all for!' A remark that made Polly momentarily quite pink with annoyance and envy. If she were not contented, what hope was there for the rest of them?

They walked on, circling the park in the clear spring light. As they approached the house, Candida commented that as the next annual Sunday luncheon was their twentieth they should do something special to celebrate it. Perhaps Neville could propose a toast and make a speech: 'After all, he was there with us in our finals year. And he does these things with such an air.'

Polly winced. Neville's view of the yearly lunch was scornful, monosyllabic and couched in words not intended for other ears. 'He might.'

'And if you don't object, Polly darling, Bernard will bring the champagne. Vintage Veuve Cliquot would be suitable, I think, don't you?'

'Marvellous,' she said faintly, galled at lacking the funds to wave such an offer aside. 'It would be marvellous.'

Both were silent as each contemplated the reaction of her husband to these suggestions.

Then Candida clapped her hands to her head. 'Drinks! Goodness, I nearly forgot . . . we have two chaps over for drinks before lunch tomorrow. Hugh Hanbury, a neighbour, and his brother Thomas. Hugh's land runs alongside ours to the east. He's pleasant – the articulate, easy to talk to sort; easy on the eye, too. He's in merchant banking, but he doesn't talk about that, thank God. They've a handsome William and Mary house that I long to get my hands on.'

'And his brother?'

'Him I know less well, though you may have met him before – he lives in Winchester.'

Polly doubted it.

'Hugh insisted on coming to see my mare.' She laughed. 'The patronising brute's been teasing me about her, said I was bound to have bought a showy shocker. He'll judge tomorrow whether she's shoeable. He breeds, or rather his wife does, in a small way. They're certain no one can know a quarter what they know about horses. I'll show him!'

When the two men arrived the next day Polly found it a pleasure to look at them, the type they represented as well as the men themselves: their height, their muscular sturdiness, that air of inbuilt confidence and intelligence, all the inheritance of centuries of privilege and public school. Hugh, the elder brother, was the more sleek and well-groomed, with a long strong nose and full sensuous lips, giving him a determined, almost greedy look, contrasting sharply with the bespectacled Tom's casual, even rumpled air, and the unruly hair that at the back overlapped the top of his coat.

When Hugh and Candida went to look at the mare amid jesting and laughter, Polly found herself alone with Tom. His background was so different from hers that all small talk promptly evaporated from her mind and she looked at him almost in terror, this big self-possessed male who would be bound to find any topic she introduced banal, and she did not want to bore him, she hated the thought that he might stare in disdain. She wanted rather to be like Candida and Hugh and Tom, to be of their world, comfortable, assured, knowledgeable about the great and the beautiful. It was a world not unlike theirs that she had once dreamed of inhabiting with Neville, yet it had never materialised.

'Would you . . .?' both began simultaneously, then stopped.

Tom Hanbury made a deprecatory gesture with his hands, Polly opened her mouth and closed it, and then somehow, she never could afterwards remember how, smiling, half-laughing, they began talking, and their talk swiftly became a conversation of great ease, managing to convey a great deal about themselves without the need for long explanations. He was an architect with a practice in Winchester. 'Of course,' Polly said, sipping her drink, 'I thought I recognised the name!' and was relieved not to seem ignorant. Not surprisingly, he was often called upon in connection with restoration work in conservation areas of the city; he found delving into the past of the city's buildings intriguing, and so did she. She confessed to being a history teacher, and he said that history fascinated him endlessly, but he wouldn't know about the teaching part. His voice was deep and rich and she found it sympathetic.

They walked from room to room as they talked, because, Tom said, he'd admired Candida's improvements and clever colour sense over the years, and it was a pleasure to renew his acquaintanceship with it all and gaze at his favourite pieces of furniture. 'She has an eye for the interesting and the unusual and her knowledge of porcelain is wide, too.' He listened to Polly's comments as if they were of real interest and offered information with diffidence, saying, 'I think we'll find those chairs are Hepplewhite – we must ask Candida when she and Hugh return' or 'Would you think that bowl could be Delft?'

When they talked his blue-grey eyes looked directly at her as if she were more attractive than anything around her, and beneath his gaze she sensed herself bloom. She felt beautiful and knowledgeable and worthwhile. She told him the dining room, with its display of oriental china, was her favourite room. His too, it seemed, or was he only pretending? She asked him where he lived; was it in Winchester or one of the local villages? In Winchester, he said, by the cathedral and the college, and then she discovered that his wife had died nearly two years ago, in a car crash, and that there were: 'Just the two of us now, me and my daughter, Laura. She's a day-girl at St Swithin's School. She's thirteen. We manage. Friends help, of course.' He said little more beyond admitting that the first year without his Kate had been a hell of pain. 'We went well together, you see. We liked the same things. I wanted to live with her to old age and die first. I asked too much, didn't I?'

She shook her head. 'It shouldn't be so,' she said in real sympathy.

'And you,' he said, 'what about you? Tell me all about you.'

But that was impossible. 'Oh,' she said. 'That's dull. I've been married for nearly twenty years and I've two nearly grown-up daughters.'

Candida and Hugh returning then, laughing and talking and demanding their attention in their squabble over her mare, Polly and Tom had no opportunity to talk again, but when he left he took her hand, smiling at her, and said as if it were definite: 'I'll see you in Winchester, Polly.'

'I'll look forward to that,' she said, and her throat was dry with anticipatory excitement.

On her drive back home that evening she concluded that she would not object to a life similar to Candida's. It would be preferable to her own. She recollected with wry amusement her shock when, all those years ago, Candida had confided her mother's advice to marry for money, not for love. 'One would need to like the man, naturally,' Mrs Jamieson-Druce had advised, 'but love, let's face the dilemma, nine times out of ten is a silly word to describe physical infatuation that does not last. Look at my own case – it barely survived the honeymoon. But money, whatever the relationship, gives one a comfortable life. One meets so many interesting people, one can amuse oneself so well. No one despises money, but to be poor is dreadful.' Now Polly found herself sympathetic to Mrs Jamieson-Druce's views. Out of love and poor herself, she wondered what other strange pieces of advice, other strange methods of living, it might not be more advantageous to follow than the romantic Western idyll, once faded. She remembered Candida's tart comment to her when she had cried out: 'I don't see how you can!' to which the reply was: 'To live a virtuous life in the days when Heaven beckoned was quite another matter from today. Virtuous poverty led to a place in God's holy mansion – but with no afterlife, I'd rather make sure of my mansion now, thank you, and to hell with virtue. What reward will you get for your poverty, Polly?'

She thought of Neville leaving her behind while he went sailing, of Neville with Vanessa last summer . . . A cold finger ran down Polly's spine. She swallowed. Candida's recent remarks about the unfaithful male acquaintance rang in her head: 'He doesn't have affairs, he has sex . . . Weekends with like-minded friends don't leave tracks . . .' Could it be? Neville had weekends with like-minded friends. But they were for sailing. And other things? Girls could go sailing too. Don't think of it, she told herself. But she did think of it. Especially after a weekend at Chilbourne House where once she'd seen him . . . Just once. With Vanessa. She'd tried to bury that memory; she hated the sickening anger that came with it.

Last summer, on a hot June day with all the friends there, half a dozen of them had gone wandering over the house; when tea was served two were still absent, Vanessa and Neville. Polly had gone to find them. And she had found them – God, yes, she had found them. In a far corner bedroom, the door ajar just three inches, hard at it. She'd seen them through the crack and at once retreated, tiptoeing back down the carpet of the long passage, heart banging in her chest. Why had she tiptoed? Why hadn't she gone in and screamed at them? Pride, yes, pride, that was why. If no one else knew of it, it hadn't occurred, not so far as the world was concerned. So she was silent, waited. Nothing significant happened, nothing at all. She had told the others Vanessa and Neville were on their way and five minutes later they sauntered out on to the terrace for tea and went to talk to other people. Polly told herself it was Vanessa's fault, she'd thrown herself at him – and indeed she flirted (as she did with most men) every time she saw him. Maybe they had done it for old time's sake. (The thought repulsed Polly.) Two months later, when at last she'd braced herself to bring up Vanessa's name, Neville had remarked grumpily: 'That woman is a ruddy nymphomaniac. She'd have the trousers off any likely man in five minutes flat, whether he wanted it or not.' By which Polly deduced he was ashamed of the episode and mentally shifting the blame. And faintly that had mollified her.

Now her heart thumped as shock hit home. Could Neville be of the sort who didn't have affairs, just sex? He had frequent committee meetings, evenings with friends, sailing weekends . . . No, it was disloyal to think it, neurotic, sick, you couldn't run a marriage that way. Put it out of mind. Neville wasn't the sort. *Was he?*

Polly had learned from the start not to object to his weekends with friends. She hadn't wanted to be a nagging, possessive wife. So many were, he had told her; he was glad she was different. Once in the early days, heavily pregnant and feeling off-colour, she'd asked if he couldn't stay at home with her: surely the friends he was playing golf with could find a fourth? Neville had given her a long sad look. 'Sweetheart, you can't expect me to let them down, not at this late stage? Besides, I'm mentally tired after a hard week's work, I need the relaxation. Working for the county council isn't my sort of work. I'll never say this again, but you do realise, don't you, the sacrificing of my true career that marrying you involved? Don't grudge me my small pleasures.' Polly had been tearfully contrite. 'I'm sorry,' she snuffled, putting her arms round his neck and feeling relief when, after a second's pause, he held her in return. 'I do love you, you know I do. I want you to have fun. I won't be mean again.'

She knew now she had been a fool; had she been a bigger fool than she thought? There were always so many weekends, days, evenings away. She could find out, watch and be wary. The idea gave her the same shiver of disgust as dealing with the contents of the dustbin.

Rose was in the kitchen as she let herself into the house, and emerged, tea-towel in hand, to greet her.

'Hi, Ma darling. You came back just too soon – I'm only halfway through dealing with the weekend's detritus. Still, the kitchen was a disaster area, now it's only a mess! Did you have a good time?'

'Wonderful,' Polly said with feeling.

'Good,' Rose approved. 'Hey, I like that shirt, it's a subtle colour, something different – and stunning with your hair. Is it new?'

'Yes. A present from Candida. Is Neville back yet?'

'Got back forty minutes ago.' Rose's voice was disapproving. 'He wanted dinner pronto. He was put out that you weren't here to wait on him. I told him to go for a bite in a pub, though God knows what he'll get at this hour on a Sunday. Oh, and Emily rang. Back soon, not to worry.'

Polly nodded and took her weekend case upstairs to unpack. Flung in the centre of the bed was the smart holdall that accompanied Neville on his sailing trips. It seemed to push itself on her attention and spurred by Heaven knew what stab of curiosity and dislike, she picked it up, emptied its contents on the bed and began to rifle through them. Changes of shirt and underwear, she noted, and nightgear too. So he had always intended to make a weekend of it. With whom? She poked further. No condoms, anyway. Deflated, she pushed his belongings into his drawers or the washbasket, then, turning to go, she saw his blazer on a chair. Feeling furtive and guilty, she searched its pockets. One Paisley-patterned handkerchief, no lipstick stains. Nothing further. But wait a minute, men have inside pockets. She slid two fingers down into the silky lining and retrieved a piece of paper. Frowning, she unfolded it.

'*Darling, just a note to say thank you for a superb and revealing weekend – in every sense. Wow! You were marvellous. Everything was marvellous. I can't wait for next time. Don't let it be long. Your J.*'

So he was! What should she do now? What could she do? She walked over to the window and looked out, trembling and breathing quickly, leaning on the sill. The garden was almost dark and very peaceful; the house was still. That was how it must stay, everything peaceful and still until Emily had taken her A levels and was off to university. The last thing she must do was to upset Emily's life at this crucial point. That would be cruel. But then what? Divorce? A new life? A thought at once terrifying and alluring. The silent hiatus over the summer months would give her time to think it all out and make her plans. And besides, the thought occurred to her with a twitch of the lips, by waiting she would get the friends' twentieth anniversary out of the way: she would not have to spoil that day with talk of adultery and divorce and settlements, all the scurrilous in-fighting and fall-out of a couple at war. In another year, yes, she'd start the inevitable fight. But time would pass before the friends met again. She wouldn't have to endure Vanessa's crocodile tears, happily married Mary's shocked sympathy.

What did she feel, truly? As she thought about it her knees stopped trembling and her breathing steadied. She felt different, quite different from anything she might have expected. For years she had clung to her love for Neville, had attempted to build an impregnable world about them so that she could feel safe and content, but faced now with the evidence of his infidelity she felt only relieved of an intolerable burden. She sucked in a deep breath, hung the blazer back on the chair with exaggerated care, slipped the note back into the inside pocket, and let out a gust of air that seemed to take with it a hundred pinpricks of irritation and release the tension in her chest and every muscle of her body. In spite of her shock and distaste she felt unexpectedly light-hearted. The indebtedness Neville had pressed upon her, and the formless fears and worries that had haunted her all her married life, vanished like mist in the morning. Now she would be free: no longer a cringing subservient Polly, but a new woman with a life of her own. And if she did meet Tom in Winchester, well, just the thought of what might happen gave her an anticipatory glow.

Chapter 4

Vanessa lived in a flat in Bayswater. It was in a cream-coloured early-Victorian terrace with big high rooms, and across the nearby Bayswater Road was a footgate into the Park, a mere three minutes away. (So smart.) The flat had two main bedrooms, one for a guest and one for Vanessa and her current lover: but there was no current incumbent. The flat was packed with furniture saved from the wreckages of her two marriages and smothered with ornaments. The ornaments came by way of gifts, some from aunts or friends, most from past lovers. Culled from such varied sources, they jostled together in an erratic and eclectic mass that her old friend Jane once observed bore a remarkable similarity to Vanessa's jumbled life. There was a carved Kashmiri box, a present from a lover who had opted out for a year in the foothills of the Himalayas, there was an art nouveau vase from a dealer met in Spain and an art deco bowl from a lecturer in Italian literature; there were bits in brass and bits in glass, together with a battered trumpet and an oddly elongated bronze cat that looked revolted by the flowery plate on a plastic stand at which it stared. Once a week they were dusted by a depressed Bosnian refugee; Vanessa rarely noticed them: her interior life attracted her far more than any exterior matter.

On Monday evening she returned to find the sitting room in darkness, its air stale. After a heavy day in the office and a return journey packed amid sweaty humanity in the Underground rush hour, she felt weary, untidy and slightly sordid. She shed jacket, bag and briefcase on to a chair and tugged back the curtains. Spring sunshine glowed dustily through the window. It was weather for lovers but she was solitary. Tears filled her eyes; it was three months since her last lover had left. The telephone rang. Vanessa's heart jumped: someone, somewhere, wanted to speak to her, someone who would break the brooding emptiness of the flat.

'Hello?'

'Hello, Vanessa. Polly here. How are you?'

Polly Ferrison. The odious cheerful voice was an offence, but Polly was inviting her to the annual Sunday lunch in June. One day of a weekend filled, no longer blank, reproaching her. 'I'll find my diary,' she said. 'Must check that I'm free.' Essential to keep up the show of a busy social life. 'Oh, good, that'll be fine.'

'Will you bring a partner?' Polly asked, her tone all bright interest.

Bitch. 'I might,' returned Vanessa, her voice full of insinuations. 'It's early days . . . one has to wait and see.'

'Yes, indeed.'

There was a brief exchange as to health and Vanessa put the telephone down. She shook with a presentiment that she would never have another companion in this place. She seized her jacket and keys and ran out in an obscure sort of terror, darting across the main road and into the Park, her feet carrying her towards the Round Pond, the nearest place where there were people. Perhaps there would be someone she knew there, someone she could invite back for a drink.

Vanessa was an associate solicitor with Newhouse & Bock, a City firm of medium size and strength. Her work was in private and commercial property law. Throughout her working hours she concentrated on leases, tenancies and possession, fighting, so she told her friends, for the underprivileged against rapacious landlords. She had failed to gain the partnership she was certain she deserved, though she allowed the friends to assume she had. It had never occurred to her that she would fail in this, but when her last hopes vanished she sensed malign forces at work, as with her degree, which was a mere pass.

She walked on across the grass. Polly had done no better than her, anyway – a school teacher, a nothing, her salary half Vanessa's. And Neville had been pulled down by Polly, who'd insisted on his marrying her when she got pregnant on purpose, tearing up his hopes of a PhD, tearing him away from her, Vanessa, taking him off to dull, prissy Winchester where he was nothing too. He could have done brilliantly; she had always known that, always believed in him. She'd told him so that wonderful day at Candida's when he had seized the chance to make love to her again. She had left the door ajar, praying that this time someone would find them and scream in shock and tell, so that everything would explode in Polly's face and Neville be restored to her, Vanessa. Once she'd thought she heard footsteps, but no one had interrupted them.

A man's status is defined by his career, she thought. For nearly half a century he is tied into the world of work, but if his success is less than he thinks it should be, then by forty he can be desperate. He could break out in various ways, seeking his lost youth. She had seen it happen. If only Neville would break out – in her direction – how wonderful it would be.

There were boats sailing on the Round Pond, white sails against the glittering water. Two labradors raced behind the green deck chairs, scattering the pottering pigeons. Birds sang. Her throat closed convulsively. Each of the people here seemed to belong to someone: fathers with excited sons sailing boats, lovers holding hands. Vanessa desperately needed to be half of a couple, to belong to someone forever.

The roots of this obsession went far back into childhood. She was the second child of her parents, born twelve years after her brother, an unintended extra. Her parents were cool, detached characters, not given to demonstrative affection; Vanessa, a child who ached for cuddles, felt left out, a feeling that never left her and was reinforced when her father, a banker, moved to Hong Kong with her mother and she was left behind at school. She was seven then and holidays were a problem. She went to Hong Kong in the summer, but at Christmas and Easter she was passed around aunts and uncles and friends like an unwanted parcel – a few days here, a weekend there. She hated it, and felt, quite simply, an outsider in their families. At thirteen she moved to a smart school in Berkshire. At this school the girls had rites, they had rituals. Vanessa did not know them, and when she did she pronounced them silly. The other girls raised their eyebrows and ignored her. She pretended she didn't care, but tried desperately to gain attention. She cheeked the mistresses in hopes of admiring giggles, she showed off, she was noisy. Nothing worked.

At eighteen she left the school's closely guarded environs and discovered boys and sex. Not only did she enjoy the novel sensations (and her sexual desires were tremendous), but she found men relished her company. Her wild tawny hair, her flashing smile, her showy clothes, her availability, which they soon discovered, charmed them, so that they could hardly credit their luck. They were, of course, very young, like her. What they also realised over the course of the next few weeks was that Vanessa's desires, unlike theirs, incorporated a great deal more than simple sex. She wanted their attention, deep and undivided, for where she had bestowed the gift of her love she required to be adored. When she found that she was not all-important she became reproachful and weepy; later she threw tantrums, in the throes of which she accused them of every sort of callousness and infidelity. Over and over again the relationships broke up, the lovers vanishing. Then she wept to her friends of men's inconstancy, of how unlucky she was and how ill-treated. Their sympathy became a drug she craved.

The boarding school years had left her with a fear of being alone.

For those who have always slept in a dormitory, to be alone is unnatural, frightening. To be on her own in her flat was devastating; night after night the least sound would waken her in a cold sweat of terror; the years had passed but it never became any better.

She walked on towards the Serpentine. There was quite a little crowd here, feeding the ducks and geese that clustered by the water's edge. She watched a small boy throwing the last of his breadcrumbs and laughing at the ducks' undignified scramble for the food. Then he turned to walk over to Peter Pan's statue, studying the pedestal, examining its bronze animals with stroking hands, identifying them to his mother, a long-haired blonde in designer jeans.

'Hare!' he concluded proudly, and began to scramble up the pedestal, at each step glancing behind himself at his mother, keeping up a running commentary on his own progress. 'Look! Look how high I am, Mummy – I'm standing on a rabbit!'

The blonde girl caught Vanessa's eye. 'I suppose he shouldn't climb it,' she said half-apologetically, 'but he's not doing any harm.'

'No,' Vanessa agreed and surprised herself by adding, 'He's sweet, isn't he?'

'He's such fun,' the girl said with enthusiasm. 'A real companion. I thought I'd miss work when I left to have him, but with Freddy around I'm never lonely or bored.'

A pang shot through Vanessa. *Never lonely or bored* . . . And then, abruptly, it was as if a vision appeared to her. The low beams of the sun shone deeply in the bronze beneath Peter Pan. *Never lonely* . . . She turned, her heart thumping, and began to walk away.

''Bye!' the girl called, jumping her child down.

Vanessa was too thrilled to hear her. A week ago she had visited a colleague to see her new baby. The colleague had complained of wakeful nights. Did she regret having her two children, Vanessa asked, instead of continuing straight through with her career? (She was a partner, and a successful one.) 'Oh no,' she said, smiling and sighing together. 'One frets and complains at this stage, Vanessa, but it's worth it . . . even the bad nights and the screams and not having a minute to call one's own. Without them there'd be a horrid void. They love you, you see, so wholeheartedly, so uncritically. It's something very special.'

A horrid void without them . . . They love you . . . wholeheartedly . . .

'I shall have a child,' Vanessa said aloud. And again: 'A child of my own!'

She walked on, exultant, nearly running in her excitement. If she had a child the sounds in the night would come from him.

'My son!' she said, and laughed. And the last rays of the sun caught and illuminated her as she spun in a dizzy circle on the grass of the Park.

Jane woke up refreshed and glowing after only five hours sleep, her short brown hair tousled above black-brown eyes, her wide mouth curved in a smile. Her mood was almost invariably good; today it was more. She stretched luxuriously between the sheets in the great bed in her handsome flat in The Boltons. Surely she was twenty-four years old, not forty-four? She wanted to laugh and dance and sing. She rolled over to turn on her music, the first thing she always did on waking. Bach's 'Magnificat'. Perfect. She walked into the bathroom to send a cascade of water plummeting into the bath, carolling: 'Magnificat! Magnificat!' at full voice. Hers was a good soprano, she'd sung the 'Magnificat' with her choir not so long since, loving it. 'Magnificat!' Sacred music was great stuff, full of vigour and fervour. 'My soul doth magnify the Lord . . .' Silent cords slid back the curtains. Jane didn't believe in God, but on days like this she believed in something and wanted to sing praises to whatever it was. The world was an amazing place, the morning magnificent, coolness and sunlight and the new leaves on the trees sparkling in the gardens beyond her window. She praised it all, her voice soaring. 'Magnificat!'

She poured bath oil into the water before turning off the taps and sinking into its luxurious depths. She had two interesting meetings this morning and then an important report to complete that might well alter not only departmental thinking but Cabinet strategy. 'Et exultavit spiritus meus!' And then . . . and then . . . Jane soaped her still excellent breasts with loving care . . . and then she would meet her lover for dinner.

Dear Jeremy. He was a deputy under-secretary in the Foreign Office. She had met him recently through her work as an assistant secretary in the Department of Trade and Industry, enjoyed pitting her mind against his, razor-sharp, decisive, liked listening to his mellow baritone as he argued. But despite the voice and the rangy figure enhanced by well-tailored pinstripe suiting, she had hardly thought of him as a man, more as a rugged mind. He'd spoken once of a son; had she assumed anything she would have pictured a solid marriage and non-availability. Then only ten days ago, they had encountered one another in the foyer at Covent Garden, each with old friends. During the interval of *Don Giovanni* they had talked together, discovering mutual interests. He confirmed that the Miss in Miss Masterson was genuine and not a title retained for work, and she discovered that he and his wife had divorced for simple reasons of incompatibility, 'Meaning boredom', many years ago. 'She's pretty, she's sweet, but she has no sharp edge,' he said. 'By the end of ten years I was at screaming point. I thought I should stay because of our two children, but a year later she lost her temper, informed me that she and her friends found me a patronising pompous bore and she wanted a divorce. We parted with mutual sighs of relief and on reasonable terms.'

Since *Don Giovanni* there had been two dinners, and then the theatre last night . . . and so to bed, she thought, rising from the bath with a beatific smile and enveloping herself in a thick towel. She had anticipated that Jeremy would be good in bed, but this had been something different, an extravaganza. He was virile, demanding, sensual; he had led and she had followed, her desire surging to match his. Afterwards, sweating and relaxed, they had lain with hands clasped, smiling at the ceiling, and she remembered turning to look at the profile of her new lover with a certain satisfaction. It was a handsome profile, after all, and he had gasped at her multiple orgasms and shouted with pleasure at his own. She was gratified by both their performances, and remembering the cynical and witty Alan Ayckbourn play they had enjoyed earlier, concluded it had been an evening of altogether excellent performances. She had chuckled.

He had turned his head. 'Why are you laughing?'

'Because I feel good.'

'So you should – you're superb.' He leaned over to plant a row of kisses from her throat to her navel and she made soft purring sounds. He looked at his watch. 'Good Lord, two o'clock – do you realise we have been making love for over an hour and a half?'

'You sound complacent, Jeremy.'

'I am.'

They both laughed. He swung his legs off the bed and sat up. 'May I have a shower before I leave?'

'Of course.'

He had made no arguments for staying, accepting with a shrug her dictum that no lover stayed overnight; it led to too many complications.

'Oh,' she'd said, 'I will spend weekends with a lover, go on holiday with him, but no more. In the week my lovers have never lived in. That leads to insidious hints about the laundering of shirts and socks, and I have to think about food-buying and preparing meals – *I*, *I* have to! No, I am a selfish creature, and serious about my needs, and I need to live alone. I don't even mind being celibate for a while. Never, ever have I desired to mother some male.'

He had played the game; had nodded equably and said: 'Fine. We play this on equal terms then. Tomorrow night I shall give you dinner at my flat and *you* will drive home in the early hours.'

Jane grinned as she towelled her body, remembering this. Tonight they would be together again. And as she thought of it, warmed to it, she wondered how she could have survived these last six months of celibacy. Yet nothing could have been worse than Marcus's tantrums. First the growing demands, then the accusations, the self-pity: 'Why can't we live together? You don't care about me or you'd let me stay – I'd matter more than missed meetings or deadlines!' At the end he had reminded her of Vanessa, and when that occurred she cut the knot and said goodbye, neither mad nor sad, but wondering with a bubble of mischief whether she shouldn't introduce them. Jeremy, she hoped, would be sensible and then there could be a long and pleasant liaison. But not tied together by indissoluble vows: a long-term sexual friendship was Jane's answer to the modern dilemma.

The telephone cut across her meditations. Could it be Jeremy?

Not Jeremy, Polly. Apologising for telephoning so early, but pointing out that Jane had not yet responded to the message on her ansaphone. 'A new man?' she enquired.

'Now, Polly, you should know better than to start gossiping at dawn. Besides, what about all those dear little adolescents over at the school, each waiting upon you – "ears open", as Keats once wrote, "like a greedy shark, to catch the tunings of the voice divine"?'

'Don't be revolting,' Polly said with vigour, 'and don't change the subject. I suppose you don't want to tell me, but to have you and Vanessa both being coy is really too much.'

'Not Vanessa as well? Dear God. Then I shall come clean and say, gorgeous new man, great hopes for the future. No more to declare. Don't tell me Vanessa is heading for bad treatment yet again? Because you know, don't you, that it is inevitable?'

'It would be a miracle if not,' Polly agreed.

Jane bent to dry between her toes. 'I thought she was between lovers, if one can call them that. Carnal companions would be a better description. Why doesn't she give up on the whole beastly cycle and become celibate, as I'm always advising her? So much more simple and peaceful for everyone concerned.'

'Ah, but she must have a lover. It isn't just for sex and show, Jane, but for comfort. She hates to be alone. She told me once she was made for love. You know, she thinks of herself as ultra-modern and liberated in her outlook – indeed she once described herself to me as an iconoclast – but in reality she is a hopeless romantic for whom love is the central point of existence. She yearns to be completely immersed in it, as only a basically stupid woman could do.'

Jane straightened, catching her towel more securely above her breasts. 'I am lost in admiration for your caustic summary. But I thought you were the great upholder of romantic love?'

'Time progresses and our ideas progress with them. But now, Jane, since both of us have to work, can you let me know whether you are free for the annual lunch in June – is your diary at the ready?'

The telephone conversation ended, Jane hastened to dress herself in her favourite pintuck shirt and lightweight wool suit and leave the flat for her day's work, but the memory of her conversation with Polly still ran around her mind. There was a tartness, a bitterness she'd not met with before. She was fond of Polly and it made her uneasy.

Mary Allwood came off the telephone at half-past six that evening, after nearly an hour's chat. It was good to talk with an old friend like Polly when you lived in a farmhouse deep in the countryside. It helped you keep in touch. Candida had a new bay mare and an enchanting spring garden, Vanessa and Jane were hinting at new lovers . . . Well! Such items would keep Mary's thoughts busy as she mucked out the pigs or fed the goats and the hens. She would telephone Vanessa in a day or two. She was sure the poor girl was lonely, bound to be after two failed marriages, first to the argumentative and bossy Adrian, and then to that sly, unfaithful Guy Kellet, and now there she was stuck in her flat without so much as a dog or a cat for company. She had looked skinny and ill the last time Mary and George saw her, and the vivid make-up, the eye-catching clothes and the forced vivacity hadn't hidden the tiredness in the once bright blue eyes, or the pale and flaky skin under the cosmetics.

Mary glanced at her own image in the glass above the telephone, her ruddy, weather-beaten face creasing into a wry smile. She had never had the looks of her friends, but George claimed that he preferred her round healthy face and the plump curves of her body to their more stylish appearances. 'I always did prefer Rubens women to skinny witches,' he said.

Time for the table to be laid for the evening meal. It was Lizzie's turn, but she wouldn't remind her, not on the first evening of a new term. Lizzie was fifteen and at the resentful stage; it was simpler to do it herself than have to nag. Besides, Lizzie was her firstborn and the sight of her clumsy adolescent body and her lovely downcast eyes made Mary's heart thump still with love and pity. Lizzie she knew was struggling to create a separate life, to discover her own self, to cut the binding cord. For Mary, there was no link to be wrenched apart, no umbilical cord to sever, because she knew that however far her children went from her she would still be bound, still suffer and anguish over their problems. But she could let them go when the time came, for hers was a contented life.

From above came familiar family sounds: a CD player pounding insistently from behind Lizzie's closed door, clangings as Ben wrestled manfully with his weight-training, mutterings from young Anna reciting her French verbs. Along with the distant hens' cluckings and creakings from Lally the labrador's basket as she settled herself, they wove themselves into a fine yet secure mesh of sounds that held together the different strands of Mary's life.

Her husband came in at the door, tossing his muddy boots into the family boot-box. He sniffed the scent of steak pie and baked potatoes coming from the Aga and shed his old Barbour jacket, giving her a companionable, fading-energy smile. 'Smells good!' he grunted. He sank into a sagging armchair, stuck his legs out before him and eased his toes in their thick knitted socks. 'Bottom field's not finished yet. Too damned wet.'

Mary poured a bottle of beer into a glass tankard and passed it to him. 'George,' she said, 'Polly has just invited us to the LSE lunch party in June. Twenty years, she said it was. Isn't it amazing?'

George switched his mind from the heavy state of the bottom field with difficulty. 'Can we manage it? We'll be away all day. And what about the children?'

'The children are invited. We can manage. Driving over the hills to Winchester is better than having to go to London. We can be back in time for the evening feeds. It'll be a lovely break.'

'Well, I suppose you'll want to go,' he conceded. 'I hope Bernard Gough will be there. There's a clever man. Knowledgeable. Fascinating, in fact. Could be a good party. Twenty years, is it? Seems like yesterday. And you haven't changed, hardly a bit.'

'I've grown older,' she said softly, smiling at the implied compliment. 'We all have.'

He picked up *The Daily Telegraph* and thought about it. 'People like Polly and Vanessa have worn,' he said. 'Their skins are grained, eyes tired. You, my love? Well, the character's come out in your face, that's something different.' He shook out the pages of his paper and began to read. Mary left him to it.

Twenty years, she thought. Well, it would be nineteen years in June since they married. And at the thought of the rewarding entirety of her life with George her mouth lifted at the corners and her face glowed. There was silence in the room and the pool of silence seemed to her inviolate, holding memories of earlier happiness.

She began to peel carrots with deft fingers, glancing at George as she worked. He was a large, big-boned man, with a good head of brown hair still, and bristling eyebrows that made their own commentaries on life's problems. They had met at a college dance in another London college, each brought to it by old school friends, each feeling out of place, Mary particularly so because in those days she had a country burr to her voice and knew herself to be from a different background from her companions. Mary's parents ran a village shop, but they came of farming stock. Both were relieved, when they were introduced, at meeting someone with whom they immediately felt at home, at no longer feeling forced to smile politely at incomprehensible insider jokes. George was then in his last year at Cirencester Agricultural College. 'My friends think I'm lucky,' he told Mary. 'My father's been troubled with arthritis for years and he can't wait to hand over the farm to me and seek the sun abroad. It's a good farm, too, eleven hundred acres.'

It had caused Mary a stab of disappointment when she discovered that old Henry Allwood ran a purely arable farm. Mary yearned for the sort of farm pictured in children's books, full of hens and ducks, pigs and ponies. Old Henry laughed at her. 'All fuss and vets' fees,' he pointed out. But they soon arrived. The hens were to produce fresh eggs for the family, then ducks to amuse her babies. Little Ben had difficulty digesting cow's milk, and so there were goats, Nubians with floppy ears. Ponies and pigs and sheep followed.

One day Mary had a telephone call from a friend; it was her eight-year-old daughter Alice's birthday soon and for her treat she wanted to bring her friends to see Mary's farm. Would that be all right? Of course it would. It was a spring day, all apple blossom and sunshine. Lambs and kids gambolled, there were baby chicks and ducklings; the children had pony rides and bottle fed the orphaned lambs, and all pronounced it the nicest treat ever. Mary laughed afterwards, telling George she felt she was living in Enid Blyton land. But unwittingly she had started something; within a year she had what her friends called 'a delightful business' and she was making money. Birthday treats had branched out into playgroup and school visits, with pamphlets and quizzes; she even gave lectures and had twice appeared on television.

Mary put her pan of carrots on the hotplate and stood for a moment by the Aga's warmth. Her mind was on her friend Vanessa; she always exclaimed over the farm animals. It was Mary who had introduced her to the group, attracted by a flamboyance so different from her own quiet ways, sympathetic to the loneliness she saw in the girl. She hoped Vanessa did have some decent man in her sights; she needed affection. Perhaps if she had, then Mary and George could invite them to stay for the weekend of the party: it would be fun to have guests and cosset them, and with everyone going to Polly's on the

Sunday then George wouldn't have too large a dose of Vanessa. Mary sensed disapproval there, but she and George were not one of those modern couples who loved to bare their souls in full and open discussion, nor did they pry after what had not been said.

There was a rustle as he folded his paper and dropped it on the floor. 'We could have Vanessa to stay for the weekend of the lunch party if you like?' he offered. 'Even have her latest man. Make something of the anniversary. How about that?'

Mary stared at him in amazement. In the mystery that was communication between humans was there such a thing as telepathy, something akin to radio waves or radar? Whatever it was, it was impressive how often they thought the same thoughts.

'That would be just the thing!' she said. Collecting cutlery from its drawer, she began to lay the table.

Chapter 5

Polly's family varied in their reactions to her writing.

While she was driving Rose back to Cambridge, along with her battered suitcases and innumerable bulging Sainsbury's plastic bags, Rose said that for her to write a novel was a brilliant scheme. She was certain it would prove excellent therapy against middle-age and boredom. 'You should have done something like this years ago, Ma,' she reiterated, hugging her goodbye at Girton. 'Something for yourself. You need more in your life than Pa and his demands and dreary old household chores and marking. I'll read the first chapters when I come home next – probably in a month, I can't promise sooner, it'll depend on the level of my Saturday night partying. As a budding publisher I'll assess it from an editorial point of view! But if you stick to the plot you've told me about it'll be terrific and everyone'll rave about it.'

Emily was less sure. 'Look, Ma, I don't see how you can go on with this. You're always saying you're pushed. What about my A levels? I'm not going to help with cooking or things, I can't. Daddy wants to write his philosophy book, but he's not trying to do it now.'

'I write at dawn, darling, when you're asleep, and be honest, you hardly know I'm doing it. It's like a hobby; it doesn't interfere with the main things in my life and I promise you I won't let it.'

Emily was often restive, suspicious. Life did not come easily to her as it did to Rose. Nor did she have Rose's looks. Her hair was more brown than red, a pleasant but unremarkable chestnut, and she was shorter than Rose, too, her figure not so eye-catching, her legs not so long. Without the constant contrast with her sister she passed as a pretty girl, with Rose about she was reduced, the colour leached from her hair and her light blue eyes, her opinions overpowered. At school she did well, applying herself with a diligence Rose scorned. 'You're so good it's not decent, Emily. Why don't you break out and have fun?' But Emily didn't want to play up, she wanted to do well to impress her father and gain his praise. She had the same extravagant admiration for Neville that Polly had once held.

Neville neither applauded nor denounced the idea of a novel. 'If you think you have time . . .' he shrugged. Fiction? Novels? He knew nothing himself about that sort of thing, but he supposed it a distraction from the teaching Polly didn't seem to care for. He only wished he could find time for the book he was researching, but a couple of hours here and there would be insufficient for the grandeur of the concepts he would expound. There was little change in his life except that Polly both rose and went to bed earlier than him, lying deeply asleep when he joined her. This meant less sex, but Neville passed no comment. Polly was sure now that he often had fun, as he would think of it, with other women, out of boredom, out of lust, or in delectable spite against Polly, who had spoiled his life. Presumably he thought the likelihood of her hearing of this fun exceedingly remote.

One other person knew of her writing ambitions – Tom Hanbury. He kept appearing and re-appearing in her life, and now that she knew him she thought it odd that she had not always known him; he must have been there to be known for years, but she had not looked. He waited next to her at the check-out at Marks & Spencers and said how charmed he was to have discovered her there: 'Queues are so boring unless one has this sort of luck!' His blue-grey eyes looking into hers made her feel breathless and slightly dizzy. A week later he sat opposite her at a table in Lloyds Bank and laughed with triumph when she looked up from filling in a slip to meet his eyes. 'I said I'd see you in Winchester, Polly, and look, I have, twice already.' They chatted and ended by walking down the street together engrossed in their talk. He asked for her telephone number: 'So that our meetings can be better regulated.' She was overjoyed and flurried, opened her mouth to mutter something about having a husband and children and instead gave it to him and watched him put it in his diary. So on a sunlit Saturday morning they met to have coffee together at Richoux in the old God Begot House, except that she had a delicious hot chocolate liberally topped with cream and a large and expensive pastry similarly wicked, and perhaps it was the feeling almost of inebriation brought about by such unaccustomed rich food and drink that led to her confidences. Or maybe it was the way he leaned forward to catch her every word, interest, concern or amusement chasing in turn across his face. She was not one to confide readily; she had suspicions about the prudence of casual chatter, but to talk to Tom was a kind of deliverance.

'It's a big project,' he said, running a hand through his untidy hair after she had told him the plot and he had elicited details she hardly knew she had thought out herself. 'Intriguing, though. Don't you find the writing a tremendous effort, weaving in all that historical background as well as developing the characters?'

She shook her head. 'I amaze myself. It is an effort, but in a way it's like putting a big puzzle together – the more you do, the more you perceive and the more fascinating it becomes. And working on each scene to catch the images and the tension I want is a challenge, and when I meet it and the words flow and I feel it coming to life . . . well, it gives me a tremendous buzz. Now I pray every day that the words won't defeat me, that they'll continue to flow, that I shan't find myself staring at a blank sheet of paper with no place to go.'

He looked shocked. 'And has that ever happened?'

'No, thank God. But you must understand that these are early days. Just once I spent my whole two dawn hours on a paragraph describing the tension between father and young daughter and the right words refused to come. The frustration was extreme. I was at screaming point, with dozens of screwed up pieces of paper flung all round the room, and still it was . . . oh, so hopeless!'

'How did you solve it?' He leaned on his elbows, his face intent.

'It was time to wake the household and a horrid wet morning it was too. I dropped it and returned to it next day in a glorious dawn with the birds singing their hearts out – and behold, in two minutes it was done.'

He sat back and laughed. 'You're like me, bad weather blocks you. Great thoughts never arrive with the clouds – how can they?'

And then they talked of his work and which buildings in and around Winchester owed their genesis to him, and she was pleased to be able to give genuine comment, because each one that he mentioned she recollected at once and had admired in terms of modern design, modern architecture. 'They're not the sort of pastiche many people cry out for in the city, they're clearly late-twentieth century but they don't jerk you up with a "Get me!" impact, they blend with their surroundings. I think they're inspired.' So then they talked happily about design and creativity and how much was due to inspiration and how much to perspiration, and laughed together about clichés in writing and clichés in design, until Polly looked at her watch and said: 'Help! I should have gone ages ago. I'm a working woman and I have things that must be done on Saturday mornings.' Feeling suddenly shy, she thanked him for a delightful interlude in the day's normal flurry and asked him not to tell anyone of her writing plans: 'Because, Tom, everyone knows everyone in Winchester and I'd feel such an idiot if I didn't make it to publication. And it's doubtful anyway, because so many try and fail and why should I be different?'

Rather to her surprise he did not rise from his chair but mumbled something about it being late and since his daughter was spending the day with friends he would lunch here at Richoux. Then he smiled up at her and said that he would preserve her secret and he was honoured by her confidences. 'But I know you will succeed,' he said. 'I'm certain of that already.'

As she turned to go he caught at her wrist and the feel of his warm firm hand made her heart give a disconcerting jump. 'Tell me,' he demanded, 'does your husband read what you have written? Is he a good critic?'

'No,' Polly said. 'He isn't a novel reader. Never has been.' She realised that from force of habit she had flown to Neville's defence, and despised herself.

Tom said: 'If my wife had been writing a novel, I'd want to read every word. I would be fascinated. I'd want to praise and encourage and help.'

'But you're a kind and decent chap who is interested in what other people do,' Polly said, and did not care what he made of her remarks. 'Goodbye, Tom.'

At home she found a note on the kitchen table in Neville's scrawl. '*Golf with Geoff. Will lunch at clubhouse. N.*' Beneath he'd added a postscript: '*Candida Gough rang. Please ring back.*'

Polly dealt with her shopping and turned to the telephone. Candida sounded pleased with herself. The head of history at the prep school where she was a governor was retiring this summer and there was a dearth of good candidates for the position: 'So I thought of you. It's a lovely place, girls as well as boys these days, half day pupils, half boarding. Far more relaxing to teach children like these, they're such happy little souls. I know they'd mostly be younger than you're used to, but the Common Entrance examinations can't be far off GCSE standards. Small classes too, think what bliss. Your marking load would be halved and you'd have more time to write.'

Polly hesitated: she hardly knew where she was in her life, she'd have to work on new syllabuses, Hamlins School was twenty miles away. She voiced some of this to Candida, but her objections were swept aside. 'Don't you dare cling to that hairshirt of yours! Break out, break away. Come and see Mr Hammond, see the school. You'll be impressed. And you'd have my recommendation.'

More to silence Candida than with any real intention of applying, Polly telephoned the headmaster and found herself with an interview booked for the following Thursday: 'Say at four forty-five, and we'll lay on some tea.' He sounded positively eager; Candida must have done her work well.

Emily was reproachful. 'But why, Ma? Why have to drive all that long way when there's no need? I thought you liked the Durngate School?'

'Sometimes,' Polly said, thinking how young Emily was for seventeen and wondering whether she had spent enough time with her of recent years. 'Sometimes one takes stock and sees a need for change.'

'At your age? But why should you?' said Emily. 'Everything's fine for you. Isn't it?'

'We like to mix the radical with old-style academic excellence,' Mr Hammond observed, showing Polly new science rooms, a computer room, 'shortly to be re-equipped', a music suite and art studios full of delightful and expressive art. 'Children move upwards in the school according to progress and ability, not chronological age. They all have their individual strengths; we aim to build on these and thereby build self-confidence.' He was tall, pleasantly scruffy and approachable. In the history room she was introduced to the retiring teacher, a jovial white-haired, tweed-jacketed man who showed her the history syllabus for each year, periods she thought she could enjoy teaching. 'We've only one form with seventeen in it,' he told her, 'the others are smaller.' She had to suppress a gasp. He opened a door to a large walk-in cupboard: 'This is the book room. Plenty of back-up material here, and we've good audio-visual material also. Stationery's kept here.'

Polly queried something strange: 'You've no lock on the door?'

Both men looked mildly taken aback. 'A lock? What for? Nobody would take these things,' the headmaster said.

Later, telling Neville of the new teaching post she had been offered and accepted, she added: 'You won't believe it – I hardly do myself – but somehow that door settled my mind for me. No locks, no thefts, children who respect the school's property.'

'Shouldn't you expect that?' Neville asked.

'In theory, yes,' she said tartly. 'But it isn't always so, not at the Durngate.'

She had liked the wide grassy acres surrounding the handsome listed building, she had liked the children with their friendly open faces and the excellent facilities, but it was everything that the unlocked door stood for that had crystallised in her mind to influence her decision. She did not dislike teaching in itself; she liked the contact with young minds, the interest of her subject that she strove to instil in them. What she detested was the endless pressure: the overlarge classes and the vast burden of marking that meant less time for individual care, and the need so many of her pupils had for social work before they could attempt to deal with schoolwork, the problems of poverty and broken families playing havoc with their concentration. She was revolted by graffiti and spitting and fights, by textbooks being vandalised or simply vanishing: 'Sorry, Miss, I must've left it on the bus' – or the train or the plane. They flew to Florida but history flew out of the window.

'So you accepted the post without consulting me?' Neville said. 'I should have liked to know about it first.'

Polly opened her mouth to say 'Sorry,' and closed it again. Instead she said: 'I wanted out. I want to have satisfaction in my work.'

'Don't you feel guilty at leaving those children?'

'Yes, but I'll cope with it. I've given them fourteen years. Now I want to give something to myself, like more time for my writing.'

'There's an ambivalence there about me and your family.'

'What d'you mean, Neville?'

'You sound as though you find selfishness praiseworthy. More time to write, more time for yourself. Yet you'll spend more time travelling there and back, let alone the after-school sherry parties you're bound to be dragged into. And Saturday events.'

'We'll manage. You could always get Saturday lunch for us.'

'My Saturdays are busy,' said Neville. 'As any normal wife would have noticed, unless she was wholly self-centred. Unlike you, I don't have time to do the writing that I've longed to do for years because my job drains me – and you'll notice I say job rather than career, for that's all it is.'

'Time to change then,' said Polly. 'More than. Twenty years without any change of course or improvement is too long. Rethink your ideas, look for something new.'

'Like what? In this pottering place? You don't imagine I haven't looked before, do you? Searched desperately for work that wouldn't destroy my brain and my soul as the rubbish I deal with at present does?'

'On the contrary. For years you've done nothing but complain and blame marriage and me and Rose. Which,' said Polly in a brisk voice, 'has been a bore as well as being unfair, because Rose's advent was equally the fault of us both. And it has affected us both. If there's nothing for you here, why don't you commute to London?'

Neville looked appalled. Then he said reproachfully: 'This isn't like you, Polly. I think of you as an understanding wife, not a shrew. You know how I would loathe to spend hours of my life on a crowded hot train. Please don't let your changing life change you.'

Jane listened to the swelling sounds from orchestra and choir, relishing the power and the excitement of the music rising like some tidal wave up to the heights of the great vaulted roof. Amateur they might be, but the sound their conductor was drawing from the choirs seemed almost unflawed. And the soloists were professionals – unless the bass, who at the last minute had replaced the original singer, down with a sore throat, was an amateur. But the resonant assured voice didn't seem untrained.

Beside her on one side were Polly and Neville, Rose and Emily, and on the other, Jeremy Locke. Jeremy's shoulder was touching hers, he was leaning slightly forward and his hands lay on his knees. As the twining strands of Beethoven's 'Mass in C' filled Winchester Cathedral he was enveloped in the stillness of intent concentration, his lips slightly pursed, his eyes unfocussed.

It was a special occasion, Polly had told her over the telephone, a concert of the sacred music she knew Jane loved, being performed by three choirs on the evening before the summer reunion lunch, so she'd suggested Jane should come for the weekend and enjoy it with them – she and her new man, of course. It was the first weekend Jane and Jeremy would be spending in the company of others; it made her wary. The wariness was not for Jeremy, whose natural male self-confidence would carry him through any trials, but for her friends. They were, after all, a strange quintet. Jeremy had said he was surprised at the length of their association, men being more clubbable than women. 'Besides,' he added, 'I used to believe that friendships were forever. Now I incline to the view that they have a shorter lifespan, like flowers. If marriages don't last, even with children, why should friendships? Mightn't yours be a touch artificial?' Jane, who had had similar thoughts herself, found herself defending the group. 'It's good to have the continuity, to be with people who need no explanations of your past. It makes sense of time; the same strands, the same relationships woven through the fabric of your life, appearing and reappearing. And Polly and Candida and I have other ties. I'm godmother to Rose, Polly's godmother to one of the Gough boys.' 'Now that,' he had agreed with a grave smile, 'is reason enough. Children need continuity.'

'Gloria in excelsis Deo!' sang the choirs as Jane looked at his stern face, thought of the powerful intellect he possessed, pondered the other things she had found in him: the thoughtfulness, the sensuality and the sense of humour that belied the sternness.

'Benedictimus te, adoramus te!' came the voices. 'Glorificamus te!' His hand stirred, moved to find hers, tucked their joined hands down between them. Jane breathed deeply, settled herself more comfortably on the hard wooden chair and felt she was being borne up by clouds.

When the final notes of the concluding work had been sung and the audience stirred preparatory to leaving, Jane spoke to Polly, her voice severe.

'Polly, you were wriggling. Several times. Why?'

To her surprise a flush rose in her friend's cheeks. 'Sorry, I know one of the soloists. It was annoying not to be able to see him as well as hear.'

'Who? The bass? Terrific voice.'

The people on their side of the nave were struggling to make their way into the south aisle; there was a crowd and progress was slow.

'We'll wait,' Neville commanded. 'I refuse to fight my way out.'

They sat down to wait. Before and behind them the seats emptied slowly as the chattering groups shuffled towards the doors. Some of the choir were filtering into the crowd and among them Jane saw Polly's friend, the bass who had replaced the absent singer, abruptly detach himself from the crowd and make his way towards her along the now empty row of seats in front of them.

'Polly!' he said. 'I'd no idea you'd be here . . .'

'Tom,' she said. 'You sang wonderfully . . . superbly. I'm so impressed. Why didn't you say? You should have told me you had a voice!'

The big man seemed at once elated and constrained. He embraced her awkwardly across the row of chairs, kissing her on both cheeks. 'You know I was a last-minute substitute? I only trust I didn't let the choirs down . . .'

'You sang like an angel, a bass angel, you know you did. I was so surprised when your name was announced. Wait. I know you're not professional – don't tell me . . . a Pilgrims School chorister and then Winchester College? I should have known it.' She stopped, flushing again, for Rose and Jane to congratulate him.

He asked: 'Is your husband here?'

'Oh, yes.' Polly indicated: 'My husband and my daughters . . . and friends of ours. Jane, this is Tom Hanbury.' She introduced them all.

'Neville,' Tom said, shaking hands, his eyes assessing. 'How do you do?'

Neville shook hands in perfunctory fashion. 'Yes. How do you do? An interesting performance. Now I'm afraid my guests and I . . .'

'Yes, indeed, your guests.' Tom's look embraced them. 'You're having a drink before you go home, aren't you? How about The Wykeham Arms? Let me take you. I've had a surprising evening and it would be good to celebrate.'

The Wykeham Arms was by the far side of The Close and heaving with life; after the cool air of the cathedral its heat was almost palpable. The old college desks which served as tables were crowded and even standing room was short. Voices called to Tom and he called back, laughing and accepting compliments as he steered his companions through and out into the peace of the garden where the June night smelt sweet. He ducked back inside to bring drinks out, and they sat on benches by a wooden table in a half-darkness burnished by the glow from nearby street lamps.

Jane sat on the end of her bench, detached and relaxed. She was feeling that mingling of contentment and heightened good health which accompanied for her the start of a new affair. Two weekends with Jeremy, one in his flat, the other in a delightful family-run riverside hotel in Berkshire, had told her that without doubt the relationship was auspicious. At his flat she had feared a display of solicitous care, perhaps even a pyrotechnic demonstration of culinary skill to force on her the knowledge that here was a man who would not lean on her – something she had met before, indeed which had once impressed her – but no, the meals he cooked had been simple, unpretentious; his flat an understated place of cool colour splashes and the warm glimmers of light that come from cherished old mahogany. There were books everywhere: on shelves, on tables, in piles on the floor. The weather proving cool and damp, they had spent much of their time in bed making love, or reclining on sofas reading in companionable silence, a glass of excellent wine to hand. In between showers they had gone for the odd walk, though, as he observed: 'We aren't lacking in exercise.' Jane had ended the weekend with her liking for him strongly reinforced and feeling somehow more cosseted than if he had fussed.

Turning her wine over on her tongue, she listened to the others discussing music.

'Of course,' Neville was saying to Tom as he finished distributing the drinks, 'it must seem very fine to sing in the cathedral, and one couldn't say other than that the performances were excellent for amateurs, but you must admit that the acoustics are nothing wonderful. My old school chapel was better.'

'Oh, really?' said Tom. 'And where was that?' And then, 'Ah, not one of the schools I have come across.'

Neville breathed deeply. 'Sacred music,' he said, 'can be moving in its remote way, but opera in the right setting – Glyndebourne, for example, as it is today – that is the *pinnacle*. I never miss an opportunity to go.'

'And you?' Tom turned to ask Polly. 'Are you also a fan?'

'Only of Mozart. Neville goes with his own friends, not me.'

Tom sat down. He said almost lazily, his eyes glinting: 'I can't agree that opera represents the pinnacle of music, Neville. Many operas have foolish stories. If the music is exquisite, as in Mozart, then the work is transformed – but not if it's Verdi.'

This was sacrilege to Neville. 'All operas have their splendours, but not everyone has the musical capacity to appreciate them,' he said with disdain.

Rose leaned across her father to tell Tom: 'For splendours substitute snob appeal. Nothing else could make otherwise normal people endure huge overdressed sopranos shrilling off key, or tenors bellowing like gelded bulls.'

'Rose, be quiet,' Neville scowled. 'You don't know what you're talking about.'

'On the contrary,' Tom returned. 'She's right. Misplaced snobbery encouraged by aficionados with no discernment.'

'Aficionados? Pa's too mean to take his family,' Rose observed with a wicked grin, 'but, God knows, Emily and I have had our ears assaulted with arias from birth onward at home. And Pa's like some raging tenor himself – he'd sell his soul to the devil for a box at the opera!'

To jeer at her father and denigrate him in front of this man Tom, with his alert eyes and his sideways glances at Polly, seemed almost a betrayal to Jane – but why should Rose want to break family ranks and make a fool of Neville? For that was what she was doing. And all the time she was smiling, making light of her own needle-sharp comments, on the verge of insult yet never quite descending to it.

There was a certain something in Rose's voice that was summoning a memory of the past to Jane's mind, someone who had used the same witty scorn, light yet steely . . . Candida, yes, Candida. God, all those years ago when she and Jane had confronted Neville over Polly's pregnancy at LSE. They'd discovered him late that evening alone in a far corner of the library. They found him first obstinate, then grudging; they left him cowed and submissive.

'Marriage, couldn't afford marriage on a grant?' Candida had said, perching herself on his table, on his books, leaning across to dominate him. 'My dear Neville, no one forces you to continue these foolish studies. You'll give them up at once to forge the excellent career we all expect of you.'

He had squirmed, protesting his affection for Polly and his pity – but how could he abandon his PhD?

'Pity?' said Jane. 'Pity. What a wretched sentiment. So condescending.'

'Quite,' said Candida. 'I wonder what the Dean and your tutor would make of your pity – or of your other libidinous activities around the college?'

'You wouldn't want such activities to be known,' Jane added, 'or you might be forced to leave.'

'Not so good for that excellent career,' Candida concurred. 'Why, it might be stopped before it began. Did I ever tell you, Jane, that my mother is acquainted with two of the governors?'

'She has the most amazing range of friends,' Jane said admiringly, 'such a powerful woman.'

Neville had muttered of blackmail, but two days later Polly had rushed to tell them the amazing, the wonderful, news that she and Neville were to be married.

Emily was protesting to Rose now, Polly was looking detached and Tom was regarding her with a curiously concentrated stare, neither questioning nor provocative, but thoughtful, almost abstracted, as if he were thinking some conundrum through to its conclusion.

'Well,' Polly stirred and said, 'your views on music may not coincide, but let's not limit ourselves to that. Life should be rich and many-faceted.'

Tom smiled at her. 'Tell me how you make it so?'

She lifted one shoulder. 'Oh, through various interests. Take art, history, architecture: the more your knowledge, the greater your opportunity for enjoyment. Take Winchester. As you walk in an old city like this you have a hundred chances of appreciation and pleasure – a statue or an ancient clock here, a façade there . . .'

'Yes!' Tom put in. 'And the remains of old castles . . . or walls whose first building was ordered by the Romans or St Swithin . . .'

'Exactly. Sometimes,' said Polly, 'sometimes I wish the years of man could be several centuries instead of three score years and ten, then there would be time to know and plumb so much more – and share it.'

'Yes, and yes again,' Tom said softly. 'You know, when I first sang as a little chorister at Pilgrims School I knew nothing of the cathedral, except that it was very big and old, and often witheringly cold, but as I learned some of the stories about the building it became a living place for me. I would amuse myself in a dull choir practice with thoughts of the Roundheads riding up the nave and throwing the ancient burial chests down from the screen and tossing the bones about, and I'd wonder if the Saxon kings' bones could have become muddled, say, with King Canute's, and if so, how the virgirs ever sorted them out. If they did. Then I'd ponder whether God had truly been so angry at the sacrilegious burial of wicked old King William Rufus's body there that he caused the tower to come tumbling down on the grave as they said. And that started me thinking of the problems of building any tower on the marshy ground of Winchester, and that was the beginning of my desire to be an architect.'

Rose said those were lovely stories and capped them with tales from Cambridge, and Jeremy, entering into the spirit of the game, told them he'd been brought up in Canterbury and added similar legends. Tom then egged Rose on in reciting bawdy limericks about her Cambridge dons, and they all drank several more rounds and ended up giggling helplessly.

As they finally left the pub, tripping and chuckling through the half-darkness of the garden and the yard, Jane saw Rose touch her mother's arm and murmur in her ear: 'He's sexy, your friend Tom, isn't he? Dangerously sexy.'

'Oh, don't be disgusting, Rose,' Emily hissed. 'Supposing Daddy heard? How could you, anyway? He's quite old.'

Chapter 6

When Sir Bernard Gough was not being chauffeur-driven in his chairman's Rolls Royce, he liked to drive his British racing green Bentley Brooklands. Although it was but one in a series of such cars its style continued to give him a pleasant conceit of himself. But that conceit was not sufficient to diminish the exasperation he felt at being forced to spend Sunday, a day he was accustomed to consider his own particular property, with a parcel of people of no real value or importance. As they passed swiftly along the Hampshire roads, Candida was hoping he would not be too afflicted by boredom at Polly and Neville's to behave amiably, but she had her moments of apprehension. 'They're your friends, my dear,' he had complained, 'why should I be forced to accompany you?' 'Because you've been invited,' she replied, 'because all the other men will come, and because it would be regarded as a slight if you didn't. Besides, you like Polly.' That sort of calm and rational appeal normally worked and it had worked this time, but she prayed he would not, as he sometimes did, simply abstract himself from the gathering, mentally if not physically, and, steepling his fingers, lean his chin upon them, stare in front of himself and fall totally silent. That was worse than staying away.

Sir Bernard was a man not strikingly tall, but wide-shouldered and thick-necked, his body solid with muscular flesh allied to big bones. His large face, full-lipped, pale and gleaming with good living, gave an impression of Roman decadence, but a closer look showed lips firm with decision, a jutting prow of a nose and hard grey eyes of a tough and penetrating intelligence. He was not an easy man, but after fourteen years she could still deal pleasantly and equably with him – mostly. When a large deal was in the making, the complicated and protracted negotiations occupying his every waking hour, then the nervous energy consumed by the demands of his work left him moody, snappish and withdrawn. Candida, who had a quick temper when provoked, could not always control her responses when he arrived home in the evenings in a foul mood, but being a woman who put head above heart, she tried to avoid him until she could lure him to the bedroom, for she had early discovered that both alcohol and sex palliated these reactions, and concluding that sex was the healthier alternative for a man who otherwise took little exercise, she concentrated on it, a course of action that had in no small way contributed to the continuing success of their life together. His capacity for sex had always been vast, taking her by surprise at the start but never alarming her; it matched her own.

It had not been matched by his first wife, and it was partly because of this that Sir Bernard, whose sense of duty to his business empire had ensured that his nefarious ways never interfered with his profits, had felt no such sense of obligation to his wife. That marriage had suffered from his neglect and his interests elsewhere – though for many years his wife had been unaware of the causes of his frequent absences, attributing them to pressure of work, which did necessarily take him to various parts of the globe. He respected Candida, who invariably knew what he was up to.

'Don't forget, will you, Bernard, to congratulate Polly on her new teaching post at Hamlins? She'll be head of history.'

'Hmm. Seems something and nothing to me.'

'But not to her,' Candida said pointedly. 'Oh, and Mary appeared recently on a children's television programme to talk about her animals and I hear it was quite a success. You might ask her how she felt in front of the cameras.' She paused for Bernard to negotiate a crowded roundabout. 'And if you want to hear a different view from our landowner friends' views on set-aside, talk to George. He's always well versed in the economics of agriculture and the EC regulations . . .' As they travelled, by car or by plane, Candida briefed her husband like a social secretary briefing royalty. Their friends and business acquaintances often remarked how well both the Goughs remembered the little details of their lives, flattered by such interest. 'Jane has a new boyfriend, a Foreign Office chap, a career diplomat; they've been together a couple of months. Now there's someone who could prove interesting . . .'

'More interesting than Neville, I hope,' Bernard said. 'He reminds me of that fellow . . . whatsisname? . . . Casaubon in *Middlemarch*. A sour would-be academic, useless away from that world, forever trying to prove some theory not worth being proven; a man hopeless in the outside world because he can't make instant decisions on the evidence available, but must search for further evidence until the time for decision has long passed. A man whose raison d'être vanished years ago.

He despises those who are not like him and sneers at them – unpleasant for the non-achievers and a singular effrontery against those of us who have made a mark that he never will. Is this where we turn?'

'Yes. Left again and then right . . . second house on the right. The champagne's in the boot, in cold bags, with ice.'

Brilliant darts of June sunlight fell through apple tree branches across the garden where the friends sat, each holding a glinting glass in their hand. Through the calm air the sounds of their voices floated to Polly in the kitchen, where she dipped her wooden spoon into bubbling curry and licked and tasted and rolled relieved eyes at the rich flavours.

'All right?' Rose asked, her face wreathed in steam as she drained quantities of rice in a colander.

Polly kissed her fingers and waved them in a gesture of mocking appreciation. 'My best yet. Wonderful Rose to have suggested it.'

'Normal genius.' She bent to slip dishes of rice into the oven. 'Fifteen minutes yet?'

'Fifteen minutes. I'll do the poppadums. You go and sit in the sun. Flirt with Bernard Gough, he's looking bored.'

'Not bored,' Rose said, glancing from the window and laughing. 'Heavy. Preoccupied with problems of unfathomable complexity. Isn't he in the middle of some takeover bid or buy-out or something?'

'God, yes, I think you're right. Electricals, electrical equipment – a big deal, a huge cash bid. He always is. Craig's.'

'Electricals,' said Rose vaguely, 'chemicals, building materials, ceramics, laminates – what other industries constitute his Group?'

'Heavens, I can't remember. They change over the years. Go and distract him from them, there's a love.'

Polly, standing watching by the window, saw Rose almost dance across the lawn in her ravishing floating dress of cool blues and greens and white, and alight on the chair next to Bernard's, the rich red of her sunlit hair seeming to reflect its glow on to his stern pallor. She saw him look round and focus his eyes, and within a minute the blankness of his face was breaking up into little wrinkles and crowsfeet of amusement and she could hear his grunting laugh. Rose, she thought appreciatively, has Neville's charm, but with the sense of mischief and fun he lacks.

The sound of the bees in a deep-throated chorus among the lavender and roses outside the window intensified the warmth of the day and lay like a low organ note beneath the voices of her guests.

'Such a pretty garden,' Vanessa was saying. 'I do think it's clever of Polly to do so much with so little.'

Vanessa was being appreciative of everything today: the champagne,

'Bernard is wonderfully generous to us all', Neville's speech of welcome and his toast to the present and the past, 'He has a way of putting our thought into words so much better than any of us could', and Candida's witty reply on their behalf, 'So very sweet – it must have taken her hours to compose it.'

The speeches had roused Polly's guests, inclined to be silent beneath the day's heat, to bursts of sentiment and eloquence about the effects of two decades on the depth and breadth of their friendship: 'It's lovely that we can still be together and share things after so long,' said Mary, her round face blushing with emotion. 'It's very special.'

'Absolutely,' said Vanessa, and confided how moved she was by the kindness of Mary and George in inviting her to stay in the country with them, and the generosity of Neville in providing this wonderful occasion for them to meet. 'And we mustn't forget that he, too, was at LSE with us. I owe much of my interest in modern thought and philosophy to his influence. I remember our sitting together at Karl Popper's feet whenever he returned to give a lecture. We influenced each other,' she declaimed, holding out her glass to him for more champagne. 'We all influence and help each other.' And Neville had sauntered across to refill her glass, his eyes examining her.

She was clad in black, a black shirt and tight black trousers, with a gilt chain belted around her thin waist and gold sandals on her feet. She also wore a silk waistcoat in diagonal stripes of brilliant blues, pinks and purples, with a row of tiny gilt balls dangling across her breasts that jiggled every time she breathed. What was she talking about with such intensity? Polly wondered, leaning forward to listen. The words floated to her through the open window as she loaded a tray with her side-dishes.

'. . . We may have entered our forties but we still have options open to us. Forty is young by today's standards. Provided we have our health, that is. My health has been excellent since I gave up eating meat. Look how good my body is.' She passed her hands down her torso caressingly, waist pulled in, breasts pushed forward, the gilt balls bouncing, her eyes challenging. 'Modern meat is full of unnatural additives. You should all look to your diets for the secret of youth.'

Candida turned not just her eyes but all her lounging body towards her. The body was clad in immaculately cut stone-coloured trousers with a self-embroidered top, and it was more sleek than Vanessa's. Her voice commented lazily: 'Today's cult of health with all its pills and potions and fads has become a substitute for religious belief. Worship not the old gods, but the god of your body. If there is no supreme purpose or design in our lives, and we have no life beyond this, then we must do our utmost to prolong it.'

'There is design and purpose in my life,' Vanessa returned, breathing quickly. 'Recently I've taken a new look at it. I have plans.'
'So has Polly,' said Candida.
Polly grabbed her tray and carried it out in fear of further revelations, but Candida only yawned. Polly unloaded dishes. The sun had moved and its glare was strong on them all.
'Teaching. She has her new teaching post,' said Vanessa. 'I heard.'
Mary said: 'Vanessa has a new man, but we haven't met him yet.'
'He had another engagement this weekend,' Vanessa stated.
'Don't worry, Vanessa,' said Jane, 'we all know you can pull them.' (But not keep them, her tone implied.)
Polly fetched bowls of curry and spiced rice and gestured to her guests: 'Do help yourselves.'
They crowded the long table she had made from her own and two borrowed garden tables and hidden under her kind friend Rachel's great white damask cloth. Glasses and cutlery gleamed, roses displayed themselves in crystal vases, the laden dishes held colourful food. Really, Polly decided with relief, it looked surprisingly respectable.
Under the influence of sun and food the conversation dwindled. Prodded by Rose, who saw when the wine in the glasses had diminished, Neville poured Beaujolais again and again for his guests, except for Vanessa, who stuck to champagne. After several glasses her face and throat, already flushed by the sun, became a rich carmine, and when Neville came near a restless hand undid the button at the top of her shirt, pushing the neckline back, displaying the powdery white cleft of her bra-less breasts.
'So hot,' she said. 'So wonderfully hot. And the champagne is deliciously reviving, Neville. It reminds me of the opera. I always drink champagne when I go to the opera. Happy times, happy times. Thinking back, you know, there have been many good times in these twenty years.' And while one hand lifted her glass towards him, to drink to those good times, the other fluttered delicately about her breasts, the dish of strawberries before her ignored.
'Twenty years,' Polly said slowly. 'At twenty you believe that you and your friends – your generation – can move mountains, change the system. By forty you've realised the impossibility of your dreams. The system is a monolith, a great mountain; at best you can only chip at it. You feel limited, you are limited. And, depressingly, the changes that have happened during that period have generally made matters worse, not better.'
'A sad and cynical viewpoint,' Jeremy said. 'But I presume you are speaking with education uppermost in your mind. Yes? Enough to

exasperate anyone – inadequate resources, under-payment at the workface. I sympathise. You pulled the short straw. You must learn detachment, like Jane. She always strikes me as being singularly content.'

Jane grinned. 'My own disgusting self-satisfaction, dear Jeremy, stems from the fact that I learned early on not to kick against the pricks. Set high targets, fail to achieve them – result? Depression. Set lower targets and more than realise them – happiness. Simple.'

Jeremy gave her a thoughtful look. 'But what about the reassessment that middle-age is generally held to force upon us?'

'In my small way I've made my mark. No regrets so far.'

'Nor for me,' Mary said. 'I, too, have had twenty good years.'

'You deserved them,' Vanessa told her. 'You're such a good kind friend. You've given me a wonderful weekend – breakfast in bed, everything – and in your busy life. You have a good husband, three healthy children – no, don't worry, Jane, I shan't say, "Everything a woman could want!" But Mary has the interest of that sweet little farm she runs for children, she's always busy and never lonely.'

'Oh, yes,' Mary said. 'But then I haven't your successful career. A partnership in a busy firm of City solicitors, that's what I call real achievement. Relatively speaking, I've done nothing. Whenever I look back at my parents' plans and hopes for me, and the effort I put into my degree, it does seem a waste.' (Her eyes begged for reassurance.)

'The nature of your life put obstacles in your way,' Sir Bernard observed, 'as it did for Candida. These days I employ women in senior positions, I have to. Mostly they're good. Some are very good. More conscientious than men. But those who are married live pressured lives torn between irreconcilable opposites. Only the tough and selfish succeed; succeed for me, that is, with God knows what damage to the other parts of their lives, or their children. And is that true success? You're better off as you are, Mary. These strawberries are excellent, Polly, thank you.'

Polly ate a strawberry without tasting its flavour. She had a lump in her throat and a pulse in her veins. In worldly terms Candida had achieved the most. (Lady Gough.) But LSE had hardly taught its students the materialistic viewpoint that applauds social position as a yardstick for achievement. Candida had never had a career and she admitted that her life was fragmented by all the different calls on her time. And I, she told herself, I am the least successful: a failing marriage with an unfaithful husband, a career that's a mere shadow of Jane's or Vanessa's, and two daughters. Two lovely daughters but no son. Lucky Rose, lucky Emily, to be their age; they have a world to explore; more, they have themselves to explore and all their potential.

Jeremy is right, by middle-age one does realise the narrow boundaries of one's capabilities. How depressing.

Vanessa was leaning forward to speak, the gilt balls swaying, saying that she had been taking stock and asking herself what she had done with her life. 'And I've seen a big gap. I've been unhappy, so terribly unhappy at times, and now I see that I've been muddled, too. I need someone to love – and I have such a lot of love to give. I thought I could find love in marriage, but marriage is a lottery, as they say, and as with a lottery most of us are lucky if we draw a prize. I pulled two dud tickets.' She glanced at Polly and her look said that the prize destined for her was stolen by Polly. 'But, like I said, we have our options. I feel if I could only have someone to love in all innocence, someone who relied on me for everything, it would be the final fulfilment of my life.' She looked at the friends seated around the long table, collected their glances and smiled beatifically. 'I'm talking about motherhood.'

There was a stunned silence. George thrust his ruddy farmer's face towards her and his eyebrows bristled. 'What exactly do you mean?'

'I shall have a child, a life experience a man can't have.'

'Are you telling us you're pregnant?'

She would not say. 'My fate is based on motherhood.'

Polly collected empty plates and disappeared into the house.

'Is it your present boyfriend who's to be the father?' Mary asked doubtfully. 'Will you marry him?'

'Marriage is not an institution I would consider again. For me it is outdated. I shall be all for my child and my child for me.'

Jane said: 'In other words, Vanessa, what you're saying is – I'm totally irresponsible, isn't it smart?'

Another silence. Eyes examined Vanessa. Young Lizzie gave a sudden nervous giggle, while her brother and sister stared open-mouthed.

Mary reached out a hand to Vanessa and touched her arm, her round country face disturbed. 'You mustn't think of it, love, you really mustn't. Children need a man in their lives. If you go it alone you deprive your child of a most basic right – and its father, too.'

'You say that because you've always lived within a paternalist society. But in other societies and at other times all sorts of variations in child rearing were acceptable.' (Whatever I choose to do will be right.)

'But this is now, Vanessa,' said Mary. 'And it's wrong.'

'And what about babies born posthumously? What about widows and their children? Nobody objects to them, nobody blames those mothers. Think, Mary, time and change sweep away old precepts and we become free to choose for ourselves. One-parent families are so common nowadays they'll soon be the norm.' (Your nuclear family is outdated and boring.)

Mary was not to be deflected. 'Look, children can lose a leg in an accident – but no parent would deliberately chop a child's limb off. That's not so far from what you're planning to do.'

'I don't accept your analogy,' Vanessa said, shaking back her wild hair. 'How could I damage the child of my own body? I love babies. They're so sweet, so cuddly. When I think of their smiles, their little dimples, their trust . . . I'll make a marvellous mother, I know I shall.'

Sir Bernard leaned forward, his grey eyes flinty with disdain. 'And the cost of this child? Are you prepared for the cost of a trained nanny, for the problems and the expense in finding good schools for such a child, for the inevitable damage to your career? Besides, you're far too old.' (The woman's a dangerous fool.)

'Nothing is insuperable. And I shall overcome. I am a free person, I shall be free. Free to be a blessing to my child, to give and receive innocent love. And I know that when you have considered it, you will all see that what I'm planning is utterly right for me as a person and then you will give me your affection and your support.'

In the kitchen Polly heard every word and wished she hadn't. She emerged from the house with the coffee tray, hot and tired, her mind seething with a variety of emotions, in which exasperation predominated, to find the group on the lawn apparently on the point of disintegration. Mary and George's three children together with Emily, by some sort of unspoken agreement, were retreating to the far end of the garden, where they flopped giggling on to their stomachs on the grass and nudged and muttered to each other interminably. Vanessa accepted white coffee and added two heaped spoonfuls of sugar; Neville demanded black, gulped at it and then complained it was too hot and so was he, he would go into the house and find himself a long cold drink. 'Me too,' exclaimed Vanessa and they drifted away with Vanessa clutching at his arm and murmuring something about having wanted for hours to talk about the latest production of *Aïda* with him. Jane and Jeremy were moving their chairs back from sun to shade. 'What an extraordinary discussion,' Jeremy was saying. 'Do your friends often drop such bombshells, my darling?'

Sir Bernard rose and went with a purposeful look to join them under the tree. 'Coffee, yes, thank you, Polly. Delicious. And a superb meal. My warmest congratulations.' In taking the cup his hand touched hers.

She sensed unspoken sympathy and was surprised at her reaction.

'Black, please, Polly,' Candida said, rising from her chair. 'But in just a minute. First I must visit the loo. Vanessa's conversation has the effect on one of a honey enema.'

Polly's and Jane's eyes met and both burst into howls of laughter.

'It isn't funny,' Polly said, shaking with the unwanted mirth and helplessly pouring a stream of scalding coffee over her cup and into its saucer. 'Oh my God, ouch! It damned well isn't funny.' But the laughter wouldn't stop.

Chapter 7

'Well,' said Rose, when they had all departed with kisses and hugs and murmurs of congratulation on the memorable occasion, 'well, Ma! You carried it off with aplomb, that's all I can say. Wasn't Vanessa impossible? She always was, of course; an absolute pain. The thought of her with a child is horrific.'

'Rose, please refrain from criticising our friends until you understand all the facts,' Neville said. 'A priori, any woman has emotional and biological needs which she yearns to fulfil, and Vanessa, who had a childhood deprived of affection and two unhappy marriages in which she felt her essential self rejected, has stronger needs than the normal to give and receive love. Personally, I hold with the modern concept of reproductive freedom.'

'What the hell does that mean?' asked Rose.

'It means that provided we don't hurt anyone, we are all free to do as we wish reproductively.'

'You mean like that woman in Italy recently, free to have babies at sixty plus? Using hormone treatment and in-vitro fertilisation and all that?'

'Men can father babies in their seventies and eighties,' Emily pointed out. 'Why shouldn't women have a late chance if that's what they want, if their lives aren't meaningful without it?'

'Oh, Emily, stop drivelling! Stop and think of the unfortunate children of such elderly parents. What sort of parenting will they have? If satisfying selfish and greedy whims is meaningful, God help them.'

Neville said: 'You're a believer in full and satisfying lives for women, Rose, you're always saying so. If the means to give happiness to infertile women are only now in the process of perfection, then ex hypothesi, you shouldn't deny those means to them. Vanessa is twenty years younger than the Italian woman.'

'That's still too old, and you're evading the problem of her personality. Frankly, when she announced it I was amazed how remarkably polite you all remained. You all pussy-footed around – except Jane. You should have told Vanessa that she was mad, irresponsible and ridiculous, and you'd never heard such romantic rubbish.' She stalked into the kitchen, went to the sink, turned the taps on forcibly and began to scrub at saucepans. Polly followed her with a tray of dirty dishes. 'I can't understand why you were friends with Vanessa, Ma, any of you. She's so weird and different. Why were you?'

'She was Mary's friend,' Polly said, recollecting. 'Mary was – is – the caring sort. Look at her animals and her children now. She discovered Vanessa sunk in misery over a missing boyfriend, took her on as her protégée and insisted we cared too. You see, LSE was so big. Four thousand students, full- and part-time; not a community, more a city. Students appeared and disappeared. No lecturer could hope to remember the names and faces of all the students he taught when lectures were given to hundreds from the stage of a theatre and face-to-face contacts were almost non-existent. We scurried like ants along the corridors from library to lectures and back. Our overdrafts oppressed us. Psychiatrists delved into our angst. Friends were essential to restore a sense of our own reality, our own worth.' She piled glasses by the sink.

'God, what a scene of gloom!'

'Yes, and yet it was good. The teaching was good. And it was an exciting place to be. You felt you were where it was happening, the place of today and the future. People talked about cultural, economic and social potentials in society, of reforming education and social engineering . . . the place was full of new ideas. The Students' Union invited politicians to come and talk to us, people shouted and heckled, we were impressed and scornful all at once. Tutors and class teachers forced us to examine and explore concepts, to analyse and think in ways that were new and exciting. Well, mine did. Vanessa's tutor was hopeless, she never saw her and God knows she was someone who needed guidance on every hand, but the woman was always abroad, pursuing her own research.' With distaste she scraped remnants of congealed curry into the bin.

'Go on,' Rose said, slapping dripping soapy glasses on to the draining board. 'Tell me more about Vanessa in those days.'

'She was different from the rest of us. We were there to get a degree, to prove something about ourselves, mostly we kept our heads down. But Vanessa liked to feel strongly about issues, she liked to be involved. South Africa, nuclear disarmament, freedom for Ulster, modern plight. She went to meetings and demos and marches, she shouted 'Fuck you!' and threw pamphlets. She had mad affairs that terminated in violent rows. We had to deal with her tears and her sufferings. We had to keep her sober. We were her friends, Mary kept urging us, we had to be responsible people and look after her. And when you've done that for three years you're involved, you're concerned, you want to know the rest of the story. Hence the parties, hence the keeping up.'

'Yeah, well, that's one way of putting it, I suppose. But please, Ma, *please*, don't think you have any responsibilities towards this child she's bound to produce. I know you, you've got a conscience. But it wouldn't be fair . . .' She stopped abruptly as Neville and Emily strolled in and began picking at the last of the strawberries in the bowl on the table. 'Pa, can't you and Emily go and sort out the chairs and tables and things in the garden? They have to be returned to Rachel and the folk next door and it wouldn't hurt you to help for once.'

'I've been on my feet pouring drinks for hours,' Neville said sourly. 'But I wouldn't expect a self-righteous sexist like you to recognise that, Rose.' He followed Emily out with an expression of reluctant forbearance.

Polly began drying glasses. Neville and Rose always argued when she returned home from Cambridge. She was impatient of his idleness, scornful of his views. Referring to their earlier discussion, Rose said now: 'Reproductive freedom? Vanessa? Pa's so anxious to appear modern he accepts even the most blatantly awful concepts of self-realisation as inherently valid.'

Polly asked helplessly why they couldn't meet without arguing. 'It's so tiring.' She shrugged. 'Not that I don't agree with you.'

'Of course,' said Rose. 'What it is, it's an intellectual power struggle, an inevitable war between the generations and the sexes. Pa, let's face it, hasn't moved an inch in years, not in knowledge, in intellectual understanding or in street credibility, whatever his mouthings. He thinks that merely saying: "I was up at Oxford" puts him in the stratosphere.'

'The statusphere,' Polly murmured.

'Yeah, that exactly. Nice to hear you be disloyal for once. What's got into you?' Without waiting for an answer she went on. 'You must take a grip of him, Ma. He's impossible. He weasels out of household chores, he's out or away most weekends. And he's always left all the emotional housework to you, all our adolescent awfulness. Well, if Emily achieves the A level grades she needs next year, and I take it she will, then she'll be off to Oxford and there'll be just you two. No other company. You must straighten him out before it's too late, or you'll have a lonely old age.'

Polly was putting dishes away. 'I don't know that I'm bothered,' she said, her head in a cupboard.

'Well, you should be,' Rose said, misinterpreting her. 'You're too easy-going.'

'I have my writing,' Polly murmured.

'Yes,' Rose said, immediately distracted. 'And that's great. Ace. If we hadn't had Jane and Jeremy about all this morning, I'd have discussed it before. Weren't they great, though? Helpful without getting underfoot. Thinking of impossible things, it does occur to me that Jane wouldn't be half so shocking as a mother as Vanessa, though she is older still. But she's sensible and her Jeremy is nice, isn't he? Quiet and dry, but nice. And clever, too. Razor sharp. He'd run rings round Pa.'

'Perhaps.'

'Has Pa read your first chapters?'

'No.'

'Why not? Isn't he interested?'

'You know Neville. He never reads fiction unless it's a great work, something well acknowledged, preferably from the distant past.'

'Well, he should do. Yours is great – and it's nothing like I thought it'd be. Disconcerting. What goes on inside people's heads, I now see, is an impenetrable mystery.' She rinsed a glass jug in a jet of hot water until it sparkled. 'The iceberg effect – endless depths beneath the surface.'

'You expected something dull,' Polly pounced, 'embarrassing even, crass?'

'No, of course not,' Rose said quickly, then grinned. 'Well, perhaps a bit. One's own quiet mother. But it really gripped me.'

'Hmm.'

'Sex too . . . Look,' said Rose, struggling, 'you have a mother-image that you try to fit your mother to, but perhaps in turn she's subduing her personality to her own fancied image of the good mother – so between the two the real person gets buried. Those pages were written by someone I didn't know – yet at the same time I could hear your voice speaking. It was very strange.'

Vanessa disliked leaving people on the wrong note, in the wrong mood; the remembrance hung over her and fretted her, and she knew that in the small hours of the night she would brood over it. It was, she told herself, as she drove back along the M3 to London, because she had no one to talk these things over with and she was a particularly sensitive person. Guy had been a bad husband with his sarcasms and his infidelities, but no one could have been more witty and sharp in party post-mortems. He'd have made her laugh at them all and forget her unease.

Usually she was the last to leave, so people couldn't talk about her after she'd gone, but today at Polly's she'd felt the tears pricking behind her eyes at their scorn for her treasured plans, so she'd left quickly. So quickly and with such dignity that she'd omitted to visit the loo and what was worse, damn it, the car had not long passed the Fleet service station and suddenly she wanted to go. Not urgent yet, but it soon would be, and it would take her an hour to reach her flat. No more service stations, no suitable garages, not driving in this direction. She'd have to hang on and find a hotel on the road into London, one of those large impersonal multi-storey hotels where no one knew or cared whether you were a guest or not.

That's typical of my life, she thought angrily, no one knowing or caring. And those I care about tried to destroy my dream. My oldest friends. Even kind Mary, who gave her weekends in the country three or four times a year and often telephoned for a chat. And Jane had been horrible. Vanessa's throat ached with the need to cry; her eyes blurred. She did not want a child for smartness' sake, she wanted a child for its own sake, to love. Jane, tough and childless, how could she understand?

The car ran swiftly along the outside lane of the motorway and Vanessa glanced in her rear mirror. No sign of a police car. She pushed her speed up to ninety-five, then a hundred, aggressive and defiant. 'Out of my way!' she muttered at a BMW driver who forced her to brake her Golf. She liked speed, the thrill and the excitement of it, the sense of defying the rules. She despised the slow potterers in their packed family cars in the inside lane. A hundred and ten. She put the window down and the warm wind rushed in and blew her hair back. She had courage, she was different, above the conformist mass. And Christ, she had to find a Ladies soon, hadn't she? She glanced in the mirror again. Oh my God! A police car, coming up fast behind her. She stood on the brakes, sweating, swerved somehow into the centre lane between a fast coach and an oil tanker. Would the police stop her, smell that she'd been drinking? The police car drew level; she held her breath, not daring to look across. The car seemed to float beside her for a couple of seconds, then powered on past. It was someone else they were after. She felt sick with relief.

The hotel in Hammersmith was enormous, newly built, ferociously clean and impersonal. A thick green and gold carpet deadened the sound of her feet; great green plants held up thick architectural leaves around a bubbling fountain. A group of Japanese ladies stood twittering among their luggage by the wide glass doors, a half-a-dozen

American men in baseball caps shook hands heartily among themselves by the desk and beamed and joked with an impassive receptionist. As Vanessa trod across the foyer no one took the least notice of her. For once she was glad. Her eyes flickered from side to side. Ah, there it was, the ubiquitous plastic female figure proclaiming the room she needed so desperately.

The loo was a delicate grass green. She was watering the pampas, she thought with a wry grin and a sigh of relief. Pale green paper too, just the shade for her own bathroom, and there were two unopened fresh rolls on a shelf. Zipping her black cotton jeans, she contemplated them. From her shoulder-bag she drew a small fabric package which, unbuttoned and shaken out, turned into a shopping bag. She took one of the lavatory rolls and slid it into her bag, paused, then with a decisive dart snatched the other.

There was no one about while she was at the elegant basins and the apple green soap was creamy and clearly expensive, like everything else in the room. She dried her hands and sniffed them, feeling cosseted. There were wrapped packets of the soap to one side of the basins. Vanessa took two of those as well. Then she put the nearly full box of paper tissues gently on top of the other objects in her bag. In a place like this they could afford to give things away. She patted her bag. Money saved was money gained, ready for her baby.

She forced herself to walk in a languid confident manner back across the foyer, her eyes averted from the people about her. The Japanese and the Americans had gone, replaced by a group of Germans, all hung about with cameras and binoculars, who were besieging the staff with questions, keeping them occupied. Outside, she breathed a sigh of relief. No one had challenged her. As she drove her car away she smiled, easing her shoulders against the car seat, relaxed and comforted now. In the game of life she'd scored.

'Well!' said Sir Bernard as the Bentley Brooklands glided silkily away from Polly and Neville's small house. 'I've notched up my score on the way to sainthood today. The food was good, I grant you, unpretentious and good, but why you all put up with that appalling woman Vanessa I shall never comprehend. Thank God the boys were both playing in cricket matches at school today and we didn't bring them – one could hardly recommend her conversation as suitable for their ears.'

'No,' Candida agreed. 'She was a trifle much, wasn't she? The sickening thing is, one could almost have anticipated this development. Having failed to find the right man to fulfil her needs it was almost inevitable that she should alight on motherhood. A child is a captive producer of love.'

'Unfortunate child.'

'My mind is boggling. I simply cannot picture it.'

'She's neurotic at the best of times. You'll have that shrill voice down the telephone splintering your eardrums over the horrors and hazards of child-rearing, complaining of exhaustion and the destruction of her sanity.'

'Please God, no,' Candida said. 'Let's pray that having a baby will make her happier and nicer. It could, you know.'

'It seems unlikely. Nothing has so far. Two marriages and X number of lovers haven't. Successful psychological development in the forties must be almost unknown. And do you realise that if the woman has this child she plans, she'll be menopausal while it's adolescent?'

'Oh, lord! One hopes she'll fail to conceive.'

'She may already have,' Sir Bernard grunted, swerving to avoid a pheasant on the road. 'She was hardly precise, and one can't tell early on.'

They were silent for several miles.

'That fellow Jeremy was interesting,' Sir Bernard said ruminatively. 'I had some worthwhile discussions with him and Jane. Useful. They're both very knowledgeable about our industrial state and the present clutch of privatisation schemes. The lunch wasn't entirely a waste of time. And one would expect a man in his position to be able to talk in detail on foreign affairs and the blasted European Union, obviously, but there are those who prefer to remain studiedly silent and look wise, and others who toe some set line, of whom, frankly, one despairs. Their opinions are received opinions. But Jeremy's views on Germany and the EC run with mine. A relief to find there are those in such circles who are still clear-sighted.'

'A pleasant change,' Candida agreed. 'I liked him too. Pleasant, our sort, and a sharp mind. Jane should hang on to him.'

Sir Bernard nosed out to speed past a large Mercedes and grunted agreement.

'How about our inviting them for a weekend?' said Candida. 'Not immediately, but say in a month or two?'

His slightly protuberant eyes glanced at her with approval. 'You took the very words from my mouth.'

'On their own or with others?'

Sir Bernard meditated. 'On their own. But a dinner party on the Saturday night to amuse them. The other guests must be carefully thought out. We should not pass up so good an opportunity for an exploration of views and information with two such useful people, but on the other hand, there is moderation in all things. Perhaps later we could have an evening at the theatre together or a good concert. Even the opera.'

'Yes. An evening like that would be better than some I can recollect.'

'I am always grateful,' her husband pointed out.

The car passed through the gates of the park and proceeded with dignity up the drive to Chilbourne House. Sir Bernard took one hand from the wheel and laid it on Candida's knee.

Driving back through London, Jane thought suddenly: We shall appreciate these lunches quite differently when we are old. Old and accepting. Remembrances of examination terrors shared, of old loves that no other people would recollect, of youthful happiness enjoyed together . . . excitements . . . experiments. Now is too soon: twenty years is a long time but it is not long enough. Our ways have diverged, common interests dwindled, but we are still competitive. Still? Perhaps more so: desperate with middle-age to prove ourselves in the short time before old age looms. Age will bring acceptance of our limitations. Perhaps then there will be a wistful pleasure in looking back from time to time. Vanessa made today's lunch quite dreadful. Poor Polly.

'Do we drive back to your place or mine?' Jeremy enquired.

'There's no food at mine,' she said. 'We'd have to eat out.'

'We could eat at mine,' he suggested. 'I've a couple of steaks and some fresh mushrooms.'

'Then yours, darling, thank you.' A pause, then with accusing laughter. 'Oh, you cunning brute, you had this planned!'

'Naturally,' he said imperturbably. 'You will be the one to leave the bed in the early hours. Your choice, sweetheart.'

There was a pause while Jane negotiated a difficult right turn. Then she observed in a thoughtful voice: 'Perhaps we might review the system.'

'Your system, my love.'

'True. Then yes, I think we might.'

Chapter 8

In early-July Polly had a lunch appointment with Tom Hanbury at The Wykeham Arms and the thought of it braced her as she plodded through a hot and difficult Friday morning. She had her most restless and unattractive class for a double period before lunch, thirteen and fourteen-year-olds, the boys testosterone-ridden and aggressive, the girls struggling with eruptions of pimples, greasy hair and their changing bodies. They swung between over-excitability and listlessness, moaning at intervals: 'It's too hot in here, Miss. We'll all be ill. Can't we go outside?'

Polly was the more exasperated, then, when the school secretary poked her head round the door of the classroom to inform her, without apology or sympathy, that she would have to take playground duties in the lunch hour. 'Mr Winterbottom told me to tell you. Mr North's off sick.'

Mr Winterbottom was the deputy head, a cadaverous and gloomy man on the verge of retirement.

'You can tell Mr Winterbottom I'm sorry but there is no way I can do it. I have a lunchtime appointment.'

The school secretary took immediate umbrage, her scanty eyebrows shooting upwards in her sallow face. 'I'm afraid you'll have to cancel it, Mrs Ferrison. The children can't be allowed to run riot on their own.'

Polly gave her a look of dislike, pushed her out of the room, followed her, and shut the classroom door. Mrs Rogers took umbrage on a daily basis and disgruntlement formed the stock-in-trade of her conversation. She formed a decided dislike to new members of staff on sight and it took a saint to cause even the smallest reversal in her stance on any matter. Why she chose to work in a school was a mystery, for she disliked children.

'These things should not be discussed in front of the children,' Polly said, determined to wrong-foot her.

Mrs Rogers was similarly determined. 'Just because you're leaving at the end of term does not give you the right to do as you wish, I'm afraid, Mrs Ferrison. We all have to do things that are inconvenient at times. We're short-staffed. I myself frequently work many more hours than I'm scheduled . . .'

'That is not the point – I simply cannot do that duty.'

It was several minutes before Polly could triumph and be rid of her, and in the meantime the sound of their voices must have penetrated to the next classroom, for as Mrs Rogers strode off its door opened and her neighbour, a hefty and volatile young man called Kevin, appeared. He was involved in a relationship with one of the female games teachers, but this did not stop him from regularly offering to 'lock loins' with Polly.

'Well fought!' he said to her. 'She got her comeuppance all right.'

'Thanks,' she said. 'If she hadn't gone off when she did, I think I'd have hit her, miserable woman. God, she made me so angry.'

'You don't want to let people like her get you down,' he said with a large gesture. 'Hell, no.' He paused for a contemplative moment. 'Tell you something, if there were only three people left in the world, her, me and scraggy old Winterbottom, I'd fancy *him* sooner than her – and I'm not that way inclined!'

Swallowing ribald laughter Polly returned to her class. Only ten days more, she told herself, only ten days more. She said the same to Tom when she arrived at the pub to find him waiting for her at the bar.

'Holidays soon. I can't wait for blissful freedom from wriggling adolescents, difficult colleagues and stuffy classrooms.'

'A bad morning?'

'A bad morning.'

She felt his sympathy. 'Don't worry,' he said. 'You look well on it.'

'That's the tan from last Sunday in Joanna and Geoffrey's garden.'

Their eyes met in laughter. Joanna and Geoffrey Brookes had thrown a Sunday morning drinks party at their house on St Giles' Hill above Winchester and Tom and Polly had been amazed to encounter one another there, for they never had before, and they had talked and talked and then talked some more. Joanna had expostulated with them. 'You're not circulating!' she said, proffering tiny smoked salmon roulades, her eyes searching the overcrowded room for guests to move each on to, her downy upper lip damp with the heat: 'That's naughty. You must circulate, you know.' As she bustled off to marshal her forces, Tom murmured to Polly: 'I like the conversation in our corner. How about you?' She nodded. 'Then we'll sneak into the garden. I refuse to be organised away from you. Besides, I want to talk to you about your writing.' They had sneaked outside into sunlight and wind and it was in Joanna's untidy garden that she had been persuaded to let him read her first chapters, dropping them through his letterbox on Monday after school. Now they were meeting to discuss his reactions.

His eyes scanned the blackboard menu. 'Trout,' he said. 'Pan-fried, all buttery. How about that? And a dryish white wine? Good.'

They agreed to sit outside and she was relieved. Fewer people would be about in the little garden. She did not misjudge the speed with which trifling news travels in small communities: Mrs Ferrison seen lunching with someone not her husband – that was an item to be chewed over, passed on, to produce a salacious ripple in the minds of parents, ex-pupils, governors, friends, in the pool of the city's consciousness.

She was differently clad from usual today, hiding the schoolteacher under Candida's silk shirt and new smart trousers when she had dressed in the early morning, slipping her bare brown feet, apricot-toenailed, into sandals kept for the better occasions in her life. For a lunch out with a friend, she told herself, just that. A lunch where he would be discussing her book, her writing, giving criticisms. And her stomach had tensed in nervous anticipation.

They sat at the wooden table where they had sat on the night of the cathedral concert. She expected Tom to sit opposite her, but he swung his legs over the bench beside her and she could feel the warmth of his shoulder and thigh against her skin, smell his male scent and the Floris aftershave he was wearing. She sipped her wine and wondered if he could sense and scent her too, in the close summer warmth in the garden.

They talked for a few minutes of this and that, and then: 'Your book,' Tom said. 'Your novel. I found it riveting. No problem in holding your reader's attention, not with this reader anyway. I want to know more, I want to read on.'

She let out pent-up breath. 'Oh, thank you. I'm glad.'

'It's something different, it hasn't got that formula feel. And your knowledge of your subject shows through in all the details – subtle things the average person wouldn't know of, yet which give a feeling of another time and place.'

He was interrupted by the arrival of their food. Polly began to eat and the trout was cooked to perfection. Tom ordered more wine and turned to her again.

'You can write, that's the tremendous thing. You make me feel I'm there with those people and connected to them, that what happens in their lives is vital to me. That's clever. If you continue it similarly, well, it'll be something people will want to read – and tell their friends to buy.'

She could feel herself blushing with relief and pleasure. 'You're very kind.'

'Kind? What's kindness got to do with it? You must have faith in yourself.' He grinned. 'When I have young people in my office designing and drawing up plans that are lacking that certain something, I don't go for the modern mode of mincing round the problem in case they're discouraged. I tell them straight what's wrong. I'm telling you your work is great.' He forked trout into his mouth and began to munch as if to say, That's the end of it.

She thought how she had suffered nervous jitters all morning, afraid of what he might say, or worse leave unsaid in embarrassed mutterings. 'Nothing's perfect. You must have some criticism.'

'I don't think so. Only a suggestion – that you develop the character of the girl's brother, Matthew, and make him into a spokesman for the local people. You've made him too articulate and lively to leave on the sidelines.'

'Oh. Yes.' She thought. 'Yes, I could. He's somehow taken over and developed himself. It's disconcerting how characters can do that.'

'Your subconscious working.'

She smiled at him. 'I didn't know I had so light-hearted a subconscious.'

'No? You expect it to be bleak and gloomy? Why? What's wrong in your life, Polly?'

She hastily filled her mouth with food to give herself time to think, but he didn't seem to expect an answer, concentrating like her on eating, his eyes lowered. They sat in silence. Polly felt constrained and stupid, as if lifting food to her mouth and chewing and swallowing were all she could do. She put down her knife and fork, lining them up with compulsive neatness. She struggled to find something they could talk about: his daughter, the city, his work. What are you designing today? No. What are you working on at the moment? So stilted, so patronising. Oh, hell.

She was more aware of Tom than she had been of any man since Neville twenty years ago. Was Tom aware of her? Why had he asked her to lunch? Was this an oblique approach to a seduction? For heaven's sake, this was no dinner by candlelight with soft music playing, but a lunch in full July sunshine, with a young couple at the next table feeding crisps to a demanding toddler to keep him quiet. Why should this gentle kindly man be interested in her body? It was no good deluding herself – she was over forty, middle-aged, her children almost grown-up. A school teacher, too, due shortly to leave the pub and return to her schoolroom. How dull, how ordinary. Everybody knows about school, everybody's been there. It's repetitive, it's boring, it smells of chalk and hot bodies, it's the antithesis of the romantic. Nothing fresh to explore in that, nothing to excite his interest. Did she want to excite his interest?

Certain friends of hers like Joanna Brookes or Vanessa were eternally hopeful, laying hot hands on men's arms, gazing into their eyes, leaning forward to display their cleavage. She despised that sort of parade.

Tom stirred and she was immediately aware of every bone and muscle in his body. The warmth of him next to her spread through her in a flow of feeling till she ached and ached for him to be closer still. Her heart beat slowly and strongly. She lifted her arm to check her watch, then let it fall back on the table, feeling the wood hard and smooth and sun-hot beneath it. His hand came over hers; his fingers were warm and dry.

He asked: 'Would you like a pudding?'

'No,' she said. 'No, thank you. Just coffee.' Her heart was beating faster now and her hand under his was developing a pulse of its own.

'Just coffee for me too,' he said. He rose, turning his head to smile down at her. 'We'll have it at my house. It's very near. I left your manuscript there. I didn't dare bring it here in case some fool – probably me – spilt beer or something all over it. Is that all right?'

'Yes,' she said huskily, and cleared her throat. 'Yes, that would be fine.'

Tom's house was tall and narrow and old. Inside the thick old door there was a darkness and stillness that contrasted strongly with the brightness of the street outside. It was a darkness that seemed to hold her in a momentary blankness. She stood in the hall on a worn and beautiful Ispahan rug and shut her eyes and smelled roses and old polished wood, and then she opened them and now she could see the roses in a great bowl on a walnut table, and the hall was cool and welcoming, with a shaft of light coming from its far end, and shoes and boots and racquets jumbled in its corners. Tom guided her into a sitting room that communicated by a large arch with a dining room.

'Sit down,' he said, gesturing towards a battered sofa covered in elderly silky cushions. 'I'll just make the coffee.' He disappeared towards the back of the house.

Polly decided not to sit down; she would wander about and look. For there was plenty to look at here: porcelains and silver and leather-bound old books crowded on to tables and shelves and window-sills, and more flowers, roses and lilies crammed into vases in a dazzle of scented beauty that intoxicated her. Above the fireplace was a great mirror in a walnut-veneered frame, with moulded borders and gilt-metal candle-holders; in its old glass she saw herself looking mistily pretty, as in a soft-focus film of the 40s or 50s. On the walls were pictures of Hampshire scenes from earlier centuries, and two portraits: one of a gentleman in an eighteenth-century wig and knee breeches, presumably an ancestor of Tom's, the other a portrait in pastels in a modern style; it was of the head and shoulders of a young woman whom Polly guessed to be his dead wife, Kate. She was a slim, pretty girl with abundant dark hair and big pellucid eyes that seemed at once to meet Polly's and to look at her and through her with a disconcerting neutrality. This and the unreality of death to that recently living face saddened her and she turned away to drift round the two rooms, looking and thinking, caressing old mahogany with the tips of her fingers, nodding at the old piano with its music piled untidily on it and under it. She pictured candles lit in its sconces and flickering softly on summer evenings throughout the centuries. The rooms had none of the gloss of perfection; pieces did not match in age or grain of wood, but they would be comfortable to be at home in, to read or play or sing or love in, as Tom had once done with that dark girl.

He came in with the coffee on an elderly wooden tray and looked for a space to put it down. Polly cleared part of a Pembroke table by pushing a medley of objects to one side.

'Thanks,' Tom said. 'I sometimes think there's too much in these rooms, but I'm a hoarder, I can't bear to part with anything.'

'You shouldn't,' she said. 'It's perfect how it is.'

He poured coffee and its aroma was strong and good. 'I'm glad you like it,' he said seriously.

She laughed, accepting her cup. 'Rooms tell tales about their owners – whether they're happy or tense, organised or chaotic, what their tastes are and their interests. Sometimes they're disconcerting. But I like what your house says.'

'Truly?' he said with a twist of a smile, faintly mocking. 'And what about your own house? What should I know of you if I saw it?'

'Ah, that's unfair, asking me to assess myself. What would you know?' She could feel herself withdrawing, shrinking. Poverty, she thought. And dreariness of the sort that comes from years of counting not just pounds but pennies to support Neville's expensive and varied interests. The house over-neat and clean because that made their basic possessions look better. Grubbiness would have finished them. Possessions that were neither in good taste nor bad, simply ordinary. Affordability had been her criterion. Her neighbours said how nice her house looked. Nice! The overworked word summed up her hopeless efforts to give charm with vases of dried leaves and flowers and water-colours of

Hampshire views. Nothing she had could compare with what was here. 'You would know me,' she replied, 'as dull and ordinary.'

'No. Your writing tells me you are not dull and ordinary. Don't run yourself down, Polly, please. Oh heavens, your writing. Your manuscript is upstairs. I must retrieve it for you before I forget. And you can't have much more time. When do you have to be back?'

She put down her coffee cup, glanced at her watch, gasped, thought, I shall be late, pictured her timetable to discover which class she was due to take and gasped again with relief as she recollected that she was timetabled for a double period with her fifth years – who had taken their GCSEs and would none of them be there. Two free periods. What a relief. She told Tom there was no hurry. 'But now we've finished our coffee, I'd love to see the rest of the house. I like houses, particularly interesting old ones like this.'

He led the way upstairs. Old polished floorboards, a scent of potpourri; bedrooms and beds. She liked everything about the rooms: the sense of age and peace, the gentle muddle of belongings, the pictures, the elderly beds – a Victorian brass bed for his daughter's room, an early nineteenth-century bed with scroll ends in the guest room, his own small four-poster with its polished narrow wooden columns, so different from the grand architectural bed that Candida slept in with Bernard Gough. She wanted to remark upon it, but she couldn't, she daren't; she was becoming flustered and confused, the ache inside her sharp in its need to be assuaged: she was afraid that to speak of beds would betray her.

They stood by the window to look down at his garden and she saw a narrow haze of green between ancient walls and was distantly aware of roses and flower spikes and an old stone bench. His arm went round her shoulders to turn her left a little to see the tower of Winchester College chapel, clean cut against a flawless sky where swifts circled.

'Yes,' she managed to say, 'Yes, it's lovely.'

And then the arm tightened and pulled her towards him. 'Polly,' he said, and kissed her. It was a gentle kiss at first, serious, explorative, almost shy, but then as she leaned into his arms it deepened and heat rose from it, and she joined in, her mind far removed from anything but the feel of his lips and his body against hers. 'Polly,' he said again. 'Tom,' she said against his mouth, dizzy with relief. One of his hands was warm against a shoulderblade, the other came to touch a breast. With urgent fingers she undid the top buttons on her shirt and put the hand inside against her skin, holding it there. 'Dearest.' His voice was very deep. He finished unbuttoning the shirt and together they moved to the bed, shedding clothes as they went.

Later she remembered his voice breathing soft words into her ear as he took her, and her blood pounding and her spirit racing, and her own voice crying out: 'Yes, yes!' and 'Yes!' again, as her body arched against his.

Afterwards they lay facing under the shady canopy of the bed, hands in each other's hands, their breathing subsiding in unison, their bodies damp and hot.

'Magnificent,' he murmured, looking into her eyes, his face intent and serious. 'I was afraid I should be too fast for you, I wanted you so much. I felt like a racing car, bursting through time and space towards eternity, but you raced with me and the excitement was like no excitement before. It took me to another time, another place.'

'Yes,' she said. 'Yes. It was splendid. It was complete. How could it not be? I'd been longing and longing for you, so much it's impossible to describe.'

The familiar faint smile flitted across his face. 'It's not fair,' he complained. 'I can't tell with you. You keep it secret.'

She laughed. 'Very unfair.'

He pulled her closer and laid his face against hers. 'When we had coffee that morning in the God Begot – do you remember? – I couldn't stand up to say goodbye to you for decency's sake. In fact,' he rumbled grumpily into her ear, 'I had to stay and have lunch there. I couldn't get you out of my mind . . . or my body.'

'Dear Tom,' A delightful confession, easing her of past confusion, illuminating the future in a lightning flash of great brilliance against black velvet peace.

He eased his arm from beneath her and sat up. 'I want to drink to this,' he said. 'I want to celebrate us.' He slipped his legs from the bed and stood and stretched, thrusting his fists towards the ceiling in an exultant gesture. Then he went off, and when he returned carrying a bottle of champagne and two glasses on a small silver salver Polly could not help but laugh at the incongruity of such sophisticated items against his big naked body, and he looked at her and down at himself and saw at once the reason for her mirth and sat beside her, the tray wobbling on his thighs, and laughed with her and tried to fill the glasses.

'Look out! Oh, Tom, you'll have the stuff all over us!'

'Then I'll lick it off you, I'll lap it up! Delicious!'

But somehow he stopped the drinks from spilling and handed her a glass and they drank to love and sex and mirth and she felt extraordinarily happy and knew that the happiness was all coming from him.

He said, holding up his glass and looking at its glints of light and not at her: 'It is the first time, you know. The first time . . . since my Kate.'

'You've been abstemious.'

'It was how I felt. Until now.'

She nodded and sipped thoughtfully. Then she said: 'It's the first occasion for me . . . outside my marriage.'

He raised his eyes to hers. 'Two very important occasions. How does it feel to you, now?'

A pause. She could not ever remember having felt better or having more of the power of assurance within her. She finished her glass of champagne, put it on the tray and leaned against his shoulder. 'Once I would have sworn it would feel wrong. But it doesn't. It feels right . . . and warm and good.'

He put his glass down too and the salver on the floor. He replenished their glasses. He said: 'Will you tell me what is wrong in your marriage? Polly . . . please.'

She leaned back on the pillows and stared at the canopy overhead, not to have to look at him while she forced herself, against her reticent nature, to share what she considered in shame to be a sad and silly story. She told him hesitantly at first, and then gradually, since he did not interrupt, but lay beside her with his hand still and somehow comforting on her thigh, she found herself able to tell it all, from the beginning. The memories were clear, the images were hard-edged; she held nothing back of her own folly, her ardent desire to love and be loved, nor of Neville's inability to respond, his desire for a son, his thwarted plans for his life, her final realisation of the extent of his infidelities. She hated to tell it, but the unspoken sympathy she felt radiating from him eased the embarrassment. She tried to be dispassionate.

Tom said; 'So your marriage has been a long lonely disappointment. And there's been hurt, too.'

She considered. 'Yes. There has. But nothing dramatic. We've never had the sort of screaming or plate-throwing quarrels I've heard about with others. Neville never cared enough, and I, fool that I was, I cared too much.'

'You had bandages over your eyes.'

She sighed. 'Oh, yes.'

'My poor love. You deserve better than that. He's the one who's a fool – an empty-headed fool for not seeing your worth.' He curved his hand round one of her breasts and held it, still and warm. 'You're twice the person he is.' For a moment he was silent. Then he said with great seriousness: 'This isn't just sex, you know. Sex comes into it in a big way, but it's liking and admiration and affection, too.'

'Yes.' She turned her head to him, wanting to kiss him again, the liking welling up inside her. She reached up with her hand and pulled his head towards her. They kissed slowly with a kind of rational tasting of each other, their eyes open.

Afterwards he said: 'You must go, sweetheart. I know that, though God knows I want to keep you here. Come back tomorrow. Come and see me when you do your shopping. Will you? Will that be possible?'

She rose from the bed and walked round it, retrieving her clothes from the floor. 'Yes,' she said steadily and tenderly, looking at him. 'That will be possible.'

He lay back watching her. 'I think I am falling in love with you.'

Polly caught her breath. Her brain was singing, Happy, happy, happy, but she was seized by a fear that if she spoke her feelings something terrible might happen. The moment was too fragile, too miraculous for her to speak; she was not sure that it was right to speak about love yet. She wanted the feeling to develop at its own pace, slowly and gently expanding from whatever chanced between them, not rushing upon her with its own demands, making complications. It was not that she distrusted him; it was herself she could not trust. She could not see the future clearly. She pulled on her trousers and was about to zip them when he scrambled from the bed and came to fling his arms about her and kiss her, but playfully. She put her arms up to him and the trousers slid down.

'How delightful!' he said.

One hand moved to the back of her head, massaging the nape of her neck, the other was on her bottom. His face was buried in the angle between her neck and her shoulder. She could feel his mouth warm and smiling against her skin. And then the flurry and tension that had been inside her for months, that had been stirred up by all the complications of her life with Neville, suddenly settled, fell still. The sadness of years dissolved. And she wanted to shout for sheer gladness.

'Here,' he said, his hands travelling about her, 'are we sure there isn't time for some more delectable activities?'

She escaped from him backwards, seized her trousers to pull them up, tripped and fell back on to the four-poster bed, laughing helplessly.

'I do love you,' he said. And then he followed her down.

Chapter 9

When her period failed to arrive on its due date in mid-August Vanessa was tense but calm; she had been late before. But by the third day she was visiting the lavatory at work at ever-decreasing intervals to see if anything was happening. And when a conference with the argumentative Scottish landlord of five rundown Battersea properties overran its allotted time she cut him short so tersely that he was mortally offended, and when later she had to contact him for a telephone conference on points of information she had failed to grasp, he called her a silly lassie. Since her visit to the loo in the intervening time had still showed nothing, the rudeness that normally would have upset her failed to disturb her mood of hopefulness and, unusually, she apologised.

By mid-afternoon she could bear the wait no longer and braved a heavy summer shower to run to the nearest chemist for a pregnancy testing kit. Back in the narrow little washroom, wet-haired and panting, she tested herself and then stood waiting for the result, breathing deeply in a conscious effort to relax, shutting her eyes and then opening them again. Two minutes, the test took to show its result: it was an eternity. At last a line appeared on the kit, which somewhat resembled a thermometer: if a second line developed she would be pregnant. It came, faint, yet definitely there. It was . . . she must be . . . having a baby! Tears of excitement came, mingling with the rain on her cheeks. She worshipped the line on the little stick. It was like witchcraft, she thought, the tossing of sticks and bones. It was magic. Her fertility was magic, that weekend had been an enchantment, her stars were for her.

I'm going to have a baby, I'm going to be a mother! She burst to tell the world. She was a great blurter of ill-considered trifles, certain that everyone must be as excited as she was with her latest triumph or excitement, disappointed when they barely managed: 'That's nice.' This time caution held her quiet. This was no trifle, this was important. Friends would not say: 'That's nice!' They would advocate abortion, thrust unwanted advice at her, even preach sermons about illegitimacy. Besides, at her age, and Vanessa did from time to time acknowledge that she could be younger, she might miscarry. Her medical dictionary said that a miscarriage was most likely in the first three months; also it was in those months that abortions were performed; afterwards would be too late. For those and other reasons Vanessa decided upon silence. She would have a wonderful secret to gloat over in private. The girl in the chemist's, from whom Vanessa regularly bought aspirin and Tampax, she knew; she'd smiled and asked about the tests and said: 'Ooh, how lovely if you are. Wish it could be me.' She was a friendly girl, a pretty girl with a regular boyfriend, she would enter into the spirit of the occasion; she would be someone to talk to. In the meantime Vanessa bought a book called: *Your Baby's Name* and visualised herself as a radiant Madonna planning for its future.

She reckoned without pregnancy nausea. The first time it hit her she was having lunch with a client, one of her most important, a large and ebullient man called Len Martin who was the owner of a chain of restaurants which were moving steadily into the serious league. They ate at his latest, The Plump Pigeon, in the West End. It was a place – a venue would be a better word – that actors and journalists had already claimed as theirs, relishing the way they were cosseted and pampered, and broadcasting its fame. Among the vanities of Vanessa's life, one from which she obtained particular pleasure, was being taken to lunch by a wealthy client who commanded attention. In return she would play up to the occasion, miming great enjoyment, laughing and exclaiming loudly for the benefit of those around them, all the while planning how she would recount the event to her friends.

Her starter being a modest tomato and basil galette, the waiters fawning and the conversation verging on the indecent (Len's way of complimenting an attractive woman), all appeared to be going well. Impossible to confess to a carnivore like Len that she'd turned vegetarian, but, thank God, salmon was on the menu and she still occasionally ate fish. But one glance at Len's grouse with celeriac purée and Vanessa's stomach heaved. She swallowed, took a couple of sips of wine, and struggled to concentrate on his conversation, which had moved when the waiters left them to problems with two of his leases. But sub-clauses floated about in her brain to no more effect than the spots before her eyes. Something horrible, she knew, was about to happen to her. She muttered, ''Scuse me!' and fled for the Ladies. There she waited to be sick; nothing happened. After four or five minutes the nausea subsided and she thought she dared return.

'You all right?' Len growled, raising hairy eyebrows. She nodded, dropping into her chair.

'Good,' he said. 'Right then . . .' and he plunged back into the complications of his leases, complications compounded by the fact that both of the premises were Grade II listed buildings.

'And the damned Fire people are driving me mad with their petty fusses. There's a new man arrived on the job to tell me his predecessor got the regulations all wrong and if I don't make all sorts of expensive new alterations yesterday then he'll close me down!'

Len grumbled as he chewed and Vanessa's nausea rose again as she viewed the dead flesh churning in his mouth. She averted her eyes and thought how disgusting food was. For politeness' sake she pushed the salmon around a bit and attempted a mouthful. She could not swallow it without gagging – she pushed back her chair and ran, napkin clutched to her mouth.

When she returned Len was hovering half out of his chair, his brows lowered. 'What's the problem?' he hissed at her. 'What's happening?'

She made a shrugging gesture. 'Sorry,' she said, seating herself with all the nonchalance she could muster. 'Just the old tummy playing up, that's all.'

'Stomach?' he snapped in a growling undertone. 'What's wrong with your stomach? I hope you're not claiming it's anything you've eaten here?'

'No, no, no! No, indeed. Just one of those things.'

'The food in my restaurants is perfect. No one is ever made ill here.'

'No, I'm sure they're not. Your food is superb. Perfection. Everyone knows that.'

He was not mollified. 'Then what's wrong with you, for heaven's sake? I hope you aren't coming down with some damned bug *I'll* get infected with next?'

'No, of course not,' she said.

'No?' he retorted. 'You go a horrible shade of green, you rush about with napkins pressed to your mouth. What do you think my clientèle are thinking?'

'Oh, all right, all right, all right,' she said, feeling sweaty and miserable and hating him for his lack of sympathy. 'I'll have to tell you, shan't I? I'm pregnant, that's what it is. I didn't know it was going to hit me like this or I'd never have come here today. Never mind your clientèle, I feel awful.'

Len's jaw dropped. He glared at her for a moment and then to her surprise he flung back his head and broke into a roar of laughter. 'Pregnant! Well. Think of that. Ho, ho, ho! God, we must drink to that

– champagne, that'll revive you!' He beckoned to a hovering waiter. 'Fred! Bring a bottle of house champagne, the lady's expecting a baby.'

His laughter was becoming theatrical. He made great play with the bottle when it arrived, standing to toast her noisily, gazing round the room for approbation. Vanessa realised that his piercing apprehension at her hasty exits to the Ladies had now been replaced by relief at so natural an explanation. The champagne settled her stomach amazingly – a few gulps of the cool bubbly stuff and she felt fine. She raised her glass, tossed her head, flashed her eyes at him.

'This is great,' she said, 'a terrific idea. I must remember it. How clever of you – but however did you know?'

'Got two kids myself,' he said. 'Hey, what about me and my problems when you have your baby? You aren't going to give up working, are you? Shove me off on to some earnest young man?'

Vanessa warmed to this show of liking, downed the remains of her glass and held it out for more, giving him her widest smile. 'No way. I'll have a short time off over the birth, of course, but I'll soon be back to work. There's too much fun and interest in solving my clients' problems for me ever to want to give it up. Now, tell me about this fire hazard problem of yours.'

Len Martin was relatively easy to deal with, others were not. Vanessa developed regular bouts of sickness that made each morning before eleven hell and the last hour or so before her evening meal scarcely less so. She cancelled so many early appointments and let down so many clients who had especially requested late conferences that angry telephone calls and complaining letters became almost routine. A friendly colleague, a quiet bespectacled man called Reg Newman, warned her in the corridor one day that the partners were becoming concerned.

'What's the matter, anyway?' he wanted to know. 'It's unlike you. You're always the life and soul of the party. Have you come down with one of those lingering things like ME, or is it an ulcer?'

'Nothing like that,' Vanessa said wearily. 'God, you can't even be unwell in peace in this game. For years I've hardly missed a day – but nobody notices that. But when for once I'm not so good they're all waiting to pounce.' Various partners and associate solicitors had been ousted over the last two or three years of the recession and Vanessa recalled with vivid clarity their white and shocked faces as they had cleared their desks and said their goodbyes. Suppose the partners decided to oust her? What would she do? With a frightened interior snarl of defiance she told herself that they couldn't dislodge her, not pregnant as she was; that would be discriminatory, sexist. They wouldn't have a leg to stand on. But she must protect herself before it reached that stage.

Abruptly she told Reg Newman that she was going to have a baby and interrupted his startled and lame congratulations to say, 'But I'm keeping it quiet for the time being.' That should ensure that kindly gossipy Reg would make it known in the right quarters without telling the whole world. And she would talk to the more approachable of the senior partners.

Despite this she felt depressed. She tried to concentrate her mind on the lovely time when her baby would be born and smiling at her – Fabian, she would call him (it hardly occurred to her that it might be a girl), Fabian Neville Peter – when all her friends would be happy for her and rushing round to see her and the child, but she felt so sick and tired that it was all she could do to drag herself through the days. This perpetual exhaustion she had not anticipated, nor the waves of drowsiness that swept over her in the afternoons so that she nodded off over her work, waking with a jolt as her head sagged on to her chest. It was all horrible; horrible and wholly unfair. Surely it would get better soon? But it didn't, it got worse.

When Polly started teaching at Hamlins School in September, Tom insisted on hearing all about it. 'Go on,' he would urge when her voice faded for fear of boring him. 'Go on, those children are so amusing and you do such fascinating things with them. It brings back memories of my own prep school days.'

Once he told her he needed to make the other parts of her life come alive to make her more his. 'I have you in the flesh from time to time,' he said, 'but your life is elsewhere . . . when I know all that you're doing I can pretend you belong to me. Although I know you don't in reality, you belong to that fellow Neville.'

'No,' Polly said. 'I don't belong to him. We exist together, in separate spheres, that's all.'

' "He comes," ' Tom murmured, ' "and passes through Spheare after Spheare, First her sheetes, then her Armes, then any where." *Do* you still sleep with him, Polly?'

She shook her head. 'We share a bed. In any other sense, no. From time to time Neville makes the suggestion, something in the nature of an alibi, I suspect . . . or perhaps he's revolted at the thought that I might believe he's suffering an early failure in that area! I plead tiredness or a headache, he shrugs, turns away, and we go to sleep. It's all pretty much of a nothingness.'

He picked up her hand, turned it to kiss the palm and on an apologetic note said: 'I know. It's hard for you. It's hard for me, too.'

'Yes,' Polly said, trying to speak lightly. 'But you see, I rather fancy you and if you feel the same way about me that makes it all quite bearable.'

'Oh, I do,' he said, pouncing on her. 'I do, I do! Do you want me to show you again?'

'Any number of times!' she said.

Because of Tom's love and the confidence she gained from his belief in her capabilities, she was at ease with the children at Hamlins and they responded well to her. At the end of the first fortnight the headmaster told her that he had received excellent reports from them. Naturally there were those who played up from time to time, testing Polly for weakness, but a few firm words brought them back into line. For they wanted to work, to do well. It was the behaviour of quite another child that gave Polly cause for concern.

The day after she and Tom had first made love she had returned to his house on the Saturday morning as he had suggested, almost dancing down the ancient narrow street in a drizzle that had no effect whatever on her spirits, and tapping a lively rhythm with the old brass knocker on his door. As it opened she had stepped forward smiling, only to be confronted by a young girl whose green eyes stared at her from a face blank of any expression.

'Oh, hello,' Polly said, disconcerted and reconstituting the smile at a more suitable level.

'Are you Polly Ferrison?' the girl demanded.

'I am, and you must be Laura.'

'Yeah,' the girl agreed, standing blocking the door and only slowly retreating to let Polly in from the rain. 'Daddy, it's her.'

So this was Tom's daughter. Polly's first reaction was of surprise at the lack of likeness. No warm sturdiness here. She was slight and skinny with long, dark, unkempt hair, a poor complexion and that unfinished look Polly had often noticed in her adolescent pupils.

Tom appeared, greeted Polly with a kiss on the mouth which was regarded by Laura with an antagonistic stare, then ushered her into the sitting room for coffee. She sat in one wing chair and he in another. Laura scuffed her feet out to bring in the coffee jug and sat at his feet with a possessive air.

'What do you do with yourself on Saturday mornings?' Polly asked her.

Silence, then: 'Nothing much. Hang about. What can you do when it's raining?'

'Laura was going to play tennis with a friend today,' Tom said, pouring coffee and catching Polly's eye over Laura's head, 'but it had to be called off.'

'What a shame,' Polly sympathised.

Laura shrugged and looked the other way. Her chin was up; the face, closed against Polly, said, Don't try to talk to me, I don't have to talk to anybody if I don't want to, you can't force me. Polly accepted a cup of coffee and studied her, not caring if Laura turned and caught her. The face was halfway between childhood and adolescence, but nature was fashioning a woman's body under the blue-checked shirt, and the well-marked brows were set and the mouth curved in a passionate line of resentment that was all woman. But why the resentment, clearly pre-dating her arrival?

'We could have gone to a modern art exhibition at the gallery in Southampton,' Laura said. 'Our art teacher told us we should go. The rain wouldn't matter there.'

Was that it? Had her plans for this morning been disrupted first by the weather and then by Polly Ferrison, this woman she didn't even know? Or did she have an instinctive awareness that Polly was closer to her father than she would want? Tom had said: No other woman since Kate. Did Laura sense a change in her father and fear competition for the place beside him that she'd held so long? Polly drank her coffee, trying to maintain an air of calm detachment, something unthreatening. And then the reason occurred to her: Laura had known nothing of Polly until, her tennis having been cancelled, and Polly's arrival imminent, her father had explained. Meeting in her house, behind her back! No wonder that resentment and fear had flared.

Abruptly Laura began questioning her about her work. A teacher, Daddy said. 'But teachers don't have red hair,' she expostulated, 'I've never had a teacher with red hair.' The way she spoke made it sound indecent, like standing at the blackboard in nothing but knickers. She added with contempt that her teachers were a pretty awful lot. They nagged. That was the sort of people they were, boring nags. They all thought their own subject was the only one that mattered and gave you far more homework than you could do in the time set, then complained when you rushed it. 'Cosmic unreality, that's what it is. Teachers are out of this world.'

'That's enough,' Tom said.

Laura had given Polly a smirk and fallen to picking at a spot of dirt on her jeans. In the days and weeks that followed Polly had tried to reach out to the antagonistic girl, to discover common interests and common grounds, but Laura refused to join in. Driving to and from Hamlins School in the early-September days, Polly mulled over the problem and worried that she had made no progress. Tom blamed himself: 'I blew it!' he had said to her later that morning when Laura finally left them alone and stomped off to play pop music loudly on her CD player.

'Why?' Polly had asked. 'How?'

'That silly woman Joanna Brookes warned Laura recently that women were bound to be interested in me. "One of these days your daddy will marry again!" she said. She believed, so she told me, that she was being helpful and far-sighted, Laura was old enough to understand these basic facts of life. But Laura was furious and since then she's been horribly wary of every woman I've spoken to. This morning when I knew she'd be around I thought it better to be open with her – I knew I couldn't keep up a pretence about you. I told her how nice you were, how kind, what fun, that I hoped you'd be a friend for us both. I thought the knowledge that you were important to me would lead her to make a good impression, to appear loveable and intelligent as she genuinely is. Clearly I was wrong.'

'I think you gave her a fright. And maybe she's afraid of losing you, as well as her mother,' Polly said. But her tentative identification of the problem was no help in solving it.

There was no doubting that Laura was shrewd. She was never rude enough to goad her father to anger. Her response to Polly's conversational efforts instead implied patience, a driven patience of the sighing and pitying sort, hinting that this woman was dull, stupid, a nonentity not worth bothering about. And the awful thing was, Polly reflected, that she could feel herself actually becoming a dull and stupid nonentity, or worse, condescending, as she struggled to talk with someone who so obviously found it a bore.

After the last class of her second week at Hamlins, Polly drove off down the country road towards Winchester relishing the deep clean blue of the sky and the breeze that blew leaves from the silver birches in a flurry of yellow confetti. There had been a shower earlier that afternoon and the lane steamed and glistened with iridescent fragments of light. She thought how contented she could be were it not for Neville – and Laura. Yet despite the difficulties of juggling with the two of them to plan their meetings, she and Tom had managed a good summer. She felt that she was coming fully alive after years of a half-existence. The sense of physical well-being was amazing; she had energy she hadn't felt for twenty years. She slept without dreams and woke to the expectation of a pleasurable day. She was at home with her body. She thought it was because Tom was at home with her body: she loved it when he undressed her, with kisses for each part he revealed; she loved the way he stroked her back, massaging the base of her spine, the slow delectable way he caressed her nipples with his tongue.

Remembering all this now, she longed for him, in a rush of delicious feeling that was almost painful in its intensity.

She liked Tom, she liked him enormously. She liked his kindness, his generosity, his boundless sexual enthusiasm for her, the way they talked together and he listened, his head cocked on one side, a little smile in his eyes, sharing her feelings and her interests. Had she ever liked Neville in this way? It was hard to remember. She had found him physically attractive, she had worshipped what she saw as his maturity and his confident and articulate way of expounding ideas. Admiration to the point of infatuation, yes. But simple liking? Real friendship? She couldn't remember. Certainly she had no liking for him now.

To be together with Tom had required ingenuity. Neville had been at work by day, but then so had Tom, intermittently, depending on the kindness of friends and relations who offered to look after Laura. Emily, Polly was thankful to find, pronounced herself old enough to do her own thing and refused to be organised. She studied in the mornings, then slouched off to her friends' houses for lunches which seemed to consist of their gleanings from refrigerator raids, followed by afternoons of gossip and listening to CDs. She was undemanding and occasionally companionable; she did not appear to notice Polly's absences from the house. It was taken for granted, Polly thought, that what a mother did must be dull, so why enquire?

At propitious moments she would slip off to Tom's house, they would fall into each other's arms and into bed, and then afterwards, in the delicious haze of post-coital languor, one of them would make an omelette, or Tom would produce one of his unusual salad concoctions, and they would talk, soft and low and intimate, until finally inexorable time would impinge and Tom would swear at the demands of his work: 'Because what I want is to talk some more and then take you back to bed, my lovely lover.'

And every morning Polly concentrated on her writing, slowly, painstakingly, creating passions and hopes and frustrations in another age, another world, enjoying the summer luxury of having the time to plot and think and deliberately craft the passage of her characters through the pages. Gradually the pile of typescript grew, and as each chapter reached its end she gave it to Tom to read. 'Riveting!' he would say, or, staring pensively at her, his head on one side: 'Nothing fundamentally wrong, but perhaps from a development point of view you might . . .?' and offer suggestions about detail or characterisation. He took her work seriously and she struggled to live up to his expectations. Once she told him that with him she felt like a plant growing towards the light. 'Truly?' he said, and then, stretching out for her, 'My gorgeous twining plant.'

There had been ten days of bliss at the end of August when Neville had sailed to France with friends. He had complained all summer about the impossibility of taking a holiday with Polly – 'So awful being tied to high summer when all those shrieking schoolchildren are about!' – and their lack of money: 'You're badly paid, I'm under-appreciated, it's quite ridiculous, how can we possibly afford a holiday of any quality?' But then had come the offer to crew for a friend: 'A simply fantastic boat, a Swan 46, if that means anything to you, darling. You wouldn't expect me to refuse, would you?' By sheer luck the dates tied up with the fortnight Emily was spending touring France with three friends on a student railcard Polly had bought her. Tom had cheered, remarked that Neville was a selfish bastard, but who cared now that he and Polly could be together? He sent Laura to stay with her cousins and Polly moved in with him.

She was free of qualms where Neville was concerned; she was even gleeful. Her original discovery of his infidelity with 'J' had been followed by clues to show that this or some other relationship was continuing. Telephone conversations were abruptly terminated when she entered the room; a letter with a handwritten envelope was stuffed into his pocket at breakfast with such an unnaturally abstracted air that she was hard put not to laugh; days out sailing or playing golf had increased. Where Rose was concerned she did feel a little guilty at keeping everything from her; deceiving her was not easy, and cynical Rose would probably laugh if she knew. Thank God she had spent the summer abroad, mostly in Austria, working for a travel company. Any real penitence Polly felt was over Emily. She must not find out about Tom or 'J'; she would be shattered and angry, and worse, she would be deeply hurt. Emily had none of Rose's confidence or objectivity to sustain her; a girl of undeveloped perceptions, she still thought of theirs as a united family and despised those of her friends' parents who had parted. But with luck Emily would know nothing for many months yet.

The road ran briefly beside the River Test. Polly slowed and then stopped her car, to sit watching the water rippling on its way down to the Solent. It was suddenly very quiet without the engine. She wound her window down and heard a faint insistent buzz reminiscent of summer. Yet the breeze that rustled through the leaves of the hazels and the dogwoods carried with it a cool scent of damp earth and mushrooms and late honeysuckle that breathed of autumn. Somewhere a skylark sang.

It was not far from here that Tom had begun to teach her fly-fishing, and she chuckled to herself as she remembered the first occasion, for in her excitement in pursuing a greedy trout she had tripped into the river and sat down with a great splash, cursing, and he had come wading to her rescue only to succumb to the tug of the same current and collapse over her legs. And then they had sat there side by side in the river, shaking with laughter, clutching one another and exchanging damp kisses, the fish quite forgotten. And the occasion, like others that followed, had inevitably led to love-making, tucked beneath the bushes, and afterwards motion had slowed to a dreamlike lingering – a gesture of his head, a smile, words that were spoken, all seemed to hang on the water-scented air. And in the close world around her, tiny things – the laughter lines round Tom's eyes, a bee crawling heavily on the rosebay willowherb, every blade of grass – all stood out with special clarity. And the sky above blazing with light till it hurt to see it.

Here Tom had said how he dreamed every night of Polly coming to live with him.

'It would be heaven,' she said, lying back naked on the grass. 'But like heaven, unattainable yet.'

He dropped small kisses on to her face. 'But I need you.'

She said: 'So does Emily. And Rose.'

'Emily could come too.'

Polly shook her head. 'She couldn't. She wouldn't. She's young and insecure and she adores her father. It would be cruel to her.'

'This is cruel to me.'

'And me. But we're older and stronger. We can bear it. We know there'll be an end. Besides, there's Laura.'

He groaned. 'You're right. We have rocks strewn in our path. Immovable rocks. Has Emily any idea about us?'

'None at all, I don't think.'

He ran a finger round each of her breasts, then tapped the nipples. 'Waiting is horrible, skulking and hiding. I want to tell everyone how much I love you. I'd shout it from the top of the Westgate if I could.'

'Dear Tom,' she said. 'But it's early days yet. We need time still. We need time to be sure.'

'I'm sure,' he stated. 'I make up my mind quickly and then there are no doubts.'

Polly said: 'I made up my mind quickly once and spent twenty years trying to suppress doubts.'

He stared at her and winced. 'I understand,' he said, and it seemed he did, but she knew he didn't like it.

There was a moment's intense silence. Then she sat up, reaching for her bag to pull out a bar of bitter chocolate and unwrap it. No one could be intense for long with a mouth full of chocolate. 'Oh, help, it's all sticky and slidy.'

'Not surprising since it's been in the sun all afternoon.'

She took the slithery thing from its wrapping, her fingers sinking into the chocolate, and they bit into it together, their faces closer and closer, both laughing. Then he kissed her.

'Hah!' he observed triumphantly. 'You're all over chocolate now!'

She popped the last damp morsel between his teeth. 'So are you!' Her eyes bright with mischief, she drew lines of chocolate down his chest with her sticky fingers.

Abruptly a dog appeared beside them, a black labrador. It sniffed excitedly and began to bark. They stiffened, clutching each other. 'Go away!' they hissed.

'Mungo!' a peremptory woman's voice called. 'Mungo, here, boy!'

Then she appeared, a stout dowager figure, standing ten feet away, staring at them. 'Good God!' she said. 'Cover yourselves up, do. I'm not shocked, I've seen it all in my time, but a child might be marred for life.'

She ordered the dog off and marched away. Floating back over her shoulder had come the words: 'Well, Mungo, I've heard of doing it with honey or champagne, but chocolate's a new one!'

Laughing at the memory, Polly started up her engine. They had licked the chocolate from one another, tongues caressing as grooming animals do, and then, dressed, he had held her and they had stood silent, smiling, transmitting, receiving, affirming all there was between them. Now in a rush of warmth she understood that in a world of ambiguities this was real, this combination of friendship and sensual joy and trust that she felt with him, different from anything she had known before with Neville. Certainty was in her. How strange that she had been afraid to admit it before. She wanted to raise her fists and shout: 'Yes! Yes! Yes!' She drove off along the road in a hurry: she must bring her certainty to Tom.

Chapter 10

Mary was aware of Lizzie's pony looking at her over the half-door of his stable. As she tidied buckets and brooms into their rightful places she could hear his snorts and snuffles, directed at her back. 'Pray give me your attention!' he was commanding her. She shut the tackroom door and turned: the pony, expert in dramatics, was registering disgust, the eye turned in her direction cold, the nostrils flared, the ears twitching. 'Why am I here and not out in the paddock?' the jerks of his head demanded. The morning dew was sparkling, the sky clear, it was going to be a fine autumn day; not surprising he wanted to be out. But Lizzie wanted to ride him in the company of friends as soon as she got in from school and Mary did not want the bother of catching him, should Aladdin, a recalcitrant fellow at times, refuse to co-operate.

'It's your own fault,' she told him.

He rolled an eyeball, stamped a hoof, swished his tail. A speech on the subject could not have been more emphatic.

'But will you be good?' Mary mused, studying him.

Aladdin blew down his nostrils.

'Probably not. Which means *I'll* have to catch you before Lizzie returns, you pest.'

As she hesitated with her hand on the bolt the telephone rang, its outside bell clear on the morning air.

'Drat! Well, you can stay there for now.' She abandoned the disgruntled pony and ran into the farmhouse.

Her caller was difficult to hear down the phone, her voice mumbling and . . . and *limp*, Mary thought, the words coming in incomprehensible spasms.

'Vanessa? Is that you, Vanessa? What is it, love?'

'Oh, Mary, I feel terrible, simply terrible . . . And it won't stop . . . sometimes I think it'll never stop.'

'What won't? Whatever's wrong?' Fear stabbed at Mary, her friend sounded so incoherent and desperate.

'I've been so ill. So sick. You just can't imagine how beastly . . .' More mumbling, then a gulp and a wail: 'Mary, you've just got to help me, please! I can't cope all on my own.'

'But what's wrong? You must tell me! Have you seen a doctor?'

'Yes, oh yes. But he's hopeless – men always are. He'll do nothing. He says it'll pass off in a few more weeks, but I can't take any more, I can't.'

Mary had a terrible suspicion. 'Vanessa love, pull yourself together and tell me what's wrong.'

More mumbled incoherences from which Mary gleaned only a few words, but they were enough. Pregnant! Vanessa had done what she'd threatened. How stupid, how incredibly foolish and wrong! So now she was suffering from morning sickness. There had to be a man in this somewhere – he should be caring for her, but clearly whoever this latest boyfriend, the father, was, he was not about. This was all too likely, it was the tawdry bleak pattern of Vanessa's life. But pregnancy sickness was horrible; Mary remembered her own sufferings, remembered wailing to George: 'I feel so awful. Why should pregnancy make you feel like death when you want to exult with new life?' Twin feelings welled up in her: exasperation with her friend's obstinacy and idiocy, and pity for her miserable state. Some women suffered worse than others, and Vanessa was not young. They must talk this through, she must give Vanessa advice from her own experience. But who would care for her?

'Can you telephone your boyfriend to help? He should be there.' A frown wrinkled her forehead. 'He's miles and miles away? Out of reach? Oh, dear. Well now, listen, love, you must have a kindly neighbour to help – no, I'm sure they wouldn't mind. Most people are surprisingly warmhearted under those busy surfaces . . . Well, if you can't, you can't.' Her country voice rich with kindliness she insisted: 'Now, remember, eat little and often and keep your fluids up. Fizzy drinks like soda-water help, God knows why, but they do seem to settle the old tum. And make yourself light soups to drink so that you never quite get hungry . . .'

The sad protesting mumbles started up again. Vanessa was saying: 'I can't cook, I can't, even the sight of food makes me gag.' A sudden wail: 'Mary, I want to die it's so bad! I shall die, I know I shall . . .'

Fright welled up in Mary again. She remembered the story she'd read of Charlotte Brontë dying of pregnancy sickness, and at about Vanessa's age, too. She took a decision, cutting off the sobs with her words. 'Go to bed. I'm coming. I'll be at your flat in an hour – no, I can't do it in less than an hour and a half. But I'll be there. Hold on.'

George was working several fields away; no time to plod the furrows to explain. She scrawled a note to leave on the kitchen table, adding: '*Do yourself bacon sandwiches for lunch.*' Then she grabbed her car keys and a coat. The animals and the poultry were fed, the labrador had been walked, dratted Aladdin must stay in his stable. All would be well here. She ran out, jumped into the big ungainly estate car she kept for ferrying the children, started it with a roar and turned its nose towards London.

Action had not relieved the fear inside her: this was too like a previous occasion. It was twenty years ago now but the images came clear as a video link. She saw a big gaunt house in North London, late at night, dark shadows on the stairs that the dismal lighting did nothing to dispel. It was a house full of bed-sitters, each with a shabby brown door. She had found Vanessa's with difficulty because the cards tacked to the doors were mostly illegible. There was silence and a dusty stillness on the landing and her anxiety level had risen steeply.

Mary turned from the farm lane on to the main road to find it almost free from traffic. She speeded up in relief. The memories were increasing her dread. It had been just such a frantic telephone call then that had made her run to Vanessa's place, in those days not far from her own.

The shabby door had not been locked; she had found Vanessa sprawled on her bed, an empty bottle clutched in her fingers. Mary spoke to her, shouted at her, at last got a mumbled incoherent reply, grabbed the bottle, read the label, found it empty of its sleeping pills. She ran for the shared kitchen on the landing . . . God, the filthy jumbled mess! She snatched up a tumbler, unearthed a packet of salt from a cupboard. How much? Never mind, plenty. The tap splashed her violently – must slow down, stay calm. Stir the stuff. Find a bucket, run back to the room. Vanessa was barely conscious: Mary lugged her up by the shoulders, slapped her face, forced her to drink.

Vanessa was very sick. Afterwards a doctor came, examined her, and pronounced with a kind of terse disdain that she'd do. He packed his bag again, said she probably hadn't taken enough to kill herself. Could Mary stay? Good, then he'd not have to waste a hospital bed. Melting with compassion for Vanessa, furious with the monosyllabic doctor, Mary said she'd stay, and was given brief instructions.

'Neville,' Vanessa moaned, weeping at intervals through the night. Neville had left her, Polly had betrayed her. She was having his child. It was a plot to force him into marriage, she knew it was all a plot, it was she who Neville cared for, not the scheming Polly. She hated Polly, she would curse her all her life, but oh God, she loved Neville, how could she live without him? She howled and hit the pillows with weak ineffectual hands.

Mary felt impotent to comfort her: she was daunted by such grief and abandonment, beyond anything she had ever been acquainted with, assuming the proportions of Greek tragedy. She doubted if she herself could ever suffer to such an extent and she saw it as something missing in her character – a lack of imagination or sensitivity – that she found herself failing to enter into Vanessa's feelings. All she could do was to make the banal gestures of ordinary life. She patted Vanessa's shoulder with the uneasy ineffectual motions of a young child trying to pet an animal; she undressed her, pulling off sour-smelling clothes, shoes and tights, disturbed by her own distaste. She brought her drinks and later food. And for three days she abandoned her college work to stay in the dull, tasteless room, sleeping in the sole armchair, nursing her.

Vanessa swore she had saved her life. 'Without you I should have died,' she told Mary later, leaning from her pillows to clutch her hand. 'You dragged me from the depths of despair. You are my saviour, my friend for life.'

Mary had been warmed by her gratitude. It occurred to her that for the first time in her pleasant but dull existence she had achieved something of real, indeed vital, importance. No longer was she merely a watcher on the stage of life, she had become a player. A fond concern for Vanessa coursed through her veins; she might have been a sister, so aware of her tribulations and her griefs had Mary become. She had rejoiced to have been of such use.

The drive from Sussex to Bayswater seemed to have taken hours, but at last she was there. Vanessa – was she all right?

The sight of her made Mary gasp as slowly the door to the flat was opened. Her face was putty-coloured and ravaged, her pale lips dragged down at the corners, her eyes bloodshot. Her hair, normally brushed wild about her head, was flattened and limp, damp strands smeared across her cheeks.

'Mary,' she said dully.

She turned and trailed across the little hall to her bedroom, where she rolled herself with a sort of floppy whimpering abandonment on to the double bed. She retched twice and lay still. The curtains were pulled across the windows and there was a dull soupy green half-light in the room. The glow of the sun behind the curtains made the floral pattern on them look dark and tawdry. A chair was covered with discarded clothing, slippery underwear cascading shoulder straps to the carpet. The room was at once cold and stuffy; it breathed a smell of stale air and caked talcum powder. It evoked a sense of sickness and disconnection, and slow insidious decay.

'Vanessa, this is awful. How long have you been like this?'

'Days. I don't know. I've lost track,' she mumbled, hardly moving her lips. 'Last weekend, I s'pose.'

'When did you last eat?'

'Can't eat. I bring it up.'

'Have you been ill, or is it all pregnancy sickness?'

'Had 'flu. Terrible. Four . . . five days ago. Oh, God, what am I going to do, Mary?'

'Let's get you properly into bed first.'

She eased the covers from beneath the inert body with difficulty, for Vanessa was heavy and not helping in any way, then covered her up.

'That's better. Now, we must get something to stop this. I'll call your doctor.'

A clammy hand grabbed Mary's wrist. 'No, not the doctor. He's hopeless and he's horrible.' Two tears trickled from beneath her eyelids.

From her broken whimperings Mary understood that the elderly doctor had no sympathy with an unmarried middle-aged woman expecting a child and suffering the more unpleasant symptoms of her condition. He was a sadist, a torturer, a devil whose grim smile as he examined her had shown a macabre pleasure in Vanessa's misery.

Mary took a deep breath, considered alternatives, fought an internal battle visualising George's disapproval, and dismissed it. There was only one thing to do and that was to take Vanessa back with her to the farmhouse and nurse her until she was sufficiently recovered to return to her flat and her work. She could not stay alone in this terrible state: Mary would never forgive herself if anything bad happened. And there were plenty of nasty things that could happen: a fall caused by Vanessa's weakness, a miscarriage . . . worse things too, that the poor soul's misery might drive her to do. Briskly, she told Vanessa of her plans. But first a little brandy and water would settle her stomach and warm her. Then a nourishing bowl of hot soup, little by little. And she'd need glucose drinks. Mary would go to the shops.

Vanessa's lips trembled as she spoke her gratitude. Mary was the best friend anyone ever had. This would be the second time she'd saved her life. She'd be in debt to her forever for her loving kindness; she had sunk into a hell of misery and Mary was pulling her out. 'You're the one person who's always been there for me. The one and only person.'

Polly and Neville's wedding anniversary fell in late-September. With dogged sentiment Polly always bought a card to mark the occasion, even if Neville forgot (and he generally did), and she cooked a special meal to be served with wine, by candlelight. There had been times in earlier days when she had dressed herself especially to attract him, gone to the expense of having her hair done, anointed her body with the sweet-smelling salves of the chemist, tried ardently to make something special of the evening. Neville was not unwilling to have sex, but to have a discussion about their marriage, an exploration of their feelings, that he dismissed as trite and sentimental, something vulgar and to be scorned. 'Feelings are feelings. Why analyse them? It would kill them!' he said once. 'You're hardly a philosopher or a poet, Polly, are you?' So the occasion for Polly was prosaic and disappointing, but at least there was an occasion. They did as lovers or their neighbours did.

This year she hesitated before committing herself to the expense and the bother and the farce of the evening, longing to pull down the whole façade of their marriage over their heads into some sort of yelling chaos, but in the end decided that she might as well keep up the pretence of normality, comforting herself for the deceit by thinking that it would be the last time. She even had a bath and changed out of her school clothes to do honour to the fillet steaks and the claret, the candles and her mother-in-law's wedding present silver cutlery, if not to their marriage.

Emily was out at a friend's house, so they ate alone and for some time in silence. Then Neville abruptly put down his knife and fork, emptied his glass of claret and pushed back his chair.

'Polly. Uh, that was a good steak. Very good. Polly, I have to talk to you. Twenty years. You've done your best. You must realise that I appreciate that. Two decades of marriage, more than many people achieve, it's something to chalk up to you . . .' Deep breath. 'Look, I know you'll be terribly upset, I'd spare you if I could. But something's come up, something vital and new and different in my life . . .'

'Neville, what are you trying to say?'

His hand toyed with his empty glass. He raised his chin and tried to look noble. His eyes avoided hers. 'There's someone else in my life. Someone very important to me. I want us to separate.'

'Good God!' said Polly.

He focussed his eyes on her. 'I'm sorry, Polly, but when you've thought about it I'm sure you'll see that it's right for us both.'

'Who is she? What's her name?'

'She's called Juliana. Juliana Wallace.'

'J for Juliana,' Polly said to herself.

'What?'

'Nothing. So what do you want to do? Go off and live with her?'

'Yes, well . . . It's not so easy as that. She's . . . the problem is, she's a barrister and she's married to another barrister, and he's found out about us and forced her to leave their flat. It's very difficult telling you this, Polly, very hard. I don't want to hurt you. In fact, it hurts me as much as it hurts you. You must be brave.'

'I'll be brave, don't worry.'

'If you want to cry,' Neville said, 'then you must cry. Look, I'll pour you some more wine to strengthen you. This must all come as a terrible shock – well, I know how much you love me.'

Polly watched her glass fill with claret, the wine bobbing and sparkling, and then said: 'Love you? I don't love you, I haven't for some time. I don't even like you.'

Neville finished refilling his own glass and put down the bottle with a thump. 'You're saying that because you're upset.'

'Upset? Not in the least. I'm long past being hurt by your infidelities. They're a matter of indifference to me.'

'What . . . what do you mean?'

'You've hardly been the loving faithful sort, have you? Serial infidelity, I think it's called. Bolstering your ego, those women, were they? You're a pretty pathetic person to need that.'

'I don't know what you're talking about.'

'God, what a trite line. Can't so brilliant a man do better than that?'

'Juliana is special to me,' he said stiffly. 'She understands me. She, too, reads the great philosophers. She's in touch with the inner reaches of my mind. She knows that I have a deep need to fulfil myself. She wants to help me do so.'

'Poor deluded fool!'

'You see? If only you knew how depressing you are to my psyche, Polly. Juliana is going to support me while I write my book. She's introduced me to a publisher who's interested in my ideas. We've talked. Talked at length, in fact. It was a meeting of minds. He was encouraging. I've never been encouraged before. I'm to write a full synopsis and three sample chapters and then he'll commission the work and give me an advance.'

'If he thinks it'll sell.'

'Naturally,' Neville said, looking annoyed that she should doubt it.

Polly leaned back in her chair and said dreamily: 'My lover supports me in my writing. He really understands what interest and encouragement mean. I'm surprised you even recognise the words, Neville.'

'Your lover?' Neville looked shattered. 'I don't believe you have a lover. You've never been the sort.'

'Tom Hanbury. You remember Tom? The singer you met in the cathedral?'

'Him?' Neville was having a struggle to keep his composure and his face reddened. 'Are you seriously saying you've been having an affair with that . . . that opinionated bastard? And sleeping in the same bed as me? You bitch! That's sickening, just sickening. How long's it been going on?'

'Oh,' Polly shrugged. 'Two or three months.'

'I'd never have dreamed you'd be unfaithful to me. Never.'

'I'd never have dreamed you'd leave me for one of your passing fancies. We've both learned something new about each other, haven't we?' She rose to clear their plates, taking them out to the kitchen and returning with crème brûlée.

He refused it. 'I couldn't eat that. I'm too upset.'

Polly ate with enjoyment. 'What a hypocrite you are, Neville. You should have some. It's delicious. Tell me, what happens next? Do you want a divorce or will you simply live with this female?'

'Her name is Juliana,' said Neville.

'So you told me. Juliana, then. Well?'

'I want a divorce. She will divorce also and then we'll be married. You see, Polly, I intended to break it to you slowly and gently, but now I've learned new terrible things about you I realise that you are a far harder woman than ever I believed. I shall tell you this straight: Juliana is expecting my child and it's a boy. She's had a scan and we're certain. I shall have my son at last and I intend to be with its mother for this great occasion.'

Polly jerked with shock. 'Oh my God, you . . . you unfeeling bastard! What about Emily, what about Rose? Don't consider them, will you?'

She stood up, suddenly, violently, wanting to hit him, wanting to throw something as an outlet for the overwhelming burst of fury that exploded in her. He was at the opposite end of the table, too far from her to hit. Her hand flashed instead for a missile, but even in her rage her prudent mind rejected a wine glass as too expensive and she snatched the butter dish, hurling it at his head. It missed him by a millimetre to hit the wall behind, marking the paper with a greasy splatter and falling in a shower of shards to the carpet.

He sat absolutely still, his mouth open, staring along the table in amazement. Polly sat down and glared back. The house was silent around them.

Finally she said in a tigress's menacing snarl: 'You do take the prize as the most self-centred shit in the country, don't you? How could you do this to the girls? Rose will cope, I suppose, but Emily will be devastated – and right in the middle of her A level courses, too. You know how she adores you – why choose this of all times? Couldn't you have waited just a few months? Oh, no, silly question. Never. Whatever

Neville wants, Neville gets, and right now – never mind the consequences to anyone else. But this isn't a new suit or a new car or sailing trips. This is people's lives and you're tearing them apart. You miserable little prick-centred creep!'

'Shut up!' he shouted.

All trace of nobility had left his face and his features were screwed up in anger. Polly thought dispassionately how ugly he looked, the confident charm dissipated.

'So what happens now?' she asked. 'What in hell's name happens now?'

Silence again while they breathed deeply. Polly saw his eyes flicker to her and away. The candles, still burning steadily away for their twenty years together, lit up his face to show the emotions moving across it. She saw anger battle with the need for conciliation and recognised that he would try for peaceful negotiations to achieve his own ends in the struggle ahead. She knew that for years she had lived with him in a gentle cloud of affection, the reality of their relationship hidden. But the cloud was thoroughly dispersed now, blown away by a wind of change that had left her world hard-edged. She saw Neville's approaching strategies with a clarity she disliked and with a fury that was alien to her, but which made her alert to his every thought and possible move.

He poured himself another glass of wine and did not offer her any. 'We shall have to talk this through rationally. Soberly and rationally. There are other people than ourselves to consider . . .'

'I'm glad you've recognised that, Neville.'

'Juliana is staying with friends for the present, but naturally I wish to be with her as soon as possible.' He paused; the candles flickered. 'Your involvement with this man Hanbury . . . is it going anywhere? Does he want you with him?'

'Yes,' Polly said proudly.

'If you want to go and live somewhere else then I wouldn't stop you.'

'Oh, no! That would solve your problem too easily. The day I leave this house is when a good fat cheque and a completed contract come in from a buyer – which could be you, of course.'

'How mercenary you are.'

'If you're so philosophical about money, then go and live with your pregnant mistress in a garret – except that it wouldn't be a garret, would it, not with the money successful barristers earn – or isn't she so successful?'

'She's successful,' he said shortly.

'Naturally. You wouldn't be interested otherwise. Then go and live somewhere with her and I'll have the house. I'm entitled to it in any case because Emily's under eighteen and still in full-time education.'

'By the time we've organised a settlement she'll be eighteen and away from home. We'll sell it and I'll take half the money.'

'Oh, you have got it all worked out, haven't you? It throws a great light on your pillow talk with Juliana – take a calculator to bed with you, do you?'

He opened his mouth to blight her, then clearly thought better of it and sat struggling with himself, his pinched nostrils and stiff expression intended to rebuke her. She watched him across the candles with icy disgust. She could still hardly credit what he had told her of the coming child. She'd heard of other men who married again or 'took on a new relationship' and produced a further family in their forties, had met some of them too. Their pride in their achievement she found nauseating, while the way in which they ignored the havoc they left behind them she considered beneath contempt. Neville, too, had been scornful, she remembered, pronouncing himself grateful that he'd had his children young and would soon be free of them. She wondered how he would cope with a screaming baby, a whining toddler? He had coped with Rose and Emily largely by ignoring them through such unpleasant stages; would this unknown Juliana allow him to ignore her child? Perhaps she could afford a nanny as well as Neville and a baby? Abruptly Polly instructed him to tell her more about this woman. She foresaw a fight and needed to know her enemy and how the battle lines would be drawn. 'Just for once come clean with me.'

His voice high with insult and unease, he began to tell her, a tale veering between self-defence and pride. They had met sailing. Juliana's husband had not often found the time for fun at the weekends; her pupil master when she had first entered Chambers, he was now Head of Chambers and possessed also of an exceptionally busy and highly lucrative civil practice. She too was busy, but not so devoted to her common law practice that she could not spare the time to relax. She resented it that her husband found his work more absorbing than her. They had no children and there were fourteen years between them: 'There are only eight between me and Juliana. The gap was too great for her husband, he's mentally middle-aged.'

'And you're so young?' Polly gibed.

'Well, of course. You know how fit I keep myself. And I still look young. You can't deny that.'

Cross with herself and him, she had to admit its truth. He had never done anything to produce the signs of wear.

'We think alike,' Neville went on. 'Our minds are in harmony.' He repeated this in various ways several times: she was relieved he didn't add how in harmony their bodies were. Juliana, it transpired, longed to give Neville time for the life of the mind, whatever that meant. More prosaically they needed the half value he had in the house to help them purchase a suitable place to live in London. The husband, whose name appeared to be Henry, had not unnaturally turned difficult when he discovered her pregnant with another man's child. 'And he is,' Neville said, 'an exceptionally difficult man.' Juliana was his third wife and she had had more staying power than the others, but only her strong inner sense of her own worth, and, naturally, Neville's support, had prevented him from destroying her confidence entirely. 'And he's being a bastard about the Kensington flat. It's big. They moved to it when they were first married and Juliana does have a share in it. But he will neither agree to sell it nor to buy her out.'

'So he's known about this for longer than I have?' Polly observed.

'Only a week,' Neville said hastily. 'It all blew up this week.'

'So her husband threw her out and she went to friends? Nowhere near here, I hope?'

'She's in Eaton Square.'

'Like that, is it? You have done well!' But the sarcasm was a mere reflex as her mind rushed to and fro among the feasible solutions to this unprecedented and wholly unexpected problem. All her gentle rational internal plans to build on the companionship between her and Tom, and eventually, when Emily was established on her own two feet at university, to sever herself without fuss from Neville and join Tom, all these were smashed now. Outrage was not too strong a word for what she felt. Neville had made a fool of himself and fools of all of them. Worse, he had made no suggestions for their futures, hers and Emily's and Rose's. In character as always, he depended upon charm and expensive aftershave to obtain what he wanted. He had no more sense of responsibility than a child, and a wilful dangerous one at that. Polly wondered which of them took responsibility for the conception of Juliana's child. She asked him.

He looked surprised. 'It was an accident, entirely unforeseen.'

But such accidents should be foreseen and forestalled. No point in arguing with him over that, though. 'Then why not abort it?'

He replied with an air of pride: 'She wanted to bear my child.'

Dear God, what folly. But twenty years ago Polly had felt the same. She had been very young, she excused herself, remembering. This woman was older, in theory infinitely more mature, yet she hadn't learned as Polly had to reject the obvious charmer. Polly thought of her with scorn. And Neville, did he really want another child, with all the responsibilities and problems it would bring, or had he in effect been seduced by the words, 'my son'? With this woman's earnings at the Bar, they could probably afford to send the boy to Eton or Winchester. How Neville would revel in that. She became aware that he was speaking again and had to force herself to listen.

'I'd like us to stay friends, you know. You haven't been a bad wife, Polly – you've never not done your best in your own way . . .'

'Dear God, damned by faint praise and a double negative! How mean-spirited you are, Neville.'

They stared at one another across the candles. One flame dipped, guttered and recovered, the other was smoking. Polly blew them out and pinched the wicks. A small side-lamp was the room's only illumination.

'Twenty years,' she said with bitterness, staring at the candle stubs. 'Twenty years guttered out. Friends? You don't know the meaning of the word. Friends take an interest in each other's lives, through good times and bad alike. Friends support one another with understanding and companionship. You never have. I've merely been your wife – a nonentity fit only to serve as your housekeeper. When did you ever seek to know how I was or what my feelings were? Friendship has never come into our relationship.'

The sound of the front door being opened and shut broke into their consciousness. Then the dining-room door opened.

'Hullo!' Emily came in. Her eyes looked at them, at their silent tight faces, at the remains of the meal and the dead candles. Then she saw the butter on the wall and the smashed dish below.

'What's this?' she said. Then as they did not answer she rushed on, her voice rising nervously: 'What's happened? What's going on?'

Chapter 11

'Emily was devastated,' Rose told Jane, dropping on to a sofa in her godmother's drawing room. 'There were sobs and tantrums and more sobs. First she shouted at Ma, then she shouted at Pa, then she rushed from the house. I came back from Austria two days later and I never saw anyone in such a state, and it's still going on. The shock was bad enough when Ma told her they were divorcing, but after they'd coaxed her back into the house, the next thing she heard was that Pa's woman was expecting a baby, and Pa said – yes, he actually *said* it to her: 'The son I've always wanted!' – well, then she roared at him. She called him a sexist pig and various other epithets like adulterous git, and ended up sweeping all the dirty plates and cutlery off the table and into his lap, and emptying his wine over his head.'

'Serve him right,' Jane said, half-laughing. Then her face sobered. 'But, oh, how sad for Emily. She thought the world of Neville, didn't she?'

Rose looked revolted. 'I know, poor fool. And the worst of it is, she feels so rejected by him. There's an anger there I'd never have believed her capable of – she's literally exploding with the shame of it all. Because he always spoke of us going to university she thought he believed in female advancement and real equality for women. Now it's clear we don't rate – we're Simone de Beauvoir's second sex. If you've worshipped somebody like she worshipped Pa, the shock of finding a sexist creep under the façade is earth-shaking. If he were capable of forgetting his own injured feelings at her outburst and apologising and fussing over her, then the anger that's burning inside her might cool down. But he's sticking to what I suppose he sees as a dignified silence. Emily and I don't know whether we'll feature at all in his new life; he simply doesn't discuss it and that's another thing that's hurting her. Not that it's relevant at the moment – he and this woman have nowhere to live together and neither of us has been invited to meet her.

Pa's still at home with Ma and Emily, and God, the atmosphere – like three spitting cats in a basket.'

Her head turned and her eyes took in the quiet charms of Jane's drawing room in The Boltons: elegantly furnished, book-crowded, a bronze statue here, a bowl of late roses there. She added with caustic scorn: 'Pa will want a place like this, always has done, but he won't get it until our house is sold and his woman's disentangled herself from her husband.'

Jane switched on two side lamps. The bronze statue shone and the evening shadows withdrew into the corners. She studied Rose, her smooth young face twisted with contempt for her father. 'Rose laughed when we told her,' Polly had said in desperation over the telephone. 'She laughed and said it was only what we might have expected of him. I thought Neville was going to hit her. Emily roared at them both. I've never seen her like this before and it's frightening. For God's sake, Jane, I'm asking you please as my friend invite Rose to stay with you for this last week of her vacation or murder'll be done.'

'Of course. Theatres, exhibitions, godmotherly things,' Jane said. 'I'll have her and distract her and it'll be fun. I'll telephone tomorrow morning all tactfully, and tell her I need her company urgently. And that'll be the truth. I took the week off to do fun things with Jeremy – but the blasted man's unexpectedly been called to Brussels so I'm alone.'

'You'll talk to her?'

'Yes, if you want me to.'

'Thank God!' poor Polly said. 'The talking stopped here years ago, real talking, I mean. Now we just take up attitudes. Look, no holds barred – no embarrassment. I'm past caring and heaven knows Rose is streetwise and cynical enough.'

'No holds barred. But do Candida and the others know?'

'Not yet. But doubtless they soon will, including Vanessa. Oh, hell!'

Rose had her feet tucked under her now and was leaning back, her face stern. Jane remarked that the conflicts at home were hard on Emily, still young and naïve. 'One hell of a shock.'

'Sure. But I tried to warn her,' said Rose.

'What do you mean, you tried to warn her? Did you know something?'

'I overheard telephone calls,' Rose said briefly. She picked up an embroidered sofa cushion, studied it for a few seconds, then held it against herself as if for comfort, her arms wrapped round it. 'The first time I was only fifteen. Pa was careful, but, well, he was arranging to meet a strange woman. I didn't want to believe the worst, who would? One's own father? But the tone was wrong for mere friendship. I felt furious for Ma. Later I overheard other calls. It was obvious he was playing games. I told Emily. She called me a nasty-minded cow and refused to believe me.'

'You didn't tell Polly of the calls?'

'Christ, no! I didn't want to upset her. She didn't deserve that. She's too nice, you know, decent, kind, generous.'

'I do know. That's why we've been friends for so long.'

'Yeah, sorry,' Rose said, head down over the cushion. 'But some people are different outside the family from in it. Ma isn't. She never varies. Pa is. The mask of charm drops. He's self-centred. And lazy and opinionated. He treats Ma with this awful off-hand condescension that makes me want to scream.' She lifted her head. 'Jane, just tell me something, will you? Why are women like my mother and my sister such fools for old-fashioned cads and bounders?'

'A familiar syndrome for me,' Jane said lightly. 'My father was one. He gave my mother hell till he died of a heart-attack at fifty-nine – in another woman's bed. Mother always hoped he'd settle down. She said after his funeral that he might have been a macho swine but at least he'd never bored her. Like you, I knew. His gift to me was cynicism . . . if it was a gift. At least I've avoided the pain of people like Polly and my mother. Why do women fall? The obvious reasons are charm and sexual attraction. Such men are clearly active and that's a challenge. Can I get him? Can I tame him? Also they have energy, they radiate an atmosphere of excitement and strength and success.'

'Pa?' Rose said disbelievingly.

'Neville wears good clothes, he speaks of golf and sailing and Glyndebourne. Girls want a part in this prosperous scenario. Oddly, too, that sort appeals to the maternal instinct. Their personalities have not developed with their physique. Like a toddler, they still expect the world to revolve round them. When it doesn't they sulk or throw tantrums, but when all goes well they show all the adorable qualities of a small child, full of charm and nonsense. It keeps us females on edge; it's exciting.'

'It's stupid,' Rose commented. 'You're right, though. Most of what you say fits Pa. And I hate him for what he's done to Ma and Emily, but at the same time I feel exasperated with them for falling for it for so long. And then I feel mean.'

'Just try to be patient. Don't crowd them. Give them time to sort it out.'

'Pa should do the sorting. He made the big mess. But he won't. He'll leave it all to Ma. She's the one who's seeing the agents and putting the house on the market. But he's bound to complain she hasn't realised a high enough price for it. God knows what she'll do for herself. Half the price of our house'll buy almost nothing.'

'We spoke on the telephone and she didn't have time to tell me much,' Jane said, treading delicately, 'but she did say she had a lover. What's happening there?'

Rose chucked the cushion back into its corner. She laughed. 'Pa's livid with fury. The sanctimonious bastard. It's amazing. Did Ma tell you it was Tom Hanbury? The chap we met at the cathedral?'

'No! I thought he was distinctly attractive. And I remember having a feeling he might be interested in Polly. Well! So where's it heading?'

'Nowhere at the moment. That's what's so tantalising. I went to see him. He was really nice, didn't mind a bit. He poured me a whisky and rhapsodised about Ma and said he was glad she had me. He wants her to go and live with him. He wants to marry her, too. But Ma says his daughter is anti and sulking, and Emily throws a fit at the very thought – she wants someone to wave a magic wand and bring back yesterday, untarnished. It'd be more cats spitting in a basket if they did shack up all together, that's clear. So the poor loves are stuck until these two silly females come round. In the meantime, if the house sells, Ma and Emily have nowhere to go.'

'Like my friends, I tend to believe that Cambridge is the centre of the civilised world,' Rose said, watching large grey buildings and large red buses pass the car windows, 'but when I go to an exhibition as stupendous as the one we've just seen, I realise how little anywhere else rates against London. It's unsettling.'

They were in Jane's BMW driving westwards back to The Boltons along the Brompton Road after spending a couple of hours at the Royal Academy studying the pictures at the great autumn exhibition of twentieth-century art.

'It's amazing what the organisers have amassed together under one roof,' Jane agreed, 'stunning, breath-taking. I'm almost speechless myself. Picasso, Mondrian, Duchamp – and more to come at the Hayward. It's put an entirely different complexion on modern art for me.'

'Yup,' Rose agreed. 'Cubism and Dadaism have taken on new meanings.'

She lapsed into silence, staring at passing museums, and Jane assumed her mind was busy in the world of art, but when she spoke it was on a different topic.

'Jane? Have you ever felt you've missed something in not marrying?'

'No, not particularly. But asking a woman who's neither married nor had children if she's missed out is a bit like asking her if she regrets not having achieved fame. I haven't sufficient information on the state to give a knowledgeable answer. Why d'you ask?'

'I was thinking. I think women who combine marriage and children and a career are heroines, they're altruists who make endless sacrifices for which they get damn-all appreciation, motherhood being so low in status these days. But heroines or not, I don't feel drawn to join them. You always seem so content, Jane, and so . . . in control of your life – not like Ma, fenced in by thoughts of the family and whether the money will stretch. You've no children, you're free to go to great exhibitions, theatres, concerts, take lovers – you know what I mean. And then I wondered why you chose your sort of life? Because we women have choices now.'

Jane's brows drew together. 'I suppose I could say my parents put me off. Dad's infidelities, his lack of contribution to the emotional life of the home, Mother's constrained life of housework and sewing. Just the thought of repeating that pattern brought me out in a cold sweat. Still does.'

'Me too. I refuse to end up like my mother, treated as a lesser form of life, with no time or money for fun.'

'Oh, yes. But you won't. You're a very different character. Hard-headed, clear-sighted. And brought up in a different generation. But don't let the tangles and miseries you've seen in her situation form the basis of your choice. Many marriages work very well. My refusal to marry was based on selfishness, or so one of my lovers once told me. He was probably right. I value my freedom. I value solitude, too.'

'That's part of it,' Rose said. 'It's so awful having to be nice to a man over breakfast when you've woken up in snarling mood. They will keep making inane remarks to force you to cheer up. Either that or they grab the entire newspaper to themselves and sulk behind it.'

Jane laughed. 'Oh, the drip, drip, drip of those petty irritations. With me it's the men who can't believe I don't long to wash their boring smelly socks and shirts.'

'I wish I'd been born a male,' Rose said regretfully. 'Life's so much more simple for them. No periods, no hormonal imbalances, no roller-coaster ups and downs. Worst of all in being a woman is the thought of my uterus, my womb, lurking inside me waiting to be filled. It makes me feel inferior, as if I counted only as a body and hadn't any brain. Pregnant women make me cringe. I see their futures contracting as their bellies bulge. I want a high-flying career. Husbands and babies get in the way.'

'Many women manage them and still succeed,' Jane observed neutrally.

'At what cost to themselves in stress and exhaustion? I'd rather be like you,' Rose said cheerfully, 'and have lovers who are friends. And no ties.'

'Is there a boyfriend around now?'

'And how! He's normally good fun, but when he phoned and I told him about Ma and Pa separating and all that, the idiot went all maudlin and wanted to rush to my side and comfort me. I told him going their own ways is the best thing they ever thought of – specially for Ma. He was shocked. I reckon I shall have to ditch him. Men are like chocolates. Yummy if they're good, but I can't stand the milky ones with soft centres!'

Jane and Rose encountered Candida in the food hall at Harrods. Candida was buying caviar or alternatively crabs: 'Or pâté de foie gras. Business entertaining, you know. These people like the flashy obvious stuff. I hope the brutes get indigestion. We've been at the Kensington house for a fortnight. Bernard has a series of important meetings and we have a Japanese couple and an American couple to stay *and* I have a garden design to complete, but on Friday we go back to the country, thank God.' She was looking elegant and painted but not in the least harrassed. 'What is Rose doing?'

'Rose is up for a week of culture and clothes shopping,' Jane said. 'We popped in here to gather the ingredients for our meal tonight.'

'In fact,' Rose said, laughing, 'I'm fleeing the wrath that's finally come at home.'

'Oh, dear,' Candida said, with a sidelong glance. 'Whatever can have happened?'

'Do you think you should tell?' Jane interposed hastily to Rose.

'Why not? It's all bound to come out when they publish their separate addresses, so why not forewarn – if the opportunity arises. Ma won't mind and Pa can go to hell!'

'Tell then,' Candida said. 'Harrods food hall is heaven for a gossip – food for the body and food for the soul, you know – and whiffs of scandal blend excellently with the fishy scents. Only break it to me quickly, there's a darling, Rose, because I've an appointment shortly.'

Rose told her with what Jane thought was unnecessary levity as well as brevity, concluding: 'So Pa's going to become a father again at an age when he could well be a grandfather. Searching for the source of eternal youth, I suppose – and other sources.'

'Well!' Candida said, peering distastefully at the large crabs an assistant was proferring her and then turning away. 'What extraordinary things men will do in middle-age! I'm shocked at your father, but not altogether surprised. Such an event was always on the cards, as you seem to have realised. How is Polly bearing up under these embarrassments?'

'I'm happy to tell you,' Rose replied on a note of triumph, 'that Ma has acquired a lover, and about time too. My view is that he's rather super, but Emily is certain he's everything that's bad. She refuses to go near him, let alone live in his house.'

'Unfortunate,' Candida returned, 'but perhaps not surprising. Still, she's almost grown up, she'll disappear off to university in another year and find new friends and recover. It's Polly's turn to take control of her life and grab some happiness while she has the chance. I'd like to see her shed that Puritan sense of duty and resignation that hangs over her like a shroud. I'd love to see her kick out and have fun.'

'Me too.'

'But do tell me, who is this lover of Polly's? Anyone I might know?'

'He's a Winchester architect called Tom Hanbury.'

'Heavens, yes,' said Candida. 'I do know him and I applaud Polly's taste.'

'Do you know him well?' Jane asked.

'Not well, not Tom. But his brother Hugh is a neighbour – him I know particularly well.' And her lips broke into an amused smile. 'They're delightful people.'

'Oh, good,' said Rose, pleased with this endorsement.

'That's something on the plus side for Polly,' Jane said, 'but even if she has got this Tom in the background, she's having a terrible time with Neville and she doesn't deserve any of it. We must give her our support.'

'I endorse that whole-heartedly.' Candida glanced at her Cartier watch. 'I must fly. I'll telephone your mother, Rose, to commiserate and congratulate, and it may be that I can give practical help. Possibly by telling Emily how silly she's being in rejecting Tom? Though one never knows, does one, whether that sort of thing will do more harm than good. But I'm sure I can do some good somewhere, even if it's only giving Polly the occasional weekend's break.'

'She'd love that.'

'Yes. Good. Moving house is invariably horrid, and particularly so in her circumstances – all that embarrassment at having to admit that you're divorcing! Really, things are impossible, aren't they? Now wait a minute . . . I've had an idea . . . it could be a good one – I must think it over. Yes, don't you worry about Polly with Tom, Rose, and tell your sister not to worry either, I'm sure he's exactly right for her. In fact I'm pleased with the rôle I played there – I introduced them – though not, I assure you, with the intention of playing Pandarus. Did you know they met through me?'

'No,' said Rose, diverted by Candida's evident self-satisfaction. 'But I'm sure she's grateful.'

'Right.' Candida turned to the white-coated assistant who had been hovering hopefully all the while. 'Yes, I will take the crabs. How much? Good. Here we are. Thank you. 'Bye, Jane, 'bye, Rose. I go to an appointment with a client who wants me to design her a whimsical rustic garden behind her formal early-Georgian house, and when I blench in horror witters of *rus in urbe*!'

Tom invited Polly, Rose and Emily to Sunday lunch in his house. Rose said: 'Good idea. Brave of him, too!' Then she added: 'Pa will be away in Belgravia as usual, I suppose. But make sure he knows, Ma, won't you? It might even hammer it home to him that it's time we met his woman.'

'I don't want to meet Tom or this Juliana,' Emily stated, and the frostiness of her voice confirmed all Polly's worst fears about the attitude she could expect over the meal. 'Look at the damage they've done. One's stolen my father, the other's trying to steal my mother. They've wrecked our family and even our home's got to go. They don't care how we feel, I don't suppose they give us a moment's thought. Why should they? But why should I be forced to go and make polite conversation with that man? I hate him and that woman for what they've done to us.'

'*He's* going to be your stepfather and *she's* going to be your stepmother,' Rose pointed out. 'You might as well get used to it sooner or later.'

'I don't see why. They're nothing to do with me.'

'Unless you want Pa and Ma to vanish from your life completely, you're stuck with them. Get wise, Emmy, for heaven's sake. And stop being so beastly to Ma. Where would she be without Tom? Deserted and lonely and miserable, facing years and years of life on her own. You should be grateful to him for wanting to love her and look after her. You should be happy for her. Anyway, you're going to this lunch if I have to drag you there kicking and screaming.'

Emily wore black. It was her latest favourite colour, the latest among the girls at the sixth-form college this year. Polly thought it looked horrid on her, particularly in the garment she had selected, a long limp-waisted linen frock that came down almost to her ankles and creased at a touch.

Rose took one look at it and said with sisterly candour: 'Christ, Emily, where did you get that dreary garment from? You look as if you're in mourning.'

'I am,' Emily snapped back. 'I'm in mourning for our lost family. Pity you aren't too. But you've got no sense of family. You don't care, do you?'

Polly thought she could not bear the feeling of pity that engulfed her. Was this how other mothers felt? A searing sense of compassion and culpability, a feeling that she alone was responsible for their hurt and she must somehow deliver them, or bear their pain as if it were hers. Compassion for Emily whose world had collapsed, compassion for Rose, brittle and cynical too early, compassion, too, for old Mrs Ferrison who had been saddened by the breakdown of their marriage, and for her own mother who had wept down the telephone for her daughter and her granddaughters' pain. 'I was so proud of you and Neville and your successful marriage. It's so rare these days. What pleasure can one have in talking of a *divorced* daughter? Of a broken family? Oh, darling, whatever will you do now?'

She caught sight of herself in the glass over the chimney piece, poised to intervene between her daughters, and thought how tired and pale she looked. Dramas and battles did nothing for the middle-aged, did not enhance their looks; even her normally springing bright hair looked dull. But in contrast she saw that Emily and Rose's indignation became them, their eyes flashing, the flush of animosity giving colour to the taut lovely faces of youth. She cut through their squabble decisively. 'No more sniping, thank you. If you're both ready, let's go.'

'Hello, my darling!'

Tom looked so familiar and real and solid it was absurd. He hugged Polly with bravado, watched by cold eyes.

Rose kissed him with the air of one greeting an old friend.

'Hello, Rose,' he said and returned the salute, then, 'Good morning, Emily, I'm glad you could come.'

A formal handshake. Her face pale and still.

Tom looked at her, then turned. 'Rose, Emily . . . this is Laura.'

'Hi,' said Rose, unbothered.

The two younger girls stared briefly, their faces blank, in retreat.

Tom poured drinks, wine for the women, whisky for himself. Laura, defiantly untidy in jeans and sweatshirt, red socks and no shoes, was given a Coke and flared her nostrils with disdain. Talk limped along about the unexpectedly warm weather and their holidays. Rose, alert but still insouciant, managed to be amusing about her Austrian adventures with elderly travellers who left their dentures and their hearing aids behind in their hotels: 'In the most peculiar places – we found one set of teeth wrapped in vast bathing shorts at the *bottom* of the pool – the mind baulks at the how and why!' And Emily, coaxed by Tom, reluctantly spoke of her tour of France and some of the areas to which it had taken her: Brittany, the Loire Valley, the Dordogne . . . 'Yeah,' she admitted, 'they were okay.'

'The girls at school are always reeling off the places they've been to,' Laura remarked, 'as if there were something clever about getting into a train or a plane and just going. Did you get to Provence?'

'No, we didn't actually.'

'Oh, you should have. We went last year. It's really different. Fun places to go and all that gorgeous sunshine. And old cafés that are toffee-coloured inside from years of Gauloise cigarette smoke, where funny old French peasant women serve you all dressed in dusty black. Like you. Just like you.' She smirked. 'Are you a French peasant woman?'

'Hardly.' Emily's small breasts rose and fell beneath the black. She stared at Laura's dirty jeans and her red-socked feet, then closed her eyes and turned her head away in a sick-at-the-sight look. 'Are you a French peasant boy?'

There was a brief and horrid silence before Tom said grimly that it was time he dished up. 'But first, is anyone ready for another drink?' Rose said she was: 'Definitely.' Tom poured, then grasped Laura by the wrist, said, 'I'll need your help, daughter mine!' and took her from the room.

Emily opened her mouth to begin. 'Well, of all the nasty . . .'

'No!' Polly interrupted. 'No. I think she meant it as a joke.'

'What rubbish. Jokes are supposed to be funny.'

'She's young, she's tense. This is a difficult occasion for her. Just remember what I've always told you – if you can't think of anything nice to say, don't say anything at all!'

Then she and Rose discussed the pictures in the room while Emily said nothing at all.

Tom had taken trouble, that was clear. The mahogany table was carefully laid with a centrepiece of roses and the sirloin of beef he'd roasted was darkly crisp on the outside, moistly pink within. He'd bothered with both roast potatoes *and* Yorkshire pudding. Polly thought how old-fashioned and comforting it all looked as he carried it in; very different from the seafood salads her acquaintance favoured when they entertained, prettily arranged on the plates for colour and pattern, but chilly and insubstantial in the stomach. Perhaps, she prayed, perhaps Tom's warm food would warm the atmosphere.

He gathered them round the table. With only five of them, Emily and Laura could not be wholly separated. They stared under their lashes and fiddled with the cutlery.

'This looks delicious,' Polly said, helping herself to roast beef from the platter Tom handed her. 'Cooked just as I like it.'

'Terrific,' said Rose, taking vast quantities of roast potatoes in her turn. 'I'm going to enjoy it, make a pig of myself, in fact.'

The false heartiness of their voices was embarrassing, it hung on the air like a dubious smell.

'You must have been working all morning, Tom,' Polly persevered, cursing herself. Anything was better than silence broken only by the clatter of cutlery.

'Not *all* morning,' Laura said, buttering a roll. 'It isn't that difficult to roast a joint, you know.'

'Ma's cooked a few in her time,' Rose said gently, passing the horse-radish to Tom. 'She knows.'

They began to eat, the sounds echoing round the room.

'Are you still at school?' Laura asked Emily.

'Yes.'

'Where?'

'Sixth-form college.'

'And before that?'

Emily told her tersely.

'Goodness,' Laura said. 'They have awful louts there. They leer and shout at us when we go down into the town. How could you bear it?'

'I'm not a snob,' said Emily.

Polly cut her roast beef into small pieces, and saw the blood run out. She felt nauseated. The food on her plate blurred in waves of colour. She forked a little into her mouth but she could hardly chew and her throat was closing with the first intimations of angry tears.

Tom asked Emily how she was enjoying her A level work and what courses she was doing. Was he right in thinking she was heading for a PPE degree at Oxford?

'What's that?' Laura demanded. 'I've never heard of that.'

'Politics, Philosophy and Economics. Like my father.' Emily scowled. 'Yeah, my courses are okay.' Her mouth closed round a crisp corner of Yorkshire pudding and it was clear she would vouchsafe nothing further.

'That's a funny degree,' Laura remarked. 'Sort of mixed and muddled. What's the point of it?'

'I wouldn't suppose you're old enough to understand,' Emily said condescendingly.

Polly saw Tom looking at her down the table. She shook her head and smiled weakly. Then she concentrated on her lunch, struggling to eat, trying to ignore the sulky antagonistic voices and the things they were saying, the point scoring and the sneering, the insensitivity to their parents' feelings. Her daughter, his daughter. Their nearest and dearest. At their most dislikable. If she'd had any expectations from this Sunday lunch they had not been great, but now those she'd had were blasted.

Why, oh why, she thought, didn't she have the courage to tell the little beasts to shut up? In the classroom she'd have done it without a moment's thought. Her cowardice stemmed from her fear of bringing the nastiness out into the open, of making too much of it, of still further antagonising Laura, with whom, against all indications to the contrary, she still hoped to build some sort of a relationship. It was too personal. It mattered too much.

Furious that Tom had stolen a march on him by inviting his daughters and Polly to lunch, Neville determined to upstage him by inviting Rose and Emily to dinner with Juliana at San Lorenzo in Beauchamp Place. This brilliant stroke would impress on them just how far their father would be moving with her and into what fascinating society.

'Completely wasted,' Rose told Polly the next day. 'Emily failed to recognise even the names of ninety per cent of these people – she never reads *Tatler* or *Vogue* or *Harpers & Queen*. When Juliana named one highly finished female to her, Emily asked blankly what she did and then said, 'Oh, a model, what awful lives they must lead, all that posing and stuff!' as if she were speaking of some cleaner scrubbing sinks. I think Juliana was amused, but Pa was thoroughly put out that such a richesse of the talented, the rich and the amusing meant nothing to us.'

And this Juliana?' Polly prodded her.

The epitome of today's successful woman, Rose told her. Fair hair, but English fair, not Scandinavian blonde. Tall and lean. The clothes, the shoes, the hair, all were narrowly cut and immaculate. Even the shape of her face had the bony clear-cut lines that one associated with the modern career woman on her way to the top. She looked tough but Rose wondered if the determined appearance weren't contrived, the clothes selected with that end in mind. 'There must be a weakness somewhere,' she added, laughing. 'After all, she's in love with Pa.'

'Did you . . . get on with her all right?' Polly asked, bracing herself. She couldn't bring herself to say 'like her' in case the answer was 'Yes', which she felt she couldn't have borne.

'Yes, in a funny way I did. She talks very briskly, very quickly, as if she feels she must constantly prove how sharp her intelligence is, but she didn't make a display of intellect, as Pa does sometimes – you know, quoting the Greeks and that sort of stuff – and she never put

Emily down, and God knows Emmy laid herself open to that, you know how she does.'

'So how did Emily cope?'

'Well . . . I could see when she dragged on that unspeakable black dress that she was working herself up for fresh bouts of beastliness, so I sat down on her bed and told her she was behaving in an immature way in judging people before she knew them and planning to hate them before she knew they were hateful. She'd do better to accept them decently than be thrust out of everyone's lives for being loathsome. She argued for a bit about intruders and how everything was spoiled by them and I nodded and said, Christ, yes, I knew how she felt, and then came out with some cliché about not being able to turn the clock back or turf Juliana's baby out of her belly, and she glowered at me, but she did change into her yellow dress and speak when she was spoken to. Pa was surprisingly tactful and said nice things about her to Juliana, including her Oxford expectations, and Juliana was briskly agreeable in return and said she'd been at Somerville and how special Oxford was with its noble and ancient buildings, its traditions of centuries, and its great learning and scholarship. "An esoteric paradise," she called it, "a different world from Redbrick, or glass and concrete towers – and girls like you who care will carry it through to the twenty-first century." This produced a marginal thaw and Emily finally did concede that Juliana might be okay.'

Chapter 12

In later years Polly was to say that she remembered the first two weeks of that October as the most afflicted and impossible time of her life: 'I felt like a child being endlessly chastised for someone else's bad behaviour!' While Emily trailed the house, disconsolate and cross, Neville carried to a fine art his self-imposed task of being difficult. He argued every step in selling the house and dividing its equity and its furniture between them, backed by the tough female solicitor he'd instructed, who swiftly succumbed to the full blast of the Ferrison charm and flung herself into harrying and hassling Polly.

Neville proclaimed himself revolted at having to sleep in the same house as the unfaithful Polly; he wanted to throw in his job, move to London and immerse himself in philosophy. But he had nowhere to go, and until the final settlement he must keep working to pay his share of the mortgage. Besides, he'd heard nothing as yet from his potential publisher. Juliana's friends invited him to stay and he did spend his weekends in London, but he refused to commute, returning instead to Winchester full of invidious comparisons between the place in Eaton Square and their own very ordinary house. 'These are people of exquisite taste who know how to live, something you've never learned to do, Polly.' Since she had abandoned her old rôle of punchball and hit back with: 'A pity then that you've never learned to earn, Neville!' the atmosphere was rancid and their conversations full of unpleasantries.

Rose fled thankfully back to Cambridge, but Emily remained, edgy, reproachful to both sides, and bemoaning her lack of interesting friends, which Polly deduced meant boyfriends. She yearned for love, special to herself. If her parents, so old for *all that sort of thing*, could find passionate new relationships, why couldn't she? But the boys in her classes were short and ugly and scruffy. Polly assured her Oxford men would be different; she had only to get there.

One Friday evening in mid-October Emily slouched home from school, feet scuffing the pavement, to find her mother seeing potential house-buyers out of the house, the third in a week whom Polly had had to dash home from school to show round. This was a couple of about her parents' own age, but both were grey-haired and overweight. They were blocking the gate. Emily sighed and stood on one leg, waiting for them to move.

'There's a lot to be done,' the woman was saying. 'We'd have to redecorate the whole place. My husband can't be doing with plain walls; nor me, come to that. We like wallpaper . . . floral, cosy, know what I mean?'

'And swagged curtains,' he nodded, 'them'n festoons – they're smart. We couldn't offer for your curtains, too plain.'

'We had a lovely house in Essex,' the woman went on. 'Tudor-style, with beams and real lattice windows. We put beams in the lounge to match, black they were, looked ever so old. You couldn't do that with this house.'

'And your garden, now,' the man chimed. 'Too much work there, all those roses. We'd have to get them out and pave it.'

Polly caught sight of Emily's face and smothered a giggle.

''Scuse me!' Emily said, and pushed her way past them.

'So long as I have a pool for my goldfish,' the woman said. 'Kidney shape, I like.'

I must get rid of them, Polly thought, agonised, or I shall bust a gut! They'll be saying they want a wishing well next. Wildly she said: 'The telephone, I'm sure I can hear the telephone. I'm expecting a call. Goodbye, goodbye! Contact the agent if there's anything you want to discuss!' and fled.

Safely inside the house she let go gust after gust of laughter, first watched and then joined by Emily. Together they staggered round the hall, Emily finally collapsing on the bottom step of the stairs.

'Weren't they awful?' she said, gasping weakly for breath. ' "Floral, cosy, know what I mean?" '

'Too much work, my lovely roses. Do you know,' said Polly, relishing hearing Emily laugh again, 'the couple I showed round yesterday complained the garden was too small, but this lot actually reckoned it was *too much*?'

'They're all so rude,' said Emily. 'So absolutely horrid. Why don't they keep their nasty remarks to themselves? You couldn't sell our house to that lot just now – could you?'

'I could sell my soul to the devil if he'd bring me good money,' Polly said, suddenly serious. 'I can't stand much more of this.'

The telephone rang, startling them.

'Keep your fingers crossed it's an offer,' said Emily, clasping her knees as she watched Polly answer.

'Candida, good to hear from you. Ah, you've heard about our mishaps, misdemeanors and miseries, have you? Mmm, it has all been a bit fraught. I sound cheerful despite everything? Yes, you could say that. A weird fat couple just came to view the house and Emily and I got the giggles. You might be able to help us? I can't imagine how, but thanks . . . What? Where? The Gatehouse? What about Bernard? He does? Oh . . . that sounds positively . . . Come now? Yes, if we could, please. And stay for the weekend? That too? Wow! Hold on, let me ask Emily.' She covered the mouthpiece with her hand and raised her eyebrows.

'No,' she hissed. 'I don't want to go to Candida's – she's so smart she makes me nervous, and talking to *him*'s like talking to God.'

'We're going,' Polly hissed back. 'You've nothing on this weekend, you told me, and Candida's talking of *Othello* at the Salisbury Playhouse.'

'Oh, Ma!'

Polly released the mouthpiece. 'We'd love to come,' she said with fervour. After a couple of minutes' chat she put down the telephone and turned to the scowling Emily. 'True friendship,' she informed her, 'exists when you can descend on someone at almost no notice to grab a break when things are bad, be left to spill it all out or keep mum – *and* have breakfast in bed. Not only is Candida giving me all that and *Othello*, but she's also offering us The Gatehouse at Chilbourne to live in until the dust settles and we know where we're at – which will make life infinitely easier all round. The least you can do, Emmy darling, is to give in with a good grace and pack a bag with the best clothes you possess. And, you'll be glad to know, Sir Bernard's in Washington.'

All the lights were on at The Gatehouse, gleaming out into the October dusk, illuminating from within the attractive shapes of the pointed Gothic windows, rendering dimly visible the carved barge-boarding along the gables, and making the cottage look like an illustration from a Victorian children's story.

'A pretty place, isn't it?' Polly said to Emily as they drove up.

'Not bad,' she answered guardedly.

Rose, Polly thought, would laugh at it and love it. Neville, though, would consider it an insult even to be offered such a place. A gatekeeper's cottage? Particularly coming from the Goughs, whom he affected to despise. 'So much naked ambition for money and social prominence,' he'd said disdainfully to his family after the summer lunch party. 'It isn't given to everyone to climb the slippery pole like

Bernard, and not everyone would wish to do so. Material success has never attracted me, as I'm sure you all know.' None of you possesses my philosophical detachment, his sad smile had implied.

Candida appeared at the heavy pointed Gothic door to embrace them both. She led them into the hall and through to the living room in a waft of expensive scent. 'I feel almost embarrassed offering you this place,' she said, waving a slim ringed hand at what Polly saw as a good-sized room, 'but I did hear from Jane and Rose something of your difficulties, and this, if you'd like it, is yours while you need it. At least you'll get away from Neville.'

The room was empty of furniture and its wooden floor gave off hollow sounds as they walked. The walls had faded patches from long-gone pictures. There was a Victorian wrought-iron fireplace and deeply embrasured dusty windows whose sills could hold a riot of geraniums in pots. The room's forlorn charm seemed to crave life and movement. Upstairs, ceilings slanted low over their heads, and there were tiny old tiled fireplaces patterned with shells or flowers in rich colours that glowed like jewels. Polly, who had dreamed of living in a country cottage, found this one delightful.

'It needs airing,' Candida commented.

'It's a dear little place,' Polly said.

'We've no more use for it. We've tried to let it, but it's too far from the nearest town, and to be honest, rather lonely. The roof and the drains and all those sorts of unspeakable things are said to be sound.'

Polly looked at Emily and Emily looked back.

'These autumn evenings are chilly,' Candida remarked dispassionately. 'I must shut the front door.' The retreating clack of her shoes sounded on the uncarpeted stairs.

'Well?' said Polly.

'It's all right,' said Emily. 'I suppose.' Her lips tightened and she added angrily: 'I don't want to leave our house.'

'We have no alternative. I'm sorry, but I can't pay the mortgage on my own. And you know how horrid those flats and little houses we've looked at were. Charmless and poky and altogether impossible. So?'

'How do I get to school?' A sulky mumble.

'There's still a bus goes along the main road.'

'It's miles from anywhere,' she burst out. 'No shops. And how'd I visit my friends?'

'I'd teach you,' Polly said with bravado, 'to drive.'

Emily's face changed. 'Would you? That would be ace. Imagine people's faces if I drove to school!'

'It's a deal?'

'Yeah, it's a deal.'

'We're coming down,' Polly called to Candida, and they clattered down the twisting staircase together. 'We'd love it,' she said, but you must let us pay a proper rent.'

'Friends,' Candida said, 'old friends who are caring for a house that would otherwise be deteriorating, don't need to pay rent.'

'This friend needs her pride,' said Polly.

'Peppercorn then, peppercorn plus the bills. And to have the garden tended would be well received.'

'With pleasure.'

'Then that's decided.' Candida's tone hinted that she was bored with the subject and wanted to change it. 'I'll send the odd-job man round to freshen up the rooms with emulsion paint straight away. Just let me know the colours.'

It was difficult during the course of the weekend for Polly not to make comparisons between handsome Chilbourne House on its rise and the little Gatehouse down by the road. They would keep surfacing and Polly could not always suppress them. Did such comparisons occur to her friend? Candida, so apparently open on the surface, said little that revealed her own views and thoughts. She had expressed a calm sympathy to Polly on the telephone, but her real feelings were more evident in the offer of The Gatehouse and this leisurely weekend away than in the sort of probing and commiserating discussions Mary or Vanessa would expect to have with her. Candida would find the free play of all those naked unsubtle emotions of anger, jealousy and sympathy embarrassing and uncalled for. She handled Emily well.

'Do you ride?' she asked her early on Saturday morning.

'Ride?' Emily said, hesitant. 'Well, it depends what you mean by ride. One of my friends has a pony and I go over to her place at the weekends and we muck about together, taking it in turns. You know.'

'Can you rise to the trot?' Camilla enquired.

'Oh, yes, and canter and all that. But I can't jump more than a little ditch.'

'I shan't ask you to jump. But I thought you might like to exercise Matthew's pony with me in half an hour when I go out?'

'Great,' Emily responded, enthusiastic for once. She had frequently badgered Polly and Neville for a pony and stamped and muttered every time her mother pointed out the impossible cost. It was, Emily had informed her only a month ago, one of the great tragedies of her childhood that she had been deprived of horses and dogs.

Candida kitted her out, remarking: 'We're much of a shape, though you haven't quite my height!' and they disappeared for an hour and a half, while Polly borrowed a tape measure from the housekeeper and went to prowl and measure and brood in The Gatehouse.

It occurred to her as she contemplated window sizes (the windows were filthy and of a difficult shape) and mentally hung curtains (the adjustments would require hours of work), that she was being ridiculously scrupulous not to throw in her lot with Tom right away. Why should it be so much better for Emily to live out here with her, miles from her school and her friends, than for them both to move to Tom's, which was infinitely more convenient? She flung open a window to let out the musty smell in the cottage and saw a robin on the topmost twig of a bush, eyeing her with interest. He hopped to the next bush and let out a ripple of notes. 'All right for you,' she informed him. 'Robin families don't share nests.' Was it inevitable that Laura and Emily would continue to regard one another with enmity? Might not Laura come to admire Emily and look up to her as a favoured elder sister? Or Emily to feel protective towards Laura and help her with her homework? But when she contemplated opening the subject with either one of them, she felt a chill run through herself and knew that it was impossible. Poor, suffering, cross Emily? Sharp and prickly Laura?

'In a pig's ear!' she told the robin.

Where was the cherubic, the adorable Emily of seventeen years ago? Gone, grown into this half-woman with all her female wails of unfairness, racked with adolescent insecurity intensified by Neville's rejection of his family (no mentions from him of having them to stay for weekends or holidays) and by his vision of her as that lesser being, a girl. Poor Emily, crawling unwillingly from the dark safety of the chrysalis stage into a piercing light that illuminated in all their ugliness the adult resentments and betrayals than had torn her parents apart and now were tearing at her. Oh, God, if only Polly could think of a way to help her.

If only . . . What sad words. If only Neville could have behaved with more sense and restraint, waited for a few more months, Polly thought for at least the fiftieth time. But he had been heading for trouble for years. She was surprised that some woman had not protested before, telephoning him – or even her – with wails of treachery or tales of pregnancy.

'You're not unfaithful, are you?' she asked the robin, and he chirped and preened himself. 'No, robins stick to one mate, sensible fellows.'

Tom had said: 'How extraordinary people are who change their bedfellows so frequently – like changing one's friends weekly. Personally I prefer to be permanently with someone whose habits and likings match mine, in bed or out of it.'

Dear Tom. Polly sighed, bade farewell, 'But not for long!' to the robin and moved on to the next room, the next window.

*

Candida had expected riding with Emily to be at best boring, more probably an ordeal. She had offered the ride on Matthew's pony as a hostess's kindly gesture, not imagining it would be taken up. But to her surprise Emily rode with a straight back and controlled the lively pony well, laughing as they cantered across the park, calling to Candida: 'He's great!'

Candida was aware that there were certain positive aspects to her invitation to Polly to live in The Gatehouse, and to gain a quid pro quo was the sort of generosity that appealed to her. She told Emily that if she liked she could help the local doctor's son to exercise the boys' ponies regularly while they were away at school. Emily was ecstatic, the nervous sullen look quite gone from her face. 'Oh, thank you, thank you! That would be terrific!'

'You'll be doing us a favour in riding one,' Candida said, to cut short the embarrassing effusions. Her hands were tight on her reins, controlling her lively mare's eagerness. 'Down this slope, through the trees, along a few hundred yards and we come to the river. I'll ride ahead and show you.'

The river path was flanked with willows and alders, and the water below was shallow and clear as glass, running over leaning, rippling strands of weeds and shining pebbles. On the opposite bank a large man on a big bay horse was watching them appraisingly. He lifted a hand in greeting.

'Candida!' he said. 'Good morning. Who's your friend?'

'Emily,' Candida said, reining in her mare, 'this is Hugh Hanbury, a neighbour of ours. Hugh, meet Emily Ferrison. She and her mother are coming to live temporarily in our Gatehouse.'

His eyebrows rose. 'Really? How delightful for you both,' he said to Emily. 'Tell me,' he added softly, leaning towards her from his horse as if they were alone, 'how does Candida manage that mare of hers? Does she behave?'

'Of course,' Emily said, indignant at the implied slur.

'She's rather a wild girl,' he said. 'One never knows how she'll behave.'

'Hugh's always making dark insinuations,' Candida told Emily. 'About my mare, I mean!' Her eyes met his in a swift flash of amusement.

Hugh asked Emily how old she was. 'Seventeen? A marvellous age for a woman. And what do you plan to do with your life?'

'Well, I hope to go up to Oxford,' she said.

'University? An intelligent woman. I like intelligent women – that's why I'm glad to have Candida as a neighbour. And now you're going to be our neighbour, with your mother. I met her once, I believe, at

Candida's place. Gorgeous red hair. Yes? I thought so. Well, if you want to ride across my property consider it yours – so long as you obey the country rules.' His horse was tossing his head against clouds of riverside insects and wheeling round. He tightened his reins. 'I must be off. Good to see you both. Goodbye.'

'He's a nice man,' Emily said shyly to Candida. 'What did you say his name was? Hugh Hanbury? Is he . . .?'

'He's Tom's brother,' Candida said, nudging her mare on. 'You've met Tom, I take it?'

'Yeah, a couple of times,' she said, and Candida saw the sullen look return.

The expression annoyed her. 'And you made your judgement on so short an aquaintance? And condemned him? How very odd. Someone who is so important to your mother, who has given her happiness?'

'I don't like him.'

Candida said softly: 'You haven't given him any real chance, have you? You know, Emily, rejecting your mother's lover isn't going to bring your father back to the fold. Can't you try to be positive about all this? There's a positive side to everything if you take the trouble to look for it.'

Emily was silent.

Candida leaned from her mare to open a field gate and went through. 'Push the gate back hard when you're through and it'll shut. That's it. You know, my mother had lovers all through my childhood. I never remember anything different. They made her much nicer – she liked me more when she was rapturous with a new man. She'd buy me presents and we'd go out together and laugh at nothing. It was her thrill of excitement spilling over on to me, and so I learned not to be jealous, but to share. Children don't own their parents. They have them for a little time but then when they grow up they must give them back to themselves, to follow their own lives. Polly isn't just Mummy the mother, or Miss the school teacher. I think you might help her re-build her own identity, don't you?'

Emily flushed, looked at her sharply and kicked the pony to a canter. Candida followed more slowly, casting her mind back to her childhood and her mother, in those long-gone days before she had become stout and overbearing, sweeping back into the house from some new lover's bed, radiant, proud, clasping in her arms the flowers he had given her, and the gifts and new clothes for her daughter that normally she would say they couldn't afford, but which now were part of the happiness overflowing into her life. If Polly and Tom could live and love together, two such gentle and affectionate people, then surely there would be a similar excess of fulfilment and happiness to spread its warmth to Emily and Rose and Laura? She wished she could paint the picture she saw with sufficiently brilliant words to persuade Emily to her own conviction, and smiled drily to herself at the thought of dwelling on something that would normally be wholly alien to her own sophisticated and incredulous nature.

Peace. Birdsong. Deer. A wide and empty sky. A gentle breeze. Grass rippling. Leaves dropping from trees. A V-formation of geese flying overhead. Having woken late and relaxed after a late return to the house from *Othello*, Polly had breakfasted in bed on boiled eggs and croissants and delicious Kenyan coffee, dressed at a leisurely pace, and now was out on the terrace with Candida and Emily, exulting with them in the morning's sunshine.

'We must walk,' she said. 'We can't miss this golden day.'

'I want to ride,' Emily chimed.

'We shall do both,' Candida promised.

They were strolling back through the long windows into the drawing room when the telephone rang. Candida perched on the arm of a Queen Anne wing chair and picked it up.

'Chilbourne House,' she said. 'Oh, hello, Vanessa. How are you? You're what? You're pregnant? Oh, lord! What am I supposed to say to that? Congratulations? You think so! Well, doubtless it *is* an achievement at our age.'

Emily looked at Polly and Polly looked at Emily, who jerked her head. Both looked at Candida, whose triangular eyebrows were near her hairline.

'You're telephoning everyone to tell them, are you? Yes, indeed. When is the infant due? April. I suppose that's as good a time as any. Yes . . . You found Polly and Neville away?' She put long fingers over the mouthpiece and murmured to Polly: 'Does Vanessa know about you and Neville parting? No? Then shall I break it to her?'

'Oh, please,' Polly murmured back, relieved to have this horrid task removed from her sphere, hating to imagine the reaction.

She listened as Candida spoke. Vanessa's high-pitched response was audible across the drawing room. 'Oh, but he is quite definitely leaving Polly,' Candida assured her. 'It's been decided for two or three weeks now . . . If you're so regularly in touch then I'm surprised he hasn't told you. No, he's in London, Eaton Square, I believe, with his girlfriend, Juliana somebody. She's the reason for the rupture. She's expecting a . . .' She was stopped abruptly and the pitch at which the interruption had come was again clearly audible to the listeners in the room.

Prompted by some wayward imp of mischief, Polly grabbed her bag and dived into it for her diary. She flipped through the pages to find the entry she wanted and thrust it at Candida.

'Ah,' Candida said, her face amused. 'It does so happen that I have a telephone number where Neville can be reached. Would you like it?' She dictated the number, said goodbye and put the receiver down. 'Goodness, the poor girl's almost hysterical. How extraordinary. I wonder why?'

'Probably,' Polly replied in sardonic tones, 'because her relationship with Neville was all that it shouldn't be. She always did feel she had special claims on him right back from the old days at LSE.'

Emily said furiously, 'It isn't true! You're disgusting.' She glared at her mother.

Polly looked back.

Emily's voice cracked with uncertainty. 'It isn't true. Say it isn't true.'

'I can't. Oh, darling, I'm sorry but I can't.'

Chapter 13

Vanessa was shaking as she came off the telephone, shuddering and sick from shock. She tried to sit in her chair and keep calm, but the horror of what she had just heard would not allow her to stay still; she jumped up and began to stagger to and fro across the room. All that the rest and tranquillity of the farm and her friend Mary's kindly nursing had done might never have had its effect: she felt as ill as she could ever remember feeling. She made for the brandy bottle, sloshed the stuff into a tumbler and took a couple of gulps, gasping as the alcohol hit her throat, remembering too late, angrily, guiltily, that it was bad for the baby.

How could Neville have left Polly for anyone other than her? She hated this woman, this Juliana, whoever she was, for worming her way into his affections, stealing him. It was Polly's fault, it must be. She was so dull, so sexless, so settled into middle-age and mediocrity that she had made him desperate, and now this woman had driven her claws into him, staking a claim when he was vulnerable. A scream rose in her throat like sickness and she had difficulty keeping it down. For all these twenty years Neville had told her he owed a duty to Polly and his daughters; that he was old-fashioned in his attitudes here. There was no love in his marriage, he implied, no passion, but his daughters needed him; they loved him, they needed a stable background. He would forego much for them – career, advancement, the philosophic life – and his life's achievement would be less than he had planned, but he would have the satisfaction of knowing that he had behaved as a father should. His stoicism had been admirable, concealing his emptiness, his grief. He had cared deeply for her, she knew he had, through all those years of stolen meetings and passion revealed in secret. They were connected together forever, and it had been so from the beginning. What did temporal distance matter? This Juliana must be a mistake, a moment's madness. She must rescue him from the madness.

She would telephone him, but first she must have her mind clear, think what she would say. Oh, God, if only the recent scan at the hospital had confirmed that the wonderful child in her womb was a boy, how thrilled Neville would be, and how much easier it would be to say all that she longed to say. But her baby – and how delightful it had been to see his minute limbs moving and waving, a miracle that had brought tears to her eyes – her darling baby had not been in the right position to show its sex. She had wanted her intuition to be confirmed as certainty before she spoke to Neville, to go to him with pride and rejoicing. But it *must* be a boy. The son Neville wanted. Her child was his child. She must tell him right away. It would change everything. She picked up the telephone.

'Neville? Oh, Neville . . .' But it was an unknown man with a well-bred incurious voice who answered. Seconds passed while he was fetched. Her nails bit into her palms. 'Hello? Oh, Neville, how lovely . . .' She took a deep breath, putting into her tone all the old liveliness and gaiety he'd said he admired. 'Darling Neville, what on earth are you doing in London? Have you escaped from Polly for the weekend?' Best to pretend she knew nothing. 'What fun! Why don't you come round and have supper with me?' Supper sounded more intimate, less formal than dinner. Please, Neville, please come, she prayed in a silent shriek.

'Oh, hello, Vanessa. Good to hear from you. No chance of a meeting, I'm afraid. I'm fully booked with friends. But we must have a chat some time. There've been great changes in my life. I wonder if you know?'

'Changes? No! How exciting.' She rushed on: 'Such exciting changes in my life, too. Neville, I'm pregnant!'

A pause. 'You are? Well, it's what you said you wanted, Vanessa. I hope you'll be happy with this new development. And I hope everything goes well for you. Is the father with you?'

'Oh, no. No! How could he be? It's *you* who's the father, Neville! And we're going to have a son. Isn't that wonderful?'

Silence. Then his voice, stiff and somehow unnatural: 'Vanessa, this sort of nonsense isn't funny. And it simply isn't possible.'

His reaction was all wrong; it wasn't meant to be like this. There was a different, unprecedented note in Neville's voice, a hard note of warning that chilled and frightened her. 'When we went to *Aïda* at Covent Garden,' she gabbled. 'That wonderful night. Remember the full moon and how we laughed at it for peering in on us? Remember how we made love? You must remember. That's when we made our son.' She wished she could see his face, wished she knew who, if anyone, was in the room with him. She waited desperately for the thrill of excitement to leap in his voice.

But his voice, when it came, was a social one, flat, non-committal. 'No, what you are saying is quite impossible. You know, Vanessa, I thought Polly or one of your other friends would have told you by now, lovers of gossip as they are, but evidently they haven't, so I must: Polly and I are separating. After twenty years it's a long process, and difficult, but when it's over I shall be leading a very different existence in London. There's someone new in my life and her name is Juliana, Juliana Wallace. She's a very wonderful person . . .' (She was in the room with him, she must be, listening with greedy suspicious ears to every word he uttered, the bitch.) '. . . I shall be living with her. Indeed, I hope to marry her when my divorce is through. And we are having a child together, and it has been confirmed as a boy. I'm sure as an old friend you will be happy for us.'

Her room seemed very pale. The colour had drained from everything around her. She began to stammer: 'You're not . . . She's not . . . Marrying her . . . a baby – say it's not true! Say it's not true!' Her voice rose to a scream. Faintly she heard his voice saying goodbye. 'No, don't go, Neville. No, you mustn't, I have to talk to you . . . I must, I must! Neville! I love you!' But she heard the click, soft and final.

She moved with uncertain steps across the room to the window and leaned against it, clutching the curtains, weak and sick. She knew the meaning of the words 'a stunning blow' now; her head was reeling, as if some brutal force had attacked her from behind, knocking the senses half from her. Outside a wind was rising; it was shaking the branches of the trees, stripping them of their shrivelled leaves to blow them along the street in a whirl of dust, cigarette ends, scraps of paper and discarded bus tickets. She had been discarded too, thrown out of Neville's life, trivial and unwanted as the detritus of the street. She had given him the most special news of his life and he had rejected her; he had cut her off. And after all these years. She had always been there for him, friend, playmate, lover, and above all his admirer and supporter. And now he told her another woman was bearing his son, another woman was preferred to her. She let out a low howl in concert with the wind and tears poured down her cheeks.

Polly, Emily and Candida had finished their lunch with cheese and fruit; wonderful cheeses, delicious fruit, Polly thought, admiring the colours of the apricots, the pears and the great bunch of black grapes that spilled over the side of their bowl. The look of the table as they rose was entrancing, like some still-life picture of the seventeenth century with its juxtaposition of the sparkling wine glasses with the cheese platter, the fruit bowl and a vase of autumn flowers and leaves; lovely shapes and colours, and an air overall of ease and diversion. It seemed almost unreal, and Polly felt unreal in this atmosphere of wealth and ease, a different person, temporarily detached from quarrels and bitterness, the trials of life held at arm's length. Delightful relaxing Chilbourne, where one was never asked to tackle tedious tasks; lucky Candida to live every day in such luxury. What heaven never to have to scrub burnt saucepans, put bleach down the loos, or stand ironing shirt after shirt to cope with the daily demand. Polly was not so naïve as to suppose that the possession of wealth was any insurance against unhappiness or infidelity, yet she was certain that to grapple with such problems without constant cash crises must make the finding of solutions so much less wearisome. If one's estranged husband laid claim to all the best furniture, well, hell, it was possible to buy afresh instead of having to argue over each chair, each bed, each pair of curtains. When Polly claimed a Christmas present picture from her mother, Neville had remarked with disdain that Juliana had abandoned her matrimonial practice at the Bar rather than endure the raging emotions of combatants fighting over every dishcloth while they divorced. 'That's my water-colour and no dishcloth!' Polly had snapped, but she understood the distaste only too well. She also understood the importance of every dishcloth to a budget stretched to snapping point.

When they rose from the table to stroll to the drawing room for coffee she stretched and sighed with contentment: here for the space of a few more hours she could forget dishcloths and other such horrid objects. They were discussing their plans for the afternoon when the telephone sounded. 'Damn!' said Candida, who had extended herself elegantly along a sofa. 'Which bore now?' She rolled on to her stomach and leaned over to pick up the instrument. 'Oh, Vanessa. Hello again. What can I do for you now?' She rolled her eyes towards Polly, mouthing: 'No peace!' and grinned. 'What was that? Oh, you rang Neville . . . You had a talk . . . Why didn't I tell you about the baby? I tried to, but you gave me no chance. My dear Vanessa . . . yes, indeed, and as Polly's friend I understand your concern. I'm as horrified as you . . .'

While her listeners in the big sunlit room could hear the babble of Vanessa's voice, the words were not distinguishable, yet it was clear that Vanessa was in a shocked and emotional state. Without knowing why, Polly felt tension mounting inside herself and in a flash anticipated dealing with a distraught Vanessa on top of everything else. But what could Neville have said to cause this near hysteria? Polly put down her coffee cup and leaned forward.

'Your baby – you're talking about *your* baby . . . Neville's *what*?' Candida swung her feet off the sofa and sat upright. 'You can't be serious! Vanessa, this is appalling. How? When?' A pause while she listened to a cascade of words, her eyes wide and flat with shock. 'No. No, I can't tell you how stunned I am. You can't help yourself to someone's sperm as if you were simply borrowing a drop of milk!'

'Good God, what a sentence!' Polly murmured in admiration.

'No,' Candida was saying, the drawl gone from her voice, the words clipped with anger. 'I don't think I do need to hear any more. No, I'm putting the telephone down. You've made this situation and you must live with it, but you cannot expect my sympathy. Goodbye!'

She replaced the telephone as if it were a explosive object. Her eyes swung to Polly and swerved away to the drinks table. 'Polly, I don't know how to tell you what that damned fool has just imparted to me, but I know strong drink will be needed. Do you prefer whisky or brandy?'

'At this time of day?' Candida's eyes were fixed on her painfully. 'Oh, very well, whisky. But I can guess what it is – Neville fathered Vanessa's baby. Am I right?'

'Oh, God, too horribly right.' She lifted the decanter. 'How in hell did you know?'

'From the sound of what you were saying and from knowing the parties concerned,' Polly said in a light voice, surprising herself with her own resilience, 'I'm only astonished it didn't occur to me earlier.'

'It's not true!' Emily said in a half-suppressed shriek. 'I don't believe it.'

'Whisky for Emily,' said Candida, and poured. 'Neat, or with a dash of water?'

'Oh, water,' said Polly, watching with concern.

'Neat!' Emily demanded dramatically. She grabbed the glass, drank, gasped and choked, tears starting to her eyes.

Candida rescued the glass. 'Steady! Poor Emily, you've had a shock. I must say, I am a trifle startled myself.'

'It's not true,' Emily managed. 'Daddy wouldn't have done that.'

Emotions were sloshing around in Polly's head like pickles in a jar and her thoughts were pure vinegar. 'Done what?' she asked. 'Been unfaithful to his new woman? He was unfaithful to me – and to us as a family. Why should you think he'd change his ways?'

'I'm afraid it is true,' Candida told Emily. 'Vanessa was quite explicit. Apparently they went to *Aïda* together, had a wonderful evening, made mad passionate love afterwards – and made the baby.'

Emily muttered: 'I want my whisky back.'

Candida added water and handed her the glass. Emily's hand shook. Her eyes were pink with unshed tears and her lips tight with the effort of controlling the fester of feelings inside her. She drank the whisky in nervous gulps. Polly went over to her and put an arm round her shoulders.

'Emmy love, I don't suppose Daddy had a clue what Vanessa was up to, except that for years, when the opportunity presented itself, well, they'd make love. For old time's sake, she'd say, or something of the sort, and Neville would oblige. She made use of him.'

'It was sick of her.'

'She wanted a child – remember her telling us so at the summer party? You and Neville agreed against Rose and me that women should be free to do as they wanted reproductively, to have a late chance if that was what they desired.'

'I didn't mean it like that!' Emily expostulated in a half-shout.

'You meant,' Candida said with interest, 'that in principle it was right, but not when it affected your family?'

'No . . . Yes. You mustn't hurt other people. That's where the principle is.'

'And Neville didn't follow it.'

There was a silence while Emily grappled again with her emotions, Polly sought for the right thing to say. Emily burst out: 'Why did Daddy have to do this to us?'

Polly struggled between detestation of her husband and affection for her daughter. 'I don't suppose he did, not consciously. And he did admit to me that Juliana's baby was a failure of contraception. But when she told him it had happened he saw all the advantages – a son and her. She's young, well-off, successful. Success could rub off on him, give him the chance to escape from county council boredom and write his book. Vanessa? Quite simply she broke the rules . . . if there are any.'

'But what about us?' Emily said. 'You and me and Rose?' She sounded desolate, her voice betraying her sense of utter rejection.

'You're nearly eighteen. You're grown-up now. When the dust's settled on all this, you'll find a new relationship with him, as friends. And as for me, after all, he never really wanted me, did he?'

'What do you mean?'

'Ours was a shotgun marriage. Neville was bullied and bribed into it. There were always undercurrents of rejection swirling about.'

Emily looked blank. 'I didn't know.'

'Oh, come on, darling. You knew that Rose was on the way when we married.'

'Well, so what? Lots of people don't marry until they're having children.'

'Not in those days, not like now.' Emily had no sense of history, of other ways of living and behaving. 'Neville nursed his resentments. We existed together politely, no more.'

'You put a damned good face on it,' Candida said. 'For years we all thought everything was fine. The friends, that is.'

Emily turned to her for support. 'I thought my parents had the best marriage around. Was that so very stupid of me? I never saw them arguing. They never fought in front of us.'

'Your mother must have worked hard to avoid that.'

'I did. I played the doormat, pretended to myself that all was well,' Polly said. 'I refused to see Neville's little games. You opened my eyes, Candida. You gave me a hint.'

'Did I? Perhaps I did. You worried me. There is such a thing as growing comfortable with your own unhappiness and pain, becoming so accustomed to it that you cease to notice the damage it's doing to your personality, growing blind to increasing problems. You had no life of your own, Polly. I was cross on your behalf.'

'Growing so accustomed,' Polly mused. 'Victorian women did that, didn't they? They had to, trapped in the marriages of their day. Becoming victims of themselves and society, of what was acceptable and what was not. They even felt they must be expiating their own sins, they were so self-deluding. One can become used to being a victim, it seems one's predestined rôle. But in our marriage it was Neville who constantly spoke of himself as the victim. He even had me believing it for years.'

'And now it's Rose and Emily who are the victims, with not one but two unwanted brothers on the way,' Candida said, smiling with rueful kindliness at Emily. 'Especially Emily, because she's still at home and now she'll have to move away from her friends.'

'Vanessa was supposed to be Ma's friend,' Emily muttered. 'I don't think much of that for friendship.' Her tone sharpened suddenly. '*Two* brothers?'

'Vanessa spoke of a son.'

'Oh my God!' said Polly. 'How ludicrous. Neville always yearned for a son but now he's truly overdone it. Now there will be some fights.'

'And expenses,' said Candida, 'whatever sex arrives. Who is going to pay those?'

'That's a thought,' Polly observed.

'You won't be so foolish as to help, I hope?' Candida remarked.

'No way!' Polly said fervently. 'I'm concentrating on my own salvation, mine and Emily's and Rose's. But whatever will his Juliana say when she finds out? Because find out she certainly will. Vanessa will ensure that. Stand by for the next instalment this evening when Neville returns to Winchester.'

'How can you joke about it?' Emily burst out, leaping to her feet and rushing for the door. 'It's all horrible and sordid. I don't want any brothers. And I don't want ever to see him again.' And she slammed the door behind her.

Polly stood up. 'I must go to her.'

'Motherly counselling? Don't rush, give her a minute or two to get hold of herself. How about you? In your place I'd be shaking with rage. You're amazingly calm. I admire you.'

Polly gave her a sidelong look and then grinned. 'Do you know, I surprise myself. I must be turning into a new cynical and accepting woman. I feel awful about Emily, and I couldn't possibly tell her this, but this latest revelation has quite restored my sense of humour. Two women in one's ex-husband's life are much better than one, aren't they? If a husband has a mad passion for some gorgeous younger woman and rushes off in her pursuit, his wife feels belittled, faded and boring. But *two* women, both pregnant? No burning longing there for the one perfect love he believes he's found. Just a skunk whose wife is better off without him!'

'It's unbelievable,' Emily said, pacing furiously up and down her bedroom. 'It's foul, it's sick, it's like a nightmare – or one of those television programmes where you can't believe the characters could really be that awful. But you can switch the telly off. How can I switch my father off? How could he be such a bastard?'

Polly sat on the bed, watching her. 'Plenty of men are like that. Having women on the side feeds their inflated egos and they can't imagine ever being found out or hurting anyone. They're sure they're unassailable. No, that's unfair. Plenty of women are like that, too.'

'Sod that. *You* were unfair. You knew. Why couldn't you have told me? Now you've made me feel just so stupid and childish and naïve, I can't bear it!' She turned to the chair where her clothes of yesterday were lying and began to hurl them across the room, but the weightless shirt and slip and tights fluttered uselessly as paper darts. She seized instead a pair of shoes and flung them at the door, which they hit with thumps loud enough to startle her into stopping. She rounded on Polly, her fists clenched. 'Well?'

'I didn't want to upset your teenage years, God knows they're difficult enough anyway. I wanted you to feel secure. And you did, didn't you?'

'Oh, yeah, I did. But how do you think I feel now? I feel betrayed. Were you and Tom laughing at me for being a baby?'

'No, never.'

'Well, you should have been, because that's what I was. Everything was good in our family, that's what I thought. We didn't make an embarrassing thing about it, but we could trust each other. Now who can I trust? Everything was a sham. Pa was a sham, you were a sham. What a fool I was!'

'No, that's not true, I loved you and I cared. I still do. I was protecting you until you were eighteen and off to college. Then I'd have told you. I promise you that's what I'd planned. You're a big part of the reason I'm not with Tom now. I'm putting you first.'

'I don't want you to,' Emily said furiously. 'I don't need that. I'm grown-up now.'

Mary liked to go for a stroll after she had shut up her poultry and checked that her animals were secure and settled for the night. She would hear little murmurs and rustlings that were homely and comfortable, and she would think her own thoughts about the lives of her children and her farm. In mid-October dusk came early, and more so each day, but the weather was good and the sun still set in an orange glow behind the trees in the orchard and the air had the bitter-sweet odour of the decaying year. Soon it would be too wet and cold and dark for her wanderings and briefly she felt the fore-taste of winter, dark and treacherous in her mind, and wondered if any ills would befall her charges. She watched a leaf or two detached from an apple tree drift sideways down to the grass, tussocky now and damp, and then she saw a late apple, tucked into a hollow between the tufts, and stooped to pick it up. It should be up with its fellows in the farmhouse apple loft, scenting the room to the rafters, and she wondered how it came to be missed when she and the children had picked them last weekend. She pulled up her old pullover to rub it clean on the shirt beneath, and then bit into it, sharp and good. The pony Aladdin whickered and she called to him: 'I'll give you the core, boy!'

Suddenly her mind was wrenched from its gentle maunderings by the sound of the farmhouse doorbell, which rang in the yard as well as indoors. Someone was leaning on it, an impatient someone who was now beginning to thump on the door. Something urgent? An accident? Her children were all in their rooms, and she hoped they were doing their homework. The bangs continued. Something was very wrong. Where was George? Soaking in the bath after his day's work outside? Robbers? Could it be evil men come to the isolated farmhouse to threaten and steal? Just such a farmhouse as this had been attacked only last week twenty miles to the east of them. Oh, nonsense, nothing worth the taking here. Mary ran to the back door, kicked off her boots and ran through the house in her stockinged feet to the front door.

'Who is it?' she called, and thought she heard a woman's voice outside. She tugged the heavy door open.

A crumpled figure collapsed on to her shoulder, a shaking distraught woman whose words she could barely distinguish.

'Vanessa! My dear, what is it? Come in.' Her voice changed, became anxious. 'The baby – is it all right? You haven't lost your baby?' Foolishly conceived or not, the child was a reality, a tiny dark entity that must be protected.

'No,' Vanessa jerked out. 'But I might as well have done. Mary, everything's gone wrong. He doesn't want me. He's rejected my baby. I've rung him and rung him, but he won't listen to me.'

'Who won't? Oh well, never mind that now, let's sit you down.'

Mary put an arm round the thin shaking shoulders and led her into the warm kitchen to sit in George's big comfortable padded chair. The apple was still in her hand; absently she took a bite, and surveyed her friend's ravaged face. 'You look terrible,' she said bluntly, crunching. You had to be blunt and commonplace with Vanessa to calm her, to move her from the clashing world of drama she inhabited into the quiet familiar world of everyday. 'Now, how about a cup of tea? And while I'm making it you can tell me what's upset you.' She reached for the kettle on the Aga and pitched the remains of her apple into the fire. 'Tell me slowly,' she ordered.

Vanessa poured it out. Under a crumpled black jacket she was wearing a soiled and skimpy scarlet wool top that revealed the angular lumps of her collar bone, and cut into the bulging flesh of her swelling breasts. Her black tights were laddered from a hole on one bony knee. Her hair was tangled and falling forward over her eyes and her hands constantly pulled and tugged at it, twisting the locks round her fingers. Beneath the hair her eyes were wild and pleading; she leaned forward in her chair and her words demanded understanding and sympathy. And at first Mary did feel a confused pity for her, for her sluttish unkempt state, and her obvious anguish. She thrust a mug of tea into her hands and Vanessa clutched it to her chest like a talisman. But even as she spoke Mary sensed the feelings of commiseration that had always reached out from her to Vanessa drain away. She spoke of such incalculable acts of folly. All that was old-fashioned, solid and decent in Mary revolted. This was no way to run your life, this grasping in greed and selfishness for what belonged to other people. If she was so unhappy and lonely then she should concentrate on her career, take up some hobbies, go to classes. Mary believed in the restorative powers of classes: they enlarged the mind, broadened the acquaintanceship, filled the empty hours. Vanessa had had too many empty hours to spend in brooding, and brooding was dangerous, a poison to the soul. There was poison in Vanessa's tale, poison against Polly.

But if Mary was perturbed by Vanessa's story, George was appalled. He came into the kitchen fresh from his bath, a big man clad in his homely evening garb of open-necked shirt, thick pullover and well-worn green corduroy trousers, greeted his guest with his usual reserved quietness, thrust his hands deep into his pockets and stood contemplating the dismal figure of Vanessa as she ended her tale, watching her flushed and crumpled face unmoving until she dissolved into tears on her final words.

'. . . so you see, I have nobody.'

Over Vanessa's sobs Mary encapsulated in a few neutral sentences all she had been told.

George took his hands from his pockets, pointed a stubby forefinger at Vanessa and said: 'You're telling me that Neville fathered Vanessa's baby through some trick of hers during an adulterous episode, and that he is now leaving Polly for some other woman, some married barrister, who is also having a child by him? It's rotten. It's atrocious. They should all be ashamed of their behaviour. What has this to do with us?'

'Vanessa is desperate with shock and unhappiness.'

He looked inconceivably shocked himself. He said: 'She deserves a good spanking!' and walked out of the room. Mary had the impression that a part of life that was good and clean and wholesome went with him, while she was sullied by association with the hysterical woman beside her. Looking down she saw the tear-smeared face staring at her. Vanessa had drawn herself up in George's chair as if jolted and disconcerted by the notion that someone might condemn her, her mouth open, a hand clutching a sodden paper tissue frozen in mid-air.

'He doesn't understand,' she said. She grabbed Mary's hand. 'You must make him understand.'

'I don't understand myself,' she said, freeing her hand. 'Polly's your friend and Neville's Polly's husband. How could you do this?'

'Polly was never my friend. She stole Neville from me with Rose. He always cared for me best. And I was first with him, not her. We've had a love that was consummated year after year, even till now with my baby.'

'What, even when you were married? What about your husbands, Vanessa?'

'I looked for love with other men but I was disappointed and betrayed. I've always been betrayed.' Her eyes held Mary's in a half-defiant, half-appealing stare. She sighed. 'But I shall always love Neville.'

Mary felt as though she was struggling in a marshmallow maze, sticky with sentiment. Her mind fixed on one thing: that Neville had apparently kept up some sort of affair with Vanessa for more than twenty years. The idea filled her with repugnance for both participants, and the thought that if anyone had been betrayed it was Polly. Vanessa was claiming the opera as an excuse: Polly was a philistine who never entered into Neville's great love of music, Vanessa the understanding friend who arranged for him to indulge his obsession – while he was staying overnight with her and claiming the indulgence of her body also. Mary, who had never cared for Neville, fixed the major part of the blame on him. Vanessa had been deceived and she had courted the deception, yet her strange and love-deprived childhood had made her the obvious prey of men like Neville, who told her he cared for her, then made use of her. She wished she had Neville in front of her now so that she could tell him what she thought of him.

Abruptly she told Vanessa to go and wash her face in cold water and pull herself together before the children caught sight of her. 'I won't have them upset by tales like this.' (Sexual selfishness and unbelievable indiscretions.) Then Vanessa must eat for herself and the coming child, and then she should go to bed. She could stay for the next day or two and Mary would care for her: 'Nervous upsets are bad for the baby.' (Poor child, doomed before its birth by two such hopeless parents.) She would ring Vanessa's office to explain that she had been taken ill. The woebegone figure in George's armchair had the same effect on her as a sick animal.

Chapter 14

'Of course, Vanessa is mad,' Neville informed Polly and Emily. 'Quite, quite mad. She's having delusions. Possibly it's a nervous collapse brought on by this late pregnancy.'

'I thought you approved of the modern concept of reproductive freedom?' Polly murmured.

'My views have not changed,' he said stiffly. 'But in this particular case the person involved seems to have the wrong mentality. Hormonal disturbance, possibly the start of an early menopause. For all we know she may not be pregnant at all, but imagining it. She needs help, psychiatric help, badly, before she spreads her nonsense around.'

'You mean Vanessa hasn't told Juliana yet that she's also expecting your child?' Polly said. 'You'd better think up a good tale very fast, because she will. And that will ditch your plans in deepest mire.' She told him that she didn't give a damn for herself (not true, she felt made to look a fool, something no woman endures with equanimity), but Rose, who had rung for a gossip and received more than even she had bargained for, and Emily, who had been vilely embarrassed by hearing such dreadful things of her father through Candida, had both been sickened. 'And no child should be put in such a position by her own father.'

Neville was examining his immaculately kept fingernails. 'I have already told you that the allegation is rubbish. It's quite impossible.' He flung his hands down in a dismissive gesture. 'I shall tell Juliana the same and she'll believe me.'

'But you slept with Vanessa. You always have done. Why shouldn't it be true?'

He threw back his head and frowned at her, the picture of a man maligned. 'Are you calling me a liar?'

'Yes!'

He looked ludicrously disconcerted. Polly could have laughed, except for Emily standing beside her, her glance nervously twisting from one to the other.

He breathed deeply. 'I have not had an affair with Vanessa.'

'Call it meaningless flutters, call it what you like, I know you've had her from time to time. I saw you once, you see.'

'What the hell are you talking about?'

'At Candida's. In a far bedroom. Sorry, Emily. I think you should go somewhere else. Why don't you go and watch television? Come to think of it, Sunday evening, it's Mastermind. Play against the contestants – you're so quick at producing the right answers.'

'No. I want to hear Daddy producing the right answers.'

'He can't. I'm sorry, darling, that's why you should go.'

'No.' She stood her ground, her eyes on her father.

'Your mother's fantasising, like Vanessa,' Neville said. 'It's jealousy. It's the shock of losing me.'

'She's got Tom,' Emily said, as if discovering an entirely new fact. 'She doesn't need to fantasise. But you – you had three women in your life all at once. How sick and stupid can you get? You're gross. You've got some gross disease. Satyriasis, that's what they call it. They told us about it in our sex classes at school. You're the one who needs to see a psychiatrist. Oh, God, my own father. You do at least think you can trust your own father.'

Tom said: 'Oh, Polly, my poor darling. Down another snake. As if you hadn't enough to contend with.' His voice over the telephone was so concerned that she stopped shaking and felt calm, restrained and rational. Just to know he was there and listening was enough. They spoke to each other every day that they couldn't meet and because of an undiscussed fear that Neville might pick up the telephone and overhear God knew what, an emotional shorthand was developing between them, little cryptic remarks that conveyed so much and made her laugh and feel that at last she belonged to someone whose thoughts were attuned to hers, someone who understood.

The failure of the Ferrisons' marriage was becoming public property, probed and dissected by their friends and neighbours, with shakes of the head and knowing looks of horror when people realised they were still forced to live under the same roof. The word spread that each had embarked upon a relationship elsewhere, and there were lively marital arguments as to who was to blame, the wives on the whole opining that dull Polly had held Neville back in life, the men contending that Neville was a selfish demanding sod and she'd blossom once he'd gone. Some of the more quick-witted of their acquaintances recognised Polly and Tom as a couple and invited them for a meal, anxious to be au fait with the latest development and determine whether, as gossip said, Neville had caught Polly and Tom in flagrante, or whether it was the other way around, for similar rumours plunged Neville into a variety of local involvements, and truth was, as always, hard to come by. Humans relish disasters, so long as they affect other people, and those at the centre of a drama are sought after for their newsworthy aspects. Joanna and Geoffrey Brookes were the first to secure Polly and Tom's presence and it was at their dinner table on Saturday evening that Polly realised how lonely she had been with Neville, lonely in having no one whose sidelong glances made some other guest's words into a secret joke, no one whose foot nudged her toes under the table, no one who looked across the flickering candles in the candelebra and saw her as a person of value, someone special in the way she'd always wanted to be.

She clutched the telephone to her ear, crouched well to her own side of the double bed she and Neville had slept in together for twenty years. He'd moved to the guest room now, but the place where he'd lain repulsed her; the print of his body was on it, and the smell of him, expensive aftershave like rank sweat to her flared nostrils. Tom was talking about Emily's reactions: despite her rudeness to him he felt for her anguish and her anger. 'A part of her world has collapsed. A big part. Worse than a bereavement. Not only has she lost the father she thought she had, but she's discovered someone new and repulsive in his clothes.' It was cold in the bedroom, but as Polly listened to him suggesting in his diffident way how Emily might be helped and comforted, she felt relief roll over her like a warm wave. God, what was it with Tom? He had a strange power of comprehension of people; explanations were unnecessary, his mind was ahead of hers. He was talking now of keeping Emily busy with her studies, her friends, anything that might reduce the effect of the emotional bludgeoning that her father's treachery made on her spirit. He spoke of the comfort of new clothes and new hair styles in restoring the stricken adolescent self-image, and she marvelled at his common sense.

Of Vanessa's behaviour he was incredulous. One of Polly's oldest friends, and she acted in such a way? What was this friendship between these five women, how had it come about, and how could someone supposed to be her friend treat her with such offhand contempt and treachery? Sitting on the bed Polly stared at her mahogany dressing-table and its stool, which recently had been the subject of intense dispute between her and Neville. But she saw neither dressing-table nor stool; their images had faded to make way for an earlier picture. She saw the London School of Economics as she had first seen it, tall grey buildings that more resembled warehouses than the stone quadrangles and gleaming spires of her imagination, standing in a dark canyon of a street. Recollection crowded the buildings with people of many nationalities: students milling about the notice boards in the foyer or waiting for the iron gates of the main lift to be dragged back; balding lecturers with distant faces meditating upon problems of macro-economics as they attended their own, more select, lift. Three stocky young men discussing rugger. Two Indian girls in saris chattering earnestly of John Stuart Mill's *Liberty*. It was a place to feel lost. A place to feel insignificant.

But she had been happy there with her friends. Chance had favoured Polly; Candida had been allocated to the same first-year classes and seminars as her. Candida, so striking and amusing; so articulate and self-possessed; so much the cynosure of male eyes. It had surprised quiet Polly that she should choose her as her friend, but perhaps it was an attraction of opposites, or possibly, she surmised, Candida saw her as a foil to her own looks and character. Knowing her had rapidly enlarged Polly's circle of friends.

Jane and Mary similarly shared seminars, and appeared odd friends; Mary quiet and on the shy side, Jane four years older and considerably more mature and self-confident, but the link here was in their determined attitude to their studies, which they pursued in the same room of the library, each beside a pile of reference books, breaking off at intervals to consume the excellent coffee available in the coffee bar, comparing progress as they did so. It was there, one wet November afternoon, over banana sandwiches and a discussion of fiscal policy in a recession, that they met Polly and Candida, struggling to prepare similar essays. They compared sources of information and an alliance was soon formed between them. They took to keeping places for one another in the lunch queue, to meeting for their cups of coffee at the same times each day, to sitting during lectures towards the back of the gallery of the Old Theatre where they could assist each other with missed notes or exchange sotto-voce comments on lecturing styles. One rotund professor, famous for the egg stains on his tie, regularly adjured them: 'Remember this point, it's worth a mark in your examinations!' Another read his lecture at a speed and a level calculated, as Candida said, to burst the sound barrier, regularly concluding it twenty minutes early and running from the platform as if heading late for Heathrow; a third spoke ponderously of Afri*cah*, Indi*ah* and Ameri*cah*, which, as the lecture droned on, struck them as ever funnier. On more than one occasion their ill-suppressed laughter caused the unfortunate man to threaten them with removal. Their group achieved minor fame. In the male-dominated college men invited them en masse to their parties to even the balance of the sexes. Polly reminisced to Tom, recalling it as huge fun.

'So where did Vanessa come into it?' he demanded to know.

'Ah, Vanessa. She was the odd one out,' Polly admitted with a certain dryness in her voice.

Looking back, it was Mary who was Vanessa's real friend, Mary who had acquired, or more accurately been acquired by her in the college pub, The Three Tuns, one evening, when each of them had been let down by a man – 'And that's the story of my life,' Vanessa had pronounced solemnly and slightly drunkenly, for the time spent waiting for her boyfriend had not passed unused, 'being let down, I mean.' Mary, whose male acquaintance had at least managed to buy her the wine she was sipping before racing off to a forgotten late tutorial, commiserated and studied her new acquaintance with interest. She was a striking-looking girl with thick yellow-brown hair like a lion's and Mary had noticed her around LSE because she had a rather rude and flamboyant face and manner; together they gave an impression of total self-confidence which Mary envied.

'Men are all the same,' the girl said. 'Hopeless, greedy, insensitive. I've had such terrible experiences, you wouldn't believe.' She looked gloomily at the circle of used glasses on the table in front of her. 'I'm low because I'm high,' she brooded, 'but it isn't only that, I've a cosmic sense of the injustice of the human condition. Particularly for female humans. We're used and abused and thrown out with the rubbish.' And she invited Mary to join her.

Mary was fascinated; she had never met anyone quite like Vanessa before. Vanessa was reading law rather than economics like the rest of them because, she said, she wanted to right the injustices suffered by the woman in the street, the woman on the Clapham omnibus. But she was missing out on the political philosophy side that the economists explored. 'I'm a busy, active person,' she said, 'with reason and incentive and desire. I feel I have the potential to be an agent for change. I'm glad I've met you, you have access to knowledge and understanding that will illuminate the side of my mind that's still dark. We need a period of evolution and revolution, a revival of the forces of change of the 60s, a revival of the individual's powers over herself. I've read Parsons and Plato and Marx and Popper and Gellner – I have to know all sides of all the arguments – but I'm not focussed yet, I'm dissipated, I need a guru.' Several drinks later and with her eyes full of tears, she told Mary about her terrible childhood and her experiences with men and how her psyche was lacerated with hurt. 'But I'm helpless before their attraction, they have such power over me.'

Mary introduced her to Polly and Jane and Candida. 'You wouldn't believe what she's been through,' she told them. 'That look of self-confidence she's got, well, it's like wearing armour made of tinsel. She needs strong friends to look after her.' So a place was kept for Vanessa too in the lunch queue, and Mary collected her from the library to join them at coffee time and insisted that she was invited to all the same parties.

'And don't tell me,' Tom said, 'the guru she ultimately found was Neville?'

Jane was at a dinner party, a party with a different social ambiance from her own friends': not higher or lower, simply different. It was in a large flat that was well furnished but in no way opulent; the few pictures and the ornaments reeked of good taste and little money after school fees had been met. There were eight people in the drawing room, all standing, all talking in voices that were penetrating and self-assured. The men were members of the Diplomatic Service, the women, with the exception of Jane, were their wives, and she knew none of them. Jane was not nervous but she was tense; she felt herself on show, she felt herself being assessed, like a candidate for some position of whom the Board had its reservations. She was not used to this and she disliked it. But she was Jeremy's partner; his mistress, a couple of the older wives might term her. All the wives had known Jeremy's wife; some of them still kept up with her. 'Such a nice girl, so sweet, such a shame their marriage went wrong.' Marital failure in their circle was something to be deprecated. A strong marriage was essential in the lives they led; postings abroad left family and friends behind, an undivided front was essential where wives performed so many unpaid tasks as hostess, amanuensis, unofficial diplomat, guide to important visitors and smoother of rifts in the lute. Divorce fluttered them as doves when a hawk passes over.

'And how is Jeremy?' a sturdy lady enquired of Jane, her head cocked to one side. She had a faint foreign accent, probably German. And her name was Ursula something. Perhaps her husband had met her on a posting to Bonn or Vienna? She could have been attractive then, young and light-hearted in a dirndl skirt. Now she looked tough and decisive, iron-grey hair skewered back into a pleat, spectacles hanging on a grey cord round her neck, a person of competence and resolution. 'Does he still go to so many concerts? "Herr Beethoven" we called him in the old days.'

'He does,' said Jane. 'We go together.'

'That's good,' she said. 'A man who works as hard as he does should have his relaxations. And how are the children, Peter and Helen?'

'They're fine,' Jane said cautiously. She had met Jeremy's children several times and talked with them easily on a surface level, for they were well brought up, well-behaved young people. But she did not feel that she knew them at all, under that smiling politeness. 'Wrestling with the usual examinations,' she ventured.

'Of course, poor dears,' Ursula nodded. Her own were at the same age and stage, the children had known one another forever, she told Jane. Another woman came across to greet Ursula; they embraced, kissing the air beside their respective faces three times.

'Lovely to see you . . .'

'Lovely . . .'

'Lovely . . . *Mmwah*! When did you get back from Prague?'

'Oh, two or three months now. It's wonderful to be back – there's nowhere like old England. I remember when we were in Kuala Lumpur, how I'd wake in those stifling mornings and yearn for frost-fresh autumn days here, and I haven't changed a bit since. Oh, don't look so shocked, Ursula, I know it's not done for people like us to say so, one should exclaim that each successive posting has been the most fascinating and delightful yet – but it's how I feel.' She looked with interest at Jane, and the flash of her eyes over Jane's hair, her make-up, her dress, took a mere second, but Jane knew she had been inspected and graded. 'Hello. I don't think we've met before, have we?'

Ursula introduced her. The name was Georgina Ellington and she was elegant, something in the Candida mode, the hair expensively smooth and lustrous, the subtle, figure-caressing oatmeal-coloured dress probably from Caroline Charles.

'You came with Jeremy? A very old friend of mine. Such a charmer. I've always been particularly fond of him.' Her words implied more than they said. 'How do you know him?' Her eyebrows slid upwards. 'From *work?* What sort of work? A civil servant! In the Department of Trade and Industry? But what do you *do* exactly?' Her eyebrows stayed elevated as Jane explained briefly. 'Well, I've never come across anybody like you before, not in our life. I hear talk about problems of spouse employment amongst the younger men, girls who insist they must work, but you . . .? Someone like you would be quite different. I daresay you've never worked anywhere but London.' And her tone was not congratulatory.

Ursula interrupted with a question about the son at Marlborough and the two of them plunged into a discussion of schools. Jane was on her own; a career woman, unmarried and childless, she had nothing to offer on this topic. She stood sipping her drink, attempting to appear at ease and fearing she was failing. Behind and beyond her she could hear other conversations which in a dreamlike manner wove words into a broken tapestry: 'The architecture in New Delhi differs entirely in conception and quality . . .' 'Suppose one's own son were at an African desk during a coup . . .?' 'Our delegations in Brussels are constantly pushing at the boundaries . . .' The occasion felt quite surreal to her.

At the dinner table her host talked to her perseveringly about travel and places she knew; they discovered affections for similar locations, Paris and Florence and Venice, and Jane began to feel less like an actress taking a part in a play she'd never studied.

There was a lull in the conversation while plates were removed and delicious roulades of venison stuffed with prunes and served with colourful roast vegetables were produced. Her neighbour on the other side, husband of the elegant Georgina, told Jane he had recently bought a small Queen Anne house in Alresford in Hampshire, and described it.

'A gem,' he said. 'It will be perfect for holidays with the children and one day we shall retire to it. Georgina threatens to live there permanently and I suppose commuting to London or even to Brussels would be a possibility. We shall see. The garden is walled and in urgent need of attention. I long to transform it but I have a horrid feeling that when we are next posted abroad our tenants will inevitably neglect it and all my efforts be wasted.'

Jane smiled and felt sorry for him in his shifting life. 'You want to preserve it at a moment of perfection, but gardens and their weeds will grow. You need a low-maintenance plan, something simple and foolproof.'

He looked at her approvingly. 'Are you a gardener? You sound knowledgeable.'

'Me? Heavens, no. No one less. But I know someone who is – Candida Gough.'

'Candida Gough?' Georgina said, leaning forward. 'Isn't she Sir Bernard Gough's wife? She's good. Do you really know her?' Her voice sounded doubtful.

Jane sipped her wine and gave a small smile. 'We've been friends for many years.'

'But she does London designs.'

'And Hampshire, I assure you. They have a place in Hampshire, Chilbourne House.' She turned back to Georgina's husband. 'I'll give you her address and telephone number, if you'd like me to?'

'I would like,' he said.

'Candida Gough,' somebody said. 'That would be quite something. How clever of you to know her.'

Her host claimed her: he was recollecting what Jeremy had told him of her work; he wanted to enquire her views on the enlargement of the

EC and whether she thought the opportunities the erstwhile Eastern Bloc countries could offer in the way of trade could in any way counter-balance the downside of their years of strangled development, their neglected infrastructure. 'Never discuss politics at the dinner table,' had been Jane's father's adage. Recollecting the words she replied briefly, but her host was not to be fobbed off, he persisted, two of the other men joined in and there was a lively discussion to which the ladies reacted by turning their shoulders coldly away and speaking of the latest acerbic Tom Stoppard play. Later their hostess collected the ladies' attention with her eyes and led them off to her bedroom to make repairs to their faces and then to the drawing room for coffee. Now they spoke in affectionate gossip of the promotions of people Jane had never met. 'Old Henry's made it to ambassador after all, isn't it amazing?' and 'Young Crispin Worcester, John and Anna's boy, you know, he's been posted to Madrid. Second Secretary. He's doing so much better than they thought he would.'

Jane was feeling quite invisible until abruptly their attention switched to her. 'Jeremy's due for a posting, positively overdue. Do tell us, has he heard anything yet?'

Tom was playing the piano, alone in his sitting room. Shading the glass of the window with her hand, Polly peered to make certain, cursing as the autumn rain lashed her. Laura must be up in her room doing her prep, thank God. She rapped with her knuckles on the glass. He looked up, smiled, and was on his feet all in a second; the door opened and he drew her in.

'God, my darling, your face is icy,' he said as he kissed her. 'Come by the fire.'

She sat on the sofa, shivering frantically and pushing wet hair away from her face. 'I didn't have an umbrella,' she said vaguely. 'So stupid.'

He sat down beside her and took her hand. 'Tell,' he commanded. 'Something more's happened, you've slid down another snake – is that it?'

She sighed, then smiled ruefully. 'Is it so obvious? Neville. His sole concern over the last couple of days has been that Juliana Wallace might discover Vanessa's allegations and wreck his plans for a life of philosophical detachment with her. And now she has. That dear old friend of mine telephoned Juliana at her Chambers today to give her the low-down in all its sordid detail. When I arrived home, Neville was waiting for me in such an evil temper, you can't imagine. He shouted, he screamed . . . I thought he was going to hit me. No suave sangfroid this time. He thought it was me who told Vanessa where and whom to ring.'

'He didn't hit you, did he?' Tom demanded, hunching his shoulders and looking large and ferocious. 'Tell me the truth.'

She shivered again. 'No, he didn't. I hopped out of the way. But I'll tell you something strange, my legs were shaking. I didn't think I was frightened, not really. Neville's a words man, not an action man; he doesn't need to lash out, his tongue inflicts far more damage. Yet subconsciously I must have been afraid. To have my knees turn to jelly like that, I mean.'

'Where is he now. Still in the house?'

'God, no. He's speeding up to Eaton Square to counter-attack and swear undying affection, but of course everything is now in a state of flux, with Vanessa, so I'm told by Mary who rang to commiserate, in a state of hysterics and almost suicidal. And there's more. I found a letter from Neville's publisher fellow on the kitchen table, which I had no compunction about reading, and guess what? It was turning him down. Oh, all very polite and wrapped up in pretty words about how they admired his writing, his meticulous research and his clear body of knowledge, but basically saying that far from going where no man's mind has inquired before, he was going down well-trodden philosophic paths, the paths of yesterday, not today.'

'No wonder he was screaming.'

'He won't accept it. He'll try other publishers. He'll keep it from Juliana, too, but I know he was longing to boast of success to her. He's in the shit now with nothing to recommend him. And although Mr and Mrs Floral Cosy came for a second look last night, no one has yet made an offer on the house. So we're stuck – locked together in loathing until The Gatehouse is cleaned and repainted. Frankly, I'm praying that Juliana will overlook his indiscretion with Vanessa and get him out of my hair. But that's expecting a miracle.'

'We'll pray for one,' he told her fervently. 'But a baby is a trifle too large an indiscretion to be overlooked.'

'Oh, God, it is!' She giggled rather wildly. 'But I don't want Neville forced to remain in Hampshire. I don't want him anywhere near me.' In a sudden fit of anguish at all the complications in her life she clutched at Tom and pressed her face against his. Wordlessly he held her, his lips against her hair. Then she giggled again and said in a voice that mocked her own tribulations: 'But what am I worrying about? If Juliana rejects him – why, he can always turn to Vanessa.'

He laughed too. 'To be the recipient of all the mad dramas and tantrums you've told me about? A just penance for his sins. But could she afford to keep him in all his expensive tastes?'

'God knows. Just so long as someone other than me does.'

'You shouldn't still be living with him,' he told her grumpily. 'It's insane when you could be living with me.'

Polly freed herself from him and rose to stand by the fire, stretching her hands to its warmth. 'Don't, Tom. You know I want to and you know why I can't. Laura apart, Emily is shattered by all she's heard about her father. It's been a dreadful trauma for her and she needs time to recover. She resents you almost as much as the women in Neville's life. It's understandable. She's terrified of losing both her parents.'

He leapt up. 'It's ridiculous, tyrannical. I would look after you, make you happy. Both of you. Emily's selfish to want you to herself. It's time she accepted our relationship. And why did Candida Gough have to interfere, offering you that Gatehouse? Everyone's combining against me!'

His anger startled her. 'We'll still get together, I promise you.' She smiled her most brilliant smile at him. 'One or other of Emily's grandmothers will be delighted to have her to stay; somehow we'll have weekends together.' To Polly's surprise both parents were supportive of her, Mrs Ferrison even going so far as to say: 'I'm surprised you put up with Neville for so long – he's his selfish father all over again.' Her own mother, voluble with indignation, wished she still had a husband who could thump him as he deserved. Both said: 'If there's anything you want me to do, you only have to ask.'

But the thought of having to make use of grandmothers and friends only served to fuel Tom's fury. 'We should be together. Have you consulted your solicitor about a divorce yet? Why not?'

'One thing at a time,' Polly said. 'I've enough on my plate with a new job included.' The task of confiding the details of Neville's behaviour to the solicitor made her despair.

'Your job isn't new now. You aren't committed, you're hedging your bets. We've been through this before!' His voice was becoming louder and louder, its deep bass resounding through the house.

'Ssh,' Polly whispered. 'Laura will hear.'

'To hell with Laura. I have to force *you* to hear,' he yelled. 'All you can think of is how that bastard Neville treated you – but give me credit, will you? *I'm not him!*'

'It's nothing to do with that!' she yelled back. 'Of course I'm committed to you. Haven't I told you a hundred times?'

The door opened and Laura stood there, her eyes examining them. 'Sorry,' she said. 'I heard my name. Didn't mean to interrupt anything.' Faintly Polly saw her smirk.

Tom opened his mouth, shut it again, then said with a quietness more deadly for the bellows before: 'Rubbish. Go away, you horrible nosy child, and do some growing up.'

Laura paused, reddened, blinked and went. She shut the door after herself.

Tom and Polly stared at each other. Tom spread his arms wide and she walked into them with great readiness. Neither uttered a word, they simply stood, wrapped together, silent.

'Oh, Polly,' he rumbled at last in her ear, 'I didn't mean all that. I'm just hopelessly frustrated, that's what it is.'

'Of course you meant it,' she said, 'and I'm not surprised. I'm surprised at myself, though. I never yelled at Neville. I hadn't the courage. It shows how much I trust you that I can break free of myself like that. And don't you see, it shows how much I love you?'

This observation was followed by remorse, apologies, forgiveness, caresses and acute frustration until Polly suggested that Laura was unlikely to break in on them again, and anyway, the door had a key and he could lock it. Sex on the sofa was not perfect, since the sofa was small and Tom large, but with great good-will and felicity they managed, assuring each other again and again of their undying love.

But later, as Polly drove back to the now hated house with the estate agents' boards outside, she wondered how many more rows there would be before they could be together finally? It made her feel quite weak with love and depression.

Chapter 15

The Goughs' elderly odd-job man, chivvied by Candida, finished the cleaning and emulsion-painting of The Gatehouse speedily and Polly and Emily moved in on Guy Fawkes' Day, with Polly feeling as exuberant as any of her schoolchildren, rockets of relief bursting in showers of sparks in her mind. She had never been so relieved to leave anyone or anywhere as she had been to get away from Neville and the house. She could have danced round The Gatehouse, though she thought it might amaze the removals men if she did. Their old house was finally being bought by Mr and Mrs Floral Cosy for a price that was nothing special, but on completion of the deal she would have more money than she'd ever had before. And it would be her own money, with no Neville to make demands on it for a new car, a new suit, or some other expensive ploy without which he'd claim that life would not be worth living. They had occupied the same house for the last three weeks in a silence broken only for essentials. Polly had decided to be calm but not friendly. Neville seemed hardly aware of her. The cracks she had seen between them in the spring when she had first contemplated leaving him had widened into a chasm with the revelations of his tangled relationships with Juliana and Vanessa.

There were chasms too in his dealings with his daughters. Rose and Emily, waiting for explanations, discussions, even possibly apologies, also found him silent. He had never been a man who thought it necessary to justify himself, because it never occurred to him that what he did could be wrong. Besides, his own erratic father had told him many years ago that only the weak and creeps apologised, and that apologies, by admitting a fault, inevitably put one in the wrong. 'Avoid them at all costs!' he'd said, advice that Neville had prided himself on always following. He was, in any case, too busy to talk to his daughters. His weekends and evenings were spent either in driving up to London to support Juliana and affirm his devotion to her, or on the telephone struggling to persuade her how sad, pathetic, and of course untrue Vanessa's allegations were.

'Juliana cares for me deeply,' he said stiffly to Polly, 'but this stupid story has come at a delicate time for her, in her condition. Small wonder she's upset.' She had asked him to give her space; she needed time to confront her reactions and define her conclusions. Neville would be staying on in the house until the completion of the sale or until Juliana felt she had had enough space and they could come together. He did not admit the possibility that she might never come round.

Polly's awakening that morning had not been good. Before she opened her eyes she had heard a drip, drip, dripping from the apple tree branches by the window, and a deeper note, splat, splat, splat, from the guttering. She remembered what day it was and her eyes flashed open to see a November fog, a thick grey blanket, fastened to the windows. The gloom seemed to attach itself to the house and to Neville, his face pinched with meanness as he reminded her item by item which furniture she might *not* take with her. But at last he had to leave for work and then there were shadowy colours appearing among the grey. She had the day off from school for her move and she was escaping him. By midday, as she parked her car by the cottage and ran up the garden path to open the door, a yellow sun was catching glimmers of light from the drops of water clustered like glass baubles on the lavender hedge, and the world was full of colour.

She was ahead of the removals van. She had time to run round the cottage opening windows to let out the smell of paint and let in the fresh air, cool and good in her lungs. She went into the smallest bedroom last and the happy thought came to her that she would use it as her writing room, spending some of the money from the sale of the house on a little Victorian desk, and a set of shelves for her paper and her books. For a moment she leaned on the windowsill in a bubble of stillness and solitude, breathing the country smells and listening to the small sounds about her, little rustlings and pigeons cooing. She took a deep breath. She said aloud: 'I am myself.' And she smiled, thinking with a lively anticipation of returning to her writing routine when the cottage was straight, recollecting the sweat and the frustration when the words refused to come, and the relief and the wonder of it when the words reflected her vision, or even transcended it. The first draft of her novel was half-finished, and while she hardly dared to hope it was good, she could admit that it was not bad, and Tom gave it warm praise and Rose said she loved it. Emily, too, had read it, and given it a guarded go-ahead in which Polly heard a note of surprise.

Poor darling. Poor muddled, hurt, vulnerable darling. When Neville had been ranting about the furniture earlier she had glimpsed Emily's overcast face. 'Daddy,' she'd said, 'you're not being fair. We need tables and chairs, the same as you. We'll only take what's agreed to be ours. If you think you can't trust Mummy, trust me. I'll see to that.' But Neville had ignored her intervention and she had fallen silent, easily put down. I used to be like her, Polly thought, but Tom is changing me. How strange, how silly, that I once felt nervous of him. Who would change Emily?

From the road came the sound of a heavy vehicle and a grinding of gears. The removals van was at the park gate. She ran downstairs, wedged open the Gothic front door, and for the next few hours there was no time to ponder anything, only to shout directions to the men as the three of them staggered in and out under the burden of packing case upon packing case and chairs and bedheads and chests of drawers, all looking somehow smaller and shabbier than she remembered them, outside in the wintry sunshine. Then suddenly the day was done, the light was going and the men went with it, leaving chaos behind. Polly collected Emily and drove at breakneck speed along narrow lanes to meet her bus, and as they arrived back at the cottage so Candida's silver Mercedes glided to a stop outside. They went in together to the main room.

'Bleak!' said Emily, casting her schoolbag to the floor and kicking it aside. Books spilled out on to the dusty floor.

'But where's the furniture?' asked Candida, staring round. 'Where are the carpets?'

'This is all,' Polly told her, suddenly tired and disenchanted. 'My part of the shareout.' There was normally elation in seeing a strange house transformed into your own place as you unpacked familiar objects and ranged them about you. But what pleasure or elation was there to be found in the two elderly armchairs, the bookcase and the side table that stood lonely on the bare boards, or the half-empty bottles of whisky and gin on a windowsill? She sighed.

Emily squatted down to rifle through the contents of two packing cases, pushed in a corner. 'Nothing much here,' she commented.

'I don't believe it,' Candida said, appalled. 'How on earth will you manage?'

'With improvisation and inspiration,' Polly said sardonically. 'We'll eat our meals off our laps for the present. Neville's taking all the dining furniture because that was a wedding present from his mother.'

'Dear God!' said Candida.

'But I have the marital bed. Neville said Juliana would not care to sleep in a bed he'd shared with me!'

'Daddy was all bitter and horrid,' Emily said in a forlorn voice. 'He never used to be like that.'

'Separations and divorces are terrible things,' Candida said. 'Remind me frequently, will you, never to contemplate such a step?' She frowned her revulsion of a catastrophe that would devastate her elegantly constructed life so completely, then she took off an expensive silk scarf, ruffled her hair and remarked: 'There's a ton of furniture doing nothing in the attics at Chilbourne House that would be better being used and polished. I know there's a Regency supper table because I noticed it particularly last time I was up there. One of the rule joints is slightly damaged, but it's really rather delightful, and there are some chairs which would go with it, and I could probably find a pretty cupboard or two. How about coming over and rooting about a bit, Polly? You won't want to be buying if your plans for your future with Tom come to fruition soon.' And she glanced at Emily, who looked away and feigned deafness. She shrugged off Polly's thanks, declined a drink from one of the bottles on the windowsill, and her Mercedes purred quietly away with her.

Polly found a stool, placed it by the window and began to hang curtains to shut out the black emptiness beyond. Emily cast her eyes round the room, shrugged off her coat on to a chair, then said to Polly: 'You look tired. Wait while I make us both a cup of tea, and then I'll help you.'

Gradually, Mary told herself, she was helping Vanessa to understand the harm she had done herself, and the mischief and unhappiness she had caused through her obsession with Neville; gradually she was cutting through the thick layers of distorted liberal thinking and yearning sentimentality and jargon that for years had screened Vanessa from reality. At first there had been little talking, for Vanessa had been genuinely near complete emotional collapse and Mary had had to nurse her and calm her. It had taken more than two weeks before she was sufficiently fit, mentally or physically, to return to her flat and her job, but slowly, with help from the local doctor, she had been brought back to some sort of equilibrium. Since then Mary had insisted, to George's distaste and annoyance, but in the end to his grumbling acquiescence, that Vanessa needed to return to the farmhouse each Friday to Monday to rest and be fed on good home cooking, and, of greater importance, to talk, and through that talk to examine her life and her future with the baby. 'To be *counselled*,' Mary told George, smiling as she herself lapsed into jargon.

Their talks covered many sessions and were punctuated by periods when Vanessa sat motionless, radiating misery, tears pouring down her face, or rose to pace the kitchen, one clenched fist pounding into the other hand, refusing to allow her thoughts to go where Mary was gently, but implacably, directing them.

Mary's first success had been Vanessa's agreement that she should stop pursuing Neville. They had talked in the afternoon, as they had several times, sitting at the big table in the warm kitchen, the labrador asleep in her basket beside the Aga.

Mary asked her, 'How was it that your relationship with Neville kept going as it did through all these years? Twenty years is a long time.'

'Through our love for each other,' Vanessa stated.

'But how did that love persist and express itself at such a distance?'

'It was always there!' she said proudly. 'And we met.'

'Yes,' Mary said pensively, looking into her mug of tea. 'So you've told me. At the annual lunch, of course. And at Covent Garden.' She looked across at Vanessa. 'You went to the opera, what, two or three times a year?'

'Yes. And every time it was perfect. First the music – and that was special with Neville because he understood it, in all its depth and its reverberent beauty, and to share it with him was utterly transcendent, always. And then in the intervals we'd drink champagne and talk and that heightened the feelings and made me all relaxed and so happy you can't imagine, and then afterwards we'd go back to my flat and drink more champagne and laugh and make love. Superb love. It was a renewal . . . every time was a renewal.'

'How did he explain his absence overnight to Polly and the girls?'

'He told her he was staying with a friend from his Oxford days, a man he did go to the opera with too.'

'Which of you paid for these evenings at the opera?'

Vanessa looked down at her twisting fingers. 'I did,' she muttered. Then she flung back her head defiantly. 'This is today. I'm a free woman, why shouldn't I? Neville had so many expenses with the family Polly foisted on him that he couldn't afford it.'

'Did he invite you to other evenings in return? Give you a present, as it might be?'

'I don't know!' Vanessa said angrily. 'I can't remember, not over all these years. What does it matter anyhow? He always bought me a box of chocolates. Don't badger me!'

Silence. Lally the labrador stirred in her basket at the sharp voice and sat up, her eyes looking from one to the other of the two women. Her tail thumped faintly, ingratiatingly. Mary drank her tea. Vanessa turned her head to stare out of the window at the farmyard beyond.

Mary's mild country voice persisted. 'Vanessa love, how did you keep in touch through all this? Did he telephone you?'

'How could he find the opportunity? It was all so impossible.' There were red poppies on the tablecloth. Vanessa drew an outline round one with a sharp red fingernail.

'So you rarely spoke?'

Vanessa's head reared up; she glared at Mary in fury. 'The situation wasn't of Neville's making, it wasn't how he wanted it. It was something dreadful we had to live with because of his children.'

'But it was of Neville's making. It takes two to make a child. He was unfaithful to you with Polly, that's why she had Rose. Rose wasn't an immaculate conception, you know.'

'He made a terrible mistake.' Her eyes dropped back to the tablecloth.

'He makes a lot of mistakes, doesn't he? And you have too. Your marriages. And Neville. He's been unfaithful to Polly – and you – with another woman and now that she's going to have his child he's talking of marrying her, as he did with Polly. Concentrate your mind on the truth of this: his history repeats itself.' She went on quietly, relentlessly: 'And when you met, did Neville say he loved you? Did you ever speak of love, of a future?'

Vanessa shaded her eyes, as if the light Mary was turning on her precious relationship with Neville was too harsh to bear. 'How could he? How could we think of the future, with Polly and the girls always there, always clinging to him?'

'So he never did. Oh, Vanessa, how cruel. He didn't care, did he? Not truly.'

'He did love me. We loved each other, I know we did! I hoped, I always hoped . . . one day . . . I thought if I could go on it would all come right one day.'

'But it hasn't, has it?' Mary's voice had hardened now, become implacable. 'Far from it. You had two marriages and they both broke down. You dreamed and your dream became a nightmare: Neville turned to yet another woman and she's bearing his son. And the nightmare grew in your mind until it reached intolerable proportions, until you nearly broke down. You hung on to that nightmare of a dream because you couldn't, wouldn't, face reality. Look it in the face now, Vanessa. Yes, look at it without flinching and recognise it. Neville used you and took from you as he's used Polly and taken from her. Oh, yes, you're an old friend, I'm sure he liked you and enjoyed your company. But that's natural. What man wouldn't like and enjoy a woman who bestowed on him not only the expensive pleasures he couldn't afford for himself, but also gave him her body and her unstinting affection? But other men wouldn't take and take in such a selfish fashion. What has he ever given you? What in all truth have you had from him? When you were lonely, has he been there for you? When you were sick, has he cared for you? When you were sad, has he comforted you?'

Vanessa wrestled with herself. She shook her head. For once she was not crying, she was beyond it. 'I . . . I've been trying not to see it. I've been afraid of seeing it. Oh, God, Mary, you must help me. If I can't have him, I have nothing. My dream's gone, everything's gone!'

For once Mary did not move to put her arms round her. She sat very still and looked across at her. 'No,' she told her, 'everything hasn't gone. Far from it. Neville has rejected you, but you have me and I'm always here for you. You have other friends, too, and your family. But far, far more important, you have a child coming. The child will be there for you.' Her voice was soft. 'I can promise you that. You've not had a baby before, love, so you don't know. But I have and I'm telling you that a baby's love is something quite different from anything you've ever known or dreamed about. That love is simple and uncomplicated, and there are no bargains or lies or deceits about it. It's always there and it's trusting and whole-hearted and . . . and beautiful.'

The labrador put her head in Vanessa's lap; her liquid dark eyes looked up at her. Vanessa reached out a hand to the warmth of her. She closed her eyes for a second and then looked back at her friend. For the first time in many weeks her pale face relaxed. 'I don't know anything about babies,' she said. 'I'll need you to teach me. This is something I have to get right.'

Mary leaned back in her chair and smiled at her. 'You will. But it will mean hard work such as you've never known in your life.'

Vanessa considered this prospect in silence. 'And I have to do it without any dreams of Neville. I don't want my baby to be let down by his father. I couldn't bear it, Mary, I couldn't bear it . . .'

'You're right, love, you're right. But we'll build a future for your baby. We'll make sure this little one has all the loving relationships he or she can possibly call upon.' She stood up. 'Now, I have to start cooking dinner for us all and you look tired, you must rest. After you've eaten we'll talk some more. We'll start that building.'

Mary hated the thought of telephoning Neville. She had always been wary of the obvious charm that he turned on and off like a tap, while now she marvelled at his capacity for adultery, deceit, insensitivity and meanness, and found him quite detestable. She was only ringing him herself because Vanessa said she was terrified for her new resolve if she heard his voice.

'Neville?' She took a deep breath. 'Mary here, Mary Allwood. I've called about Vanessa, who's been with me while she's been so ill.'

'Ill?' he demanded sharply. 'Has she miscarried the child?'

She heard the hopeful note in his voice and wanted to swear at him, to scream abuse, and had to clench her teeth to stop herself, she, Mary, always so calm and in control. 'That's just what you'd like, isn't it? Something, anything, to get you out of trouble. No, she hasn't. But small thanks to you. She's heartbroken over your cruelty.'

'Let me make one thing quite clear,' Neville said in a haughty voice. 'If Vanessa is carrying a child, it is not mine. But I am concerned as an old friend that she should be having such delusions.'

'Then let your concern carry you into doing something positive for her. She has spoken freely to me and I am certain in my own mind that the child is yours. A DNA test would confirm that – no, please don't interrupt, let me speak. You may find that what I have to say is for your benefit. Vanessa has decided that she will have this baby on her own and she will make no claims upon you. There will be no request for maintenance. She asks only one thing from you, and in this George and I uphold her completely, as I am certain our other friends will do too. She asks that you will always behave to her child as a friend, an unofficial uncle.'

His voice was full of suspicion. 'What's she mean by that? Any gesture I might make she'll turn against me as evidence that I'm the father, and I'm damned if I'm having that!'

'You're damned anyway,' Mary said tersely. 'You be grateful for what you're getting, Neville. No, she's decided that as a liberated and modern woman she will tell the world that her baby's father is an old friend of great intellect and attainment, carefully selected as a parent whose genes should prove biologically excellent, but that she feels the trammels of marriage are not for such a free-living person as herself. The identity of the friend will not be common knowledge. But you will send a generous present at the birth, and presents at birthdays and Christmas, and you will take a proper interest in the child's progress.'

Silence. He finally managed a hurt voice: 'As an old friend I would do that in any case.'

'You're off the hook. She's let you off the hook. She won't contact your woman Juliana or whoever she is again. She's being generous with you. Frankly, I don't think you deserve it.' A moment's pause. He said nothing. Miserable ungrateful bastard! she thought, and added in a burst of detestation: 'And keep to the bargain, because I promise you, if you don't she'll give you hell. And so shall I!' She slammed the telephone down.

*

One of the things Polly liked most at The Gatehouse was the log fires. Tom had given her a load of applewood that smelt delicious, and mid-morning on the second Saturday after the move, she blew the fire to life with the bellows Candida had found for her in the attic. As the wood blazed up and its heat began to warm her she smiled with pleasure: in the house she had just left there had been only radiators. She propped the bellows at the side of the hearth, rose and turned to see Neville darting up the path through a thin sharp rain.

'What is this?' he demanded as soon as he was through the door, waving a letter in her face. 'I never thought *you*'d stoop to blackmail, Polly!'

'Whitemail, not blackmail,' she said. 'Intentions strictly good. Like a white witch as against a wicked black witch.' She laughed.

'How dare you threaten me!' he said. 'Juliana and I are working through our problems and we don't need your malice. And that's all it is. And I shall visit my daughters when I choose to do so.'

'Fine,' she said equably. 'Then do so. You never have so far. I let you know Rose was here last weekend. You couldn't even be bothered to telephone. Have you *ever* telephoned her at Cambridge – never mind visiting her?'

'You were the one who liked to run up bills gossiping. There was no need for us both to waste money.'

'Then you haven't. Nor, a far worse crime, have you contacted Emily. She's deeply hurt. That was why I wrote to you – and have no doubt about it, Neville, I mean every word.'

Tom had given her the idea. Polly thought it wickedly brilliant and acted on it. The letter said, in simplest terms, that, with the sole exception of the lunch party at San Lorenzo, Neville had behaved like a bastard to Rose and Emily. He'd committed every crime in the matrimonial and paternal calendars, yet he had given them no apology, no explanation, none of the reassurance that Emily in particular craved. Nor had they seen any place for themselves in his future life. Polly gave him five days to put this right. If he failed then she would telephone Juliana Wallace to reveal all that she knew of his liaison with Vanessa, and spell out in detail what a miserable self-centred arrogant brute he was to live with, and how useless as a father. Her blood was up and on behalf of her daughters, she told herself, she could become a real tigress.

'What right have you to give me ultimata?' he shouted.

Ultimata? Silly pedant. How could she ever have admired him? 'Rights don't come into this. We're talking about feelings. Rose's and Emily's feelings.'

They walked into the sitting room. Neville stopped short and looked around, his mouth half-open in shock. 'What's all this? Where did you get that furniture?'

Polly gazed too, seeing for the first time the room through someone else's eyes: the oak floor, newly sanded and sealed by Tom, gleaming ruddily with the flames from the fire; the pair of pleasantly faded oriental rugs Candida had found for her that looked so right with the Bergère sofa and the corner cupboard and mahogany supper table that had all come from the attics of Chilbourne House. She had placed a great bowl of fruit that Joanna Brookes had brought her on the table and pots of flowering chrysanthemums on the windowsills, while on the mantlepiece sat a pair of old silver candlesticks that Polly had found in a little cottage shop in the village and polished till they shone. There were water-colours grouped on the walls. She had thought it looked good; now she was surprised how good.

'Candida and Bernard kindly lent us various items when they saw how little we had.'

'And I don't suppose,' Neville said in a tone of bitter hurt, 'that you flinched for a moment at laying the blame on me for that?'

'I didn't have to,' Polly said. 'After the way you've behaved, how could anyone doubt whose is the blame?'

'Why do you have to keep digging at me?' he asked. 'You never used to. This man Tom is changing you and spoiling you. If Emily is as unhappy as you say she is, that's probably why. Where is she anyway?'

'She's out riding. She's helping to exercise the Gough boys' ponies.'

'I might have known it,' he said. 'They're making use of her, and you let it happen. You're so overwhelmed by their wealth and prestige, you think it's an honour.'

Polly felt a wave of fury sweep over her, and had to battle to overcome it before she could respond to Neville with the determined cheerfulness she had vowed to stick to with him, firstly because it made her feel better, and secondly because she knew it annoyed him. 'Oh, no,' she said. 'Emily is thrilled to be able to ride regularly, and to be paid for it as well, as she is, has put her in seventh heaven. No one could have been kinder than Candida, or more understanding of Emily's feelings of loss and hurt where you're concerned. And then there's this lovely furniture. We count ourselves lucky to have such supportive friends.'

Balked, Neville looked out at the November weather and scowled. 'Your friends are a herd of interfering cows. Riding in the rain? She's bound to catch a cold and she'll be lucky if it doesn't turn to pneumonia.'

Polly glanced out too. 'The rain's stopping – oh, and look, here she is in Candida's Mercedes.'

She saw Emily emerge from the car, laughing and calling something, and Candida and a tall boy waving and calling in return as they drove on. Then Emily recognised Neville's car in front of her, stopped momentarily and seemed to ponder before slowly walking on up the path. She appeared in the sitting-room doorway shaking drops from her hair with flicks of her head. She gave her father a suspicious reflective look, then addressed herself to Polly. 'Candida brought us back in the car because Mark and I were a bit damp. Wasn't that sweet of her? We could have made her carpets all muddy. What's Pa doing here?'

Neville moved forward to give her an ostentatious hug and kiss. 'I came to take you out to lunch, my darling daughter.'

'Oh?' she said stiffly, not returning his embrace. 'Why?'

'I want to talk to you. I've been worried about you. I want to hear how you are now that your mother's moved you so far from your friends and your school.'

'I'm fine. I go to school by bus. It's only twenty miles. But Ma's teaching me to drive.' At the thought of this her face seemed to relax and she began to speak more normally. 'It's terrifying but fun at the same time. I nearly drove into the Test last weekend!' She turned to Polly. 'Mark can drive, Ma, he passed his test four months ago. There's a party in Winchester he's been invited to tonight and he wants to take me. Is that all right?'

'I should think so.' Mark was the local doctor's son, a quiet eighteen-year-old who exercised the Gough boys' ponies in company with Emily, and had ambitions to follow his father into medicine. Polly had met him on three or four occasions now, and liked him.

'Who is this boy?' Neville asked. 'How long have you known him, Emily? Are you certain he can be trusted to drive safely on a bad winter's night?'

Polly interrupted. 'Can't that wait? Emily's pretty wet. She needs a hot bath and a change of clothes – now.' She gestured to Emily to go, and she stared at her father, shrugged a shoulder, turned and went. Polly added to Neville with savage sarcastic precision: 'You can interrogate her about Mark over lunch. That is, if Emily does want to eat with you, and if you really think that this sort of approach is going to build bridges with her.'

She bent to fling another log on the fire and sparks flew up the chimney.

Candida stood looking down the river, past clumps of red-twigged dogwood and yellow willow shoots, away from him. She did not want to look at him, at the face that blazed at hers. They had met by the gate that led into one of his fields and now he was leaning on it, his arms folded on the top bar, his face turned sideways to hers. 'Ride with me tomorrow morning, Candida?'

She did not speak, but turned her head instead to look at her house. Across the meadows she could see its roof and chimneys, but she could not recollect that it was possible to see his field or the river from its upper windows. She sighed. Finally, softly, she said: 'Where, Hugh?'

'Meet me at the base of Flintpen Ring. It's far enough away to answer even your notions of security. No one but mad us would want to be there on a November dawn.'

'I hope,' she said. 'I hope.'

He was impatient. 'We skulk around too much,' he said. 'It's not what I want.'

'Nor I,' she said with unexpected vehemence. 'But it's what we have to do, both of us.'

He turned to her. 'It makes it all so impossibly difficult when it should be bloody marvellous. Damn Bernard.'

'The winter makes it impossible,' she said, laughing unexpectedly. 'No passionate love in bowery spinneys!'

Hugh laughed too. 'You fell off your mare,' he said in reminiscent tones. 'I knew she'd throw you if I waited long enough.'

'And then you pounced on me! Taking unfair advantage.'

Suddenly she found him pressed against her, his thighs hard next to hers, his gloved hands holding her neck. The low sun spun in her eyes, and somewhere beyond them a woodpecker laughed. It was cold and his mouth was very hot.

'Oh, God,' she said.

Bang! Bang! From across the meadow came the sound of shooting. It startled Candida into leaping away from him. She straightened her shoulders and pushed at her hair.

'It'll be my boys,' Hugh said. 'By Pike's Wood. They'll be after pigeon.'

'Oh, God,' she said again. 'You see? We're not even safe from your sons. You don't know where they'll be. Or do you?' Annoyed, she began to stalk away.

'They don't come down here,' he said, catching her arm and walking beside her.

She turned her face to his, her heavy-lidded eyes examining him. 'Danger,' she said, 'may be a stimulant. Folly is not. Not at any time. Kindly remember that, my love.'

Chapter 16

Neville dropped Emily off by The Gatehouse in the late afternoon, refusing to come in. 'I spoke to your mother this morning. I don't think there's anything more we have to say.' Then, seeing her face stiffen, he added swiftly: 'But it was good talking to you over lunch, Emily. I was conscious that you're developing a mature and understanding mind, one open to new ideas. You're seventeen, yet you're grown-up. It's a tremendous progression that, the move from adolescence to maturity. I'll look forward to taking you out again – soon!'

Emily found Polly in the kitchen: 'Hello, Ma, what are you doing?'

Polly glanced at her as if she were a barometer, to gauge her mental weather. It was clearly marked Fair and she smiled with relief. 'I'm making a pudding for Tom. He gave me a Roux Brothers book because I said I hadn't tried anything new for years. So now I'm making something called *Gratin de fruits frais au sabayon de caramel* for him for dinner tonight.'

'Fresh fruits with a caramel sauce. Sounds good.'

'Tom has a sweet tooth. The fruits are soaked in rum. How was your lunch?' She measured caster sugar into a thick-bottomed pan and turned on the heat.

'Fine. We went to a cottagy pub in a village on the way to Salisbury and the food was great. And Daddy and I really talked.'

'Good.' Polly sought for the tactful words which would encourage Emily to spill all. 'And, er, how are things with him?'

'He was different when we were out, he was so nice. He told me lots. He said I was old enough now for him to confide in me.' Her face flushed with pleasure. 'He thinks things are sorting themselves out. He said – you won't believe this, Ma – well, he said Vanessa's been terribly sick with her pregnancy, and she's been at Mary's farmhouse with Mary looking after her. Well, you know how old-fashioned and moral Mary is, she must have made Vanessa see the error of her ways and all that, because she, Mary, I mean, telephoned Pa a couple of days ago and said Vanessa had faced up to things and wouldn't be asking him for any help with her child's upbringing, no maintenance or anything like that. She was perfectly capable of looking after the child herself. So he told Mary that he was glad to hear that she was in a . . . in a mentally more settled condition and now able to cope as she should.'

'That must be a weight off his mind.'

'Yeah. In a big way. It looks as if things are going to go ahead with him and Juliana. Maybe she believes him now about the baby not being his. He reckons they could be moving into a flat together soon and all that. How would you feel if they did, Ma?'

'Relieved!' Polly said drily.

'Oh. That's nice of you. I reckon I feel the same. I mean, her child ought to have his father, oughtn't he? At least that'd be something put right. And things need to be put right. Pa said something else. Apparently he told Mary that despite all the trouble Vanessa had stirred up for him he hoped that as an old friend she would allow him to give her child birthday presents and so on. He believed that a child without a father needed the concern and affection of males in its life in order to grow up normal and balanced.'

'How interesting,' Polly said in determinedly neutral tones, watching her liquified sugar turning the colour of dark honey. 'Go on. What else did he say?'

'He said Mary was very cold and abrupt, so he was cool back. He still says it's not his child. But I don't see why Vanessa should claim that if it's not. I mean, she's a bit over the top, but not that peculiar. It doesn't make sense. You believe it's Daddy's, don't you?'

'I'm certain it is.' Polly put cream into the caramelised sugar and stood back as the mixture spat and bubbled ferociously. She thought it expressed her feelings exactly.

'That's fierce!' Emily observed. 'Is it supposed to do that?'

'Oh, yes.' Polly stirred with caution.

'I suppose I'm beginning to get used to the idea that Pa's like he is. I mean, I don't like it, but it won't go away, will it? Perhaps all the Vanessa business has given him a fright, perhaps he'll behave differently now?' Polly said nothing. Emily added wistfully: 'Oh, hell, we just don't know, do we? When I was little I thought he was amazing. But he still is my father, whatever he's done. I thought I'd never want to have anything to do with him again, but you just can't do away with your past and wipe out your own father, can you?'

Polly shook her head and smiled reassurance. So many questions, she thought, unanswerable questions. But her daughter didn't seem to want any reply. These were the rhetorical questions that only time could answer.

Emily walked over to the window and looked out at the naked trees in the park. She said: 'Pa asked me about Tom. You know, if he comes here and how I feel about that?'

Polly slid egg yokes into the caramel cream, added lemon juice and whisked the mixture. 'And how do you feel?'

'Okay.'

Polly glanced at the averted head and back at the mixture she was heating.

'Well, I do. I don't even mind him staying. I mean, like I said to Pa, he's done such a lot for you. Helping to move furniture around, and fixing things, and polishing the floorboards. And then he put up those bookshelves for me and made an extension lead so I could put my anglepoise lamp back on my desk to study by. And I hadn't been very nice to him, had I?' Their eyes met. 'Well, I hadn't,' Emily said, lowering her eyes and drawing circles on the floor with a foot. 'And I think he's all right. Kind. He's mad about you, too.'

'Is that what you told Neville?'

'Yeah. He wanted to know so I told him.'

'I'm glad,' Polly said. 'Thanks.' She dipped a finger into her mixture, tasted, nodded and removed the pan from the heat. She offered it to her daughter for trial.

Emily smiled at her. 'Mark says he's met Tom and his brother Hugh. He reckons they're great characters.' She put her forefinger into the sauce, withdrew it hastily, and licked it. 'Mmm. Wicked. Tom'll like that.'

As Jane sat beside Jeremy in his car, driving away from the Festival Hall on a dark and rainswept night, she wondered what was going on in his mind. She sat with her eyes fixed on the traffic ahead of them, a line of sleek cars gleaming wetly beneath the street lights, all held up by a lumbering red London bus, while in their rear Jeremy stopped and started and stopped again, uttering not a word, not even of exasperation. She could not conceive what he had been thinking about all evening to make him so silent and abstracted. Normally after an excellent concert such as the one they had just left, they would be exchanging comments, analysing, appraising, taking pleasure in each other's enjoyment, comfortable together.

She glanced at his profile and saw that not even Mozart's Thirty-ninth Symphony had altered the mood she had first noticed during dinner, but attributed then to the pressure they were under to arrive on time for the music. During the intervals she had spoken to him of this and that, but his replies, while courteous, had been brief, the kind to conclude conversation rather than encourage it. So she had kept quiet, acknowledging his right to mull over his thoughts uninterrupted. The rain drummed down on the car roof and the windscreen wipers swept to and fro, to and fro. What thoughts?

Jeremy waited until they were in his flat. He poured two glasses of wine, pushed Jane's into her hand. Then he put it plainly. 'I've been posted,' he said. 'I'm being appointed our Ambassador to Warsaw.'

She stared at him in horror. 'Warsaw? Oh my God, I never visualised this happening. When?'

'Not immediately. I'll have a month or two, more, in fact, to prepare.'

One word rang loud bells in her head. 'Ambassador! Goodness, that's an upward move all right. Congratulations, Jeremy. It's brilliant, isn't it?'

'It's good. You could say that.'

'You're too modest.' She raised her glass and forced herself to say the words: 'To your success. I'm thrilled for you, Jeremy.' She drank. Inside her head another voice was screaming: *What about me?* But she couldn't bring herself to say the words aloud. She remembered that Polish was one of his languages. French and German he'd studied at school, speaking of holidays with friends in Provence and the Black Forest. 'I was always abroad,' he'd said, 'whenever I had the chance. I found languages fascinating, foreign travel enthralling.' Russian had followed at university. There had been postings to Moscow and Warsaw, a crash course in Polish in which a friend of Jeremy's had told her he'd done brilliantly. 'But then,' the friend said, shrugging, 'He's always shown himself exceptional.' She'd picked herself a shooting star and now he was vanishing into the great firmament of success.

The thoughts were whirling: I'll lose him. Oh, at first he'll want me to fly over as often as I can, and doubtless he'll be here for meetings and conferences, but over time we'll move apart, the feelings between us will fade. She felt cold with an icy chill that had nothing to do with the December rain beating on the window panes.

Jeremy said abruptly: 'I want you to marry me. I want you to come with me.'

She sucked in a deep breath of shock. She could not think what to say. Life without him would be lonely and empty, but it was impossible to think of giving up her career and her lovely flat and her life here. She looked at him and said softly: 'Oh, Jeremy.'

'I've been thinking about this all day since I heard,' he said. 'I know I'm asking the impossible, but I'm asking it anyway. I want you with me. We get on so damned well together, you and I.' A faint taut smile. 'In bed and out of it.'

'We do . . .'

'It's a big decision,' he went on swiftly. 'Don't answer now. Take your time to think about it in all its implications. Take a month if you need. I know how much you put into your work, and how you love it. I'm pinning my hopes on your caring more for me, that's all I can do.' They looked at each other in silence and she knew that he expected her to agree. He took her hand. 'I want you with me. I love you, you see.'

Her throat closed and her eyes burned with tears. They had never spoken of love before; theirs had been an adult relationship with none of the fond declarations and vows of young love. They had not needed them. A great wave of feeling rushed over her.

'I love you, too,' she said. And then: 'Oh, God, this is awful.'

People had warned Polly that she and Emily might be lonely at The Gatehouse, away from their old neighbours and friends, but the warnings were wrong. They were alone here, but not lonely. Tom often drove over, friends from Winchester called, intrigued to know how they were coping without Neville, bringing flowers wrapped in cellophane or baskets of fruit. 'As if we were patients to be cheered up,' Emily commented. 'As if divorce were an illness.' Candida appeared twice, sometimes three times a week, driving down after dinner at Chilbourne House, accepting a cup of coffee or a glass of wine, watching Polly alter curtains and commenting how good The Gatehouse looked, or talking to Emily about her studies or her riding and what she and Mark might do with the ponies next. At times she seemed abstracted, almost dreamy, quite unlike herself; other times she was full of some inner elation and bubbling with wit and humour. She would never stay long; after half an hour or so she would murmur about visiting a friend or an elderly onetime housekeeper in the village, and disappear again in her car.

She came one Sunday evening, unusually, remarking that Bernard had driven off to London immediately after lunch, which she considered very boring and dreary of him. 'He's flying Concorde to New York at dawn tomorrow. He's all caught up in his latest ploy, an American drugs acquisition, and when he's like that he's moody and difficult and shuts himself up with sheafs of paperwork, or else he vanishes off to God knows where, which simply does not improve a grey December weekend.'

'No,' Polly sympathised.

'So I have to amuse myself and here I am, come to see my Polly.'

'What's Bernard looking to achieve with this acquisition?'

'He wants to give the group a pharmaceutical business that will produce some non-cyclical earnings to plug any gap that the next downturn in chemicals will create.'

'You keep up with all this?'

'I must. I suppose to you it sounds complicated and remote, but when one's husband's engaged in it all the time it becomes essential to know all that's happening. And it has its own fascination. For me, anyway. Hugh Hanbury, you know, he's a man after Bernard's own heart, they talk together. When he and his wife come to dinner the pair of them stay up till all hours, immersed in discussion and quite oblivious to the time, while I'm left chatting to Hugh's wife Anne about children and education. Bernard thinks Hugh's brilliant.'

'Yes, of course, he's a merchant banker, isn't he? Tom always says he's particularly successful.'

'No one could dispute that. A pity that he wasn't more successful in picking his wife. She's one of those awfully nice and good people one avoids like the plague because they're so crashingly dull. And she's an intellectual lightweight. She hardly understands anything of what he does. He made the mistake so many public schoolboys make, after living so much of their lives without females around, of marrying too soon, and without having fully analysed and understood his own needs. He was certain he didn't want a career woman competing with him in his own home – and then, of course, too, in his early-twenties he was more concerned with his sexual needs than his wife's intellectual capacity. The same mistake Bernard made with his first wife.'

'Hugh's told you of this?'

'Oh, no,' she said quickly, 'no, it's the assessment Bernard and I have made.' She smiled. 'Pillow talk after I'd been landed with Anne's exceedingly small small-talk all evening while Hugh and Bernard happily delved deep into the latest movements in the nation's industry and trade figures and exchanged useful information they'd turned up.' She glanced at her watch. 'I mustn't stay long. I promised I'd visit poor old Dorothy in the village again, and this is a good opportunity. She loves to hear what's happening to the Goughs, item by item. After all, she worked for the family for twenty years. We're as good as a soap opera to her. Better, because we're real! Besides, the poor darling's virtually housebound now. But before I do go, Polly, can you come to dinner on Saturday week – with Tom, naturally? Short notice, I know, but we've Jane and Jeremy coming for the weekend, so they'll be there, and we've also some intelligent local people coming you might like to meet to enlarge your acquaintance here.'

Polly accepted: 'Though I'll have to check with Tom!' and wondered, in normal female fashion, what on earth she should wear. She knew without looking that her wardrobe contained nothing sufficiently glamorous for Chilbourne House and the Goughs' friends. She remembered that completion of the sale of the Winchester house was due to take place next Thursday, and thought that she might celebrate that significant severing of the bonds between her and Neville by treating herself. She would use a part of the money it brought her to buy something of exceptional style and quality, something that would make Tom widen his eyes and feel proud of her, something that would make her feel equal to this new and sparkling community she was moving into. The thought filled her with pleasant anticipation.

As dusk fell on an icy blustery Friday Mary ducked in through the back door of her kitchen with a gasp of relief: warmth and peace from the buffeting wind at last, and a chance to ease a back aching from mucking out Aladdin's loose box. She sighed contentedly. She would have a mug of tea and a scone warmed up in the Aga, thick with butter and her own homemade strawberry jam, and she would read the paper. She liked to stay in touch. But she mustn't spend too long reading. Vanessa was coming from London and Mary must prepare the meal for the six of them and check the guest room.

Her scone and her tea ready beside her, Mary shook the paper open and her eyes fell upon the headline of an article: *Borderline Personality Disorder: Manipulative Women on the Edge of Madness*. Not her usual choice of topic, but something clicked in her mind and made her fold the pages back and start to read. The symptoms of the condition – reckless behaviour such as promiscuity, addiction to drink or drugs, shop-lifting or mad spending bouts; wild variations in mood; desperately intense but rocky relationships; a terror of being deserted and alone – mostly reminded her all too horribly of Vanessa. So what was this condition she'd never heard discussed before? Disturbed, Mary read on. When she had finished, she sat looking in front of herself, thinking hard. Twenty minutes later she picked up the telephone.

'Polly,' she said, and plunged at once into the deep end. 'Look, you aren't going to accept what I'm about to say with any enthusiasm, if at all, but I'm going to say it, ask it, anyhow. Blast me if you must. You know I've been trying to help Vanessa over her emotional traumas with Neville, and looking after her while she was having terrible bouts of pregnancy sickness?'

'Yes,' Polly said.

'I intend to help her after the baby comes as well. She's not . . . she hasn't a very stable personality, has she? I can help her through those first difficult six weeks after it's born, and try to ensure that she isn't hit by post-natal depression. But she and her baby will need other people, too. We must all try to make certain that the child . . .'

Polly interrupted. 'Mary, why are you still Vanessa's friend?' Her voice was cold.

'I always have been. She's talked to me. She's had hard times. She's needed me.'

'I'm sure she has. But has it ever occurred to you that she's a waste of time? Worse, a cosmic waste of space? She's leant on you, taken from you, financially as well as emotionally, I suspect. Her sort would suck you dry. Do you ever have anything positive from her?'

'I don't mind that, help and support are what friends are for.'

'However badly a friend behaves? Right or wrong? You can forgive the unforgivable?'

'If you truly care. Forgiveness means a lot to someone in Vanessa's situation. To know that you're not condemned by everyone unheard. To have someone who understands. God knows I'm not condoning what she's done, Polly, and I've made that very clear. And I understand if you find her loathsome. But I'm here for her and this child that's coming.'

'Friend isn't the word, is it?'

'What is?'

'Muggins. Sucker. Fool.' The line went dead; Polly had put the phone down.

Mary peeled potatoes and thought. Ten minutes later she picked the telephone up again.

'Polly?'

Her voice was edgy and sharp. 'Look, Mary, there's anger in me, a great deal of anger. It isn't just on my own behalf, it's on my daughters' too.'

'It's about Rose and Emily that I'm ringing. You're a generous woman, Polly. Don't hang up on me, hear me out. Please.'

'What then?'

'Vanessa could be said to have a personality disorder. She over-reacts to events, she's manipulative, she finds close relationships difficult to sustain and more than once she's been on the edge of breakdown.'

'I shan't argue with any of that!'

'Blame her upbringing, blame her parents, blame that same personality that makes such a mess of her relationships only to do more damage to herself. None of that matters, it's in the past. Let's look to the future. What I'm frightened about where Vanessa's concerned is that if we all reject her and her child, we'll push her into a further downward spiral. She'll be lonely and desperate with a child demanding the maternal response and care she'll be incapable of giving. Remember how exhausting, mentally and physically, a screaming baby can be? Then what?'

Silence. 'Go on,' Polly said grumpily.

'Do you know what people really need? More than anything else?'

'You tell me,' Polly said.

'Someone who's wholly for them. Vanessa thought Neville was, but he's turned his back in total rejection of her and the child. I'm afraid that either she'll resent the poor little thing for the hurt its coming caused, or she'll invest huge amounts of emotional energy in it and demand the same emotional response back – which naturally the child won't know how to give. She's already told me they have to be all in all to each other. I'm sure you'll see the dangers in that?'

Polly was silent.

'She'll need help now more than ever. Yes, I know, she's impossible, she's gone way over the top. But her mental state's never been good, precisely because of that, because of the damage her behaviour does to herself, because even when she was a child no one was there for her. Her parents were never around to give her that sort of commitment. But there must be people around for that baby if Vanessa's not to repeat the pattern of her past again, to produce another damaged person.' Mary paused for breath.

'You're asking me to be wholly for *her*?' Polly demanded incredulously.

'Oh, heavens, no. That would be more than a saint could give. No, what I'm suggesting is that Rose and Emily should take an interest in the child. After all, it's their half-brother. And it's going to need them badly – two young people who'll be real family, more like young aunts than sisters, I suppose. But wholly for the little one, poor scrap. And there to rejoice with Vanessa over its progress. She has a much older brother who never married and is barely in touch, while her parents retired from Hong Kong to Devon and see almost nothing of her. They never have. Children should have family.' She waited.

'Mary,' Polly said, 'you're sentimental, you're revoltingly idealistic, you ask the earth – and damn you, you're right! I'll talk to Rose and Emily.'

Saturday night and Polly was on her own. Emily was at the cinema with Mark in Southampton, Rose was in Cambridge – 'Big parties this weekend, Ma!' – and Tom was taking Laura and a couple of her friends to the theatre in Winchester. Polly didn't mind being alone, she told Tom when he was apologetic, she would whisk through various chores she'd been meaning to do for weeks, have a meal on her lap by the fire and then settle down to an evening's writing on the Victorian writing table she'd given herself as a special present. The novel was racing along now; its characters as real to her as her colleagues and friends, and making them act and speak in character no longer demanded a conscious effort. She might finish her present chapter if its final scene developed no unforeseen problems. She was in another time and another world when the telephone rang, and swore with annoyance at being dragged back to the present.

'Hello?'

'Am I speaking to Polly . . . Polly Ferrison?' an unknown voice enquired.

A well-modulated contralto: one of Candida's friends inviting her and Tom to dinner, perhaps? 'Yes,' Polly said. 'This is Polly Ferrison.'

'I'm Juliana Wallace,' the voice said. 'I imagine the name won't be unknown to you.'

Oh. 'No,' Polly agreed, her heart bumping. 'It isn't. What can I do for you?' How condescending that sounded, but better than the mincing alternative, 'How may I help you?'

She listened as Juliana explained briskly that she and Neville were hoping to have Rose and Emily to lunch over the Christmas period, now that they had their new flat in Notting Hill straight: 'But I thought I should clear it with you first.' Polly said she had no objections. Indeed, how could she have? She was anxious that Neville should keep in touch with his daughters. She gave Juliana Rose's telephone number in Cambridge and suggested that Emily was best contacted on weekday evenings, when she stayed in to study. In a dry voice she requested the telephone number and address of this new flat so that she could contact Neville in any emergency concerning their daughters. Juliana gave them, seeming surprised that Polly hadn't been told. Of course, she said, Neville had been under considerable stress recently, and cited her husband Henry's impossible behaviour as well as the traumas of the moves and the pending divorces. (She did not mention Vanessa.) Without these pressures she was sure Neville would have seen far more of the girls. Polly listened with admiration to the deft manner in which she implied an apology for Neville's behaviour without in fact making one. She said she quite understood.

Something like a sigh of relief sounded in her ear. How very reasonable she was, how civilised, said Juliana, admitting with a half-laugh that she had been dreading this telephone call and yet it had proved perfectly pleasant and easy, no accusations, no vituperations, none of the hysterical reactions she had been dreading, not like Henry or . . . She stopped. There was a brief silence impregnated with meaning.

Polly brought it out: 'Or Vanessa,' she said.

Another silence.

Polly said: 'I understand from my friend, Mary Allwood, who has been caring for her, that Vanessa has relinquished any thought of demanding maintenance for her baby from Neville.'

'Then there is a baby?'

'I don't think there is any doubt about that, God help it.'

'Neville maintains, firstly, that he does not believe there is a baby, and secondly, if there is, that it could not be his.'

'Yes, that's what I've been told. I don't think I should comment further.'

A sigh. 'You believe that it is. Why?'

Polly hesitated.

'Tell me, please.'

'They've had a sexual relationship in the past.'

'Go on.' Grimly.

'I saw them at it once, though they didn't know it. We were with our friends at Chilbourne House for the day. I went to find them in the far reaches of the house and I wished I hadn't.' She added irrelevantly: 'It was teatime!' and then nervous tension overcame her and she giggled. She added kindly: 'But that was eighteen months ago.'

'How do I know whom to believe?' Juliana demanded in a cynical voice. 'Men are such bastards and women aren't much better – certainly not that raving neurotic friend of yours.'

'Ex-friend.' Unexpectedly Polly found herself experiencing a moment's total empathy with Juliana over Neville's infidelities with Vanessa, and this sense of identity was the last thing she would have expected. She admired Juliana's courage in speaking to her; she thought that at another time, in other circumstances, they could have been friends. She saw that Juliana had, as the cliché had it, burned her boats. She had left her husband, committed herself publicly to Neville, and her world knew that she was carrying his child. Presumably she had jointly signed the lease with him for the flat they had moved into temporarily. She was struggling to force her ex-husband, Henry Wallace, to disgorge her share of the value in their old matrimonial flat to give them sufficient funds to buy somewhere more permanent. Hers was not a situation or a relationship to be lightly abandoned.

Picking her words carefully, Polly said: 'I believe Vanessa engineered situations in which Neville would find it difficult not to have sex with her. The opera was her lure, and since he disliked driving home in the small hours she would offer to put him up for the night. The bed in the guest room would not be made up, her bed and she would be available instead. Sex was his thanks for the music and she was his fun friend. No more than that.'

'You don't know. You're guessing.' Juliana's voice was flat.

'On sound evidence and twenty years' knowledge of Neville.' Visualising the situation in its entirety, Polly realised with a thump of her heart that it would be better for them all, especially Rose and Emily, if Neville and Juliana did stay together and made a success of their relationship. To have her ex-husband satisfied and reasonable, happy to see his daughters and impress them, was an alternative vastly to be preferred than the nasty glimpse her mind gave her of Neville rejected and bitter. No money then for all his varied pleasures, no chance to commit his philosophical theories and reflections to paper, instead only the malicious comfort of letters and telephone calls to Polly accusing her of deliberately ruining his life, while her closeness to Emily and Rose would be so derided and assailed that her poor darlings would hardly know where they were or whom to trust.

She shuddered and told Juliana: 'Of course I don't know the whole truth, but I do know that his feelings for you are genuine. Believe that. His feelings for me I can recognise and admit now were at best never more than mild liking. I can see the difference between reality and polite pretence.' She paused. Juliana said nothing. Polly added: 'Look, I don't want bad feeling between us. It's counter-productive for our offspring. Civilised, you said, and that's what I want this to be for all our sakes.'

'It feels unreal to talk to you like this,' Juliana said. 'So different from anything I expected. Especially after Henry.'

'Neville said he was being difficult.'

'Difficult? Do you know what I had to do to get hold of my own furniture? Presents from my family? Even my own clothes? He wouldn't let me collect a thing – the bastard actually changed the locks on the door! I waited till I was certain he'd be stuck in court one day, then I got the removals men over and wailed to a local locksmith that in the panic of moving I'd mislaid my keys. The man was a bit suspicious, but I was able to show him my driving licence with that address still on it, thank God, and then he was lovely and helpful. Henry was livid – even threatened me with court action – but at least our flat is decently furnished now!'

They both laughed.

Chapter 17

Candida took a voluptuous pleasure in preparing herself for her dinner party, revelling in the deep scented warmth of her bath, in the cool luxurious feel of silk against her skin as she drew on each garment, and when she was ready she turned herself this way and that before the looking-glass, striving to see herself as her lover would when he came. Her skin shivered with a fierce sparkle of anticipation. The cut and line of the new dress showed off her figure to perfection, how could he help but desire her? Besides, the interior excitement of her affair and its sensual pleasures had given to her skin and her hair a glow and sheen as if she were ten years younger.

'Tremendous,' came Bernard's voice from behind her and she spun round, smiling.

'A success, I think, don't you?'

'I do. And who is to be impressed with it tonight?' he enquired. 'Remind me just who it is we are entertaining.' His voice was smooth, but his eyes seemed somehow blank and possessive.

For a moment she felt a flicker of fear, then she said, her voice as smooth as his: 'You know who our guests are, I reminded you only last night.'

'Remind me again.'

'Jeremy and Jane, of course. Polly and Tom. Victoria and Edmund Lockwood. Then I tried to get the Poultons, but they were away, so I thought of Anne and Hugh Hanbury.'

'It seems,' he said, 'a trifle odd to have both brothers.'

'Polly tells me she has hardly met Hugh. Their circumstances, I suppose. I thought it might be pleasant for them to meet here and chat, without the antagonistic offspring around.'

His hard grey eyes considered this. He nodded. 'I see.'

Candida turned away with a swirl of ivory silk, breathed out a sort of joyous sigh and said she was going down. She raised her eyebrows at Bernard who said he would be down shortly. In the drawing room she found Jane, leafing through a *Country Life*. She looked up and smiled as Candida came in. 'Such a delightful walled garden here,' she commented. 'Formal structure, informal planting. Even a non-gardener like myself might be tempted to potter with secateurs in such surroundings.'

'Gorgeous, isn't it?' Candida agreed. 'And walled gardens reminds me . . . I owe you thanks for recommending me to the Ellingtons. My latest commission is to re-design their garden in Alresford, and they're giving me just the sort of free hand with it that I enjoy.'

'I thought you and they would agree well together.'

'Distinctly. Foreign Office people, aren't they? Friends of Jeremy's. Georgina Ellington was saying that she'll hate to leave the house and garden when they're next posted, and I can't say that I should care for that life myself. Besides, the poor dears can't choose where or when they go – imagine the inconvenience!'

'Those,' said Jane, 'are problems I am mulling over at this very time.'

'You are? Don't tell me Jeremy is due to go shortly?'

'To Warsaw. And he wants me to go with him.'

'You? Oh, Jane, you mean – as his wife?'

'Yes.' A wry smile, a spreading of the hands, a shrug of the shoulders.

'Oh my God! What an impossible decision to take.' Realisation of its magnitude passed swiftly through Candida's mind as she stared at Jane. 'And which weighs heavier in the scale? The career or the man?'

'I don't know,' Jane said. 'I don't know, I don't damned well know!'

Over her despairing voice came the sound of the doorbell jangling. 'Hell,' said Candida. 'No time to talk now. Listen, Polly's suggested we three should have coffee tomorrow morning at The Gatehouse. We'll talk then. We could well think of things you haven't considered, help you put it all in perspective.'

Jane gave a smile that was nearer to a grimace. 'The objective viewpoint. God knows I need it. All I have is feelings – opposing feelings in a hopeless battle. Thanks.'

The double doors opened. Bernard strode in looking bull-necked and unnaturally tough in his dinner jacket, followed by Jeremy, lean, alert-eyed and smiling at Jane, and then the first guests were ushered in, Victoria and Edmund Lockwood, a highly vocal couple in their mid-fifties wearing the air of self-confidence natural to those who have spent their lives in positions of privilege, followed shortly by Polly and Tom.

Candida moved to stand beside Bernard, falling automatically into her role as hostess, welcoming, introducing, chatting lightly. Where was Hugh? Why did he always have to be late? She wanted him here now, his eyes upon her, laughing, caressing, greedy. Heavens, Polly looked amazing, her lovely hair, well-cut for once, dramatically contrasting with the black of a designer dress Candida would not have minded for herself. And so happy beside her Tom, who managed to look rumpled and crumpled even in a well-tailored dinner jacket. Tom was like his brother, big, virile, good-looking, yet he was not like, she thought absently, scrutinising him. He was milder, gentler. He had none of the male greed, none of the exciting edge of Hugh, he lacked for her those chemicals in the blood – the pheromones, was it? The something she'd sworn she didn't believe existed.

'Victoria, how well you look, and Edmund, too . . . Victoria, this is Polly Ferrison, a very old friend . . . Polly, Victoria and Edmund have that lovely William and Mary house by the village church and their garden is the scene of our annual fêtes. And Jane Masterson . . .'

Hugh, come soon! Infatuation, she decided, made you dreadfully vulnerable, every nerve-end alert and tingling to each separate look or move of the adored object, your awareness high-tuned to the point of pain. How was it that she, always before so detached and cool, could now be so involved in another person? Other affairs, brief flares of passion that she had found exhilarating but too dangerous to dare continue for long, had never affected her in this way; she had been in control, standing outside the emotions. Her desire for Hugh shocked her. Like the healthy woman who despises her sisters for their susceptibility to illness, so Candida had rejected the fevers of love. It seemed preposterous that she should now pass the small hours tossing beside Bernard in their great four-poster bed as she analysed every word Hugh had uttered, every gesture he had made.

Beside her Victoria was talking with great vigour to Tom, complaining that she hadn't seen him for an age, demanding to know why he came to the village so rarely. 'You're an architect, you could have advised us on a decent design for our new village hall, instead of which we have the inevitable eyesore. Why don't people nowadays plan buildings that are good to look at, write music that's good to listen to, or paint pictures that gladden the eye?'

'Oh,' Tom said mockingly, 'that would be too simple for the ambitious among us. But they are all *meaningful*. We have to study to understand them, to appreciate them with the brain rather than the eye or ear.'

'Then the point of them is lost,' she expostulated. 'And explanations are a bore.'

'Darling,' her husband said with a small laugh, 'you surely wouldn't want a pastiche!'

'Oh, wouldn't I?' she retorted.

Where was Hugh? Didn't he long to see her as Candida yearned towards him? Oh, this was ridiculous. Forget him, take your eyes from the door and concentrate upon your guests before Bernard's tough and intuitive intelligence grasps that something is wrong. The door swung open. Hugh was here, half-hidden behind his wife, Anne, an eyebrow lifted towards her, a half-smile on his lips. He had seen, he knew she was dressed just for him. His wife advanced towards her, plump and bosomy in a black lace frock of indeterminate length, her copious frizzy brown hair showing needle-thin streaks of grey.

'Anne, how lovely to see you,' Candida said, kissing her with the warmth of guilt.

The evening proceeded. Hugh was next to her at table, she had taken the risk deliberately, and besides, in point of precedence he should be there. Beyond him Polly was talking swiftly, gesticulating, amusing him, while the chubby Anne, opposite, watched and listened. Polly, the girlfriend of Tom, had considerably more confidence than Polly, the repressed wife of Neville. She looked and sounded a different person. Was there a similar betraying change in her, Candida? She half-jumped as something caressed her ankle: Hugh's warm stockinged toes. The madman must be wearing his Gucci loafers to have achieved the action unseen. Without looking at him she lifted her glass of wine with an answering flourish, and drank. Take care, my love.

Along the table Victoria leaned over to cross-question Polly. She loved to know all about everyone in her friends' social circles: genealogies, social strata and social niceties absorbed her, and she recollected every detail with the tenacity of an elephant. Candida listened.

Yes, Polly had known Tom for some months. No, she agreed, she and Victoria had not met before. Polly had lived many years in Winchester; now she was staying in the Goughs' Gatehouse with her younger daughter. Victoria looked non-plussed at having to reconcile an employee's cottage with Polly's expensive attire and the Hanbury and Gough connections; her intent look betrayed the curiosity that devoured her. But their family house? (Candida swallowed mirth at the remembrance.) Sold just weeks ago, as part of a divorce settlement? Victoria shook her head at the devastation this must have caused. An amicable separation? Not noticeably, Polly said with a wry smile, not since her husband had made two women pregnant at the same time, one an old friend. A frisson of sympathy passed round the table. Victoria's eyes glistened. 'How dreadful!' she said happily. 'Oh, you poor girl.' Polly must tell her what this ex-husband did that would support such folly. Polly's response was airy and she had the nous not to mention the loathed county council: Neville, Victoria was told, was engaged in writing a philosophical treatise, dwelling at present upon social ethics. 'We met at university, where he was brilliant,' she said. Neville's persona pinned among the strata, Victoria sighed her commiseration. Acceptable, yes, but hopelessly dry and arid. 'When academics emerge from among their dusty tomes, they really do go mad, don't they?' she breathed. Later, she turned her attention to Jeremy beside her. 'Didn't someone say you're a diplomat? Fascinating. Do tell me more.'

The evening wore on. Hugh's fingers touched Candida's as he passed her a dish of cream. Her heart pounded and she was conscious of her hands shaking. She drew him and Edmund into a lively and witty conversation on how best to deal with hunt saboteurs. She ached to be alone with him.

She woke the next morning with a heavy head. She was not used to the feeling of electrical excitement that kept flashing through her at the thought of Hugh, it was something new and intrusive, disturbing the balance of her carefully planned life, and again she had passed a night of restless and fitful sleep. It was not simply the burning physical desire that tormented her, it was also the amorphous but powerful yearning to surrender herself completely to this man and the waves of questions thrown up by such sensations, that threatened to overwhelm her. Did he care for her in the same extravagant fashion? Would he risk everything for her? Could he be trusted? What of her sons? Of her mother? Was she mad to think that concealment could be carried on indefinitely? Her brain ached as the unanswerable questions swirled round and round within it.

At The Gatehouse mid-morning she sank into a chair by the log fire and sipped Polly's excellent coffee, relieved to divert her mind to Jane's quandary.

Polly was demanding to know Jane's thoughts on the complex life she would lead as an ambassador's wife. It would be a life in the public eye, one demanding endless tact and judicious handling of all those with whom her husband would have contact. There could be disagreeable or even dangerous situations. Nevertheless, wouldn't she find its varied possibilities stimulating? Jane laughed shortly and asked whether either she or Candida could really imagine her as the gracious hostess at great receptions or dinners, exerting her charm to support her husband, welding together possibly antagonistic guests, promoting United Kingdom interests at every turn?

Candida thought she would be excellent: Jane had the personality, the poise and the capacity for intelligent interest that were necessary, and besides, the extensive knowledge of trade and industry and their finance that her work at the DTI had given her would put her in an exceptional position. 'Instead of advising the Minister,' she observed, 'you'll be advising His Excellency the Ambassador – not so very different!' Jane grumbled that while she might be a useful adjunct, she would still be only an adjunct. Candida said she could assure her that there were compensations: she would be in stately surroundings, in daily contact with people of power and importance, at the heart of what was happening: the fascination would be endless. She could have a surprising influence. 'An *éminence grise?*' Polly suggested, smiling, but Jane grimaced and said she was used to more than that. Candida leaned forward to put down her coffee cup and remark in a detached voice that Jeremy was already to be an ambassador and given that he continued in the same swift and brilliant mode, his next appointment could mean a knighthood. 'To be Lady Locke would be something not to be despised.'

There was a silence. 'Supposing the marriage didn't work out?' Jane said. 'I'd be left with nothing. My career would be finished, and I couldn't go back. What's a title worth then? Besides, you know how I love my work, my freedom, my flat that's mine and no one else's. An embassy in essence is the equivalent of a tied cottage!'

'A very large tied cottage!' Polly pointed out with some amusement.

'But in a foreign land, and one that's going through a particularly difficult transitional stage as it moves to a market economy. Oh, Jeremy assures me the Deputy Head of Mission is an old friend, and his wife is sharply intelligent and just my sort of person and all that – but I don't know, I just don't know! I can't picture myself there.'

'What sort of language is Polish?'

'It's a western Slavonic tongue. If I were to go with him, I'd take a crash course in it beforehand. God, what a bore!'

'How's it written? Cyrillic?'

'Latin alphabet, I believe.'

'Well, that's something,' Polly said encouragingly.

Candida had a sudden sense of unreality. Here they were, Polly and she, urging the arguments for marriage when both of them were unfaithful to their husbands and Polly on the edge of divorce. It was bizarre. Jane's independent spirit was the one women should be urging upon each other, not the rôle of the supportive and subordinate wife, that hangover from a bygone era. Scratch a feminist and find a romantic under the skin? What strange expectations of happiness we still have, despite everything. And Jane must have of Jeremy, or the scales would have tilted the other way from the start. Polly was saying now that Jane should keep her flat and let it for the income it would bring her. That wouldn't have to go; something would remain of her old life. But was she certain that Jeremy and she were soul mates?

Jane sighed and said that Jeremy was the most interesting man she had ever met, and the easiest to be with – and the most amusing lover. 'But life is such a gamble. I feel as if I'm waiting on the flip of a card, the fall of a coin. All of us live on such a narrow edge of circumstance that the least thing can upset everything. One day our base seems firm – love, respect, security – then, whoops! The card turns, the coin falls, and all is lost.'

They looked at her with sadness and understanding. They could not tell her whether to resist the gamble or take it. They could only listen and sympathise.

Vanessa became used to pregnancy, and once the sickness had stopped she found herself revelling in the state. She was growing a future person inside her and it was an amazing thought. Her belly swelled and people noticed it, even strangers, even with her winter coat over it. They smiled and offered their seats on the Underground, while colleagues at work brought her cups of tea and coffee, cosseting her. Mary rang from the farm for reassuring chats and she had a standing invitation to go there for weekends. Her doctor, her midwife, her consultant at the hospital where she would give birth, all were concerned for her. They wrote 'Elderly Primipara' on her record and gave her special care. They prodded this, they measured that, they tested the other, they took her blood pressure, she had to undergo amniocentesis because of her age, but everything came out fine. And each time it did they beamed on her as if she were a child who'd been particularly clever. 'Well done!' they said, and a strange feeling of warmth enveloped her. She had never known such attention before.

For a while she had suffered genuine grief over Neville, but she struggled to control her sufferings, 'For the baby's sake!' as Mary told her, and then one morning, just at the time when her health began to bloom, she conjured up his name on waking and felt nothing but indifference. She opened her eyes and her bedroom was full of light, and the light persisted. She went to the window, pushing back the curtains and looking out. It was a bright winter's day with a light blue sky and a little mist, and from the lacework of twigs on the trees in the street and from its iron railings water hung in brilliant sparkling drops. A distant plane was leaving a white trail across the sky. Not a soul was about; there were no sounds in the road but the chattering of the starlings on the rooftops. The scene, familiar and ordinary, yet now somehow special, delighted and uplifted her. Depression was dissolved and she felt well and full of energy. She remembered how often she had walked wet streets in anguish, how many nights she had lain awake in the lonely darkness of her flat and wept, and was full of wonderment at the transformation of her world.

On Mary's instructions she wrote to her parents and her brother to tell them she was pregnant. They were not a close family. They saw one another only occasionally at Christmas or family funerals, and the telephone might not have been invented for all the use they made of it. So she was surprised and heartened when her father not only phoned to announce his pleasure: 'I'd given up all hope of a grandchild years ago and I have to admit I'm delighted!' but added, 'What do you say to celebrating with a theatre trip or a concert together? I could stay overnight with you, couldn't I?' He admitted that her mother was not impressed by single parenthood, and she heard nothing from her brother, but when they met in the Savoy's River Room her father gave her a hug as if he meant it, not the usual cool peck on the cheek, and he thrust into her arms a gift-wrapped parcel which, its coverings removed, revealed a small honey-coloured snub-nosed teddy bear. It was the first gift Vanessa had received for the baby and somehow it symbolised for her the reality of her coming motherhood; she pulled its stubby legs forward and sat it on the table beside her throughout their dinner and each time her eyes fell on it she was filled with pleasure. She couldn't get over its charm. 'It's lovely,' she kept saying. 'It's really lovely.'

After the show, a lively comedy they both enjoyed, he stayed the night, and for most of the next day they talked in an intermittent, relaxed sort of way, between bouts with the Sunday papers, about Vanessa's health, about the coming child and whom it might resemble, of her father's boredom in retirement, of her mother's worsening arthritis, of nurseries versus nannies, and anything else that happened to cross their minds. There was nothing deep in their conversation, it did not probe old injuries or resentments from Vanessa's childhood, or discuss the rights or wrongs of bringing up a child without its father. It rambled gently as a meadow stream. They ate a leisurely lunch and took a reviving nap after it, each confessing to relief that the other shared this need. Finally they had tea with toasted muffins and discussed without heat the short-comings of the present government, surprised to find themselves so pleasantly in accord. It occurred to each, though neither mentioned it, that they really had never known one another very well. They agreed that both parents should join Vanessa for Christmas.

'Your mother's not come to terms with your news yet,' her father acknowledged with a sideways look and a little nod, 'but she will. I'll see to that. And she'll be here.'

Vanessa had never before managed the Christmas festivities for anyone, not even her husbands, but the thought of it, instead of appalling her with the work entailed, gave her a thrill. She would make it special; it would be a practice for the Christmas she would give her baby next year.

Polly found Christmas trying. It was a matter, she said to Rose, of wanting to keep too many people happy too much of the time, and being quite unable to do anything for any of them most of the time. She sluiced crossly at the washing-up (Neville had awarded himself and Juliana the dishwasher), turning the taps noisily on and off and splashing herself. She had dreamed of being with Tom, but Laura had insisted that her father must accept her Uncle Hugh and Aunt Anne's invitation to spend three days with them and their boys: she was bowled over by her seventeen and fifteen-year-old cousins' recent assumption of cool masculinity, by their rumbling deep voices. Polly's mother was with her at The Gatehouse, still lamenting Neville's appalling behaviour: 'I can't believe it, I just can't believe it! So degrading for you, my poor Polly!', still muttering, 'And if your father had been alive he'd have dealt with him properly. He'd have hit him. If ever I see him again, I shall. A good slap in the face.' She was asleep now on the sofa, audibly snoring as she digested roast turkey and mince pies and brandy butter. She was due to meet Tom for the first time tomorrow, Boxing Day, and Polly hoped she would fall for his gentle and untidy charm.

Emily's boyfriend, Mark, had joined Polly's small party for the festive lunch and now they both appeared in the kitchen doorway, forgotten paper hats lopsided on their heads, their eyes large with over-eating and young love. At least, she thought, those two were happy. Knowing Emily's yearning for someone of her own, Polly had lived in wretched anticipation of the day when she would turn up with some opinionated spotty youth in tow, her dreams of the unique, assured, brilliant leader of the class abandoned for the sake of something, anything, rather than nothing. The advent of the distinctly personable Mark had come as a huge relief, and what was more, he was *nice*, a mother's dream.

The nice young man said with his usual mixture of self-consciousness and composure, that if it was all right with Polly, he and Emily would drive over to Flintpen Ring and run round the encircling banks of the old iron age fort. 'We don't have our regular rides now the Gough boys are home from prep school, but we must get out and take some exercise.'

Rose muttered over her drying-up cloth that she bet they didn't go short of it. She was between boyfriends herself and cross.

Polly looked at her and then out of the kitchen window into that most subtle of all lights, winter sunshine, glowing on the frost-whitened park meadows and their tall grey trees, picking out the darker curves of the hedges dividing the land. The quiet colours lay under a clear pale sky. She envied Emily and Mark their freedom to drive out and run and shout and take in great gasps of the invigorating cold air, and from the height of the hill see the wide Hampshire landscape, pale field upon field contrasting with the darker masses of woods and spinneys, with here and there grey-flint towered churches showing where the villages lay.

'Flintpen Ring sounds fun,' she said, leaning against the sink and adding with mischievous wistfulness: 'I wouldn't mind going there too.'

Emily backed away hastily, feeling for the backdoor handle, dragging the politely smiling Mark with her. 'See you later,' she breathed. The door banged behind them.

Polly and Rose laughed.

'Someone like Mark would drive me mad,' Rose said, polishing a wineglass with vigour. 'All that scrubbed and earnest decency. Perhaps it's something to do with living in the country. Oscar Wilde said *anybody* can be good in the country. Mind you, I don't think he ever considered the temptations offered by haylofts!'

'More hints?'

'What? About sex? Oh, Ma, why haven't you just yelled at Emmy – "Are you having sex yet?" Anyway, nowadays it's out of the good or bad category. It just *is*. Yeah, she's getting it.'

'I thought so.'

Rose raised her eyebrows.

'She's changed,' Polly said, starting on the saucepans with a pan-scrubber. 'Even her clothes have changed. She's wearing colours instead of that dusty black, fun clothes – when she's not in riding clothes, that is. And she's content as a purring kitten.'

It was not only sex had done that, she thought, though Emily was suddenly full of herself, talking and laughing with an assurance that had been lacking before. It was also that worrying withdrawn intensity of anger which had been broken down, the anger that had sprung from the shock of her father's rejection of his family, the hurt of the break-up. Polly supposed it was inevitable that something of it would always linger in her subconscious. But now in Mark she had someone of her own generation who sought her out and shared her private thoughts, whose eyes showed his approval. Mark was changing her.

'You're changing too,' Rose told Polly. 'I hated it when you were all patience and forgiveness. Like one of those animals at the zoo, a gnu or something, a sad caged herbivore, but now you've broken out of your cage and you're full of energy and rippling muscles. I really go for that. And the sexy new clothes and the hair. You never think of your mother as sexy – but it does give you hope for the future, doesn't it?'

Hugh and Candida managed occasional evening meetings during the week in an empty thatched cottage that belonged to him, once a tied cottage but now no longer needed. Winter hadn't made it impossible after all; winter had made it easier, with the villagers out of sight behind drawn curtains. Candida found it fun to wear something different each time: this way she could surprise him, presenting changing facets to her personality, preserving some element of mystery about her as she flitted from the dark into the glimmering candlelit room. The electricity had been cut off, but the quiet soft light somehow enhanced the secrecy and fear of detection which gave such guilty excitement and allure to their meetings. Besides, those little flames were flattering. As she slipped in and flung her coat on to a chair, his eyes appraised her, her clothes enhancing the curving complexities of the body beneath. She knew he liked it, this rich and tantalising show of taste and colour and charm, and the subtle flattery that lay behind it.

'Ah!' he said. 'Candida. At last.' He rose swiftly from the little carved oak bed by the window that had once been a crippled grandmother's whole world, left behind with other unwanted sticks of furniture when the last tenants moved out. He caught her by the shoulders, holding her at arm's length, looking at her, silent.

'What are you thinking about?'

'You. Who else?'

'Liking me?'

'Admiring you. Adoring you. Wanting you. It's ridiculous, the way I want you.'

'And I you. It's meant,' she said with a little smile. 'Meant by the Fates, and we can't escape it.'

He kissed her, brief and hard, and released her. He had brought a bottle of Chablis in a cold bag, together with two glasses. He turned to pull the cork and pour. As he thrust her glass into her hand he demanded to know why she was late. He had been uneasy, and besides, he hated to wait.

'I went to see Polly. I have a running alibi of visits to cheer her loneliness. And I visit old Dorothy too.' She drank, eyes laughing at him over the rim of her glass.

'My clever Candida. I like Polly and her quiet intelligence. Exactly the sort for Tom. But not for me. I prefer something more finely honed, with a real sharpness of edge. And a capacity for passion, that wonderful passion that you give me.' He drank too, then put down his glass to pull her against him, warm thigh against thigh. For a moment she resisted him, the muscles of her stomach tensed, her head flung back from the hunger that blazed in his face.

'How did you escape from the house and Anne? Was it all right?'

'Candida, for God's sake! Relax, let go, throw away the world, fall into me so that I can fall into you . . . Anne has a most reassuring picture of me immersed in discussions of EC regulations with my farm manager. And I tucked my car away behind the pub. We're unsuspected, unquestioned, safe! Now, kiss me, you wonderful, irresistible, gorgeous creature whom I adore!'

Chapter 18

Emily was spending the evening lolling on her bed, devouring a book Mark had insisted she must read, Scott Fitzgerald's *Tender is the Night*; Rose was out with friends in Winchester and Polly was sitting by the living-room fire with a pad on her lap, pleased to have the peace to write. The spring term would start soon and with thoughts in her head of the marking and lesson preparation that would crowd upon her then, she was making use of these last free days to push on. The first draft was tantalisingly near its end and there were nights when inspiration came to her with such a sense of vivid reality that she wrote until one or two o'clock in the morning, knowing from experience that she must capture her visions at once or risk their disappearing like mountain views glimpsed in a lowering mist.

Before she started she reached for the telephone to have the usual evening chat with Tom, murmurs of love and nonsense interspersed with more down-to-earth items. Today Tom was worried about Laura, off-colour and gloomy, complaining of indeterminate aches 'low-down' for which the doctor could find no specific reason. Polly tried to reassure him. 'Probably growing pains. Adolescents do have them from time to time.' 'Do you think so?' he said doubtfully. 'Yes,' she said.

At about ten she heard a flurry of rain against the windows and thought of Candida who had called on foot to see her earlier, wondering whether she had an umbrella, thinking in puzzlement how odd that she should choose to walk on a damp January night. Candida had stopped to drink a cup of coffee, but confided she was worried over old Dorothy and her bronchitic chest and soon left. Perhaps Dorothy would lend her an umbrella? Perhaps Bernard would pick her up? Polly shrugged and switched her thoughts back to the suffragettes and how best to illuminate the hard choices forced on her heroine by her involvement with them.

The peremptory sound of the front-door knocker aroused her from her Edwardian scene. Bernard Gough was in her porch, outlined against the rain by searchlight-powerful beams from his Bentley Brooklands.

'Oh, hello, Bernard,' Polly said. 'Have you come to collect Candida? She left for the village some time ago.'

'Really?' said Bernard, pushing against her as he hustled her back into her hallway. He slammed the door behind himself, forgetful of his headlights which continued to illuminate the wild and empty night. 'The rain drove me to collect my wife for fear she'd be half-drowned. So where has she gone in the village?'

'Oh, to Dorothy's. She's concerned over her chest.'

'How long was she with you?'

His voice sounded odd. Without knowing why Polly felt a disagreeable, unspecified foreboding. 'Half-an-hour or so.'

'She did come in?'

'Yes. Why not? She often does. I'm grateful for her company.'

'I shall telephone Dorothy.' He picked up the telephone and dialled without looking at her. 'Dorothy? Bernard Gough. Is my wife with you?' The conversation was short and to the point. 'Then you haven't seen her tonight? Thank you. Goodbye.'

He turned to stare at Polly with a cold and level gaze. His eyes drilled through her skull, through her brain; she felt he could read every thought that was in her.

'So where is Candida?'

Apprehension was sharp in her. 'If she's not there then I don't know.'

'Oh, I think you do,' he said slowly, nastily. 'I think she is having an affair and that you have been lying and conniving with her to give her an alibi.' His voice turned falsetto in bitter parody: ' "I'm just visiting poor Polly, so lonely at The Gatehouse." But the alibi's broken now. What do you say to that?'

Emotions succeeded one another in Polly's head – shock, horror, and then anger, and the anger was fierce and sharp. 'I know nothing of this whatsoever. And what's more, Bernard, I don't believe it.' Could he be right? Was Candida involved with someone of whom Polly knew nothing? But how dare Bernard accuse her of complicity? And how dare Candida – if it was true – how dare she involve Polly, her friend, without warning her?

'I think you do know. You stand there, playing the gentle innocent, mild and sweet as ever, certain you can get away with any deceit because nobody could believe it of someone like you.' His voice was rough. 'But I know from your affair with Tom Hanbury, and from what I've proved to myself tonight, that you're happy to lie and cheat and act a part like the rest of your friends, like that disgusting woman Vanessa – even when you're living in my property, when you've sat at my table!'

He had advanced on her while he was speaking and now his large pale face glared at her from only a foot away. She could see bloodshot threads on the whites of his eyes and the bristling whiskers in his nostrils. His full lips had become a tight line.

'Well?' he snarled.

His ferocity alarmed her, but it also intensified her anger. 'You're wrong. How dare you? You'd better go,' she said. She flung herself across the room and into the little hall to open the front door. Outside the rain was lashing down in noisy fury and icy water splashed her legs. Her knees were trembling, just as novelists wrote. How ridiculous.

He stood for a moment staring in front of himself and she saw that he too was shaking, his face suddenly haggard. Poor Bernard, poor old Bernard, he was shattered. He needed sympathy but she could not give it, not until she knew the truth from Candida, not while he was in this mood. She held the door open and after a moment he stamped past her into the cold glare of his car's headlights.

Candida knew something was wrong before she entered the house. The main door was open to the night, all the doors were open, too many lights were on. Oh, God, and she was wet, so treacherously, ruinously wet. What a fool. If she could but reach her bedroom . . . Where were the boys, Matthew and Harry? They'd been in the billiard room when she left. Please God they were in bed and lost to the world. Sounds . . . Bernard stood there, big-boned, heavy, menacing. They stared at one another. He seized her wrist, marched her into his study, flung her from him. She heard the door thump to behind them.

'You bitch!' he said. 'You stupid cheating bitch!'

'You'd better inform me what this is about,' she told him coldly, playing for time.

He gave her none. 'Adultery,' he said. 'Hugh Hanbury.' His voice sneered, his tongue lashed her. 'Philanderers should never have personalised number plates. So vulgar. So obvious. His pretext was the pub, was it? Pathetic. And yours was Polly and Dorothy. Playing the caring friend, the good woman? You hypocrite!'

Her heart lurched. He knew. No sense in pretending. No sense in grovelling, either. She must hide her anguish; weakness he despised. Thoughts rushed in swift succession through her mind. What could he do? Nothing overt that would not make him look a fool, an old man betrayed. Divorce would be unpleasant and costly. Would he really want that? What of his sons? He could damage Hugh, and his marriage. She rubbed her smarting wrist, concentrating. She must shrug and apply an emotional brake on his anger: each of life's episodes is only as important as you make it. First she must put him on the defensive.

She said with cool dignity: 'Not a hypocrite. I care for them both. I trust you haven't been bullying them and shouting?'

He glared at her and his pugnacity was formidable. 'You're admitting the affair?'

She made herself look him calmly in the eyes. 'No point in doing otherwise.' He appeared disconcerted and she pressed him, making her voice insistent. 'Is Dorothy all right?'

'So far as I am aware from a two-minute telephone conversation confirming that you were not at her cottage.'

'And Polly?'

'I told her what I thought of her connivance and treachery.'

'You were wrong. Polly knows nothing of this – or she didn't until you started cursing her for it. How very unpleasant and unnecessary.' Bernard's anger and grief were making it ridiculously easy for her to wrongfoot him. In his boardroom no one would outflank him.

'I don't believe you. She's been covering for you for weeks – you and her future brother-in-law.'

'I assure you, Polly and Tom are so naïve and innocent and good it's almost unnatural. I'd never have involved her, she'd have hated it. She admires and likes you.'

There was a pause. Bernard's face was set in its hardest lines but his hands were trembling. She thought, He's getting old, and pushed away a stab of sympathy. She could afford no weakness. She enquired as if she were speaking of some minor house repair: 'What are you going to do about it?'

He made his way round his large and handsome mahogany desk to sit heavily in its chair. 'Get me a whisky,' he ordered.

She poured them both whiskies, adding a splash of water. He gulped in a silence that seemed profound. A blast of wind threw rain against the window and howled in the chimney.

'Why him?' Bernard put down his glass. 'Why someone so obvious as Hugh Hanbury?'

Left standing before him, she felt vulnerable, a naughty schoolchild interviewed by the Head. Would it be expulsion? She moved to sit down, realised that she still had her sodden coat on and flung it off. Her feet were very cold. She craved a long hot soak in the bath. She sat with her head up. 'He concentrates on me, something you don't do. He makes me feel real.'

'What rubbish! What tawdry rubbish. He's a nothing. Smooth and sleek on the surface, but lacking in depth. Lacking in weight, too.'

Hugh? No depth? Was that true? Never. Bernard's depths were granite. The thought of their sons lanced through her. She was not a demonstrative mother but she put their needs high. She must protect them. 'You seem to relish Hugh's company. You talk to him a great deal.'

'He's knowledgeable, I'll grant you that. I made use of him,' Bernard said with contempt.

'You could say I did too.'

'Oh, yes?'

'An outside interest,' she observed almost lightly. 'Fun. Something of my own.'

'You have plenty of your own.' He gestured widely. 'All this.'

'No, it's yours. I feel like a short-lease tenant. You acquired this long before I knew you.'

'So all that I've given you isn't enough?'

'In terms of wealth, more than. But one must do something positive to get oneself through life and preserve one's self-esteem. The very minimum is to buy presents for you, Bernard, with money I've earned and not from what you've given me. I must have some life of my own. But you're scornful of my charities and my design work – they're a distraction, a bagatelle. "*Your little amusements!*" What does that make me?'

He rose abruptly, supporting himself with his fists on the desk, leaning forward to spit the words at her: 'You're a miserable, cheating, self-centred bitch. And a manipulative bitch, too. How dare you twist your grubby behaviour to make the fault mine?' He hurled his whisky glass at her head. It missed by a millimetre and crashed in fragments against the wall. 'Get out!' he shouted. 'Get out of my sight!'

Silently she rose and walked to the door. She had no idea what he intended to do next.

His voice dropped and followed her, pulsating with scorn. 'Let me advise you not to ring Hanbury. Preserve what dignity remains to you. He'll do anything to avoid Anne's finding out. She might divorce him. Did you know your weak-kneed lover's dependent on his wife's money to keep up the house and his hunters? What a poor little creep.'

Candida stalked from the room as if he had not spoken.

Polly was back with the suffragettes when the telephone call came the next morning; she was on her own and happily writing. Clutching her A4 pad and pencil, she picked up the receiver.

'Candida? I don't think I really want to speak to you, thank you.

What the hell do you mean by dropping me in it with Bernard like that?'

'Polly, don't go! I apologise, I truly do. You must be furious. Was Bernard awful?'

'Unspeakable. He was ferocious and foul. I tell you, I was shaking for a full hour afterwards. And over something of which I knew absolutely nothing. It was unfair of you, and wrong.'

Candida spoke quickly, rushing out the words: 'I know, I know, I'm sorry. Don't hang up on me, please. I did think of telling you, but then I thought, no, you'd hate it and you'd probably despise me, being married to Bernard and living off the fat of the land and all that, and having an affair with your future brother-in-law which would be such an invidious position for you with Tom. Not to mention the embarrassment with Bernard. You'd be bound to tell Tom and then that would be impossible for *him* with his dreary sister-in-law – and I do know that Anne is always having Laura to stay so he'd hate to upset *her* if it all came out . . .' She paused for breath, then said plaintively: 'You do see, don't you, how circuitous and impossible it all was?'

'I do see, very clearly,' Polly replied crossly. 'Impossible for us all. So why do it?'

'Don't be cross with me, Polly darling, please! Look, can I come round and talk to you? I must talk to someone and you're my oldest friend or something pretty near it.'

She was struggling to be flippant but her voice sounded tremulous. 'Please.'

'I suppose so,' Polly conceded. 'But not for long. I'm busy.'

'Bless you.'

'And don't bring Bernard down on me again.'

'He's in London, on his way to New York for conferences and negotiations, thank God. I'll see you shortly, my poor battered Polly.'

Polly replaced the receiver. She was put out; fascinated, but put out. Candida had taken advantage of her, used her, and having escaped from Neville who had used her blithely and without gratitude for twenty years, she resented being used again. Impotently, she seized a log from its basket and flung it on the fire in a shower of sparks. Besides, despite the upset with Bernard, she found herself in a writing mood, which could too easily slip away. At least Rose and Emily were out, gone to London to see an exhibition of African art: 'Must keep up with the latest icons!' Rose had confided, kissing her goodbye. Rose would know at once that something was wrong with Candida, and probe with cynical relish for the truth of it. Damage limitation, Polly thought, was of the essence in this sort of situation.

When the Mercedes drew to a stop outside the cottage Polly went to the door. Candida looked dire. Her face was white and the absence of the usual cosmetics made it look curiously naked; her lips were blue. Old Mrs Jamieson-Druce would shudder with horror. She was wearing several layers of old pullovers over trousers and short boots; the topmost pullover, a forest green heavily ribbed affair, looked dusty and bits of hay were stuck in its wool. 'I caught cold last night,' she said vaguely, 'and now I can't seem to get warm again. I went to groom my mare but the exercise didn't do anything . . .' She fell silent, frowning. From the doorstep she stared into the long distances of the park, as if searching for someone, or something. It could have been for the truth of some matter long concealed from her.

Polly tried not to show her shock. 'Sit by the fire,' she said, 'and I'll find you a drink. No brandy, but would whisky do? Or would you prefer coffee?'

Candida sank on to her own elderly Tabriz rug and held out her hands to the flames. 'Whisky.'

Polly went to find the whisky and poured herself some as well. She thought she'd need it. She was poised between exasperation and sympathy. 'Well,' she said, 'tell me. Was it terrible?'

'Yes. Horrible. When Bernard wants to be truly beastly he really gets down to it. Oh,' she added, looking up, her eyes deeply melancholy, 'I assured him you knew nothing. He may have decided to believe me, he may not. I don't know. Polly, he was waiting for me when I arrived back at the house. It was bad then, but I took it for a bit and then I walked away. But ten minutes later he was up in the bedroom shouting again. Do you know, I saw a man in a road-rage once, way beyond any comprehension of the people trying to calm him, stamping on the bonnet of the other man's car and shaking and shaking with the sort of fury that demands violence to express it. That's how Bernard was.'

'But he wasn't violent,' Polly protested, shocked. 'Or was he?'

'He threw his whisky glass at me. That wasn't so bad,' Candida said with the ghost of a smile. 'He missed. But upstairs he took hold of me and shook and shook me. He's very strong. I swear my head's loosened on my neck.' She put her hand up. 'It still hurts. The worst thing was, I daren't scream or shout because of the boys. I had to struggle to keep everything damped down so they wouldn't hear.'

'How awful. What happens now?'

'I haven't been told. He says he will think over our future while he's away. That's supposed to terrify me. But when I consider his options, well, he hasn't that many, has he? He can't want to appear a fool in the divorce courts. Besides, rich men like him would die rather than relinquish half their fortune. And while he doesn't see much of the boys, they're very much *his*. He gave me an ultimatum about seeing Hugh –

not seeing him, that is. Oh, I shan't bore you with all the revolting things he said about Hugh . . .' Her voice thickened for a moment, then recovered. 'But if we ever meet I'm to cut him. But it doesn't seem that we shall meet. Bernard rang Anne, to make sure she was miserable too.' She stopped, choked.

Polly waited. 'Have you managed to contact Hugh?'

'He telephoned.' She drank some of her whisky in desperate gulps and recovered a little. 'Anne allowed him three minutes to tell me he won't be seeing me again!'

'Oh, poor Candida.' For someone like her, a beauty, a leader, someone respected and admired, that must have been the ultimate indignity.

Candida clasped her hands round her knees, holding them tightly to control the shaking. 'Hugh caved in like a coward. Complete surrender. Oh, he dressed it up in fine words about his love for his children and how he couldn't risk losing them . . . but he might have been reading from an autocue. Middle-aged responsibilities bear heavily on the middle-aged, don't they? Children and school fees, houses, professional standing. Bernard called him pathetic and he was. Did Tom tell you Hugh's a Lloyds loser? On the verge of bankruptcy. No? No one had told me, either.' Candida's head went down on her knees and Polly saw that she was crying. The tears ran down on to her trousers and she ignored them. 'Love's strange, isn't it, the way it pushes you and hurts you?'

'I thought you didn't believe in love?'

'I didn't,' she said, her voice muffled. 'Now I suppose I shan't again. But it got to me, you see. It seized me in its talons and flew me up to the heavens and I saw stars and moons and angels and discovered bliss, just like the songs say. All that feeling, existing at a different level from anything I'd ever known.' She lifted her head and mocked herself: 'I was twenty again, excited, exhilarated. I charmed myself, I charmed him. Ridiculous.'

'Isn't it known as sexual gratification?' Polly asked impassively.

'I had that, too,' she said, and laughed reluctantly. Then she added: 'But it isn't only that. It's the mysterious ingredient in your feelings for one another. The magic. The warmth. I like Bernard, you know. Some people hate him for being such a tough bastard. I don't dislike him even now. Mostly I admire him. He's powerful, even exciting in his own way. But there's no magic. Our minds may touch but our souls never have.'

'And Hugh?' Polly probed gently.

'Everything touched.' She ran a fingernail round the outline of a medallion on the rug. 'We both gave it everything. It was the things we could do together. Riding. Fishing. Walking in the woods. Talking and laughing. We had fun. We were frivolous. Have you ever seen Bernard frivolous?'

'No. No, I haven't.'

'I loved that in Hugh. I used to be frivolous, but Bernard wore it out of me. It didn't suit my style, he said. But I missed being me, the original me. I was back in my old personality with Hugh and it was amazing.' Silently she began again to cry. 'Oh God, I don't want to lose him.'

Mrs Jamieson-Druce did not look so desperate as her daughter, but then she had made up her face in her usual ferociously exact fashion and was, as always, oppressively fashionable. When Polly opened the door to her after her loud summons on the knocker she thrust her way into the house like a great ocean liner breasting a tidal wave, knocking Polly's pencil and pad from her grasp as mere flotsam.

'You have betrayed my daughter!' she accused her, surging through the sitting-room door. 'What sort of a friend is it that can do such a thing? And after all she has done for you?'

'I beg your pardon?' Polly responded indignantly, retrieving pencil and pad and following her willy-nilly. 'I have done no such thing.'

'You could have covered for her, and you failed her!' She flung her black crocodile bag on to the sofa and folded her arms across her chest.

'Since she failed to confide in me that she was having an affair –' and Polly made of the last words something foolish and regrettable, her tone repressive – 'there was little I could do save tell Bernard what she had told me: that she was visiting Dorothy.'

'You could have done better than that – mentioned old friends like the Poultons or the Lockwoods or the Manningfords. Where was your imagination? You obviously can't conceive of the damage you have caused.' Mrs Jamieson-Druce was in a high state of fury and shock.

'Bernard was in such a mood that he'd immediately have checked all of them and despised me. He already knew.'

Mrs Jamieson-Druce clapped her hands to her face, and then collapsed awkwardly on to the sofa, her tiny feet sticking out at an odd angle from the ends of her stout legs, reminding Polly of castors on a bulbous-legged Victorian table. 'Who would ever believe that Candida would be so foolish? Bernard is not a man to be cheated. God knows what will happen now!'

Polly considered her. 'You had better have a whisky.'

The old woman's face crumpled. Her eyes were suddenly pink with tears. 'I have such a headache, I feel terrible. Bernard was always so good to me, so good to us both.'

'And two aspirins.' She went to find what was needed and handed the pills and the whisky glass to her unwelcome guest.

Mrs Jamieson-Druce took them and swallowed as if unaware of what she was doing. 'Supposing he divorces her?' She burst into loud rasping sobs, through which the words eventually emerged: 'What will become of me? Oh God, oh God, oh God, if he doesn't forgive her, whatever shall I do?'

When Mrs Jamieson-Druce had gone, dragging the remnants of her lost dignity round her like an old cloak, Polly poured herself another whisky and contemplated the ruin of her day. To try yet again to write would be impossible, she was too agitated and upset. She had comforted two women, trying to enter their feelings and relieve their distress, and now she felt wrung out. She wanted to be comforted herself. Tom, she must go to see Tom. She glanced at her watch: twenty minutes past twelve. Vast aeons of time seemed to have passed, yet it was only twenty past twelve. But Tom would be working now, and working all afternoon. She decided to make herself some lunch and then spend an hour or two typing up her new pages. She might not be in a writing mood, but that would pass the time usefully. Then she'd drive to Winchester and fall into his arms. Relieved, she thought how wonderful it was to have such arms available.

It was not Tom who opened his door to her knock, it was Laura. Damn, thought Polly, summoning a smile to her lips and then losing it again as she focussed fully on the girl. Laura looked quite as agitated and upset as Candida or Mrs Jamieson-Druce. Reddened eyes, a tear-dampened white face – whatever could have happened to her?

'Laura! What's the matter? What's upset you?'

She gasped, hesitated, then pulled Polly in, shutting the door sharply.

'What is it?'

The wet green eyes gave her a look of appeal. 'I don't know! I don't know what to do. I was waiting for Daddy, but he's late. I think there's something horrid wrong with me.'

Polly put her arm round the girl's thin shoulders, and noted that for once it was not shrugged off. Laura was shaking. Polly held her firmly. 'Tell me about it.'

Laura tried to stifle a sob. 'I feel terrible – and I'm bleeding.'

'Go on. Where? What?' Gently.

'I've had funny pains – in my back and things. Daddy took me to the doctor and he wanted a sample – you know – and he said it might be a kidney infection. I had a rest on my bed this afternoon because I felt draggy, and then . . . then when I woke up I went to the loo and it was all bloody after . . .' She gulped.

'Ah.' Polly had a shrewd idea what was wrong. 'Let's go upstairs and then you can show me, tell me.'

They went upstairs and after a couple of minutes Polly said: 'Here, take this wad of tissues. You're fourteen now, aren't you? Yes, of course you are. You haven't started your periods yet?'

Laura shook her head. 'No. Ohh . . .' A look of helpless embarrassment. 'Is that what . . . all that blood? So much?'

'Yes. All that blood. Someone should have warned you. What a pity your doctor's a man, so it didn't jump to his mind. A woman could have saved you a nasty fright.' Polly put an arm round Laura once more. 'Congratulations. Today you've become a woman!'

Laura clutched her, her cheek against Polly's. 'Thanks.' A pause, then: 'Hey! A woman! I'm sort of grown-up now.' She giggled unexpectedly. Her face was red but satisfied.

'It's a special occasion. Tell me, I suppose you hadn't any supplies put by for this day?'

'No, nothing.' She blinked, thoughtful, pushing her lank damp hair away from her eyes. 'If Mummy'd been here . . . she would've had something.'

'Of course she would. But don't blame your father – he wouldn't have the same knowledge. Right, you lie on the sofa and I'll go to the local shop for what you need, which won't take more than three minutes, and then you'd better have a hot drink and some aspirin. I'll put the kettle on before I go out.'

'Thanks, Polly. Thanks a lot.' She lifted her eyes as if to say something, then dropped them again, blinking. 'I'll see you in a minute.'

When Polly returned from the shop, Laura darted to meet her at the door. 'Daddy's back. Listen, I haven't told him, I couldn't. I mean, I didn't know what to say.'

'You want me to tell him?' A fervent nod. 'All right, I will. Oh, and Laura, don't worry about getting a fright when it all started. I thought I was dying at that time myself!'

'Did you?' Laura said with obvious relief. 'I'm glad someone else did. I hate feeling an idiot all on my own.' She grinned and disappeared with the package Polly thrust into her hands.

Tom was shocked at the news. He hadn't been expecting it yet, his daughter was such a skinny little thing. 'Oh, lord,' he said. 'Thank God you were here. I supposed we'd have managed somehow . . . though heaven knows how!'

'Look,' Polly said somewhat mendaciously, 'I have to go, Tom, I only popped in for a second anyhow.' She wouldn't tell him of the uproar concerning his brother and the Goughs now. Better he should concentrate on Laura; it was an important day in her life and it was imperative that it should be made positive, not regarded as a curse. She told him so. 'Make a big fuss of her. I think wine, or even champagne, would be called for with her dinner, don't you?'

'Whatever you say,' he told her, amused and admiring.

She went to say goodbye to Laura, back on the sofa and sipping tea with a thoughtful face. 'I still feel a bit achy and dreary,' she commented, 'but I'm fine underneath. Thanks for being so kind. And hey, listen,' she took Polly's wrist and pulled her down towards her, 'you're okay. I mean, you know, you really are. I'm sorry I wasn't very nice before. I didn't understand. If you want to come and live with Daddy and me, you can, you know. Another woman about would be, well, it wouldn't be so bad, would it? Not now I'm one.'

'And Emily too?' Polly asked her, smiling.

'Yeah. She'd be okay. Yeah, her too.'

Remembering the storm at Chilbourne House that had come roaring down to her Gatehouse today, Polly thought it might be okay, too. This was an option to be considered.

Chapter 19

In early-January Mary telephoned Jane to wish her a happy New Year. Then she said: 'Jane, you told me of your dilemma with Jeremy, but then you left me dangling all over Christmas, longing to know what your answer was. Tell me now, please – are you going to marry him?'

A short silence. 'Oh, hell,' Jane brought out, 'I was hoping you wouldn't ask that question. I know I'm an absolute pig, but Jeremy's dangling too. He's on a brief trip to Warsaw, but he'll be back the day after tomorrow and then I just must say. But what?'

'I don't believe this,' Mary said. 'I really don't.' She sounded disapproving and cross, as if Jane were a shop manager who had failed to deliver her goods. 'You can't treat the poor man like that. If he were staying in London, what would your answer be?'

Again a second's hesitation. 'I suppose I'd say, "Why upset the status quo? Life's fine as it is."'

'Oh, Jane, you're impossible.'

'I know,' she agreed meekly.

'Does the thought of his son and daughter worry you?'

'No. No, it doesn't. We were together for the New Year and it was very pleasant. Civilised. They live largely with their mother, anyway, and they're almost adults; one's already at university. I like them, and strangely enough I think they like me.'

'But Jeremy. You do care for him?'

'Oh, yes. More than I ever have for anyone. That's the problem. With anyone else I'd have said, "You must be joking!" Marriage simply isn't my thing, Mary. That's why I'm hesitating. Yes, I'm sure about him, but I'm not sure that I could cope with changing my life and myself in such a radical manner. I'm forty-five, hardly a reckless impulsive girl to abandon all for love. Frankly, I'm terrified.'

Mary reflected. Echoes of conversations at recent country dinner parties sounded in her head. 'You don't want to abandon your career, I understand that. But job security now isn't what it was, even in the once famously secure civil service. Aren't the Government and the Treasury looking for up to twenty-five per cent shrinkage in costs in many areas?'

'Something of that order.'

'That's not a matter of cutting down on paper shuffling. It's cutting out people, too. One reads of significant reductions being sought one day and the next it's sweeping redundancies. Early retirement is taken as a matter of course. The Armed Services have been decimated – more than. Suppose you had to retire early?'

'People in their fifties are disappearing from the scene,' Jane admitted.

'Then where would you be, alone in your flat and nothing to do all day? Think, Jane, you could live to ninety – imagine all the long years of your life over again and nothing in them, then put that against the years of companionship and interest and stimulation you would have with a man like Jeremy.'

'Mary, you terrify me!'

'I want to make you think,' she said. 'And personally I can recommend marriage – though I know that's unusual among us.'

Vanessa's flat was dark when she came home from the City in the winter, dark and empty and silent, and she hated it. She would rush from room to room snapping on lights and pulling curtains in an effort to make it cosy, but cosiness eluded her. Satin lampshades and elaborate curtains could not fill its large empty spaces. The television news programmes that spoke of disasters and death and disgruntled politicians could not give her a feeling of companionship either. January and February were the worst months of the year: Christmas, with all its lights and tinsel and friendly bustle, was over; rain then had been hardly noticeable as you darted from one bright and glittering shop to another, and there were drinks parties with neighbours and a theatre trip with a friend and the companionship of her parents for three days. That had been good. But in January and February all was dark and quiet, only the uncompromising rain was the same, drip, drip, dripping and cold, emphasising her loneliness.

It was further emphasised on this January evening by the constant tapping of feet on the bare boards of the empty flat above her's. Someone must be moving in. Driven equally by irritation and the desire for human contact, Vanessa decided to visit the someone.

As she walked up the stairs she saw a female standing at the top struggling to lift a large and evidently heavy cardboard box. She had tugged it up roughly a foot before its bottom abruptly sagged open and books spilled out, several sliding over the lip of the stairs to cascade down upon Vanessa, clouting her feet and ankles.

'Oh, hell!' the woman called, laughing ruefully. 'Oh, Christ, I'm sorry. Nothing like throwing Wesley and Trollope at one's neighbours for making friends and influencing people. Are you all right? Are you sure?'

Vanessa winced, rubbed her smarting ankles and said: 'Yes, fine!' and began to retrieve a book or two.

'Don't bother, don't bother!' the woman said, running her fingers through her hair before ineffectively pawing at the books. 'God, isn't moving hell!' She was a few years younger than Vanessa, smallish, plumpish, blonde, with a rather bad complexion. There was a beading of sweat along her downy upper lip, and she rubbed it away with the back of a grubby hand. She was wearing a man's loose black sweater with the sleeves pushed back and purple leggings. She had bangles on her wrists and looked vaguely artistic.

Vanessa introduced herself and told her that she had come up to welcome her to the house. 'Would you care for a break and a cup of coffee? I'm just about to make some.'

The woman straightened, shoving the last of the books aside with a black-shoed foot. 'I'd adore some. Shall I come down now? God, I'm glad you arrived – I'm so parched and lonely and bored, you wouldn't believe. I'd have probably started howling or planning suicide if you hadn't.'

Vanessa was touched and impressed by this admission; she had thought herself the only person who had such searing feelings. Over coffee she discovered that the woman was called Carol Fenn, that she was a stage designer, that she had a two-year-old daughter named Edwina and thought all men were mean shits. She accompanied this last announcement with a cackle of laughter and added that she was on her second divorce. 'We've just parted.'

'I'm twice divorced, too,' Vanessa told her, and they eyed each other in awe before Carol burst into further laughter, in which Vanessa, to her surprise, found herself joining.

'Was the second the father of your bump?' Carol asked. 'Or is that someone else's?'

'Oh, someone else's entirely,' Vanessa said, copying her airy style and smiling broadly. 'Only the husband of one of my oldest friends. But the brute was being unfaithful to us both with a third love and she's expecting his son, too. He's shacked up with her now.'

Carol widened her eyes in amazement before going off into a semi-hysterical paroxysm of mirth. 'You have been through it, haven't you?' she gasped, recovering. 'Is he going to pay? You should make him pay.

I couldn't manage without Peter's contributions for my little Edwina. I can recommend you a good solicitor.'

'I am a solicitor,' Vanessa told her, pleased with the effect she was making. 'But, Carol, I've vowed not to accept contributions, they lead to interference and disputes that could fracture the shell of calm that should surround every child. I shall do everything for him myself and we shall be all in all to each other.' She added after a contemplative moment: 'But I shall have support. The father's two daughters – both sort-of university age – have written to say that they're looking forward to being big sisters to my baby. Of course, they've known me since they were born, but I believe that sort of open-hearted kinship is a beautiful sign for the future, don't you?'

Carol was admiring. She accepted Vanessa's offer of a mushroom omelette, 'Oh, how blissful to sit down while someone else cooks!' and talked with her about personal options and choices – 'Women must always keep all their lines open between eath other!' – and the altruism and sacrifice that motherhood demanded: 'When the kids are ill, men always have an important meeting – a mother's career doesn't count!' Carol's two year old was with her granny for the night, she said, but she couldn't wait to show her to Vanessa tomorrow evening. She could assure her that having a child was absolutely the best thing ever, and of course Vanessa was not in the least too old, widening her eyes in seemingly unfeigned surprise when she divulged her true years and saying with more flattering laughter: 'I'd never have suspected if you hadn't told!' She insisted that Vanessa tell her the story of her life, meaning her love-life, and appeared transfixed with wonder by each anecdote. Vanessa had never known herself to be so lively and entertaining a talker before, while in turn she found herself impressed with the profundities Carol produced about men: 'Men aren't interested in relationships, only conquests!' or 'If men had to bear the babies even China would be underpopulated!' She must be, Vanessa concluded, the most intelligent and perceptive person she had come across in years. She asked her who looked after her toddler.

'I've been managing with a living-in girl. She's conscientious enough – but boring? Oh my God, constipated in mind and body! And never a flicker of a smile, even at my best jokes. I'd sooner have had a real trained nanny, but they charge their weight in gold. Hey! D'you know what I'm thinking, though, Vanessa? We might share one, mightn't we? Halve the horrific cost.' She glanced at her wrist and jumped to her feet. 'Christ, look at the time and I haven't made me up a bed to sleep in yet. Keep the nanny in mind, think it over, why don't you? Thanks for the meal, its been great talking to you. Bye!'

*

Jeremy and Jane had dinner together in her flat when he came back from Warsaw. They ate grilled salmon and drank wine, and they looked at one another, then looked away again. He spoke quietly about Warsaw and Jane knew she should be concentrating and responding, but her brain refused to take in the words: she was too edgy. Normally when he came they would make love first, talking in bed, relaxing together, but Jeremy had turned away after a quick kiss and said he was tired and hungry. The plane had been delayed, the food at lunch had been dreadful, his belly was flapping against his spine with emptiness, and how soon could she feed him? There was tension between them, the tension of the unanswered question, the suspense and frustration of his absence in Poland which had prevented any discussion of it. And thank God, Jane told herself, for without his presence she had been able to think objectively.

She picked up pretty Victorian silver scissors to cut a sprig of grapes from a bunch on her fruit bowl, then she plucked the succulent green globes off one by one to put them in her mouth, grateful for the juice that salved its dryness. Jeremy watched her. Silence grew between them.

She leaned over to sever more grapes with the scissors. 'Jeremy?'

He shook his head, looking at her with deep intent. Her breath was short. He put out his hand to capture hers. His hand was very warm. The scissors clattered loudly on to the table.

'Jane, I've asked you before, now I need my answer. You know I love you. Will you marry me?'

His eyes held hers; mesmerised, she could not look away. 'Yes,' she found herself saying. 'I will.' Her heart thumped strongly in her chest; these were not the words she had intended. What the hell had impelled her to say that? What had she done now?

He was smiling. He came round the table to pull her to her feet. 'I adore you,' he said, and held her silently and tightly against him before bending his head to kiss her.

Later, as they lay naked and replete in bed, he suggested that the marriage ceremony should be at the end of March and she agreed. 'Registrar or clergyman?'

'Registrar,' Jane said, and thought how foolish it was to feel so happy when she had just consigned to oblivion everything she had worked for. Was she being a fool?

Polly was reassuring on the telephone. 'You've done the right thing – it'll be fine.'

'How do you know?' Jane enquired. 'You're not me.'

'I just do,' Polly said.

'You sound atrociously sentimental.'

'Too bad. I know I'm right. You're heading for a fascinating life with a fascinating man. I'm tremendously pleased.'

'Thank you. And you? How are things with you and Tom? And Candida and Bernard? Give me the latest news.'

It was a struggle for Polly to speak of Candida without telling tales out of school. She was still angry with her for taking advantage of their friendship and using her in such an unscrupulous fashion. She understood the forces that had driven Candida, but in her own uncomfortable position as the recipient of the Goughs' charity she felt used and despised. Candida should have confided in her, or looked for some other subterfuge. Bernard had come to apologise for shouting at her, very stiff and brusque, and she had felt red-hot with embarrassment; it was unfair on them both. How could they ever meet comfortably now that her knowledge of his cuckolding lay between them? Oh, damn Candida! And damn Hugh Hanbury too. She had told Tom, who called his brother a fool. 'And it isn't the first time, either. Not by a long way.' That knowledge made Polly feel worse about Candida. The whole thing was impossible.

She told Jane that Candida was working on the garden design she was doing for Georgina Ellington: 'Someone in your world, I gather, or what soon will be. I hear they have similar ideas and it's going well. Candida's grateful to you, and I imagine this Georgina will be also.'

Jane grunted. 'Georgina's a great friend of Jeremy's first wife. Cold currents swirl in the air between us, though I have to admit, snobbishly, that she's impressed by Candida. I wonder sometimes how many other of the wives will resent my appearing at Jeremy's side. The thought has added a new dimension to my difficulties.'

'The rôle of the second wife? Me, too. But Tom's Kate is dead.'

'How horrid to have to be thankful for that. But it should lessen the resentment. How are things going with his daughter – Laura, is it?'

'We're friends. Surprisingly, suddenly we're friends. Jane, I haven't told you this yet but the decree absolute's through on my divorce, I'm leaving The Gatehouse very shortly to move in with Tom, and we plan to be married at Easter. Will you and Jeremy be able to come to the wedding? Registrar's office and small, but I can't imagine it without you.'

'Oh, how lovely. Congratulations. And it goes without saying that you're coming to mine. Yes, we'll just have finished our own honeymoon, and we depart for Warsaw the following week. Well! How extraordinary that both of us should be marrying within days of one another, and at our ages, too!'

'It is, isn't it?' Polly said. She added in her driest voice: 'And it's then that Vanessa will be producing her baby too.'

'God help us, so she will. If our changes of direction were unimaginable a year ago, how much more so hers!' A pause, a change of tone, then Jane said: 'A different angle on such subjects . . . and a touch embarrassing, but I have to ask you . . . or possibly to warn you, Polly. Is Tom's brother . . . what's his name? Hugh? Is it possible he's having an affair with Candida?'

Polly breathed slowly. 'Why d'you ask?' she hedged.

'I saw him playing footsie with her at the dinner party at Chilbourne House. My napkin slipped from my knees and I had to retrieve it from under the table. Polly, my breath just went from me. I could hardly believe it – but I couldn't miss it. What a risk to take!'

'Then, yes, she was, but it's over now. At least I sincerely hope it is.'

'Oh, dear. Tell me.'

Polly told her, adding: 'I'm sorry for Candida, but at the same time I'm furious with her, and I can't think yet which predominates. And when I see poor Bernard I don't know where to look.'

'An invidious position. What a relief that you're able to get away. Really, Candida was being very silly, wasn't she? And silliness isn't the sort of thing one connects with her. Not her usual style!'

'I doubt she thought of that. It seems to have overwhelmed her.'

'Our cool detached Candida? How extraordinary. You know, when she married Bernard I was admiring. Shocked that anyone could be so cynical, but admiring nevertheless. Poverty is soul-destroying, isn't it? Yet we English still cling to our Puritan notions of wealth as basically immoral. I thought it terrific of her to act as if such serious views had no existence.'

'Their relationship has worked until now. She admires that ruthless intelligence of his and his power. One would imagine him a sensual man, too. I suspect she was not unmoved by that.'

'The thought had occurred to me also. But it was many years ago. Oh, dear. Oh, dear. We speak of youth as being torn and tempestuous but it seems to be that middle-age can be quite as unpredictable.'

'Worse. We're so much less free to indulge in eruptions of passion – and when we do the aftershocks reverberate on and on. Have you thought of the problems of our wedding guests at the small and intimate receptions we're planning? What do I do about Candida and Bernard? Tom's bound to have Hugh and Anne there! We can't have them jostling together. And Vanessa? I don't think I could bring myself to speak to her yet.'

'Yet? I think you and Rose and Emily are behaving like saints. I should be more inclined to throttle her. And just think if she should turn up to either ceremony – she'd be bound to go into labour on the spot. Can you imagine the drama? The shrieks and the fuss?'

They both began to laugh.

When Polly and Emily moved to Tom's house, the first thing that happened after their arrival was the delivery of a bouquet. It was enormous, a mass of forced spring flowers and roses, and the card proclaimed it to be from Candida and Bernard.

'For beauty amid chaos – or sops to salve pangs of conscience?' Tom queried.

'Sops to something,' Polly said. 'I'll have to put them in the kitchen sink for now.'

They were lovely, but like the flowers that tactless dinner guests bring, they required arranging and there simply wasn't time, for the second thing that happened was an icy January rain that came spitting down the narrow street. Furniture and clothes and books and pictures all had to be rushed into the house and found places of their own or at least be stowed out of the way. Moving to The Gatehouse had been easier, then there had been room to spare for their belongings, but settling into Tom's house meant either displacing his furniture (and his was more handsome than theirs) or overcrowding. Alternatively Polly could have the excess stored. For the moment most of her pieces disappeared into the dark depths of the cellar, and while she was not cast down at putting them out of sight, it annoyed her to recognise how little of value there had been in her life. Her water-colours of Hampshire views were piled in a cupboard: 'We'll find places for the best of them at half-term,' she told Tom in a tight voice, 'when we've had time to consider.'

It was a shock, moving house again, and she disliked the disorder, the upheaval, and the responsibility for Laura's and Emily's reaction to it all. It made her edgy and nervous. She and Tom had each managed a day off work to supervise the process, but she had set written work for her classes to complete in her absence and thoughts of the inevitable piles of marking hung over her, dark and heavy as the rain clouds over the street. And then there would be running the house and shopping and cooking for four people rather than two, and always having to give consideration to someone's odd tastes, and trying in spare moments to find places to store her linen and her towels and her china, and leaving her warm place in the bed beside Tom at half-past five in the morning in order to put in her two hours writing, not unattractive in the summer dawns with the birds singing beyond the curtains, but cold and unalluring now. And the twenty-mile drive to

Hamlins. She had been looking forward for so long to being with Tom; why did she have to feel exhausted and slightly nauseated? Stress, of course. It would be hard to get everything right. She decided she had taken too much on and the thought worried at her as she rushed from room to room and up and down the stairs.

Then suddenly, blocking the hallway, came her writing table, her own special purchase. Where would it live now? Where would she do her writing in this house which immediately felt overcrowded with furniture and people? She leaned on the table, unable to think. Her throat felt dry and her shoulder muscles hurt. She jumped as Tom kissed her neck from behind, then put an arm round her shoulders.

'You'll have the small front bedroom as your study,' he pronounced in his deep bass, 'and we'll put your table in the window. Then as you're musing in the early mornings on your next scene you can watch the street come to life, see the milkman plodding from doorstep to doorstep, and glimpse the local robin and the postman. And I'll deal with breakfast. I've been used to that with Laura.' He gave her a sideways glance of sympathy and added: 'I'll put the kettle on for tea to revive us. Then afterwards we can take the table up together.' He disappeared down the passage to the kitchen.

She was instantly at peace within herself. There was a quietness in the old house; nothing was moving, no one was speaking. Tom had switched on lamps as the afternoon light began to die and the rooms beyond her glowed with a kind of transparent luminosity. In a second had come the realisation of how greatly her life had changed. This was Tom she would be living with, not Neville, an emotional bankrupt. Tom would respond to her needs, she wouldn't have to labour for every inch of ground she made. She followed him into the kitchen, made him show her where the flower bowls were kept, and smiling to herself, lifted Candida's flowers from the sink and began to arrange them in the largest bowl she could find.

The arrangement looked lavish when she had finished it, lavish and beautiful. She carried it to the drawing room and placed it on the Pembroke table by the window, where its mingled colours glinted in the light from a nearby lamp and its scents hung in the air. Later she would telephone Candida to thank her, though she knew her thanks would be forced. The flowers might merit genuine gratitude, but she was still grumpy with Candida. And after all, what were lavish armfuls of flowers to a woman in her circumstances? A telephone call to a shop, a brief detailing of the numbers on one of her many credit cards. They could not wipe out Polly's sense of having been used, nor take back the insults hurled at her by Bernard or Mrs Jamieson-Druce.

She leaned over to settle a rose more firmly into place, and sighed.

She could not maintain anger for long with anyone, and not with Candida who had come to her rescue when her need was desperate. And even now Candida was making her own form of oblique apology to Polly through her kindness to Emily.

Emily, who had protested her aversion to the original move to The Gatehouse, had mutinied still more strongly at moving back to Winchester and living in Tom's house. It could never be her home in any way, she said, it might become Polly's place, but never hers. She would be living there on sufferance surrounded by people who longed for the time when they could push her off to university. Silently Polly had acknowledged a grain of truth in that, and disliked the admission. Emily proclaimed a much better idea. She would stay on at The Gatehouse – why not? There she could continue to exercise the Gough boys' ponies for Candida and, naturally, see Mark. It would be terrible to part the two of them now, she stated, how could her mother contemplate anything so cruel? And if Polly were worried about her safety all alone in The Gatehouse, well, Mark could move in with her, couldn't he? That would be really sensible. Polly's rejection of what she dubbed 'this ludicrous notion' was proceeding with some vigour when Candida's car had slid to a stop outside the windows, and it was she who, appealed to by Emily, had found a sensible compromise. Emily, she said, must spend the week in Winchester, which, after all, was where she was at school – but why should she not come to Chilbourne House for the weekend whenever she wished? Candida would issue an open invitation; she was fond of Emily and so was Bernard.

When Emily had left the room, satisfied and flattered, Candida remarked in her sardonic fashion that there was no end to the benefits from this arrangement: 'Should Bernard be away, he'll be all for having Emily about the house to act as my chaperon, while you and Tom will have one less disgruntled teenager under your feet. The adoring Mark will be delighted, and the ponies will relish the exercise.' She would, naturally, keep an eye on the amount of time Emily spent with Mark. 'The chaperoned will be the chaperon. How ironic!'

Tom took mugs of tea to the removals men and then paid them off. Polly drank her tea on her feet, clearing tea-chests of kitchen equipment. Laura and Emily would be back from school shortly and the sooner everything was in place the better.

Laura arrived home, frowning and thoughtful. Her behaviour after she had removed her coat and slung down her school bag reminded Polly of a cat, checking its territory for change. She prowled into the drawing room first, sniffed at the bowl of flowers, then investigated with her round green eyes, item by item, everything that was in the room.

Finally she stared at her father and Polly. 'Nothing's different,' she said, giving him a dubious look.

'No,' Tom agreed.

'It's a lovely room as it is,' Polly said, smiling.

Laura rubbed an eyebrow. 'The flowers are nice,' she commented off-handedly, touching a rose with the tip of a finger. 'Mummy used often to have flowers here, in this bowl.' She blinked. 'They look as if they're meant to be there.' A pause, then very straight: 'Are you going to take Mummy's portrait down?'

'No,' Polly said.

Laura considered. 'Or the photographs?' She pointed to silver-framed portraits on a side-table, one clearly of herself as a baby, another of her mother and Tom on their wedding day.

'No. Why should we? They belong there. And I like them.' It was important that the house should be as Laura had always seen it; changes could be made gradually. Besides, Polly felt at home in it as it was.

Laura visibly relaxed. 'What about your own photographs and pictures and things?'

It was Polly's turn to consider. 'I don't have that many. For the moment I think I might put them in the little front room Tom says I should use for my writing.'

'Your writing?' Laura was immediately distracted. 'What writing? Are you writing a history textbook or something?'

'No, a novel.' Polly explained her twin themes of women's education and the suffragettes. 'I've been plodding on with it for months. It seems incredible now but it's three-quarters done, the final pages are coming into sight.' Her novel was at the stage where to finish it was no longer a distant shimmering mirage whose reality it was impossible to believe could exist, but a point coming steadily into focus, gaining shape and meaning as it approached. Two more months, three more months, and it would be reached.

'Will it be published?'

'Yes!' said Tom, and 'I should be so lucky!' said Polly.

'It would be great if you did have it published,' Laura said in a pleased voice. 'We'd have a real author living in the house.'

Emily arriving at that moment there was some disturbance while she dumped her schoolbag on a chair, flung off rain-soaked clothes and stared about herself. 'It looks all right,' she said. 'It looks almost tidy.'

'Not your room,' Polly said. 'It's full of your stuff in boxes and the contents of your wardrobe are all over your bed.'

Emily groaned. 'Oh, hell. And I've hours of homework to do.'

'I'll help you hang your stuff up,' Laura offered in a gruff voice. 'If you want?'

'Thanks,' Emily said after a second. 'Okay.'

They went up the stairs together. As they went their voices floated back down. Laura hadn't known that Polly wrote, she remarked off-handedly. That was something different. Had Emily read any of this book?

'Yeah, I've read it,' Emily told her. 'It's not half bad. In fact, I reckon it's good. Interesting, you know, about what life was like a hundred years ago for women and girls. It makes you gasp how different things were then from what we've reached now.'

'Do you think she'd let me read it?' Laura asked.

'Why not? Ask her. You'd like it.'

Chapter 20

Vanessa stopped work six weeks before her baby was due. Her new friend Carol boasted that she herself had worked until only a fortnight before Edwina was born, but Vanessa's doctor informed her that her blood pressure was rising slightly, and stated that at her age and stage she should be taking things easy. Vanessa relished the thought of pottering her way through the days. The stress of travelling by Tube to the City every day, inane battles with argumentative clients who refused to accept her advice, the strain of attending court and standing to argue the case – they all took their toll. Now she could shop for her baby, catch up with the latest in innovative literary fiction, tidy out her cupboards and be ready to welcome her son as the radiant Madonna figure she'd visualised herself.

On a fine blowy March day she decided to go shopping. She had taken a leisurely breakfast in bed of warm croissants and hot chocolate, spreading the newspaper across the duvet as she read her way through its pages, and now the sun darting through the window had sent a shadow-pattern of leaves flickering on the newsprint while the baby seemed to be jigging inside her in happy response. Spring. It made her feel lively too, made her feel that action to prepare for the baby was imperative; suppose he came early and she had nothing for him? She would have lunch at Peter Jones in Sloane Square and explore their baby department.

At the Coffee Shop on the top floor she selected a vegetarian canneloni with a side salad, added a pot of Earl Grey tea and a fresh fruit pastry with cream. Now she wouldn't need to cook tonight. Vanessa hated cooking for herself alone. But she knew that when she had a child to feed everything would be different; she would plan marvellous menus for them both. She found herself an empty table and sat down.

The Coffee Shop was full of women shopping together, many of them mothers with adult daughters. Soon such a pair came to take the other seats at her table, parking a baby in a pushchair between them. They displayed a cheerful preoccupation with themselves – what they should eat and the fabulous clothes they planned to buy – and with the infant, chatting, smiling, bobbing at it, while it responded to them with wide toothless grins, its whole body wriggling with pleasure at their attention. That was how the generations should be, Vanessa thought. For there was affection there, and interest in each other's needs and opinions. She could not remember one occasion when she had gone on a shopping and lunch spree with her own mother. They had never been involved in each other's lives. Even the coming grandchild failed to arouse real interest; over Christmas there had been no more than a non-committal agreeableness between them: to her mother and brother Vanessa could have been a distant cousin, the sort you think of once a decade. Yet her father was thoroughly involved. She smiled as she thought of him.

He telephoned her every Sunday night for a talk as if this had always been part of their lives, gossiping about the baby, chiding her about her demanding profession, grumbling that life was passing him by, that he felt less than a person without his work. 'I *was* my work – it identified me. Now who am I?' He wanted distractions and activities. He'd offered to buy her baby its cot, why shouldn't they enjoy a day's shopping and lunch together? She looked around the Coffee Shop. Yes, there were men here, elderly couples mostly; her father would not look out of place. Then afterwards they could go to the theatre again. This time she would buy the tickets and take him – if he'd let her. It had been a surprise to Vanessa how agreeable it was to be together with a male companion in a relationship independent of sexual undertones and tension. She was discovering a real liking for her father.

She finished her cup of tea (coffee made her nauseous), and rose to move on. The baby in its pushchair waved its little arms excitedly as it looked up at her. A fresh smile broke across its face. Vanessa smiled back, liking its friendly acceptance of her, thinking on an indrawn breath that soon she would have her own child with just such a simple attitude to life and her, needing love and sustenance and confident that she would give him those things. A companion. *Needing her* . . . Without her knowing it, something within her clicked and changed, the balance of her life altered. She would be the one responsible for their relationship. As she made her way through Carpets and down the stairs in search of Babywear she felt she understood what Mary had been trying to tell her. For more than twenty years she had always been the needy one, demanding attention, grasping for affection, craving reassurance from her husbands and her lovers and finding it lacking. With her baby she would be in control, the one he looked up to in trust, the one who made things happen.

The baby department was alluring, but overwhelming too. How should she choose between the elaborate swinging cradles on their stands or the Moses baskets or the more mundane carrycots? Her eyes fell on baby baths, bottles, sterilisers – help! These came from another world, strange to her. What had she taken on? How did the steriliser work? Did you have to sterilise everything the baby might touch? Oh, God, how terrifyingly ignorant she was. She must ask the midwife and Mary about these things. Or maybe her new friend Carol could tell her. Carol was such fun with her apparently infinite enjoyment of everything Vanessa told her, with her rippling mirth and wide-eyed amazement. An evening with Carol never left Vanessa with a sense of her own imperfections and folly, as many people did, so that afterwards her mind went restlessly over and over the event, searching every sentence for some implication she might have missed, some subtle disparagement which would haunt and hurt her for days. There was nothing devious about Carol. Yes, she must ask her about these things. If she did laugh at Vanessa's ignorance it wouldn't be hurtful mirth. She'd once said her first husband divorced her for laughing too much.

The best way to start would be by buying simple clothes. Vanessa looked at baby body suits, baby stretch suits, designer baby co-ordinates. Which were suitable for what? The designer baby co-ordinates looked so very chic in blue and white – but no, she dared not risk the colour blue, unkind fate might send her a girl, the gods must be propitiated. (Though she was certain the baby *was* a boy.) There was a pack containing white and primrose suits. They were ridiculously expensive. Vanessa's heart began to beat heavily. Tuck the pack under the arm, wander towards the dear little white-painted wardrobes . . . on their far side she could transfer it to her shopping bag . . . She had a strange feeling of being watched. She turned and saw the baby from the Coffee Shop lying in his pushchair, his eyes upon her, round and solemn, his mother and grandmother examining some item on the far side of a display of prams. Something caught in her throat. Her heart thumped on, punishingly. Suppose she were arrested? Newhouse & Bock would never employ anyone with a criminal conviction. Disaster . . . her baby . . . Sweat prickled under her arms. Vanessa thrust the pack back on its shelf. Then she seized it again. No, she would pay for the suits, she wanted them. Once more she had the feeling of propitiating jealous gods. She stroked her belly: I am great with child, she told herself. Her baby must be kept safe. As she walked away the baby in the pushchair gurgled at her.

*

Jane woke early in Jeremy's bed on her wedding day, her senses alerted by the March squall that threw its rain against the windows. She did not take the rain as an omen, rather as a tease that made her laugh inwardly. She and Jeremy had no need for sunshine and flowers, they were past that sort of nonsense, this would be a good day whatever the weather. Beside her in the bed she could hear his breath ticking away regularly, peacefully. Dear Jeremy. Her mind passed over events, checking them off. Her flat in The Boltons had been dealt with, with all her usual calm competence, its cupboards and wardrobes emptied, its curtains and carpets cleaned, inventories taken, keys handed over, ready for the agents to introduce its new inhabitants. The personal belongings she would need in Warsaw were packed in boxes and tea-chests and suitcases and forwarded on. Her old life, tidied up and packed away. Did she regret it? Did she have qualms? She recollected her farewell party at the DTI. Colleagues had asked such questions then. Probing, half-laughing, half-perturbed that she should have rejected for the man beside her a successful and well-paid career, and by choosing to abandon it somehow brought into question their own similar careers, even subtly perhaps belittled them. She would travel the world while they toiled at home; she would meet and entertain foreign diplomats and personalities of international repute. It made them uneasy. Some had intimated that she was too old at forty-five to make such a change, to turn from today's new ground-breaking, power-dressed female rising in her own right, to play the traditional wife, admiring and self-deprecating, living in her husband's shadow. They prophesied that she would be lonely, that she would miss her friends and her family, that she would be bored with no real point to her day: they prophesied disaster.

They had no need, these people, to make such points, God knew she had made them to herself often enough in those trying weeks when she had struggled to make her choice. Jane slid from the bed to stand by the window, looking out, reflecting. The rain was slackening and the grey sky breaking up with the light of dawn. She watched the milkman coming down the road, dumping his bottles on wet doorsteps, wondering at his life. I shall have something I never knew I wanted until I met Jeremy, she thought. I shall have comforts now of a different kind from ambition realised. A husband, an embassy, servants, international acquaintanceships. Companionship . . . Jeremy.

The rain stopped. Puddles of water lay on the street, and were ruffled by the wind. In the east the light intensified. Maybe it would be a fine day after all.

In the bed Jeremy stirred and put out his hand to feel for her. He lifted his head. 'Jane? Everything all right?'

'Yes,' she said.

He left the bed and came up beside her. He took her hand in his and she was surprised at its warmth. 'Then what are you doing standing here in the morning cold?'

'I was thinking how right this is.'

He drew her hand up to his face and held it there a moment before kissing it, on the back and in the palm, his eyes on her face.

She said: 'I shall miss my friends, but they can visit us.'

'Any time. And now come back to bed and I shall warm you and your cold feet.'

Polly was typing up the last page of her novel when the telephone rang. The last page, the actual last page, finished, ended, the long, long slog over – and some idiot had to break into her concentration with unwanted messages. In another five minutes she would be going to show Tom her great pile of typescript, laughing triumphantly, knowing that he would open the bottle of champagne she'd discovered he already had hidden in the bottom fridge drawer, ready for this moment . . . She wouldn't answer the damned thing. But the ringing went on and on, her fingers fumbled on the keys. Oh, hell!

'Yes?' A growl.

'Polly? Hello, Polly, it's Juliana here.' She sounded breathless, happy, triumphant even. 'I thought I should telephone to tell you and Rose and Emily that I've had my baby and he's big and bouncing and everything's present that should be.'

'Oh . . . good,' Polly said. 'Well, congratulations and all that. I'll tell the girls. How was the birth? How is the child? Give me more information, they're bound to want to know it.' She didn't suppose Neville would communicate with them. It struck her that it ought to seem extraordinary that Juliana should ring her like this, her ex-husband's mistress – and wife to be, if the awful Henry could be persuaded to co-operate in a divorce – and yet, somehow it wasn't strange, it was right. They had never met but they could communicate without friction, basically, she thought, because they were women of good will.

'He arrived half an hour ago. I'm afraid I can't boast about him at all – in fact, he's quite hideous. Things became a bit protracted at the end and his poor little face looks squashed and bruised like some awful boxer's after a lost fight. But the midwife says he'll improve. Oh, and he'll only open one eye, and that with a baleful squinting look. You never saw anyone so sweet and comic. I adore him already. Oh, and Polly, he's bald!'

Polly began to laugh. 'What does Neville say? Was he there for the birth?'

'No. I threw him out when things got tough. He was useless, he was going green. I told him to go home and write his philosophy, that would soothe him.'

'And did he?'

'No, to give him credit he hung around. But then when he saw his son he went green again. He hadn't had any food for hours, poor love, so I sent him off to our friends in Eaton Square for dinner and celebratory drinks and all that.'

'And has the baby a name?'

'Don't laugh, he's Lionel Bertram Neville Alban. Mostly Neville's choice – did you ever hear anything so pompous? But I quite like Lionel, so I didn't argue.'

After she had rung off Polly stared at the last page of her novel with unfocussed eyes. Juliana's cynical attitude to Neville struck her with admiration. With her flow of mockery and her light-hearted ease he would be kept off balance, concerned as to the direction of her thoughts and her true judgment of him. He would be held in an insidious confusion that would be at once exciting and worrying. Did she truly believe in his brilliance? What if she derided him to their friends? He would struggle for the dominance he had always held with Polly, and, she thought, would be far from certain of winning. For a moment Polly almost pitied him. Rose and Emily had told her that he had resigned from the Hampshire County Council to take up a post with Westminster City Council. No more commuting, but time therefore, Juliana had decreed, to continue with his writing. He already had the first three chapters completed to show the publisher who'd expressed interest, now he must continue, backing or no backing. She would let him off his half share of the responsibility for cooking their dinner if he was writing; instead, he could put in a couple of hours before they ate at eight-thirty. 'Juliana believes in his ability but not his stickability, so she's twisting his arm,' Rose pointed out. 'She's clever, isn't she?' Perhaps as a barrister she enjoyed these power games.

Polly smiled to herself: Tom needed no such arm-twisting. She breathed deeply and stretched. Then, concentrating, she typed out the last paragraphs of her book, checked them for errors and slipped the final page in at the bottom of the pile of typescript. Eureka! She was tired but triumphant. She felt as if she, too, had given birth. Her novel was her baby.

Vanessa had her first pains between two and three o'clock in the morning. At the first one she woke to mutter to herself about fierce backache, and fell back asleep as it ebbed. At the second she woke in immediate awareness of what it was, and with a great sense of drama.

Her baby was ready to be born! She switched on the bedside lamp, blinked at the light and wished she had a companion. She ached to spread the news, but the clock said it was ten to three. What should she do? She couldn't wake Mary (and her disapproving George) at this hour, nor would Carol with her lively toddler relish a ring on her doorbell. Tears of loneliness came to her eyes, but she blinked them away. Mary said emotion was bad for the baby, she must be quietly positive in all her thoughts. She would make tea, listen to the radio – there must be something on some channel somewhere – read a book.

Time passed with a slowness she had never known in all her life. Half-past three. She finished packing her case for the hospital, adding her telephone book so that she could call everyone she knew when the miraculous birth had occurred. She dressed, thinking that it was the last time she would wear these voluminous unbecoming clothes, the last time she would have such difficulty in pulling on her shoes. Four o'clock. When I come back, she told herself, my child will be familiar to me, a real person. She pictured herself carrying him tenderly into the flat. That would be when she came back from Mary's; dear kind Mary was going to look after her for the first fortnight after she left hospital. It occurred to her how horrible it would be to return to dirty cups, stale food in the fridge, the bin unemptied. Everything must be ready and perfect for her baby. She dealt with the kitchen, wiping in grubby nooks and cranies she'd never noticed before, scrubbing out the cutlery drawer. Contractions gripped her, then ebbed. The sense of doing something worthwhile and motherly was curiously pleasant. Quarter past five. She stood in what would be the nursery, admiring the new cot with its stencils of Winnie-the-Pooh and Piglet and Eeyore, that she and her father had chosen together, and as she stood another pain gripped her, stronger this time, then she felt a gushing wet warmth on her legs and stared down and realised that her waters had broken. Her pains were fifteen or twenty minutes apart still but she should go into hospital, that was that the pamphlet she had been given told her. Lights, company, people who would appreciate her great drama, the most important day of her life. She rang for the ambulance.

Polly came down the stairs to breakfast, yawning and sleepy, just as the morning post fell through the letter-box on to the mat. As the date of their marriage was only three days hence, the amount of mail she and Tom were receiving seemed prodigious: cards and letters of good wishes from old friends who had seen the announcement in the papers, jumbled daily together with every sort of advertisement possible, from wedding photographers to suppliers of expensive kitchenware, from hire cars to honeymoon hotels. She scooped them up and carried them into the kitchen, where Tom was making coffee. There she sorted them into piles and sat down to start on hers.

'A big card signed from my old colleagues at the Durngate School – look, Tom, how sweet of them. And a cheque. Wow! Next one . . . *Take your Honeymoon in Tahiti* – no thanks, Paris is fine by me. *Make your Big Day a Sensation – Drive to Church in a Coach and Four* . . . Hmm. Who's this?' She tore open a smaller typewritten envelope and flicked her eyes over the letter inside. She breathed deeply. 'Oh, Tom, *listen*! It's from the literary agent that friend of yours recommended I should try. "Dear Polly Ferrison, I enjoyed reading the script of *Wit of Woman* and find it a most impressive piece of writing. You've certainly succeeded in exposing the raw nerves of family relationships and in painting sharply-defined characters who caught my sympathy, and who also represented well the views of their time. I feel that the standard of writing merits publication and we want to take it on with a view to finding a publisher for you."'

'Tremendous!' Tom said, hugging her. 'Congratulations. The first one you've tried and she's saying "Yes!"' He grinned and added: 'Of course, I knew she would.'

Polly laughed and hugged him back. 'Know-all. What a terrific note on which to go off on honeymoon!'

'What else does she say?'

She read on: '"I have to warn you that the market for historical fiction is not strong at present but this is certainly an excellent example of the genre. We shall do our best with it. I would find it useful if we could meet at my office to talk about the book in general terms and discuss such matters as whether you have plans for further books. Please ring me to arrange a convenient time." Well . . . Oh, Tom, I can hardly believe it!'

'Hardly believe what?' Emily asked, trailing into the kitchen followed by Laura. 'Oh, Tom, coffee. Lovely, thanks.'

'Polly's found herself a literary agent who wants to handle her novel. Who loves it, in fact.'

'That's great,' Emily said. She reached out for the letter. 'Well done, Ma.'

Tom was anxious to impress upon both girls the full implications. 'They say agents are harder to persuade than publishers. It's tremendous.'

Laura and Emily read the letter together. 'She says it's a most impressive piece of writing,' Laura said, looking up at Polly. 'She's right. That's what I think.'

'How do you know?' Tom scoffed. 'You haven't read it.'

'Yes, I have, too.' Laura looked faintly embarrassed. She said to Polly: 'I picked up the first few pages off your writing table to see what the story was about and I sort of got hooked, so I've been sneaking a chapter to my room whenever I had time to read. You don't mind, do you? Anyway, I think it's amazing. I think it's one of the best books I've ever read.'

'Oh, thank you,' Polly said, putting her arms round her. 'No, I don't mind a bit, certainly not when you tell me it's good.'

Laura leaned against her. 'It'd be ace to have a stepma who was a real author.'

'Hey,' said Emily, looking up from reading the letter for the third time. 'But this woman wants to meet you, Ma. Do you think you'll have time before your wedding?'

'She'll make time,' Tom said. 'Even if I have to drive her every inch of the way.'

'I could drive her,' Emily said proudly, 'now I've passed my driving test.'

Vanessa felt as if the hand of God was upon her, grinding her and wringing her out. The pain of the contractions was tremendous, overwhelming. She yelled for an epidural injection. The midwife was disapproving. 'I didn't think you would be one to give in at the first sign of discomfort,' she told Vanessa. Vanessa was past caring. 'Just get the doctor to give it to me, for God's sake,' she said. When the midwife stalked off, a woman who'd had her baby eighteen hours previously poked her head round the door to tell her that midwife was equally scathing to everybody: 'And she's never had a baby. How the hell can she know, silly cow?' she added disdainfully. 'Next time I'm not even going to start trying to do without. Me for the easy way, every time.'

The epidural given, the pain went; the relief was immense. Vanessa closed her eyes and rested; she was aware of being on a drip and of a monitor showing the baby's heartbeat and the contractions, which she was assured was normal. The contractions continued, but now they were squeezing and releasing her in what seemed quite a neutral detached sort of way after their previous vicious and personal attacks. Time went past in waves. She opened her eyes and the tall window showed a grey sky and she was aware of rain drumming on the glass. A little later nurses were fussing round her doing something, she didn't know what. Someone said she was doing well considering her age. The grey clouds were smaller now and bisected by shafts of low watery sunlight.

Suddenly she was aware of changes in herself, that she was calling out. The midwife was checking her and her hands were cold. 'Ah, the head,' she said. There was a bustle. A voice said: 'Push now!' and then, bossily: 'No, harder than that!' The hand of God feeling came over her again. She pushed and pushed once more. 'Stop! Stop pushing! Pant!' Then, 'Goodness, that was quick!' She was aware of some tremendous happening – was that the head? – and a need for another push and then there was a gush and a warm slithering between her legs and she felt her baby being born, her son. A blur of relief.

The bossy voice said almost coyly: 'What have we here? Why, it's a girl!'

'No!' Vanessa said, her eyes shut. 'No, it can't be. It's a boy.'

'I can assure you, no mistake, it's a perfect little girl.'

'I don't want a girl,' Vanessa said furiously. 'I indented for a boy.'

Laughter. Another voice said: 'Half-past six on April the sixth.'

Movements. Sounds. The short angry cries of a tiny baby. Someone put another pillow under Vanessa's head.

A hand touched her shoulder. 'Here she is, your beautiful daughter.'

Vanessa opened her eyes with reluctance and a young nurse bent to hand the crying baby over, the still damp head peeping from a piece of white hospital blanket. A soft Irish voice said: 'You can welcome her to the world now, so you can.'

She looked down and big blue eyes gazed back at her in wonderment. The crying stopped; the mouth which had been open in shock and protest, closed. There was pure silence in the room. You can't be mine, Vanessa thought, I don't know you, you're a stranger. But her hands closed upon the child. The eyes blinked, the hair was very fair. Neville's hair, she thought, and pushed the thought aside. 'Welcome to life, Fabia,' she whispered.

She shifted the baby more comfortably into the crook of her arm and a minute waving hand emerged from the blanket. Shyly, breathlessly, she touched the hand and instantly it curled around her forefinger. And suddenly, feeling this living, breathing child gazing at her and grasping on to her, the first person in all the world it had ever seen, a wave of emotion swept over her so that she wanted to laugh and sing and shout. But instead she lay there in silence with a great warmth about her heart, the most tender, the most compelling and purposeful love she had felt in all her life.

Chapter 21

Polly drove to the annual lunch party on a hazy bright morning that gave promise of a scorching day, nursing her elderly car along as she headed for Sussex and Mary's farmhouse. She passed through high woods of beeches and down into prosperous small villages and on through cornfields and downland, her mind preoccupied. Drives such as this frequently put her into a taking-stock mood. It would not be an easy day. For this occasion Mary had decreed no husbands or boyfriends or children; there would be just the four of them, Jane being in Warsaw. Was that sensible, tactful? There were, Mary had murmured, things that might be said . . . matters to be sorted. Husbands and offspring would have dissipated the tension, prevented post-mortems. Unease stirred in Polly. She had tried to refuse the invitation – what, after all that had happened, had she and Vanessa to say to one another? But Mary, unexpectedly strong, had implored her not to let the friendship between them all fail. – 'If you won't come, Candida won't come, and where shall we be then?' – and at her insistence Polly had given in.

'Oh, hell,' she said aloud. 'What's it matter? Nothing Vanessa can say or do can hurt me. Not now that Neville's out of my life so completely and I'm married to my lovely Tom.' But she would rather have spent the day with him. What was all this *for*, anyway?

She put her foot down on the accelerator and let her car swoop onwards through the undulating farmlands, hardly noticing her surroundings. A year since the party in her own garden. In a year so many things had happened . . . such trials of their friendship. She looked back, seeing, as in old slides shown on a screen, disconnected images of the past. The awful shuffling poverty that had dominated her planning of that day's food, dominated her life. Vanessa, hanging on Neville's arm, jiggling the gilt balls on her breasts, talking drunkenly of *Aïda*. The note, signed '*Your J*' she had earlier found in Neville's blazer pocket. Her own strange shy ache of pleasure each time she encountered Tom in Winchester. Candida stealing out to meet her lover while lying to Bernard of her pity for Polly. Mary, not asking, but rather demanding that Polly's children should connect themselves in help and affection to Vanessa's brat, ignoring Polly's hurt. What had their lunch parties, their ancient memories, to do with any of this? Perhaps Mary was seeing an interdependence that had never been, perhaps they none of them should be struggling to keep in touch with the whimpering ghost of their dead past?

Polly tightened her lips with a feeling of irritability, and saw from familiar passing cottages and the tower of a tree-framed mediaeval church that she was driving through George and Mary's village. Turn left at the end of the street, she reminded herself, then right after half a mile, on to their farm track. The once rutted track was now gravelled and firm. Here she must steel herself in earnest.

She pulled up outside the farmhouse beside Candida's Mercedes, from which she was just emerging, brows lowered, a crease between her eyes. She stood to watch Polly in turn wriggle from her own small car. After a second she walked over to her. Shadow kisses. An elusive, exclusive scent. A sigh. Candida looked white and tired. She was wearing something loose and silky and expensive that made no concessions to the working farm around them.

'Gird your loins for the fray,' she said, and then, 'Why do we allow ourselves to be cajoled into such things as this lunch?'

'God knows. I don't.' Polly pulled at the neck of her frock. 'It's turning hot. Why is it invariably frying hot on the day our group chooses to meet?'

The sky was very blue and a dusty scent of grass and dry dung tickled Polly's nose. There were sheep with their lambs scattered across a field to one side of the farm, and from a paddock a pony was watching them, swishing its tail against the flies. The midday farmyard silence was enhanced by the occasional bleat from the lambs and the insistent faint buzz of insects. Female voices came from the garden to the side of the house.

'Oh, well. Forward,' Candida said, stalking on long legs towards the voices. 'Into the breach. Or something.'

Polly followed her through the little wooden gate into a garden so flooded with sunlight that it seemed to shimmer. Across the lawn she could see Mary and Vanessa sitting on an old wooden seat in the shade of a lime tree, a pram beside them. Mary was on her feet in a second, rushing to press a rounded downy cheek against their faces. Her kisses were warm smacks.

'How lovely!' she said. 'How lovely to see you.' She stood back to survey them with affectionate solicitude. 'And looking so good, too. But you must be hot from your drives. You need long and cooling drinks and I've a fresh jug of the very thing in the fridge – a *cup*, you know – it's all lemony and delicious. I'll go and find it straight away.' She pounded with plump vigour into the house, leaving them to meet Vanessa without the help of her comfortable good humour to steer the way through the first awkward, possibly acid, moments.

'Well,' Candida said in a sharp spasm of annoyance, 'heavens, we may as well sit down.' She stalked on towards the seats in the shade of the tree.

Vanessa had been adjusting something in the pram, her face averted from them, but as they approached she straightened and gave them a swift exploratory look. 'Hello,' she said, her voice rasping. She cleared her throat.

Polly and Candida each gave her a nod. There was a moment's silence, then from the pram came the sound of sneezes, one, two, a pause, and then a third.

'Aah!' said Vanessa.

'Bless you!' said Polly. She bent over the pram in incomparable gratitude for the distraction. The baby was wearing the minimum of fine white cotton clothing, delicately embroidered in white. She was kicking bare legs and waving small arms. As Polly's eyes examined her, so she examined Polly. Her limbs stilled. Then she produced a sweet and gummy smile and began once more to kick. The wisps of hair on her head were fair, her eyes were blue; the shape of the head and the features of the face were curiously familiar. Yes, I know who your father is, Polly silently told her, her heart thumping.

Aloud she said: 'Well, little one, you're very cheerful!'

'She always is,' Vanessa said, pressing close to Polly to gaze down at her daughter. 'She's so good, my Fabia. She hardly ever cries. And she sleeps right through the night already.'

Polly recoiled from her approach, from the too-close warm body with its remembered heavy scent, from the swollen milk-filled breasts that pushed against the straining cotton of her shirt. Beside her Candida was inspecting the baby in silence, ignoring Vanessa. Polly retreated to a cushioned garden chair and sat down. She wished Mary would come with her drinks and her chatter. She felt the atmosphere becoming one of growing piercing embarrassment.

'Well,' Candida said finally, her eyebrows in her hair, 'no one could argue about her being Neville's child. Mostly when people coo over some baby with features like dabs of putty and say the squalling object's exactly like its Auntie Karen or whoever, one wonders whether they're suffering from delusions. Not here, I think.' She seated herself in a chair beside Polly.

'No,' Polly agreed.

A further and longer silence followed.

'Poor child. Not the best of heritages,' Candida commented to Vanessa with an aloof, supercilious air. 'Does Neville acknowledge her as his?'

'No.'

'Has he seen her?'

'No. But he sent a present, a picture for her room, as an old friend.' She spoke in an even tone, lacking the defensive edge that once would have been there. She looked different, too, the usual flamboyance missing, her shirt and skirt a dull blue, her sandals even sensible.

Candida's lips tightened. 'How very generous of him!' she commented sardonically. 'And you're not asking for money from him? God, mean adulterous sods like him get away with everything nowadays! Three women! And Polly's divorce never mentioned fault. Society today allows these adulterous brutes to do as they like.'

Polly cocked her head to one side. 'We're all adulterers these days, aren't we?' she commented softly.

Candida gave her a sharp arrested look and changed her angle of approach like a skater veering away from thin ice. 'Vanessa's produced a child, Polly, a child with no father.'

'That was my decision,' Vanessa said. 'And it's common enough today. What are you worried about? There's no social stigma left for my Fabia to suffer.'

'But there are other problems that should be concerning you,' Candida said. 'I had no father that I can remember, and I wouldn't point to my upbringing as one of the best. With my mother there was never a balanced approach. She had no one to talk things through with, so according to her mood I was either the most wonderful child ever conceived or a worthless brat. I never knew where I was. A balanced upbringing requires two parents – one alone can become over-involved, tense and resentful, saying, "My child, right or wrong!" till the child ceases to know right *from* wrong.'

'I've seen that among children I've taught,' Polly said. 'It's frighteningly common these days. And I've been threatened with thumping by an aggressive dad of that sort myself. I've also known single parents with over-high expectations and no concerned partner to say "Hey, steady on", wrecking their children with their pushing.' Both Neville and Vanessa had failed to realise their potential on the career ladder – would Vanessa insist that Fabia must succeed where they had not?

'Vanessa won't be like that.' Mary unexpectedly loomed close to them with her tray of drinks. 'She'll have us. Experienced friends she can turn to for help.' She placed her tray noisily in the middle of the garden table and her face had a stony look that brooked no more criticism.

Love me, love my dog – or should I say bitch? Polly thought to herself. How Mary has fought for the woman over these last months . . . a determination to wrench her back to the paths of righteousness and sanity such as I've never seen in my life. And to make us follow that lead, however much we're shocked and hurt. But then this is the modern mode, turning morality on its head and comforting the sinner instead of the sinned against. Aloud she said: 'Yes, I think we three know the problems she'll be facing.'

Mary lifted a glass jug to pour them all long cooling drinks, ice and mint and lemon tumbling out into the glasses along with the amber liquid. They sipped in silence, the drink seeming to glide down their throats, deliciously cool, slightly sparkling, refreshing.

'Wonderful,' Polly said. 'Cool and unusual. It has that certain something . . . I don't know what it is . . . Cointreau?'

'Secret ingredients! It's old-fashioned,' Mary said, 'a recipe from the past that I found in an old book, but I think it's just the thing for days like today when the sun is so unbelievably bright and the heat seems to intensify with every moment. It's alcoholic all right, but not so much so that one can't drink plenty of it. The first time I made it I thought it fairly danced down my throat!' She laughed awkwardly, her eyes imploring her three friends to loosen up, relax, talk together.

'It's amazing,' Vanessa said.

'Very good, very refreshing,' Candida produced.

A thrush sang on a branch. In the meadow beyond the garden the sound of the grasshopper chorus deepened, while above them bees murmured in the scented flowers of the lime tree. Somewhere a hen was clucking.

Mary said: 'I've had a card from Jane to wish us all a happy day today, together with a letter.' From beneath a bowl of nuts she fished them out, then passed the nuts around. 'The card shows the column of King Sigismund III in Warsaw. I'll pass it round. The letter is in the usual cryptic Jane style. She says little about herself, except for some comments on the life of one married to a Someone – capital S – and how that had made her a *someone*, albeit with a small s, and that she is rather taken with herself in that rôle. She's struggling daily with the language, so that she can extract all possible innuendo and fun from the conversation at the many functions she attends . . . She's been pleasantly surprised by the food, especially the vegetables. "These," she writes, "are all organic, being produced by peasants on smallholdings. Root vegetables like carrots and potatoes look knobbly and odd, but taste superb. When Jeremy and I drive out into the country we are at once horrified and enchanted by the antiquity of the farming methods. They use machines which in England would be housed in some agricultural museum, dusty, dead and gone. These look so charmingly unhurried in action, horse-drawn and creaking, that we're overwhelmed with nostalgia for our lost past. Western experts naturally advise the industrialisation of agriculture, with all that this means by way of chemicals and hormones and vast capital-intensive fume-belching machines. But others are concerned about this, not only because of the destruction of the present rural way of life, but because of the rise in unemployment which would follow. The new factories need fewer workers than the old did and the transition to a market economy is not being received rapturously by the seventeen per cent or thereabouts who are presently unemployed, to say the least of it. It has proved singularly painful."'

'Yes, I'd heard that,' Polly said. 'It's sad. It'll be interesting to hear more from her.'

'Already Jane's busy analysing the economy,' Candida said, looking amused. 'You can't keep a good economist down.'

'Not Jane!'

Mary looked up. 'She sends an invitation to us all to go and visit her. Says she's making friends, but that old friends are the best.' She folded up the letter.

'So giving up her freedom and solitude and her job has proved bearable so far?' Vanessa asked.

'Surprisingly so, from what she says. She's keeping her mind alive, anyway.'

'That's the most important thing,' Polly said. 'To be bored is soul-destroying.'

'Not something that's going to trouble you in your life!' Candida said.

'I never thought Jane would do it,' Vanessa said thoughtfully. 'Of all of us she was the genuine determined career woman. But the most unexpected people can change.'

The baby, who had been cooing intermittently at the leaves above her, let out a wail. Vanessa reached out to rock the pram, which Polly now recognised as Mary's old one. Presumably little Fabia used it when she came for the weekends with her mother. A grumbling grizzle came from its interior, gradually working itself up to a yell that became insistent, drowning their discussion of Jane's letter.

'Oh, dear,' Vanessa said, leaning over to study her daughter. 'I hoped she'd wait for her feed until we'd had lunch, but she isn't going to, is she?'

'You feed her here and now,' Mary said with authority, pushing herself up from her chair, 'and then you'll be done when I bring the lunch out.'

She walked across the lawn towards the farmhouse and Polly saw that her walk was heavy and that she had put on weight, not a lot, but enough to put a stamp on her that was suddenly middle-aged. She thought: We are middle-aged. I am middle-aged. It's not so bad.

Vanessa lifted the baby from the pram and the yells stopped.

Candida let out her breath in a sigh. 'That's a relief.'

Vanessa sat down with a bump, the baby on her lap. She unbuttoned her shirt and opened her bra. Fabia clamped her mouth greedily on to the exposed nipple and began to suckle. Vanessa clasped her closely and leaned back. 'I enjoy this,' she remarked. Her breast was white and delicately veined, hanging down like a pendant flower, full and luscious in the heat.

Polly was at once repelled and fascinated. To see Vanessa, of all people, and at her age, revelling in feeding a baby, seemed quite unreal. She swallowed. She was trembling with some emotion she couldn't quite identify. This was a shock to her system and part of her found it offensive. This was Neville's child.

Candida stood, eyes averted. 'I shall go and talk to Mary,' she said. 'I may even find that I can help her, though she's always so efficient that I doubt it.' She moved away at a brisk pace.

Polly had a sensation of being trapped, claustrophobically enclosed in the small space created by Vanessa and herself and the baby, though the lawn surrounding them was large and empty. There was nothing she wanted to say to Vanessa that would not have been sharp with dislike and disapproval, but Mary had not brought them together here to vomit up their spleen, to indulge in childish displays of hate or hysteria. She expected that they should swallow their resentment and allow their English sense of fairplay to dominate. Vanessa needed support; she should have it. Mary's idea of friendship, Polly thought, is akin to motherly love, cherishing and nurturing, as she does her children and her animals. Vanessa was quiet, her eyes wary. She lifted the baby to her shoulder, patting her gently. Polly's sense of fairplay suddenly reminded her that she had been cheerful with Juliana over the telephone, that they had become in some strange way almost friends. She did not doubt that Juliana, no more than Vanessa, had let no moment's thought of Polly interfere with her fling with Neville. But then . . . Oh, come on, she told herself, you were a stranger to Juliana, but Vanessa was supposed to be a friend. Does friendship make its own intolerance? Oh, damn the woman!

Vanessa's voice broke into her reverie. 'Polly?'

'Yes?' She felt fierce. Sweat trickled between her breasts.

'I think I owe you an apology.' Then she corrected herself: 'No, I mean . . . I do owe you an apology.'

Polly raised her eyebrows. She waited.

Vanessa stopped patting her child. 'I apologise, Polly. For everything that has happened. I was in a muddle and I was stupid. I misunderstood Neville. I misunderstood the situation. I must have hurt you.'

Polly thought she'd practised that for a long time. She believed she detected Mary's hand. Nevertheless, she was mollified; apologies always had disarmed her. She remembered Neville's scorn of them and thought the better of Vanessa. She said: 'Yes, what you did was hurtful. Very. But then for me it's all over, because now I have my Tom, and he's very different. He's . . . well, he's *real*, not a fake personality like Neville.' She felt an overwhelming sense of relief, wondered at her own boastfulness and thought, Take that how you like. She added in a detached voice, 'Neville has immense charm when he chooses to use it, but essentially he's a miserable, self-centred, constantly dissatisfied person, greedy and unreliable. What amazes me now is how long it took me to see it.'

'Me too,' Vanessa said. 'I shall never feel the same about charm again.'

Their eyes met for a long moment. A faint breeze rose and momentarily stirred their hair. Vanessa's face was hot and reddened by the sun, her eyes blinked against the light. She looked unusually serious, intent. She nodded her head slowly. Insects buzzed and murmured and the heart-shaped leaves of the tree moved above them; the breeze seemed to sigh. Polly put out her hand for the glass jug and emptied it into their glasses.

Fabia burped. 'There's my sweetheart,' Vanessa said absently and put her to the other breast. 'Tell me, Polly, how long did you breastfeed your girls for?'

When Polly reached home in the late afternoon she walked through the shadowy house and out again to the bright garden, to find Tom standing waiting for her. He was wearing an open-necked Tattersall shirt tucked into an old pair of jeans and his sleeves were rolled up. He held out his hands to pull her to him, and as she took them she was aware all in one second of the movement of the muscles in his brown arms, and the faint beading of perspiration on his upper lip, and the wonderful relief of being with him after a day that had not been altogether easy.

He told her: 'I heard the front door and it had to be you. Laura and Emily won't be back for some time yet.'

He bent his head and they kissed; his lips tasted salty and fresh. She remembered that Laura was with her cousins and her Uncle Hugh, and Emily was spending the day out riding with Mark. There would be peace for an hour or two. Around them she was aware of bees making a blurry buzzing sound in the climbing roses and that somewhere bells were ringing.

She sank into a canvas garden chair on the paving stones. 'It was so hot in Sussex,' she said in a smiling thread of a voice, 'impossibly hot, but it's cool here.' She pushed her hair back from where it was clinging to her face and stretched out her legs.

'We have the shade of old walls. I'll find you a long drink, you look in need of reviving.' He disappeared into the darkness of the house, emerging with glasses of Pimms.

'Lovely, just lovely. Thank you, Tom.'

He seated himself beside her. 'So how did it go, this annual lunch of yours? Was it so very bad?'

She drew in a quick breath. 'No . . . Not in the end. Not at all. It was . . . strange. Strange to be without Jane and various husbands. And tense at first, very tense.' She looked along the garden and across ancient walls and irregular roofs towards the tower of Winchester College chapel. Swifts were wheeling and swooping about it, wild arrows against the paling summer sky. She said slowly: 'Mary had Vanessa staying with her. I'd wondered if she'd have the nerve to appear but Mary was determined to force the issue. She refused to let the friendship break up, the group dissolve. Candida and I arrived together . . . when we encountered Vanessa there was a dreadful moment's silence. The baby saved us – she sneezed. We all turned to jelly and said: "Aah!" and "Bless you!" and so the silence was broken.' A wry smile. 'We were calm and reserved and English. No bitching, no fights.'

Tom put his hand on her thigh. It was warm and heavy and reassuring. He asked: 'What was she like, the baby?'

'Enchanting, as Rose and Emily said when they went to see their little half-sister last month. I gathered from Vanessa that she was both startled and gratified that they'd chosen to become involved with Fabia – and thrilled with their admiration of her. I must admit, I doubt I've ever seen a prettier baby. Wisps of fair hair, big blue eyes; plump and contented and friendly. But, oh God, Tom, it was strange, almost eerie . . . apart from the wrong hair colour she could have been one of my own babies, her face looked so familiar. The shape of the head, the features. I . . . I felt I recognised her.'

'The abominable Neville leaving his mark. Let's hope it's all she inherits from him.'

'Please God.'

'And Vanessa? I remember Mary at our wedding – a sturdy pleasant woman – but you've never introduced me to the shocker, Vanessa.'

Polly smiled and shook her head. 'Changed. I thought she was changed. It could be she'd been scolded by Mary into her best behaviour, but I thought – I don't know why – that it went deeper than that. Maybe motherhood was what she always needed. She was quieter, less edgy than I've ever seen her. Unobtrusive clothes, quite different. She handled the baby well, there were none of the awkwardnesses or complaints of broken nights that I expected.' She sipped her Pimms meditatively, then laughed. 'I was knocked sideways by her breastfeeding it, that was the last thing I'd expected. She was always so proud of her figure, I thought the boobs would be sacrosanct, but no, she fed little Fabia with all the expertise and complacency of some Mediterranean peasant woman on her fifth!'

Tom chuckled. 'Reassuring.'

'Yes. Yes, it was. Pleasing. Rose and Emily said that too.'

'And did she make any attempt at an apology to you for her horrendous behaviour?'

'Yes, strangely. Yes, she did. Briefly, but to the point.'

'Hmm. So I should think.' He leaned over and they exchanged a kiss.

'After that things became easier. We talked about babies and how she and a friend plan to share a nanny when she returns to work in two or three months' time. Later, when no one was listening, she asked me rather stiffly if Neville's other child had been born and I told her what I knew about baby Lionel. She nodded and swallowed and changed the subject. I don't think she visualises that particular half-brother and sister being allowed to meet.'

'No!'

'She did congratulate me surprisingly nicely on having had my novel accepted for publication and said she'd order a copy as soon as I let her know the publication date.'

'Ah, yes. When did you tell the friends of that wonderful success?'

'Over lunch. Having only heard the day before yesterday, I was still so amazed and excited I had to let it out.'

'What are friends for,' Tom asked, laughing, 'but to share one's triumphs and sorrows with? Were they pleased with your triumph? And properly impressed?'

'They were amazed. Mary could hardly believe her ears. She had to be told the plot and how long it was, and how long it had taken to write, and even when she'd had every detail that I knew – and some I wasn't sure I did – she was still incredulous. "But you're a teacher," she said, "and you've got marking to do!" She couldn't believe a townswoman would rise as disgustingly early as I've been doing – I beat her routine by half-an-hour!'

'I'm not surprised she was surprised,' Tom said. 'And impressed.'

'Candida declared she'd throw a party for us, and anyone I wanted to invite, when it's launched. A truly big affair. She was very pleased with herself because, as she told the others, it was she who'd challenged me to have a go, she who'd believed in me. And she'd been proved right – her dark horse had won where so many fail! Vanessa, who isn't slow to see worthwhile angles on anything, said the party must be held at some well-known venue and given maximum publicity, then I'd have a great start, with the Gough name behind me. But I don't think I could face that. Suppose it were a flop? I'd feel a fool.'

'It won't be. It'll be a success. Your agent and your publisher believe in it and they should know. You must let Candida do it – as a friend's prerogative. It'll keep her mind from my regrettable brother.'

Polly sighed. 'At least Candida is busy. She's become Chairman of one of her charitable societies, which she says is excellent. More interest, more kudos. It should mean less work than she did as its secretary, rather than more, but she has plans for big changes with new policies which will require detailed working out. And she's acquired two commissions to do both interior *and* garden designs for handsome but neglected Georgian country houses – the sort of money-no-object commissions that every designer dreams about. Unusual these days. I mentioned Hugh once in connection with Laura and she glanced at me from under her lashes and said nothing. But then she never has been one to reveal her emotions. She's the antithesis of Vanessa in that. Except that one time when she did let go, when she talked to me at The Gatehouse. She did care for Hugh, you know, deeply. And may still do so.'

Polly felt uncomfortable every time she thought of Candida, worse when she saw her. She wished she could have helped her. She had a sudden remembrance of her sitting silently after lunch earlier in the day, drinking coffee and staring with wide still eyes in front of her, detached from the others, her face bleak. There had been something about that straight-backed, uncomplaining stance that had pierced her with pity. Polly refused to accept the guilt that Mrs Jamieson-Druce had tried to foist on her for her inability to help in the concealment that had been of such desperate importance to Candida. None of that outbreak of anger and emotion had been of Polly's making, and yet people had wanted to blame and punish her. At the same time it was impossible to forget the one occasion when Candida had let fall her social mask to reveal the face of tragedy beneath it. Polly was deeply sad for her. She saw a great emptiness in Candida's inner self, and in her life, and recognised that in the midst of that emptiness something wholly unexpected had happened to her friend. Candida had felt a great yearning for a man and given way to it, despite her avowed belief that no such feelings of yearning or commitment to another being existed or could exist in her. Inevitably she had been hurt. In time the episode would recede into the past and blend its sadness with the emptiness. There had been no confidences today, perhaps there had been nothing to confide. Candida had chosen her life and stayed with that choice. Polly wondered about its compensations: could Candida extract the same cynical amusement and enjoyment from it that Jane did from hers?

Tom's voice broke into her thoughts. 'Polly, what about the future? Have you decided what you want to do next? Your novel is going to be published, your publishers, like your agent, what's her name? – Holly Hammond – they're going to ask about your plans for a second book. I know you've plans for a novel about women's contribution and advancement during the First World War – but when are you going to do this writing? And what about your teaching?'

Switching her thoughts over and stretching herself with lazy pleasure, she said: 'I don't know, I haven't made plans yet – how can I? My life's so full of wonderful shiny new components it'll take me time to sort them all out. There's you for a start, and how what's happened will fit in with you – and Laura and Emily and Rose. Thank God, Emily says she reckons she did all right in her A levels – and if she says that, her papers must have been super-good. She's never been over-confident or one of nature's natural boasters! But I'll have to give her support through university, and support means money besides everything else. Suppose I make the discovery that I'm a one-book person, with nothing more to say? I must keep teaching.'

'Rubbish!' He opened his mouth to contradict her and she laid her fingers across his lips.

'No, darling Tom, that's not rubbish. And anyway, I like it at Hamlins. Teaching those bright well-disposed children with their capacity for absorbing information still amazes me daily with how pleasant it is. I'll continue as I am and see how things go.'

'I earn very well myself,' he reminded her.

She was most comfortably aware of that, she told him, smiling, and she loved him for his support and generosity, but if any man had to pay towards Rose and Emily's upkeep over the years until they were earning (so she hoped) vast sums for themselves, it would be Neville . . .

and she didn't see much likelihood of that without endless bickering . . . *so*, she must earn herself. 'And,' she added firmly, 'that I am happy to do.'

'Have you told Neville of your writing success?'

'No,' she said. 'Not yet.'

'But you will.'

'Oh, yes.' She smiled. 'But his reaction won't be quite as ecstatic as my mother's!'

Her mother had rung her up three times in three hours, tearful with excitement, asking question after question, to make certain she had every detail right and more: 'Because,' she said, 'everyone will be so pleased, and I must be ready to tell them the full story. My daughter a writer, the author of *Wit of Woman* – doesn't it sound amazing? You are clever, darling.'

'No, Neville won't be so ecstatic,' Tom mused. 'If he manages to congratulate you gracefully, especially in view of his failure to attract backing for his own writing so far, I shall view him with a less jaundiced eye. But I doubt it. I doubt it.'

Polly doubted it too. It didn't matter, though. Neville had ceased to matter in any way. He was a part of her past that had also started at LSE but was now over, its dubious memories faded and overlaid with a new and luminous scene. She relaxed in her chair, her hand on Tom's. They were silent. The air was warm and soft, filled with the scent of the roses that in these last hot days had rushed into lush flowering on the old brick walls. Insects danced in the sunlight and somewhere in the lilac tree a blackbird was singing. From the sky beyond the chapel tower came a strange regular sound, and she looked up to see two swans flying together across the summer sky towards the River Itchen.

The sun moved down the sky; the shadows lengthened. Polly's thoughts of Vanessa and tiny Fabia developed and crystallised. With the clarity lent by distance she saw that the events of the day had been right. Quiet Mary's vision had been the right one. Polly wanted no unkindness nor blame, instead she wanted the chance for Fabia to grow up without handicaps, not to become the scarred and needy person that an emotionally deprived childhood had made of her mother. The friendships that had begun more than twenty years ago had not all flourished in this last year, indeed, they had undergone something of a sea-change – and yet they had not dissolved. Affection had been given, and support, despite the anger and the traumas and the hostilities. There were reserves of strength to be drawn on for the future. And Polly visualised Vanessa taking Fabia for her first visit abroad: 'We'll be staying in Warsaw with the Ambassador and his wife – a friendship of many years!'

She looked across at Tom and saw that he was asleep, neatly, soundlessly, his brow unfurrowed. From the other side of the house she could hear the girls' voices as they came home. She smiled. She rose to her feet and walked softly indoors to make the evening meal for them all.